VAL McDERMID

Val McDermid grew up in a Scottish mining community then read English at Oxford. She was a journalist for sixteen years, spending the last three years as Northern Bureau Chief of a national Sunday tabloid. Now a full-time writer, she lives in Cheshire.

By the same author

The Distant Echo
Killing the Shadows
A Place of Execution

Tony Hill Novels

The Last Temptation
The Wire in the Blood
The Mermaids Singing
The Torment of Others

Kate Brannigan novels

Star Struck
Crack Down
Kick Back
Dead Beat

Lindsay Gordon novels

Hostage to Murder
Booked for Murder
Union Jack
Final Edition
Common Murder
Report for Murder

Non-fiction

A Suitable Job for a Woman

VAL McDERMID

Blue Genes
Clean Break

Grafton

HarperCollins*Publishers*
77–85 Fulham Palace Road,
London, W6 8JB

The HarperCollins website address is:
www.harpercollins.co.uk

This omnibus edition published in 2005
by HarperCollins*Publishers*

ISBN 0 00 773411 5

Typeset in Meridien by Palimpsest Book Production Limited,
Polmont, Stirlingshire

Printed and bound in Great Britain by
Clays Ltd, St Ives plc

Blue Genes

ACKNOWLEDGEMENTS

What is outlined in this novel is entirely within the realms of possible science. Somebody somewhere is almost certainly carrying out these procedures, probably for very large sums of money.

I'm grateful to Dr Gill Lockwood for most of my medical and scientific information, and to David Hartshorn of Cellmark Diagnostics for background on DNA testing. For other matters, I'm indebted to Lee D'Courcy, Diana Cooper, Yvonne Twiby, Jai Penna, Paula Tyler, Brigid Baillie and the press office of the Human Fertility and Embryology Authority.

*For Fairy, Lesley and all the other lesbian mothers
who prove that moulds are there to be broken.
And for Robyn and Andrew and Jack*

1

The day Richard's death announcement appeared in the *Manchester Evening Chronicle*, I knew I couldn't postpone clearing up the mess any longer. But there was something I had to do first. I stood in the doorway of the living room of the man who'd been my lover for three years, Polaroid in hand, surveying the chaos. Slowly, I swept the camera lens round the room, carefully recording every detail of the shambles, section by section. This was one time I wasn't prepared to rely on memory. Richard might be gone, but that didn't mean I was going to take any unnecessary risks. Private eyes who do that have as much chance of collecting their pensions as a Robert Maxwell employee.

Once I had a complete chronicle of exactly how things had been left in the room that was a mirror image of my own bungalow next door, I started my mammoth task. First, I sorted things into piles: books, magazines, CDs, tapes, promo videos, the detritus of a rock journalist's life. Then I arranged them. Books, alphabetically, on the shelf unit. CDs ditto. The tapes I stacked in the storage unit Richard had bought for the purpose one Sunday when I'd managed to drag him round Ikea, the 1990s equivalent of buying an engagement ring. I'd even put the cabinet together for him, but he'd never got into the habit of using it, preferring the haphazard stacks and heaps strewn all over the floor. I buried the surge of emotion that came with the memory and carried on doggedly. The magazines I shoved out of sight in the conservatory that runs along the back of both our houses, linking them together more firmly than we'd ever been prepared to do in any formal sense with our lives.

I leaned against the wall and looked around the room. When people say, 'It's a dirty job, but somebody's got to do it,' how come we never really believe we'll be the ones left clutching the sticky end? I sighed and forced myself on. I emptied ashtrays of the roaches left from Richard's joints, gathered together pens and pencils and stuffed them into the sawn-off Sapporo beer can he'd used for the purpose for as long as I'd known him. I picked up the assorted notepads, sheets of scrap paper and envelopes where he'd scribbled down vital phone numbers and quotes, careful not to render them any more disordered than they were already, and took them through to the room he used as his office when it wasn't occupied by his nine-year-old son Davy on one of his regular visits.

I dumped them on the desk on top of a remarkably similar-looking pile already there.

Back in the living room, I was amazed by the effect. It almost looked like a room I could sit comfortably in. Cleared of the usual junk, it was possible to see the pattern on the elderly Moroccan rug that covered most of the floor and the sofas could for once accommodate the five people they were designed for. I realized for the first time that the coffee table had a central panel of glass. I'd been trying for ages to get him to put the room into something approaching a civilized state, but he'd always resisted me. Even though I'd finally got my own way, I can't say it made me happy. But then, I couldn't get out of my mind the reason behind what I was doing here, and what lay ahead. The announcement of Richard's death was only the beginning of a chain of events that would be a hell of a lot more testing than tidying a room.

I thought about brushing the rug, but I figured that was probably gilding the lily, the kind of activity that people found a little bizarre after the death of a lover. And bizarre was not the impression I wanted to give. I went back through to my house and changed from the sweat pants and T-shirt I'd worn to do the cleaning into something more appropriate for a grieving relict. A charcoal wool wraparound skirt from the French Connection sale and a black lamb's-wool turtleneck I'd chosen for the one and only reason that it made me look like death. There are times in a private eye's working life when looking like she's about to keel over is an image preferable to that of Wonder Woman on whizz.

I was about to close the conservatory door behind me as I returned to Richard's house when his doorbell belted out an inappropriate blast of the guitar riff from Eric Clapton's 'Layla'. 'Shit,' I muttered. No matter how careful you are, there's always something you forget. I couldn't remember what the other choices were on Richard's 'Twenty Great Rock Riffs' doorbell, but I was sure there must be something more fitting than Clapton's wailing guitar. Maybe something from the Smiths, I thought vaguely as I tried to compose my face into a suitable expression for a woman who's just lost her partner. Just how was I supposed to look, I found a second to wonder. What's the well-bereft woman wearing on her face this season? You can't even go for the mascara tracks down the cheeks in these days of lash tints.

I took a deep breath, hoped for the best and opened the door. The crime correspondent of the *Manchester Evening Chronicle* stood on the step, her black hair even more like an explosion in a wig factory than usual. 'Kate,' my best friend Alexis said, stepping forward and pulling me into a hug. 'I can't believe it,' she added, a catch in her voice. She moved back to look at me, tears in her eyes. So much for the hard-bitten newshound. 'Why didn't you call us? When I saw it in the paper . . . Kate, what the hell happened?'

I looked past her. All quiet in the street outside. I put my arm round her shoulders and firmly drew her inside, closing the door behind her. 'Nothing. Richard's fine,' I said, leading the way down the hall.

'Do what?' Alexis demanded, stopping and frowning at me. 'If he's fine, how come I just read he's dead in tonight's paper? And if he's fine, how come you're doing the "Baby's in Black" number when you know that's the one colour that makes you look like the Bride of Frankenstein?'

'If you'd let me get a word in edgeways, I'll explain,' I said, going through to the living room. 'Take my word for it, Richard is absolutely OK.'

Alexis stopped dead on the threshold, taking in the pristine tidiness of the room. 'Oh no, he's not,' she said, suspicion running through her heavy Scouse accent like the stripe in the toothpaste. 'He's not fine if he's left his living room looking like this. At the very least, he's having a nervous breakdown. What the hell's going on here, KB?'

'I can't believe you read the death notices,' I said, throwing myself down on the nearest sofa.

'I don't normally,' Alexis admitted, subsiding on the sofa opposite me. 'I was down Moss Side nick waiting for a statement from the duty inspector about a little bit of aggravation involving an Uzi and a dead Rottweiler, and they were taking so long about it I'd read everything else in the paper except the ads for the dinner dances. And it's just as well I did. What's going on? If he's not dead, who's he upset enough to get heavy-metal hassle like this?' She stabbed the paper she carried with a nicotine-stained index finger.

'It was me who put the announcement in,' I said.

'That's one way of telling him it's over,' Alexis interrupted before I could continue. 'I thought you two had got things sorted?'

'We have,' I said through clenched teeth. Ironing out the problems in my relationship with Richard would have taken the entire staff of an industrial laundry a month. It had taken us rather longer.

'So what's going on?' Alexis demanded belligerently. 'What's so important that you have to give everybody a heart attack thinking me laddo's popped his clogs?'

'Can't you resist the journalistic exaggeration for once?' I sighed. 'You know and I know that nobody under sixty routinely reads the deaths column. I had to use a real name and address, and I figured with Richard out of town till the end of the week, nobody's going to be any the wiser if I used his,' I explained. 'And he won't be, unless you tell him.'

'That depends on whether you tell me what this is all in aid of,' Alexis said cunningly, her outrage at having wasted her sympathy a distant memory now she had the scent of a possible story in her nostrils. 'I mean, I think he's going to notice something's going on,' she added, sweeping an eloquent arm through the air. 'I don't think he knows that carpet has a pattern.'

'I took Polaroids before I started,' I told her. 'When I'm finished, I'll put it back the way it was before. He won't notice a thing.'

'He will when I show him the cutting,' Alexis countered. 'Spill, KB. What're you playing at? What's with the grieving widow number?' She leaned back and lit a cigarette. So much for my clean ashtrays.

'Can't tell you,' I said sweetly. 'Client confidentiality.'

'Bollocks,' Alexis scoffed. 'It's me you're talking to, KB, not the bizzies. Come on, give. Or else the first thing Richard sees when he comes home is . . .'

I closed my eyes and muttered an old gypsy curse under my breath. It's not that I speak Romany; it's just that I've refused to buy lucky white heather once too often. Believe me, I know exactly what those old gypsies say. I weighed up my options. I could always call her bluff and hope she wouldn't tell Richard, on the basis that the two of them maintain this pretence of despising each other's area of professional expertise and extend that into the personal arena at every possible opportunity. On the other hand, the prospect of explaining to Richard that I was responsible for the report of his death didn't appeal either. I gave in. 'It's got to be off the record, then,' I said ungraciously.

'Why?' Alexis demanded.

7

'Because with a bit of luck it will be sub judice in a day or two. And if you blow it before then, the bad guys will be out of town on the next train and we'll never nail them.'

'Anybody ever tell you you've got melodramatic tendencies, KB?' Alexis asked with a grin.

'A bit rich, coming from a woman who started today's story with, "Undercover police swooped on a top drug dealer's love nest in a dawn raid this morning," when we both know that all that happened was a couple of guys from the Drugs Squad turned over some two-bit dealer's girlfriend's bedsit,' I commented.

'Yeah, well, you gotta give it a bit of topspin or the boy racers on the newsdesk kill it. But that's not what we're talking about. I want to know why Richard's supposed to be dead.'

'It's a long and complicated story,' I started in a last attempt to lose her interest.

Alexis grinned and blew a long stream of smoke down her nostrils. Puff the Magic Dragon would have signed up for a training course on the spot. 'Great,' she enthused. 'My favourite kind.'

'The client's a firm of monumental masons,' I said. 'They're the biggest provider of stone memorials in South Manchester. They came to us because they've been getting a string of complaints from people saying they've paid for gravestones that haven't turned up.'

'Somebody's been nicking *gravestones*?'

'Worse than that,' I said, meaning it. Far as I

was concerned, I was dealing with total scumbags on this one. 'My clients are the incidental victims of a really nasty scam. From what I've managed to find out so far, there are at least two people involved, a man and a woman. They turn up on the doorsteps of the recently bereaved and claim to be representing my client's firm. They produce these business cards which have the name of my clients, complete with address and phone number, all absolutely kosher. The only thing wrong with them is that the names on the cards are completely unknown to my client. They're not using the names of his staff. But this pair are smart. They always come in the evening, out of business hours, so anyone who's a bit suspicious can't ring my client's office and check up on them. And they come single-handed. Nothing heavy. Where it's a woman who's died, it's the woman who shows up. Where it's a man, it's the bloke.'

'So what's the pitch?' Alexis asked.

'They do the tea-and-sympathy routine, then they explain that they're adopting the new practice of visiting people in their homes because it's a more personal approach to choosing an appropriate memorial. Then they go into a special-offer routine, just like they were selling double glazing or something. You know the sort of thing – unique opportunity, special shipment of Italian marble or Aberdeen granite, you could be one of the people we use for testimonial purposes, limited period offer.'

'Yeah, yeah, yeah,' Alexis groaned. 'And if they don't sign up tonight, they've lost the opportunity, am I right, or am I right?'

'You're right. So these poor sods whose lives are already in bits because they've just lost their partner or husband or wife, or mother or father, or son or daughter get done up like a kipper just so some smart bastard can go out and buy another designer suit or a mobile bloody phone,' I said angrily. I know all the rules about never letting yourself get emotionally involved with the jobs, but there are times when staying cool and disinterested would be the mark of inhumanity rather than good sense. This was one of them.

Alexis lit another cigarette, shaking her head. 'Pure gobshites,' she said in disgust. 'Twenty-four-carat shysters. So they take the cash and disappear into the night, leaving your clients to pick up the pieces when the headstone remains a ghostly presence?'

'Something like that. They really are a pair of unscrupulous bastards. I've been interviewing some of the people who have been had over, and a couple of them have told me the woman has actually driven them to holes in the wall to get money for a cash deposit.' I shook my head, remembering the faces of the victims again. They showed a procession of emotions, each more painful to watch than the last. There was grief revisited in the setting of the scene for me, then anger as they recalled how they'd been stung, then a mixture of shame and resentment that they'd fallen for it. 'And there's no point in me telling them that in their shoes even a streetwise old cynic like me would probably have fallen for it. Because I probably would have done, that's the worst of it,' I added bitterly.

'Grief gets you like that,' Alexis agreed. 'The last thing you're expecting is to be taken for a ride. Look at how many families end up not speaking to each other for years because someone has done something outrageous in the immediate aftermath of death, when everyone's staggering round feeling like their brain's in the food processor along with their emotions. After my Uncle Jos's second wife Theresa wore my gran's fur coat to the old dear's funeral, she might as well have been dead too. My dad wouldn't even let my mum send them a Christmas card for about ten years. Until Uncle Jos got cancer himself, poor sod.'

'Yeah, well, us knowing these people haven't been particularly gullible doesn't make it any easier for them. The only thing that might help them would be for me to nail the bastards responsible.'

'What about the bizzies? Haven't they reported it to them?'

I shrugged. 'Only one or two of them. Most of them left it at phoning my client. It's pride, isn't it? People don't want everybody thinking they can't cope just because they've lost somebody. Especially if they're getting on a bit. So all Officer Dibble has to go on is a few isolated incidents.'

I didn't need to tell a crime correspondent that it wasn't something that was going to assume a high priority for a police force struggling to deal with an epidemic of crack and guns that seemed to claim fresh victims every week in spite of an alleged truce between the gangs.

Alexis gave a cynical smile. 'Not exactly the kind of glamorous case the CID's glory boys are dying to take on, either. The only way they'd have started to take proper notice would have been if some journo like me had stumbled across the story and given it some headlines. Then they'd have had to get their finger out.'

'Too late for that now,' I said firmly.

'Toerags,' Alexis said. 'So you've put Richard's death notice in to try and flush them out?'

'Seemed like the only way to get a fix on them,' I said. 'It's clear from what the victims have said that they operate by using the deaths column. Richard's out of town on the road with some band, so I thought I'd get it done and dusted while he's not around to object to having his name taken in vain. If everything goes according to plan, someone should be here within the next half-hour.'

'Nice thinking,' Alexis said approvingly. 'Hope it works. So why didn't you use Bill's name and address? He's still in Australia, isn't he?'

I shook my head. 'I would have done, except he was flying in this afternoon.' Bill Mortensen, the senior partner of Mortensen and Brannigan,

Private Investigators and Security Consultants, had been in Australia for the last three weeks, his second trip Down Under in the past six months, an occurrence that was starting to feel a lot like double trouble to me. 'He'll be using his house as a jet-lag recovery zone. So that left Richard. Sorry you had a wasted journey of condolence. And I'm sorry if it upset you,' I added.

'You're all right. I don't think I really believed he was dead, you know? I figured it must be some sick puppy's idea of a joke, on account of I couldn't work out how come you hadn't told me he'd kicked it. If you see what I mean. Anyway, it wasn't a wasted journey. I was coming round anyway. There's something I wanted to tell you.'

For some reason, Alexis had suddenly stopped meeting my eye. She was looking vaguely round the room, as if Richard's walls were the source of all inspiration. Then she dragged her eyes away from the no longer brilliant white emulsion and started rootling round in a handbag so vast it makes mine look like an evening purse. 'So tell me,' I said impatiently after a silence long enough for Alexis to unearth a fresh packet of cigarettes, unwrap them and light one.

'It's Chris,' she exhaled ominously. More silence. Chris, Alexis's partner, is an architect in a community practice. It feels like they've been together longer than Mickey and Minnie. The pair of them had just finished building their dream home beyond the borders of civilization as we know it, part of a

13

self-build scheme. And now Alexis was using the tone of voice that BBC announcers adopt when a member of the Royal family has died or separated from a spouse.

'What about Chris?' I asked nervously.

Alexis ran a hand through her hair then looked up at me from under her eyebrows. 'She's pregnant.'

Before I could say anything, the doorbell blasted out the riff from 'Layla' again.

2

I looked at her and she looked at me. What I saw was genuine happiness accompanied by a faint flicker of apprehension. What Alexis saw, I suspect, was every piece of dental work I've ever had done. Before I could get my vocal cords unjammed Alexis was on her feet and heading for the conservatory. 'That'll be your scam merchant. I'd better leg it,' she said. 'I'll let myself out through your house. Give me a bell later,' she added to her slipstream.

Feeling stunned enough to resemble someone whose entire family has been wiped out by a freak accident, I walked to the front door in a bewildered daze. The guy on the other side of it looked like a high-class undertaker's apprentice. Dark suit, white shirt that gleamed in the streetlights like an advert for soap powder, plain dark tie. Even his hair was a gleaming black that matched his shoeshine. The only incongruity was that instead of a graveyard pallor, his skin had the kind of light

15

tan most of us can't afford in April. 'Mrs Barclay?'
he asked, his voice deep and dignified.

'That's right,' I said, trying for tremulous.

A hand snaked into his top pocket and came out
with a business card. 'Will Allen, Mrs Barclay. I'm
very sorry for your loss,' he said, not yet offering
the card.

'Are you a friend of Richard's? Someone he
works – *worked* – with?'

'I'm afraid not, Mrs Barclay. I didn't have the
good fortune to know your late husband. No,
I'm with Greenhalgh and Edwards.' He handed
the card over with a small flourish. 'I wonder if
I might have a quiet word with you?'

I looked at the card. I recognized it right away
as one of the ones that come out of machines at
the motorway-service areas. The ones on the M6
at Hilton Park are the best; they've got really smart
textured card. Drop three quid in the slot, choose
a logo, type in the text and you get sixty instant
business cards. No questions asked. One of the
great mysteries of the universe is how villains catch
on to the potential of new technology way ahead of
the straight community. While most punters were
still eyeing the business card machines warily on
their way to the toilets, the bad guys were queuing
up to arm themselves with bullshit IDs. This particular piece of fiction told me Will Allen was
Senior Bereavement Consultant with Greenhalgh
and Edwards, Monumental Masons, The Garth,
Cheadle Hulme. 'You'd better come in,' I said

tonelessly and stepped back to let him pass me. As I closed the door, I noticed Alexis emerging from my house with a cheery wave in my direction.

Allen was moving tentatively towards the living room, the one open door off the hallway. I'd drawn the line at cleaning the whole house. 'Come on through,' I said, ushering him in and pointing him at the sofa Alexis had just vacated. He sat down, carefully hitching up his trousers at the knees. In the light, the charcoal grey suit looked more like Jasper Conran than Marks and Spencer; ripping off widows was clearly a profitable business.

'Thanks for agreeing to see me, Mrs Barclay,' Allen said, concern dripping from his warm voice. He was clean cut and clean shaven, with a disturbing resemblance to John Cusack at his most disarming. 'Was your husband's death very sudden?' he asked, his eyebrows wrinkling in concern.

'Car accident,' I said, gulping back a sob. Hard work, acting. Almost convinces you Kevin Costner earns every dollar of the millions he gets for a movie.

'Tragic,' he intoned. 'To lose him in his prime. Tragic.' Much more of this and I wasn't going to be acting. I was going to be weeping for real. And not from sorrow.

I made a point of looking at his business card again. 'I don't understand, Mr Allen. What is it you're here about?'

'My company is in the business of providing high quality memorials for loved ones who pass away.

The quality element is especially important for someone like yourself, losing a loved one so young. You'll want to be certain that whatever you choose to remember him by will more than stand the test of time.' His solemn smile was close to passing the sincerity test. If I really was a grief-stricken widow, I'd have been half in love with him by now.

'But the undertaker said he'd get that all sorted out for me,' I said, going for the sensible-but-confused line.

'Traditionally, we have relied on funeral directors to refer people on to us, but we've found that this doesn't really lead to a satisfactory conclusion,' Allen said confidentially. 'When you're making the arrangements for a funeral, there are so many different matters to consider. It's hard under those circumstances to give a memorial the undivided attention it deserves.'

I nodded. 'I know what you mean,' I said wearily. 'It all starts to blur into one after a while.'

'And that's exactly why we decided that a radical rethink was needed. A memorial is something that lasts, and it's important for those of us left behind that it symbolizes the love and respect we have for the person we have lost. We at Greenhalgh and Edwards feel that the crucial issue here is that you make the decision about how to commemorate your dear husband in the peace of your own home, uncluttered by thoughts of the various elements that will make up the funeral.'

'I see,' I said. 'It sounds sensible, I suppose.'

'We think so. Tell me, Mrs Barclay, have you opted for interment or cremation?'

'Not cremation,' I said very firmly. 'A proper burial, that's what Richard would have wanted.' But only after he was actually dead, I added mentally.

He snapped open the locks on the slim black briefcase he'd placed next to him on the sofa. 'An excellent choice, if I may say so, Mrs Barclay. It's important to have a place where you can mourn properly, a focus for the communication I'm sure you'll feel between yourself and Mr Barclay for a long time to come. Now, because we're still in the trial period of this new way of communicating with our customers, we are able to offer our high quality memorials at a significant discount of twenty per cent less than the prices quoted on our behalf by funeral directors. So that means you get much better value for your money; a memorial that previously might have seemed out of your price range suddenly becomes affordable. Because, of course, we all want the very best for our loved ones,' he added, his voice oozing sympathy.

I bit back the overwhelming desire to rip his testicles off and have them nickel-plated as a memorial to his crass opportunism and nodded weakly. 'I suppose,' I said.

'I wonder if I might take this opportunity to show you our range?' The briefcase was as open as the expression on his face. How could I refuse?

'I don't know . . .'

'There's absolutely no obligation, though obviously it would be in your best interests to go down the road that offers you the best value for money.' He was on his feet and across the room to sit next to me in one fluid movement, a display file from his briefcase in his hand as if by magic. Sleight of hand like his, he could have been the new David Copperfield if he'd gone straight.

He flipped the book open in front of me. I stared at a modest granite slab, letters stuck on it like Letraset rather than incised in the stone. 'This is the most basic model we offer,' he said. 'But even that is finest Scottish granite, quarried by traditional methods and hand-finished by our own craftsmen.' He quoted a price that made my daily rate seem like buttons. He placed the file on my lap.

'Is that with or without the discount?' I asked.

'We always quote prices without discount, Mrs Barclay. So you're looking at a price that is twenty per cent less than that. And if you want to go ahead and you're prepared to pay a cash deposit plus cheque for the full amount tonight, I am authorized to offer you a further five per cent discount, making a total of one quarter less than the quoted price.' His hand had moved to cover mine, gently patting it.

That was when the front door crashed open. 'Careful with that bag, it's got the hot and sour soup in it,' I heard a familiar voice shout. I closed my eyes momentarily. Now I knew how Mary Magdalene felt on Easter Sunday.

'Kate? You in here?' Richard's voice beat him into the room by a couple of seconds. He arrived in the doorway clutching a fragrant plastic carrier bag, a smoking spliff in his other hand. He looked around his living room incredulously. 'What the hell's going on? What have you done to the place?'

He stepped into the room, followed by a pair of burly neopunks, each with a familiar Chinese takeaway carrier bag. It was the only remotely normal thing about them. Each wore heavy black work boots laced halfway up their calves, ragged black leggings and heavy tartan knee-length kilts. Above the waist, they had black granddad shirts with strategic rips held together by kilt pins and Celtic brooches. Across their chests, each had a diagonal tartan sash of the kind worn on television on Hogmanay by the dancers on those terrible ethnic fantasias the Scottish TV companies broadcast to warm the cockles of their exiles' hearts and make the rest of us throw up into our champagne. The one on Richard's left had bright red hair left long and floppy on top. The sides of his head were stubbled. The other had a permed, rainbow striped Mohican. Each was big enough to merit his own postcode. They looked like Rob Roy dressed by Vivienne Westwood. Will Allen goggled at the three of them, aghast.

Richard dropped the bag of Chinese food and his jaw as the transformation to the room really sank in. 'Jesus, Brannigan, I turn my back for five minutes and you trash the place. And who

21

the hell are you?' he demanded, glowering at Allen.

Allen reassembled his face into something approaching a smile. 'I'm Will Allen. From Greenhalgh and Edwards, the monumental masons. About Mr Barclay's memorial?'

Richard frowned. 'Mr Barclay's memorial? You mean, as in gravestone?'

Allen nodded. 'That's not the term we prefer to use, but yes, as in gravestone.'

'Mr Richard Barclay, would that be?'

'That's right.'

Richard shook his head in disbelief. He stuck his hand into the inside pocket of his leather jacket and pulled out a press card with his photograph on it. He thrust it towards Allen. 'Do I look dead to you?'

Allen was on his feet, his folder pulled out of my grasp. He threw it into the briefcase, grabbed it and shouldered past Richard and the two Celtic warriors. 'Ah shit,' I swore, jumping to my feet and pushing through the doorway in Allen's wake.

'Come back here, Brannigan, you've got some explaining to do,' I heard Richard yell as I reached the door. Allen was sprinting down the path towards the car-parking area. I didn't have my car keys on me; the last thing I'd anticipated was a chase. But Allen was my only lead and he was getting away. I had to do something. I ran down the path after him, glad that the only respectable pair of black shoes in my wardrobe had been flat pumps.

As he approached a silver Mazda saloon, the lights flashed and I heard the doors unlock. Allen jumped into the car. The engine started first time. Another one of the joys of modern technology that makes life simpler for the bad guys. He reversed in a scream of tyres and engine, threw the car into a three-point turn and swept out of the cul-de-sac where I live. Anyone seeing him burn rubber as he swung on to the main drag would only mark him down as one of the local car thieves being a little indiscreet.

Dispirited, I sighed and walked back to the house. I'd got the number of his car, but I had a funny feeling that wasn't going to take me a whole lot further forward. These people were too professional for that. At least I had the whole thing on tape, I reminded myself. I stopped in my tracks. Oh no, I didn't. In the confusion of Alexis's visit and the fallout from her shock announcement, I'd forgotten to switch on the radio mikes I'd planted in Richard's living room. The whole operation was a bust.

Not only that, but I was going to have to deal with an irate and very much alive Richard, who was by now standing on his doorstep, arms folded, face scowling. Swallowing a sigh, I walked towards him. If I'd been wearing heels, I'd have been dragging them. 'I know you think being on the road with a neo-punk band is a fate worse than death, but it doesn't actually call for a tombstone,' Richard said sarcastically as I approached.

'It was work,' I said wearily.

'Am I supposed to be *grateful* for that? There's a man in my living room – at least, I *thought* it was my living room, but looking at it, I'm not so sure any more. Maybe I walked into the wrong house by mistake? Anyway, there's some smooth bastard in *my* living room, sitting on *my* settee discussing *my* gravestone with *my* so-called girlfriend –'

'Partner,' I interjected. 'Twenty-nine, remember? Not a girl any more.'

He ignored me and steamrollered on. 'Presumably because I'm supposedly dead. And I'm supposed to be calm and laid back about it because it was *work*?' he yelled.

'Are you going to let me in, or shall I sell tickets?' I asked calmly, gesturing over my shoulder with my thumb at the rest of the close. I didn't have to look to know that half a dozen windows would be occupied by now. TV drama's been so dire lately that the locals have taken up competitive Neighbourhood Watching.

'Let you in? Why? Are we expecting the undertaker next? Coffin due to be delivered, is it?' Richard demanded, thrusting his head forward so we were practically nose to nose. I could smell the sweetness of the marijuana on his breath, see the specks of gold in his hazel eyes. Good technique for dealing with anger, focusing on small details of your environment.

I pushed him in the chest. Not hard, just enough

24

to make him back off. 'I'll explain inside,' I said, lips tight against my teeth.

'Well, big fat hairy deal,' Richard muttered, turning on his heel and pushing past the two neopunks who were leaning against the wall behind him, desperately trying to pretend they were far too cool to be interested in the war raging around them.

I followed him back into the living room and returned to my seat. Richard sat opposite me, the coffee table between us. He started emptying the contents of the three carrier bags on to the table. 'You'll find bowls and chopsticks in the kitchen,' he said to his giant Gaelic gargoyles. 'First on the right down the hall. That's if she hasn't emptied it as well.' The redhead left in search of eating implements. 'This had better be good, Brannigan,' Richard added threateningly.

'It *smells* good,' I said brightly. 'Yang Sing, is it?'

'Never mind the bloody Chinese!' I waited for the jolt while the world stopped turning. Never mind the bloody Chinese? From the man who thinks it's not food if it doesn't have soy sauce in it? 'What was that creep doing here?' Richard persisted.

'Pitching me into a gravestone,' I said as the redhead returned and dumped bowls, chopsticks and serving spoons in front of us. I grabbed a carton of hot and sour soup and a spoon.

'I realized *that*. But why here? And why *my* gravestone?' Richard almost howled.

The punk with the Mohican exchanged apprehensive looks with his mate. The redhead nodded. 'Look,' the Mohican said. 'This mebbe isnae a good time for this, Richard, know what ah mean, but?' The Glasgow accent was so strong you could have built a bridge with it and known it would outlast the civilization that spawned it. Once I'd deciphered his sentiment, I couldn't help agreeing with him.

'We could come back another time, by the way,' the redhead chipped in, accent matching. Like aural bookends.

'Never mind coming back, you're here now,' Richard said. 'Get stuck in. She loves an audience, don't you, Brannigan?' He piled his bowl with fried noodles and beansprouts, added some chunks of aromatic stuffed duck and balanced a couple of prawn wontons on top, then leaned back in his seat to munch. 'So why am I dead?'

He always does it to me. As soon as there's the remotest chance of me getting my fair share of a Chinese takeaway, Richard asks the kind of questions that require long and complicated answers. He knows perfectly well that my mother has rendered me incapable of speaking with my mouth full. Some injunctions you can rebel against; others are in the grain. Between mouthfuls of hot and sour soup so powerful it steam-cleaned my sinuses, I filled him in on the scam.

Then, Richard being too busy with his chopsticks to comment, I went on the offensive. 'And it would all have gone off perfectly if you hadn't come blundering through the door and blowing my cover sky-high. Two days early, I might point out. You're supposed to be in Milton Keynes with some band that sounds like it was chosen at random from the Neanderthal's dictionary of grunts. What was it? Blurt? Grope? Fart?'

'Prole,' Richard mumbled through the Singapore vermicelli. He swallowed. 'But we're not talking about me coming back early to my own house. We're talking about this mess,' he said, waving his chopsticks in the air.

'It's cleaner and tidier than it's ever been,' I said firmly.

'Bad news, but,' the Mohican muttered. 'Hey, missus, have you thought about getting your chakras balanced? Your energy flow's well blocked in your third.'

'Shut up, Lice. Not everybody's into being enlightened and that,' the redhead said, giving him a dig in the side that would have left most people with three cracked ribs. Lice only grunted.

'You still haven't said why you came home early,' I pointed out.

'It was two things really. Though looking at what I've come home to, I don't know why I bothered about one of them,' Richard said, as if that were some kind of explanation.

'Do I have to guess? Animal, vegetable or mineral?'

'I'd got all the material I needed for the pieces

I've got lined up on Prole, and then I bumped into the lads here. Boys, meet Kate Brannigan, who, in spite of appearances to the contrary, is a private investigator. Kate, meet Dan Druff, front man with Glasgow's top nouveau punk band, Dan Druff and the Scabby Heided Bairns.' The redhead nodded gravely and sketched a salute with his chopsticks. 'And Lice, the band's drummer.' Lice looked up from his bowl and nodded. I found a moment to wonder if their guitar players were called Al O'Pecia and Nits.

'Delighted to make your acquaintance,' I said. 'Richard, pleased though I am to be sharing my evening with Dan and Lice, why exactly have you brought them home?' My subtlety, good manners and discretion had passed their sell-by date. Besides, Dan and Lice didn't look like the kind who'd notice anyone being offensive until the half-bricks started swinging.

'My good deed for the year,' he said nonchalantly. 'They need a private eye, and I've never seen you turn down a case.'

'A paying case,' I muttered.

'We'll pay you,' Dan said.

'Something,' Lice added ominously.

'For your trouble,' Dan added, even more ominously.

'Why do you need a private eye?' I asked. It wouldn't be the first time Richard's dropped me in it, and this time I was determined that if I agreed, it was going to be an informed decision.

'Somebody's trying to see us off,' Dan said bluntly.

'You mean . . . ?' I asked.

'How plain do you need it?' Lice demanded. 'They're trying to wipe us off the map. Finish us. Render us history. Consign us to our next karmic state.'

There didn't seem to be two ways of taking Lice's words. I was hooked, no question.

3

This was definitely a lot more interesting than rehashing the cockup of my gravestone inquiries. There would be plenty of time for me to beat myself up about that later. Dealing with the seriously menaced, even if they were barely comprehensible Glaswegian musicians, has always seemed a better way of passing the time than contemplating my failures. 'You've had death threats?' I asked.

Lice looked at Dan, shaking his head pityingly. Dan looked at Richard, his eyebrows steepling in a demand for help. 'Not as such,' Richard explained. 'When Lice talks about being wiped out, he means metaphorically.'

'That's right,' Lice confirmed. 'Poetic licence and that.' My interest was dropping faster than a gun barrel faced with Clint Eastwood.

'Somebody's out to get us *professionally* is what we're trying to say,' Dan butted in. 'We're getting stuffed tighter than a red pudding.'

'What's a red pudding?' Richard demanded. I was glad about that; we private eyes never like to display our ignorance.

'For fuck's sake,' Lice groaned.

'What do you expect from a country where the fish and chip shops only sell fish and chips?' Dan said. 'It's like a sausage only it's red and it's got oatmeal in it and you deep-fry it, OK? In batter,' he added for the benefit of us Sassenachs.

I wasn't about to ask any more. I still hadn't recovered from the shock of asking for a pizza in a Scottish chip shop. I'd watched in horrified amazement as the fryer expertly folded it in half and dumped it in the deep fat. No, I didn't eat it. I fed it to the seagulls and watched them plummet into the waves afterwards, their ability to defeat gravity wiped out in one meal. 'So this meta-phorical, poetically licensed professional stitch-up consists of what, exactly?'

'Essentially, the boys are being sabotaged,' Richard said.

'Every time we're doing a gig around the town, some bastard covers all our posters up,' Dan said. 'Somebody's been phoning the promoters and telling them not to sell any more tickets for our gigs because they're already sold out. And then we get to a gig and there's hardly any genuine fans there.'

'But there's always a busload of Nazis on super lager that tear the place to bits and close the gig down,' Lice kicked in bitterly. 'Now we've been barred from half the decent venues in the north and we're getting tarred with the same brush as they fascist bastards that are wrecking our gigs. The punters are starting to mutter that if these guys follow us around from place to place, it must be because there's something in our music that appeals to brainless racists.'

'And actually, the boys' lyrics are quite the opposite of that.' Richard with the truly crucial information as usual. 'Even the most PC of your friends would be hard pressed to take offence.'

'The only PC friend I've got is the one next door with the Pentium processor,' I snapped. To my surprise, Dan and Lice guffawed.

'Nice one,' Dan said. 'Anyway, last night put the tin lid on it. We were doing this gig in Bedford, and while we were inside watching the usual wrecking crew smashing the place up, some total toerag torched our Transit.'

'Have you talked to the police about this?' I said. Silly me. The boys scowled and shook their heads. Richard cast his eyes heavenward and sighed deeply. I tried again. 'This sounds like a campaign of systematic harassment to me. They've got the resources to pursue something like that properly. And they're free,' I added.

'I thought you said she knew her arse from a hole in the ground?' Lice demanded of Richard. '"Have you talked to the police about this,"' he mimicked cruelly. The last time I felt that mimsy I was nine years old and forced to wear my cousin's cast-off party frock in lemon nylon with blue roses, complete with crackling petticoat, to my best friend's birthday party. 'For fuck's sake, look at us. If we walked into the local nick, they'd arrest us. If we told them we were being harassed, they'd piss themselves laughing. I don't think that's the answer, missus.'

Dan picked up the last salt and pepper rib and stood up. 'Come on, Lice,' he said. 'I don't want to embarrass the woman. Richard, I know you meant well, but hey, your missus obviously isnae up to it. You know what they're like, women today. They cannae bring themselves to admit there are things that are way beyond them.'

That did it. Through clenched teeth, I said, 'I am nobody's missus and I am more than capable of sorting out any of the assorted scumbags that have doubtless got their own very good reasons for having it in for Dan Druff and the Scabby Heided Bairns. You want this sorting, I'll sort it. No messing.'

When I saw the smile of complicity that flashed between Richard and Dan, I nearly decked the pair of them with the flying sweep kick I'd been perfecting down the Thai boxing gym. But there's no point in petulance once you've been well and truly had over. 'I think that little routine makes us quits,' I told Richard. He grinned. 'I'm going to need a lot more details.'

Dan sat down again. 'It all started with the flyposting,' he said, stretching his long legs out in front of him. I had the feeling it was going to be a long story.

It was just after midnight when Dan and Lice left Richard and me staring across the coffee table at each other. It had taken a while to get the whole story, what with Lice's digressions into the relationship between rock music and politics, with particular reference to right-wing racists and the oppression of the Scots. The one clear thread in their story that seemed impossible to deny was that someone was definitely out to get them. Any single incident in the Scabby Heided Bairns's catalogue of disaster could have been explained away, but not the accumulation of cockups that had characterized the last few weeks in the band's career.

They'd moved down to Manchester, supposedly the alternative music capital of the UK, from their native Glasgow in a bid to climb on to the next rung of the ladder that would lead them to becoming the Bay City Rollers of the nineties. Now, the boys were days away from throwing in the towel and heading north again. Bewildered that they could have made so serious an enemy so quickly, they wanted me to find out who was behind the campaign. Then, I suspected, it would be a matter of summoning their friends and having the Tartan Army march on some poor unsuspecting Manchester villain. I wasn't entirely sure whose side I was on here.

'You are going to sort it out for them?' Richard asked.

I shrugged. 'If they've got the money, I've got the time.'

'This isn't just about money. You owe me, Brannigan, and these lads are kicking. They deserve a break.'

'So give them a good write-up in all those magazines you contribute to,' I told him.

'They need more than that. They need word of mouth, a following. Without that, they're not exactly an attractive proposition to a record company.'

'It would take more fans than Elvis to make Dan Druff and his team attractive to me,' I muttered. 'And besides, I don't owe you. It was you and your merry men who screwed up my job earlier tonight, if you remember.'

Richard looked astonished, his big tortoiseshell glasses slipping down his nose faster than Eddie the Eagle on a ski jump. 'And what about this place?' he wailed, waving his arm at the neat and tidy room.

'Out of the goodness of my heart, I'm not going to demand the ten quid an hour that good industrial cleaners get,' I said sweetly, getting up and tossing the empty tinfoil containers into plastic bags.

'What about killing me off?' he demanded, his voice rising like a Bee Gee. 'How do you think I felt, coming home to find my partner sitting discussing my gravestone with a complete stranger? And while we're on the subject, I hope you weren't going to settle for some cheap crap,' he added indignantly.

I finished what I was doing and moved across to the sofa. 'Richard, behave,' I said, slipping my legs over his, straddling him.

'It's not very nice, being dead,' he muttered as my mouth descended on his.

Eventually, I moved my lips along his jaw, tongue flickering against the angle of the bone. 'Maybe not,' I said softly, tickling his ear. 'But isn't resurrection fun?'

Richard barely stirred when I left his bed next morning just after seven. I scribbled, 'Gone 2 work, C U 2night?' on a Post-It note and stuck it on the forearm that was flung out across the pillow. I used to write messages straight on to his arm with a felt-tip pen until he complained it ruined his street cred to have 'Buy milk' stencilled indelibly across his wrist. Nothing if not sensitive to people's needs, I switched to Post-Its.

Back in my own home, I stood under the shower, taking my first opportunity to consider Alexis's ballistic missile. I knew that having a baby had climbed to the top of her and Chris's partnership agenda now that they had put the finishing touches to their house on the edge of the Pennines, but somehow I hadn't realized parenthood was quite so imminent a project. I'd had this mental picture of it being something that would rumble on for ages before anything actually happened, given that it's such a complicated business for lesbian couples to arrange.

First they've got to decide whether they want an anonymous donor, in which case their baby could end up having the same father as half the children of lesbians in the Greater Manchester area, with all the potential horrors that lines up for the future.

But if they decide to go for a donor they know, they've got to be careful that everyone agrees in advance what his relationship to the child is going to be. Then they've got to wait while he has two AIDS tests with a gap of at least six months in between. Finally, they've got to juggle things so that sperm and womb are in the same place at the optimum moment. According to Alexis, it's not like a straight couple where the woman can take her temperature every five minutes till the time is right then seize her bloke by the appropriate body part and demand sex. So I'd been banking on a breathing space to get used to the idea of Chris and Alexis as parents.

I've never been smitten with the maternal urge, which means I always feel a bit bemused when my friends get sandbagged by their hormones and turn from perfectly normal women into monomaniacs desperate to pass their genes on to a waiting world. Maybe it's because my biological clock has still got a way to go before anything in my universe starts turning pumpkin-shaped. Or maybe, as Richard suggests when he's in sentimental father mode, it's because I'm a cold-hearted bastard with all the emotional warmth of Robocop. Either way, I didn't want a child and I never knew if I was saying the right thing to those who did.

Selfishly, my first thought was for the difference it was going to make to my life. Alexis is my best friend. We go shopping for clothes together. We play seriously competitive and acrimonious Scrabble games together. When Chris and Richard aren't there to complain about the results, we concoct exotic and bizarre snacks (oatcakes with French mayonnaise and strawberry jam; green banana, coconut and chicken curry . . .) and wash them down with copious amounts of good vodka. We pick each other's brains and exploit each other's contacts. Most of all, we're there for each other when it counts.

As the hot water cascaded over me, I felt like I was already in mourning for the friendship. Nothing was ever going to be the same again. Alexis would have responsibilities. When Chris's commitments as a partner in a firm of community architects took her out of town, Alexis would be shackled without time off for good behaviour. Instead of hanging out with me after work, she'd be rushing home for bathtime and nursery tea. Her conversation would shrink to the latest exploits of the incredible child. And it would be incredible, no two ways about it. They always are. There would be endless photographs to pore over. Instead of calling me to say, 'Get down here, girl, I've just found a fabulous silk shirt in your size in Kendal's sale,' Alexis would be putting the child on the phone to say, 'Wo, gay,' and claiming it as 'Hello, Kate'. Worst of all, I had this horrible suspicion I was going to become Auntie Kate. Even Richard's son Davy has never tried to do that to me.

I rinsed the last of the shampoo out of my auburn hair and stepped out of the shower. At least I didn't have to live under the same roof as it, I thought as I towelled my head. Besides, I told myself, nothing healthy stays the same. Friendships change and grow, they shift their emphases and sometimes they even die. 'Everything must change,' I said out loud. Then I noticed a grey hair. So much for healthy change.

I brushed my hair into the neat bob I've opted for recently. Time to get my brain into gear. I knew where I needed to go next on Dan and Lice's problem, but that was a source that might take a little time and a lot of deviousness to tap. More straightforward was a visit to the dark side of the moon.

Gizmo is one of my silver linings. The cloud was a Telecom engineer that I'd had a brief fling with. He'd caught me at one of those weak moments when you kid yourself into believing a nice smile and cute bum are a reasonable basis for a meaningful relationship. After all, if it's a good enough principle for most of the male population . . . His lectures on telephone technology had been mildly interesting the first time round. After a month of them, there wasn't a court in the land that would have convicted me of anything other than self-defence if I'd succumbed to the temptation of burying a meat cleaver in his skull. But he had introduced me to Gizmo, which gave me something good to remember him by.

If Judy Garland was born in a trunk, Gizmo was born in an anorak. In spite of having the soul of a nerd, he had too much attitude for the passivity of train spotting. So he became a computer whizz. That was back in the steam age of computers, when the most powerful of machines took so long to scroll to the end of a ten-page document that you could go off and drip a pot of filter coffee without missing a thing. When 99.99% of the population still thought bulletin boards were things you found on office walls, Gizmo was on line to people all over the world. The teenagers who invented phone phreaking and hacking into the Pentagon were close personal friends of his. He'd never met them, you understand, just spent his nights typing his end of conversations with them and like-minded nutters all over the planet.

When the FBI started arresting hackers and phreakers on the grounds that America has never known what to do with nonconformists, and the British police started to take an interest, Gizmo decided it was time to stop playing Butch Cassidy and the Sundance Kid and come out into the sunlit uplands. So he started working for Telecom. And he manages to keep his face straight when he tells people that he's a computer systems manager there. Which is another way of saying he actually gets paid to keep abreast of all the information technology that allows him to remain king of the darkside hackers. Gizmo's like Bruce Wayne in reverse. When darkness falls on Gotham City, instead of donning mask and cape and taking on the bad guys, Gizmo goes on line and becomes one of the growing army who see cyberspace as the ultimate subversive, anarchic community. And Telecom still haven't noticed that their northern systems manager is a renegade. It's no wonder none of Gizmo's friends have Telecom shares.

If I had to pick one thing that demonstrates the key difference between the UK and the USA, it would be their attitudes to information. Americans get everything unless there's a damn good reason why not. Brits get nothing unless a High Court judge and an Act of Parliament have said there's a damn good reason why we should. And private eyes are just like ordinary citizens in that respect. We don't have any privileges. What we have are sources. They fall into two groups: the ones who are motivated by money and the ones who are driven by principle. Gizmo's belief that information is born free but everywhere is in chains has saved my clients a small fortune. Police records, driver and vehicle licensing information, credit ratings: they're all there at his fingertips and, for a small donation to Gizmo's Hardware Upgrade Fund, at mine. The only information he won't pass on to me is anything relating to BT phone bills or numbers. That would be a breach of confidence. Or something equally arbitrary. We all have to draw the line somewhere.

I draw it at passing Gizmo's info on to clients. I use him either when I've hit a dead end or I know he can get something a lot faster than I can by official routes, which means the client saves money. I know I can be trusted not to abuse that information. I can't say the same about the people who hire me, so I don't tell them. I've had people waving wads of dosh under my nose for an ex-directory phone number or the address that goes with a car licence plate. Call me a control freak, but I won't do that kind of work. I know there are agencies who do, but that doesn't keep me awake at night. The only conscience I can afford to worry about is my own.

Gizmo had recently moved from a bedsit in the busiest red-light street in Whalley Range to a two-bedroomed flat above a shop in Levenshulme, a stretch of bandit country grouped around Stockport Road. The shop sells reconditioned vacuum cleaners. If you've ever wondered where Hoovers go when they die, this is the place. I've never seen a customer enter or leave the place, though there's so much grime on the windows they could be running live sex shows in there and nobody would be any the wiser. And Gizmo reckons he's moved up in the world.

I was going against the traffic flow on the busy arterial road, so it didn't take me long to drive the short distance to Levenshulme and find a parking space on a side street of red-brick terraces. I pressed the bell and waited, contemplating a front door so coated with inner-city pollution that it was no longer possible to tell what colour it had originally been. The only clean part of the door was the glass on the spyhole. After about thirty seconds, I pressed the bell again. This time, there was a thunder of clattering feet, a brief pause and then the door opened a cautious couple of inches. 'Kate,' Gizmo said, showing no inclination to invite me in. His skin looked grey in the harsh morning light, his eyes red-rimmed like a laboratory white rat.

'All right, Giz?'

'No, since you ask.' He rubbed a hand along his stubbled jaw and scratched behind one ear with the knuckle of his index finger.

'What's the problem? Trouble with the Dibble?'

His lips twisted in the kind of smile dogs give before they remove your liver without benefit of anaesthetic. 'No way. I'm always well ahead of the woodentops. No, this is serious. I've got the bullet.'

'From Telecom?'

'Who else?'

I was taken aback. The only thing I could think of was that someone had got wise to Gizmo's extra-curricular activities. 'They catch you with your hand in somebody's digital traffic?'

'Get real,' he said indignantly. 'Staff cuts. The section head doesn't like the fact that I know more than anybody else in the section, including him. So it's good night Vienna, Gizmo.'

'You'll get another job,' I said. I would have found it easier to convince myself if I hadn't been looking at him as I spoke. As well as the red-rimmed eyes and the stubble, a prospective employer had to contend with a haircut that looked like Edward Scissorhands on a bad hair day, and a dress sense that would embarrass a jumble sale.

'I'm too old.'

'How old?'

'Thirty-two,' he mumbled with a suspicious scowl, as if he thought I was going to laugh. I didn't have enough years on him for that.

'You're winding me up,' I said.

'The guys who do the hiring are in their forties and scared shitless that they're going to get the tin handshake any day now, and they know nothing about computer systems except that someone told them it's a young man's game. If you're over twenty-five, twenty-seven if you've got a PhD, they won't even look at your CV. Believe me, Kate, I'm too old.'

'What a bummer,' I said, meaning it.

'Yeah, well. Shit happens. But it's nicer when it happens to somebody else. So what did you come round for? Last orders before I have to put my rates up?'

I handed him the piece of paper where I'd noted Will Allen's licence plate. 'The name and address that goes with the car.'

He didn't even look at it. He just said, 'Some time this afternoon,' then started to close the door.

'Hey, Giz?' He paused. 'I'm really sorry,' I said. He nodded and shut the door.

I walked back towards the street where I'd parked the zippy Rover 216 that Mortensen and Brannigan had bought for me a couple of months before. Until then, I'd been driving a top-of-the-range sports coupé that we'd taken in part payment for a long and complicated car-finance fraud case, but I'd known in my heart of hearts it was far too conspicuous a set of wheels for the kind of work I do. Given how much I enjoy driving, it had been a wrench to part with it, but I'd learned to love the Rover. Especially after my mate Handbrake had done something double wicked to the engine which made it nippier than any of its German siblings from BMW.

As I rounded the corner, I couldn't believe what I saw. There was a spray of glittering glass chunks like hundreds of tiny mosaic tiles all over the pavement by the driver's door of the Rover. The car was twenty yards from the main road, it was half past eight in the morning and I'd been gone less than ten minutes, but someone had had it away on their toes with my stereo.

4

It took me an hour and a half round at Handbrake's backstreet garage to get a new window and stereo cassette. I knew the window had come from a scrapyard, but it would have been bad manners to ask about the origins of the cassette. I wouldn't have been entirely surprised if my own deck had arrived in the bike pannier of one of the young lads who supply Handbrake with spare parts as an alternative to drug-running round Moss Side, but it clearly wasn't my lucky day and I had to settle for a less sophisticated machine. While that might increase the shelf life of my new driver's-door window, it wouldn't improve the quality of my life in Manchester's orbital motorway traffic jams, so I wasn't in the best of moods when I finally staggered through the door of the office just after ten.

I knew at once that something was badly wrong. Shelley, our office manager, made no comment about my lateness. In all the years I've been working with her, she'd never before missed the opportunity to whip me into line like one of her two teenage kids. I'd once found her son Donovan, a six-foot three-inch basketball player, engineering student and occasional rapper with a local band, having to give up a weekend to paint my office because he hadn't come home till four in the morning. After that, I'd always had a good excuse for being late into work. But this morning, she scarcely glanced up from her screen when I walked in. 'Bill's in,' was all she said.

Worrying. 'Already? I thought he only flew in yesterday afternoon?'

Shelley's lips pursed. 'That's right,' she said stiffly. 'He said to tell you he needs a word,' she added, gesturing with her head towards the closed door of my partner's office. Even more worrying. Shelley is Bill's biggest fan. Normally when he returns from one of his foreign security consultancy trips, we all sit around in the outside office and schmooze the morning away over coffee, catching up. Bill's a friendly soul; I'd never known him to hide behind a closed door unless he needed absolute peace and quiet to work out some thorny computer problem.

I tapped on the door but didn't wait for an answer before I opened it and walked in on the sort of scene that would have been more appropriate in the new Dancehouse a few doors down Oxford Road. Bill Mortensen, a bearded blond giant of a man, was standing behind his desk, leaning over a dark woman whose body was curved back under his in an arc that would have had my spine screaming for mercy. One of Bill's bunch-of-bananas hands supported the small of her back, the other her shoulders. Unlike the ballet, however, their lips were welded together. I cleared my throat.

Bill jumped, his mouth leaving the woman's with a nauseating smack as he straightened and half turned, releasing his grip on the woman. Just as well her arms were wrapped round his neck or she'd have been on the fast track to quadriplegia. 'Kate,' Bill gasped. His face did a double act, the mouth smiling, the eyes panicking.

'Welcome back, Bill. I wasn't expecting to see you this morning,' I said calmly, closing the door behind me and making for my usual perch on the table that runs along one wall.

Bill stuttered something about wanting to see me while the woman disentangled herself from him. She was a good six inches taller than my five feet and three inches. Strike one. Her hair was as dark as Bill's was blond, cut in the sort of spiky urchin cut I'd recently abandoned when even I'd noticed it was getting a bit passé. On her, it looked terrific. Strike two. Her skin was burnished bronze, an impossible dream for those of us with the skin that matches auburn hair. Strike three. I didn't have the faintest idea who Bill's latest companion was, but I hated her already. She grinned and moved towards me, hand stuck out in front of her with all the enthusiasm of an extrovert teenager who hasn't been put down yet. 'Kate, it's great to meet you,' she announced in an Australian accent that made Crocodile Dundee sound like a BBC newsreader. 'Bill's told me so much about you, I feel like I know you already.' I tentatively put out a hand which she gripped fervently and pumped up and down. 'I just know we're going to be mates,' she added, clapping her other hand on my shoulder.

I looked past her at Bill, my eyebrows raised. He moved towards us and the woman released my hand to slip hers into his. 'Kate,' he finally said. 'This is Sheila.' His eyes warned me not to laugh.

'Don't tell me, let me guess,' I said. 'You met in Australia.'

Sheila roared with laughter. I could feel her excessive response thrusting me into the role of repressed English-woman. 'God, Kate, he was right about your sense of humour,' she said. I forced my lips into what I seemed to remember was a smile. 'Hey, Bill, you better tell her the news.'

Bill stood chewing his beard for a moment, then said, 'Sheila and I are getting married.'

To say I was gobsmacked would be like saying Tom Hanks can act a bit. It's not that Bill doesn't like women. He does. Lots of them. He also likes variety. As a serial monogamist, he makes Casanova and Don Juan look like absolute beginners. But he'd always been choosy about who he hung out with. While he preferred his girlfriends good-looking, brains and ambition had always been just as high on his agenda. So while Sheila might appear more of a bimbo than anyone I'd ever seen Bill with, I wasn't about to make a snap judgement on the basis of what I'd seen so far. 'Congratulations,' I managed without tripping over too many of the syllables.

'Thanks; Kate,' Sheila said warmly. 'It's big of you to be generous about losing your partner.'

I looked at Bill. He looked like he'd swallowed an ice cube. 'I thought that in these situations one said something like, "Not so much losing a partner as gaining a secretary,"' I said ominously. 'I have this feeling that there's something you haven't got round to telling me yet, William.'

'Sheila, Kate and I need to have boring business talks. Why don't you get Shelley to point you in the direction of all the best clothes shops? You can come back at lunch time and we'll all go to the Brasserie?' Bill said desperately, one eye on the toe I was tapping on the floor.

'No problems, Billy boy,' Sheila said, planting a kiss smack on his lips. On her way past me, she sketched a wave. 'Can't wait to get to know you better, Kate.'

When the door closed behind her, there was a long silence. '"Why don't you get Shelley to point you in the direction of the clothes shops?"' I mimicked as cruelly as I could manage.

'She owns three dress shops in Sydney,' Bill said mildly. I might have known. That explained the tailored black dress she'd almost been wearing.

'This is not a good way to start the day, Bill,' I said. 'What does she mean, I'll be losing a partner? Is she the pathologically jealous type who doesn't want her man working alongside another woman? Is Shelley getting the bum's rush from Waltzing Matilda too?'

Bill threw himself into his chair and sighed. 'Sheila knows I was dreading this conversation, and she said what she did to force me into having it,' he explained. 'Kate, this is it. Sheila's the one I want.'

'Let's face it, Bill, you've run enough consumer tests to make an informed decision,' I said bitterly. I wanted to be happy for him. I would have been happy for him if it hadn't been for the stab of fear that Sheila's words had triggered in me.

He looked me in the eye and smiled. 'True. Which means that now I've found her, I don't want to let her go. Marriage seems like the sensible option.' He looked away. 'And that means either Sheila moves over here or I move to Australia.'

Silence. I knew what was coming but I didn't see why I should let him off the hook. I leaned back against the wall and folded my arms across my chest. Bill the Bear was turning from teddy to grizzly before my eyes, and I didn't like the transformation. Finally, a few sighs later, Bill said, 'Me moving is the logical step. My work's more portable than hers. The jobs I've already been doing in Australia have given me some good contacts, while she has none in the rag trade over here. Besides, the weather's nicer. And the wine.' He tried a pleading, little-boy-lost smile on me.

It didn't play. 'So what happens to Mortensen and Brannigan?' I demanded, my voice surprising even me with its harshness.

Bill picked up the curly Sherlock Holmes pipe he occasionally smokes when he's stuck on a problem, and started fiddling with it. 'I'm sorry, Kate, but I'm going to have to sell my share of the partnership. The problem I've got is that I need to realize the capital I've got tied up in the business so I can start again in Sydney.'

'I don't believe I'm hearing this,' I said. 'You think you can just *sell* us to the highest bidder? Your parents own half the farmland in Cheshire. Can't you get them to stake you?'

Bill scowled. 'Of course I bloody can't,' he growled. 'You didn't go cap in hand to your father when you wanted to become a partner. You funded it yourself. Besides, life's not exactly a bed of roses in cattle farming right now. I doubt they've got the cash to throw around.'

'Fine,' I said angrily. 'So who have you sold out to?'

Bill looked shocked. 'I haven't sold to anyone,' he protested. 'How could you think I'd go behind your back like that?'

I shrugged. 'Everything else seems to have been cut and dried without consulting me. Why should that be any different?'

'Didn't you bother reading the partnership

agreement when we drew it up? Paragraph sixteen. If either of us wants to sell our share of the business, we have to offer first refusal to the other partner. And if the remaining partner doesn't want to buy, they have the power of veto over the sale to any third party on any reasonable ground.'

' "The final decision as to the reasonableness or otherwise of that ground to be taken by the partners in consultation with any employees of the firm," ' I quoted from memory. I'd written most of the agreement; it wasn't surprising I knew by heart what the key parts of it said. 'It's academic, Bill. You know I can't afford to buy you out. And you also know damn well that I'm far too fond of you to stand in the way of what you want. So pick your buyer.'

I jumped to my feet and wrenched the door open. 'I'm out of here,' I said, hoping the disgust and anger I felt was as vivid to him as it was to me. Sometimes, the only things that make you feel good are the same ones that worked when you were five. Yes, I slammed the door.

I sat staring into the froth of a cappuccino in the Cigar Store café. The waitress was having an animated conversation with a couple of her friends drinking espressos in the corner, but apart from them, I had the place to myself. It wasn't hard to tune out their gossip and focus on the implications of what Bill had said. I couldn't believe what he planned to do to me. It undercut everything I thought I knew about Bill. It made me feel that my judgement wasn't worth a bag of used cat litter. The man had been my friend before he became my business partner. I'd started my career process-serving for him as a way of eking out my student grant because the hours and the cash were better than bar work. I'd toiled with him or for him ever since I'd jacked in my law degree after the second year, when I realized I could never spend my working days in the company of wolves and settled for the blond bear instead.

There was no way I could afford to buy him out. The deal we'd done when I'd become a partner had been simple enough. Bill had had the business valued, and I'd worked out I could afford to buy thirty-five per cent. I'd borrowed the money on a short-term loan from the bank and paid it back over four years. I'd managed that by paying the bank every penny I earned over and above my previous salary, including my annual profit shares. I'd only finished paying the loan off three months previously, thanks in part to a windfall that couldn't be explained either to another living soul or to the taxman without risking the knowledge getting back to the organized criminals who had inadvertently made me the gift. It had been a struggle to meet the payments on the loan, and I had no intention of standing under the kind of trees that deliver such dangerous windfalls ever again.

I had to face it. There was no way I could raise the cash to buy out Bill's sixty-five per cent at the prices of four years ago, never mind what the agency would now be worth, given the new clients we'd both brought in since then. I was going to be the victim of anyone who decided a two-thirds share in a profitable detective agency was a good investment.

A second cup clattered on to the table in front of me. Startled, I looked up and found myself staring into Shelley's amber eyes. 'I thought I'd find you here,' she said, tossing her mac over a chair and sitting down opposite me. Her face looked like one of those carved African ceremonial masks, all polished planes and immobility, especially now she'd abandoned the beads she used to wear plaited in her hair and moved on to neat cornrows. I couldn't tell from looking at her if she'd come to sympathize or to tell me off for my tantrum and plead Bill's case.

'And we thought Lincoln freed the slaves,' I said bitterly. 'How do you feel about being bought and sold?'

'It's not as bad for me as it is for you,' Shelley said. 'I don't like the new boss, I just walk out the door and get me another job. But you're tied to whoever Bill sells his share to, am I right?'

'As usual. Back on the chain gang, Shell, that's what I am. Like Chrissie Hynde says, circumstance beyond our control.'

Shelley's eyebrows flickered. 'Doesn't have to be that way, does it?'

'I'm not with you.'

'This behaviour from Bill is not what we're used to.'

'Of course it's bloody not,' I interrupted petulantly. 'It's this Sheila, isn't it? Like the man said, when you've got them by the balls, their hearts and minds will follow. And there's no doubting which part of Bill's anatomy Sheila's got a grip on.'

'Doesn't matter who's behind it, the end result is the same,' Shelley pointed out. 'Bottom line is, Bill is not behaving like your friend, and in my book that absolves you from behaving like his friend.'

'And?'

'You own thirty-five per cent of the business, don't you?'

I nodded. 'Free and clear.'

'So you put your share on the market. Either as an independent entity, or as part of the whole package.'

I frowned. 'But that would devalue the business quite a lot. It's a different kettle of fish buying into an established agency where one of the partners is staying on to maintain the existing clients and another thing altogether to go for something that's nothing more really than a name and a bunch of office equipment.'

'My point exactly,' Shelley said.

'But I'd lose a lot of the money I've put in,' I said.

'But Bill would stand to lose a hell of a lot more,' Shelley said. 'And he needs the cash a lot more than you do right now. What it would do is buy

56

you a bit of time and a lot of say-so on the deal. It gives you a bargaining chip.'

Slowly, I nodded. 'Shelley, you are one mean mother,' I said, admiration in my voice. 'And I thought Bill was your blue-eyed boy.'

Shelley's lips tightened. I noticed that between her nose and mouth, a couple of creases were graduating to lines. 'Listen, Kate, when I was growing up, I saw a lot of women doing the "my kids, right or wrong" routine with teachers, with cops. And I see their kids now, running drugs, living behind bars. I've seen the funerals when another one gets shot in some stupid gang war. I don't like the end result of blind loyalty. Bill has been my friend and my boss a long time, but he's behaving like an arsehole to us both, and that's how he deserves to be treated.'

I admired her cold determination to get the best result for both of us. I just didn't know if I could carry it through as ruthlessly as Shelley would doubtless demand. 'You're right,' I said. 'I'll tell him I want to sell too.'

Shelley smiled. 'I bet you feel better already,' she said shrewdly. She wasn't wrong. 'So, haven't you got any work to do?'

I told her about the previous evening's adventures, and, predictably enough, she had a good laugh at my expense. 'So now I need to see Dennis,' I finished up. 'Richard might know all there is to know about the music side of the rock business, but when it comes to the criminal side, he thinks seedy is something you listen to on your stereo. Whereas Dennis might not know his Ice T from his Enya, but he could figure out where to make a bent earner in the "Hallelujah Chorus".' The only problem was, as I didn't have to remind Shelley, my friend and sometime mentor Dennis wasn't quite as accessible as normal, Her Majesty the Queen being unreasonably fussy about keeping her guests to herself.

When I met Dennis, like so many people in their late thirties, he'd just gone through a major career change. After a stretch in prison, he'd given up his previous job as a professional and highly successful burglar to the rich and famous and taken up the more demanding but less dangerous occupation of 'a bit of ducking and diving' on the fringes of the law. Which included, on occasion, a bit of consultancy work for Mortensen and Brannigan. Thanks to Dennis, I'd learned how to pick locks, defeat alarm systems and ransack filing cabinets without leaving a trace.

Unfortunately, a little enterprise of Dennis's aimed at separating criminals from their cash flow had turned sour when he'd inadvertently arranged one of his handovers in the middle of a Drugs Squad surveillance. Instead of grabbing a couple of major-league traffickers and one of those cocaine hauls that get mentioned in the news, the cops ended up with a small-time villain and the kind of nothing case that barely makes three paragraphs in the local paper. Inevitably, Dennis paid the price of their pique, seeing his scam blown sufficiently out of proportion in court to land him with an eighteen-month sentence. Some might say he got off lightly, given his CV and what else I happened to know he'd been up to lately, but speaking as someone who would go quietly mad serving an eighteen-day sentence, I wouldn't be one of them.

'When can you get in to see him?' Shelley asked.

Good question. I didn't have a Visiting Order nor any immediate prospect of getting one. Once upon a time, I'd have rung up and pretended to be a legal executive from his firm of solicitors and asked for an appointment the next day. But security had grown tighter recently. Too many prisoners had been going walkabout from jails that weren't supposed to be open prisons. Now, when you booked a brief's appointment at Strangeways, they took the details then rang back the firm you allegedly represented to confirm the name of the person attending and to give them a code consisting of two letters and four numbers. Without the code, you couldn't get in. 'I thought about asking Ruth to let me pose as one of her legal execs,' I said.

Shelley snorted. 'After the last time? I don't think so!'

The last time I'd pretended to be one of Ruth Hunter's junior employees it had strained our friendship so severely it had to wear a truss for months afterwards. Shelley was right. Ruth wasn't going to play.

'I don't mean to teach you to suck eggs,' Shelley said without a trace of humility or apology. 'And I know this goes against the grain. But had you thought about doing it the straight way?'

5

I pivoted on the ball of my right foot, bending the knee as I straightened my left leg, using the momentum to drive me forward and round in a quarter-circle. The well-muscled leg whistled past me, just grazing the hip that moments before had been right in its path. I grunted with effort as I sidestepped and jabbed a short kick at the knee of my assailant.

I was too slow. Next thing I knew, my right leg was swept from under me and I was lying on my back, lungs screaming for anything to replace the air that had been slammed out of them. Christie O'Brien stood above me, grinning. 'You're slowing down,' she observed with the casual cruelty of adolescence. Of course I was slow compared to her; she was, after all, a former British under-fourteen championship finalist. But Christie – Christine until she discovered fashion and lads – was above all her father's daughter. She'd learned at an early age that nothing succeeds like kicking them when they're down.

One of the other things I'd learned thanks to Dennis was Thai kick boxing, a sport he insisted every woman should know. The theory goes, a woman as small as I am is never going to beat a guy in a fair fight, so the key to personal safety is to land one good kick either in the shins or the gonads. Then it's 'legs, don't let me down' time. Kick boxing teaches you how to land the kick and keeps you fit enough to leg it afterwards.

When he'd been sent down, Dennis had asked me to keep an eye on Christie. She'd inherited her mother's gleaming blonde hair and wide blue eyes, but her brains had come from a father who knew only too well the damage a teenage girl can wreak when the only adult around to keep an eye on things has a generous spirit and fewer brain cells than the average goldfish. Because she'd always been accustomed to seeing me around the gym, Christie had either failed to notice or decided not to resent the fact that I'd been spending a lot more time with her recently.

She filled me in on the latest school dramas of who was hanging out with whom and why as we showered next to each other – our club's strictly breeze block. You want cubicles, go somewhere else and pay four times as much to join. By the time we were towelling ourselves dry, I'd managed to swing the conversation round to Dennis. 'You told your dad about this Jason, then,' I asked her casually. She'd mentioned the lad's name once too often.

'You've got to be joking,' she said. 'Tell him about somebody he can't check out for himself and have the heavy mob kicking Jason's door in for a reference? No way. When he comes out'll be well soon enough.'

'When you seeing him next?' I asked.

'Mum's got a VO for Thursday afternoon. I'm supposed to be going with her, but I've got cross-country trials and I don't want to miss them,' she grumbled as she pulled a sweatshirt over her head. 'Dad wouldn't mind. He'll be the one giving me a go-along if I miss getting on the team. But Mum gets really depressed going to Strangeways on her own, so I feel like I've got to go with her.'

'I could go instead of you,' I suggested.

Christie's face lit up. 'Would you? You don't mind? I'm warning you, it's a three-hankie job coming home.'

'I don't mind,' I said. 'I'd like to see your dad. I miss him.'

Christie sighed and stared at her trainers. 'Me too.' She looked up at me, her eyes candid. 'I'm really angry with him, you know? After he came out last time, he promised me he'd never do anything that would get him banged up again.'

I leaned over and gave her a hug. 'He knows he's let you down. It's hard, recognizing that your dad's not perfect, but he's just like the rest of us. He needs you to forgive him, Christie.'

'Yeah, well,' she said. 'I'll tell Mum you'll pick her up dinner time Thursday, then.' She got to her feet and stuffed her sweaty sports clothes into one of the counterfeit Head holdalls Dennis had been turning out the previous spring. 'See ya, Kate,' she said on her way out the door.

Knowing I was doing her a favour made me feel less like the exploitation queen of South Manchester. But not a lot less. So much for doing it the straight way.

When I emerged from the gym, I decided to swing round by Gizmo's to see if he'd got anywhere with my earlier request. If the old axiom, 'If I was going there, I wouldn't start from here,' didn't exist, they'd have to invent it for the journey from Sale to Levenshulme in mid-morning traffic. I knew before I started it was going to be hell on wheels, but for once, I didn't care. Me, reluctant to face Bill?

I crawled along in second while Cyndi Lauper reminded me that girls just wanna have fun. I growled at the cassette deck and swapped Cyndi for Tanita Tikaram's more gloomy take on the world. I knew exactly what she meant when she accused someone of making the whole world cry. I sat in the queue of traffic at the lights where Wilbraham Road meets Oxford Road in the heart of undergraduate city, watching them going about their student lives, backpacked and badly barbered. I couldn't believe it when the fashion world created a whole industry round grunge as if it was something that had just happened. The rest of us knew it wasn't anything new: students have been wearing layers against the cold, and workmen's heavy-duty checked shirts for cheapness, ever since I was a student a dozen years ago. Shaking my head, I glanced at the wall alongside the car. Plastered along it were posters for bands appearing at the local clubs. Some of the venues I recognized from razzing with Richard; others I knew nothing about. I hadn't realized quite how many live music venues there were in the city these days. I looked more closely at the posters, noticing one that had peeled away on the top right corner. Underneath, I could see, in large red letters, 'UFF'. It looked like Dan and Lice hadn't been making it up as they went along.

The impatient horn of the suit in the company car behind me dragged my attention away from the posters and back to the road. After the lights, the traffic eased up, and I actually managed to get into fourth gear before I reached Gizmo's. This time, I reckoned it would be cheaper to take my chances with the traffic wardens than the locals, so I left the car illegally parked on the main drag. Judging by the other drivers doing the same thing, the wardens were about as fond of hanging out in Levenshulme as I was. I hit the hole in the wall for some cash for Gizmo, then I crossed the road and rang his bell.

Gizmo frowned when he saw me. 'Didn't you get the e-mail?' he asked.

'I've not been back to the office,' I said, holding a

tightly rolled wad of notes towards him. 'Do I take it you've had some joy?'

'Yeah. You better come in,' he said reluctantly, delicately removing the cash from my hand and slipping it into the watch pocket of a pair of grey flannels that looked as if they'd first drawn breath around the time of the Great War. 'Somebody dressed as smart as you on the pavement around here looks well suspicious to the local plod. I mean, you're obviously not a native, are you?' he added as I followed him up the narrow stairs, the soles of my shoes sticking to the elderly cord carpet. It was the first time he'd let me past his front door, and frankly, I wasn't surprised.

I followed Gizmo into the front room of the flat. It was a dislocating experience. Instead of the dingy grime and chipped paint of the stairway, I was in a spotlessly clean room. New woodblock flooring, matt grey walls, no curtains, double-glazed windows. A leather sofa. Two desks with computer monitors, one a Mac, one a PC. A long table with an assortment of old computers – an Atari, a Spectrum, an Amiga, an Amstrad PCW and an ancient Pet. A couple of modems, a flat-bed scanner, a hand-held scanner, a couple of printers and a shelf stacked with software boxes. There was no fabric anywhere in the room. Even the chair in front of the PC monitor was upholstered in leather. Gizmo might look like Pigpen, but the environment he'd created for his beloved computers was as near to the perfect dust-free room as he could get.

'Nice one,' I said.

He thrust his hands into the pockets of a woollen waistcoat most bag ladies would be ashamed to own and said, 'Got to look after them, haven't you? I've had that Pet since 1980, and it still runs like a dream.'

'Strange dreams you have, Giz,' I commented as he hit some keys on his PC and located the information I'd asked for. Within seconds, a sheet of paper was spitting out of one of the laser printers. I picked up the paper and read, 'Sell Phones, 1 Beaumaris Road, Higher Crumpsall, Manchester.' There was a phone number too. I raised an eyebrow. 'That it?'

'All I could get,' he said.

'No names?'

'No names. They're not listed at Companies House. They sound like they're into mobies. I suppose if you wanted to go to the trouble and *expense*' – stressing the last word heavily – 'I could do a trawl through the mobile phone service providers and see if this lot are among their customers. But –'

'Thanks, but no thanks,' I said. Breaking the law too many times on any given job is tempting fate. 'Once is sufficient,' I added. 'Anything more would be vulgar.'

'I'll be seeing you then,' Gizmo said pointedly, staring past my shoulder at the door. I took the hint. Find what you're good at and stick to it, that's what I say.

*　　*　　*

Beaumaris Road was a red-brick back street running parallel to the main drag of Cheetham Hill Road. Unsurprisingly, number one was on the corner. Sell Phones occupied what had obviously once been a corner shop, though it had been tarted up since it had last sold pints of milk at all hours and grossly inflated prices. I parked further down the street and pulled on a floppy green velvet cap and a pair of granny specs with clear glass to complete the transformation from desolate widow to total stranger. They didn't really go with my Levis and beige blazer, but fashion's so eclectic these days that you can mix anything if you don't mind looking like a borderline care-in-the-community case or a social worker.

I walked back to the corner, noting the heavy grilles over the window of Sell Phones. I paused and looked through to an interior that was all grey carpet, white walls and display cabinets of mobile phones. A good-looking black guy was leaning languidly against a display cabinet, head cocked, listening to a woman who was clearly telling the kind of lengthy tale that involves a lot of body language and lines like, 'So she goes, "You didn't!" and I go, "I did. No messing." And she looks at me gone out and she goes, "You never!"' She was a couple of inches taller than me, but slimmer through the shoulders and hips. Her hair was a glossy black bob, her eyes dark, her skin pale, her cheekbones Slavic, scarlet lips reminding me irresistibly of Cruella De Vil. She looked like a Pole crossed with a racehorse. She was too engrossed in her tale to notice me, and the black guy was too busy looking exquisite in a suit that screamed, '*Ciao, bambino.*'

I peered more closely through the glass and there, at the back of the shop, sitting behind a desk, head lowered as he took notes of the phone call he was engrossed in, was Will Allen in all his glory. I might not know his real name, but at least now I knew where he worked. I carried on round the corner and there, in the back alley behind the shop, was the Mazda I'd last seen parked outside my house the night before. At last something was working out today.

Now for the boring bit. I figured Will Allen wouldn't be going anywhere for the next hour or two, but that didn't mean I could wander off and amble back later in the hope he'd still be around. I reckoned it was probably safe to nip round the corner to the McDonald's on Cheetham Hill Road and stock up with some doughnuts and coffee to make me feel like an authentic private eye as I staked out Sell Phones, but that was as far away as I wanted to get.

I moved my Rover on to the street that ran at right angles to Beaumaris Road and the alley so that I had a good view of the end of Allen's car bonnet, though it meant losing sight of the front of the shop. I slid into the passenger seat to make it look like I was waiting for someone and took off the cap. I kept the glasses in place, though. I slouched in my seat and brooded on Bill's perfidy. I sipped my coffee very slowly, just enough to keep me alert, not enough to make me want to pee. By the time I saw some action, the coffee was cold and so was I.

The nose of the silver Mazda slipped out of the alleyway and turned left towards Cheetham Hill Road. Just on five, with traffic tight as haemoglobin in the bloodstream. Born lucky, that's me. I scrambled across the gear stick and started the engine, easing out into the road behind the car. As we waited to turn left at the busy main road, I had the chance to see who was in the car. Allen was driving, but there was also someone in the passenger seat. She conveniently reached over into the back seat for something, and I identified the woman who had been in Sell Phones talking to the Emporio Armani mannequin. I wondered if she was the other half of the scam, the woman who went out to chat up the widowers. They don't call me a detective for nothing.

The Mazda slid into a gap in the traffic heading into Manchester. I didn't. By the time I squeezed out into a space that wasn't really there, the Mazda was three cars ahead and I was the target of a car-horn voluntary. I gave the kind of cheery wave that makes me crazy when arseholes do it to me and smartly switched lanes in the hope that I'd be less visible to my target. The traffic was so slow down Cheetham Hill that I was able to stay in touch, as well as check out the furniture stores for bargains. But then, just as we hit the straight, he peeled off left down North Street. I was in the right-hand lane and I couldn't get across, but I figured he must be heading down Red Bank to cut through the back doubles down to Ancoats and on to South Manchester. If I didn't catch him before Red Bank swept under the railway viaduct, he'd be anywhere in a maze of back streets and gone forever.

I swung the nose of the Rover over to the left, which pissed off the driver of the Porsche I'd just cut up. At least now the day wasn't a complete waste. I squeezed round the corner of Derby Street and hammered it for the junction that would sweep me down Red Bank. I cornered on a prayer that nothing was coming up the hill and screamed down the steep incline.

There was no silver Mazda in sight. I sat fuming at the junction for a moment, then slowly swung the car round and back up the hill. There was always the chance that they'd stopped off at one of the dozens of small-time wholesalers and middle-men whose tatty warehouses and storefronts occupy the streets of Strangeways. Maybe they were buying some jewellery or a fur coat with their ill-gotten gains. I gave it ten minutes, cruising every street and alley between Red Bank and Cheetham Hill Road. Then I accepted they were gone. I'd lost them.

I'd had enough for one day. Come to that, I'd had enough for the whole week. So I switched off my mobile, wearily slotted myself back into the thick of the traffic and drove home. Plan A was to run a hot bath lavishly laced with essential oils, Cowboy Junkies on the stereo, the pile of computer magazines I'd been ignoring for the last month and the biggest Stoly and grapefruit juice in the world on the side. Plan B involved Richard, if he was around.

I walked through my front door and down the hall, shedding layers like some sixties starlet, then started running the bath. I wrapped myself in my bathrobe which had been hanging strategically over a radiator, and headed for the freezer. I'd just gripped the neck of the vodka bottle when the doorbell rang. I considered ignoring it, but curiosity won. Story of my life. So I dumped the bottle and headed for the door.

They say it's not over till the fat lady sings. Alexis is far from fat, and from her expression I guessed singing wasn't on the agenda. Seeing the stricken look on her face, I kissed Plan A goodbye and prepared for the worst.

6

'Chris?' I asked, stepping back to let Alexis in.

She looked dumbly back at me, frowning, as if trying to call to mind why I should be concerned about her partner.

'Has something happened to Chris?' I tried. 'The baby?'

Alexis shook her head. 'Chris is all right,' she said impatiently, as if I'd asked the kind of stupid question TV reporters pose to disaster victims. She pushed past me and walked like an automaton into the living room, where she subsided onto a sofa with the slack-limbed collapse of a marionette.

I left her staring blankly at the floor and turned off the bath taps. By the time I came back with two stiff drinks, she was smoking with the desperate concentration of an addict on the edge of cold turkey. 'What's happened, Alexis?' I said softly, sitting down beside her.

'She's dead,' she said. I wasn't entirely surprised that somebody she knew was. I couldn't imagine anything else that would destroy the composure of a hard-bitten crime reporter like this.

'Who is?'

Alexis pulled a scrunched up copy of the *Yorkshire Post* out of her handbag. I knew it was one of the out-of-town papers that the *Chronicle* subscribed to. 'I was going through the regionals, looking to see if anybody had any decent crime feature ideas,' Alexis said bleakly as she spread the *YP* out on the table. DOCTOR DIES IN RAID, I read in the top right-hand section of the front page. Under the headline was a photograph of a dark-haired woman with strong features and a wide, smiling mouth. I read the first paragraph.

> *Consultant gynaecologist Sarah Blackstone was fatally stabbed last night when she disturbed an intruder in her Headingley home.*

'You knew her?' I asked.

'That's the doctor who worked with us on Christine's pregnancy.'

It was a strange way of expressing it, but I let it pass. Alexis clearly wasn't in command of herself, never mind the English language. 'I'm so sorry, Alexis,' I said inadequately.

'Never mind being sorry. I want you working,' she said abruptly. She crushed out her cigarette, lit another and swallowed half her vodka and Diet Coke. 'Kate, there's something going on here. That's definitely the woman we dealt with. But

74

she wasn't a consultant in Leeds called Sarah Blackstone. She had consulting rooms here in Manchester and her name was Helen Maitland.'

There are days when I'm overwhelmed with the conviction that somebody's stolen my perfectly nice life and left me with this pile of shit to deal with. Right then, I was inches away from calling the cops and demanding they track down the robber. After the day I'd had, I just wasn't in the mood for chapter one of an Agatha Christie mystery. 'Are you sure?' I asked. 'I mean, newspaper photographs . . .'

Alexis snorted. 'Look at her. She's not got a face that blends into the background, has she? Of course it's Helen Maitland.'

I shrugged. 'So she uses an assumed name when she's treating lesbians. Maybe she just doesn't want the notoriety of being the dykes' baby doctor.'

'It's more than that, KB,' Alexis insisted, swallowing smoke as if her life depended on it. 'She's got a prescription pad and she writes prescriptions in the name of Helen Maitland. We've not had any trouble getting them filled, and it's not like it was a one-off, believe me. There's been plenty. Which also makes me worried, because if the bizzies figure out that Sarah Blackstone and Helen Maitland are the same person, and they try and track down her patients, all they've got to do is start asking around the local chemists. And there we are, right in the middle of the frame.'

All of which was true, but I couldn't see why

Alexis was getting so wound up. I knew the rules on human fertility treatment were pretty strict, but as far as I was aware, it wasn't a crime yet to give lesbians artificial insemination, though if the Tories started to get really hysterical about losing the next election, I could see it might have its attractions as a possible vote winner. 'Alexis,' I said gently. 'Why exactly is that a problem?'

She looked blankly at me. 'Because they'll take the baby off us,' she said in a tone of voice I recognized as the one I used to explain to Richard why you can't wash your jeans in the dishwasher.

'I think you might be overreacting,' I said cautiously, aware that I wasn't wearing protective clothing. 'This is a straightforward case, Alexis,' I continued, skimming the story. 'Burglar gets disturbed, struggle, burglar panics, pulls a blade and lashes out. Tragic waste of talented test-tube baby doctor.' I looked up. 'The cops aren't going to be interviewing her Leeds patients, never mind trying to trace people she treated in a different city under a different name.'

'Maybe so, but maybe there's more to it than meets the eye,' Alexis said stubbornly. 'I've been doing the crime beat long enough to know that the Old Bill only tell you what they want you to know. It wouldn't be the first time there's been a whole other investigation going on beneath the surface.' She finished her drink and her cigarette, for some reason avoiding my eye.

I had a strong feeling that I didn't know what the real story was here. I wasn't entirely sure that I wanted to know what it was that could disconcert my normally stable best buddy as much as this, but I knew I couldn't dodge the issue. 'What's really going on here, Alexis?' I asked.

She ran both hands through her wild tangle of black hair and looked up at me, her face worried and frightened, her eyes as hollow as a politician's promises. 'Any chance of another drink?'

I fetched her another Stoly and Diet Coke, this one more than a little weaker than the last. If she was going to swallow them like water, I didn't want her passing out before she'd explained why she was in such a state about the death of a woman with whom she'd had nothing more than a professional relationship. I slid the drink across the table to her, and when she reached out for it, I covered her hand with mine. 'Tell me,' I said.

Alexis tightened her lips and shook her head. 'We haven't told another living soul,' she said, reaching for another cigarette. I hoped she wasn't smoking like this around Chris or the baby was going to need nicotine patches to get through its first twenty-four hours.

'You said a minute ago you wanted me working on this. If I don't know what's going on, there's not a lot I can do,' I reminded her.

Alexis lifted her eyes and gazed into mine. 'This has got to stay between us,' she said, her voice a plea I'd never heard from her before. 'I mean it,

KB. Nobody gets to hear this one. Not Della, not Ruth, not even Richard. Nobody.'

'That serious, eh?' I said, trying to lighten the oppressiveness of the atmosphere.

'Yeah, that serious,' Alexis said, not noticeably lightened.

'You know you can trust me.'

'That's why I'm here,' she admitted after a pause. The hand that wasn't hanging on to the cigarette swept through her hair again. 'I didn't realize how hard it was going to be to tell you.'

I leaned back against the sofa, trying to look as relaxed and unshockable as I could. 'Alexis, I'm bombproof. Whatever it is, I've heard it before. Or something very like it.'

Her mouth twisted in a strange, inward smile. 'Not like this, KB, I promise you. This is one hundred per cent one-off.' Alexis sat up straight, squaring her shoulders. I saw she'd made the decision to reveal what was eating her. 'This baby that Chris is carrying – it's ours.' She looked expectantly at me.

I didn't want to believe what I was afraid she was trying to tell me. So I smiled and said, 'Hey, that's a really healthy attitude, acting like you've really got a stake in it.'

'I'm not talking attitude, KB. I'm talking reality.' She sighed. 'I'm talking making a baby from two women.'

The trouble with modern life is that there isn't any etiquette any more. Things change so much and so fast that even if Emily Post were still around, she wouldn't be able to devise a set of protocols that stay abreast of tortured human relationships. If Alexis had dropped her bombshell in my mother's day, I could have said, 'That's nice, dear. Now, do you like your milk in first?' In my Granny Brannigan's day, I could have crossed myself vigorously and sent for the priest. But in the face of the encroaching millennium, all I could do was gape and say, 'What?'

'I'm not making this up, you know,' Alexis said defensively. 'It's possible. It's not even very difficult. It's just very illegal.'

'I'm having a bit of trouble with this,' I stammered. 'How do you mean, it's possible? Are we talking cloning here, or what?'

'Nothing so high tech. Look, all you need to make a baby are a womb, an egg and something to fertilize it with.'

'Which traditionally has been sperm,' I remarked drily.

'Which traditionally has been sperm,' Alexis agreed. 'But all you actually need is a collision of chromosomes. You get one from each side of the exchange. Women have two X chromosomes and men have an X and a Y. With me so far?'

'I might not have A level biology, but I do know the basics,' I said.

'Right. So you'll know that if it's the man's Y chromosome that links up with the woman's X chromosome, you get a little baby boy. And if it's his X chromosome that does the business, you get a girl. So everybody knew that you could make babies out of two X chromosomes. Only they didn't shout too much about it, did they? Because if they did more than mention it in passing, like, it wouldn't take a lot of working out to understand that if all you need for baby girls is a pair of X chromosomes from two different sources, you wouldn't need men.'

'You're telling me that after twenty-five years of feminist theory, scientists have only just noticed that?' I couldn't keep the irony out of my voice.

'No, they've always known it. But certain kinds of experiments are against the law. That includes almost anything involving human embryos. Unless, of course, it's aimed at letting men who produce crap sperm make babies. So although loads of people knew that theoretically it was possible to make babies from two women, nobody could officially do any research on it, so the technology that would make it possible science instead of fantasy just wasn't happening.' The journalist was in control now, and Alexis paused for effect. She couldn't help herself.

'So what happened to change that?' I asked, responding to my cue.

'There was a load of research done which showed that men didn't react well to having their wives inseminated with donor sperm. Surprise, surprise, they didn't feel connected to the kids and more often than not, families were breaking up because the men didn't feel like they were proper families. Given that more men are having problems with their sperm production than ever before, the pressure was really on for doctors to find a way of helping inadequate sperm to make babies. A couple of years ago, they came up with a really thin needle that could be inserted right into the very nucleus of an egg so that they could deliver a single sperm right to the place where it would count.'

I nodded, light dawning. 'And somebody somewhere figured that if they could do it with a sperm, they could do it with another egg.'

'Give the girl a coconut,' Alexis said, incapable of being solemn and scared for long.

'And this doctor, whatever her real name is, has been doing this in *Manchester*?' I asked. I know they say that what Manchester does today, London does tomorrow, but this seemed to be taking things a bit far.

'Yeah.'

'Totally illegally?'

'Yeah.'

'With lesbian couples?'

'Yeah.'

'Who are therefore technically also breaking the law?'

'I suppose so.'

We looked at each other across the table. I didn't know about Alexis, but I couldn't help banner headlines flashing across my mind. The thought of what the tabloids would do with a story like this was enough in itself to bring me out fighting for the women who had gone underground to make their dreams come true, let alone my feelings for Alexis and Chris. 'And the baby Chris is carrying belongs to both of you?' I asked.

'That's right. We both had to have a course of drugs to maximize our fertility, then Helen harvested our eggs and took them off to the lab to join them up and grow them on till she was sure they were OK. She did four altogether.'

If I looked as aghast as I felt, Alexis's face didn't reflect it. 'Chris is having *quads*?' I gasped.

'Don't be soft. 'Course she's not. There's a lousy success rate. You have to transplant at least three embryos to be in with a shout, and then it's only a seventy per cent chance that one of them's going to do the business. Helen transplanted three, and one of them survived. Believe me, in this game, that's a result.'

'So what happened to the other one?' I asked. I had a horrible feeling I wasn't going to like the answer.

'It's in the freezer at home. In a flask of liquid nitrogen.'

I'd been right. I felt slightly queasy at the thought and reminded myself never to go looking for a snack in Alexis's kitchen. I cleared my throat. 'How do you know it works? How do you know the babies are . . . OK?'

Alexis frowned. 'There was no way of proving

it objectively. We had to take Helen's word for it. She introduced us to the first couple she had a success with. Their little girl's about eighteen months now. She's a really bright kid. And yes, I know they could have been bullshitting us, that it could have been a racket to rip us off, but I believed those two women. You had to be there, KB.'

I thought I could probably make it through the night without the experience. 'I see now why you thought they'd take the baby off you,' was all I said.

'You've got to help us,' Alexis said.

'What exactly did you have in mind?' I asked.

'Helen Maitland's files,' Alexis said. 'We've got to get rid of them before the police find them.'

'Why would the police be looking for them in the first place?' I asked. 'Like I said, it's a straightforward burglary gone wrong.'

'OK, OK, I know you think I'm being paranoid. But this is our child's future that's at stake here. I'm entitled to go a bit over the top. But there's two reasons why I'm worried. One, suppose it didn't happen like the *YP* says? Suppose the person who killed Helen Maitland wasn't a burglar. Suppose it was some woman whose treatment hadn't worked and she'd gone off her box? Or suppose it was somebody who'd found out what was going on and was blackmailing Helen? Once the cops start digging, you know they won't stop. They might not be well bright, but you know as well as I do that when it comes to murder the bizzies don't ignore anything that looks like it might be a lead.'

I sighed. She was right. Coppers on murder inquiries are never satisfied till they've got somebody firmly in the frame. And if the obvious paths don't come up with a viable suspect, they start unravelling every loose end they can find. 'What's the second reason?' I asked.

'She had consulting rooms in Manchester. Sooner or later, somebody is going to notice she's not where she should be when she should be. And eventually, somebody's going to be emptying her filing cabinet. And if I know anything about people, whoever goes through those files isn't going to be dumping them straight in the bucket. It's only human nature to have a good root through. And then me and Chris are chopped liver, along with all the other dykes Helen Maitland has given babies to.' Alexis finished her cigarette and washed it down with a couple of gulps of her drink. 'We need you to find those files.'

I crossed my legs at the ankles and hugged my knees. 'You're asking a lot here. Interfering with a murder inquiry. Probably burglary, not to mention data theft.'

'I'm not asking for a *favour* here, KB. We'll pay you.'

I snorted with ironic laughter. 'Alexis, is this how you really think my professional life works? People walk in and ask me to break the law for money? I thought you knew me! When punters walk into my office and ask me to do things that are illegal, they don't stay in the room long enough to notice the colour of the carpet. When I have to break the law, I go out of my way to make sure my clients are the last to know. If I do this for you, it won't be because you're offering to *pay* me for it, it'll be because I decide it needs to be done.'

She had the grace to look abashed. 'I'm sorry,' she groaned. 'My head's cabbaged with all this. I know you're not some mad maverick burglar for hire. It's just that you're the only person I know who's got the skills to get us out from under whatever's going to happen now Helen Maitland's dead. Will you do the business for us?' The look of desperation that had temporarily disappeared was back.

'And what if the things I find out point to a conclusion you won't like?' I asked, stalling.

'You mean, if you uncover evidence that makes it look like one of her lesbian patients killed her?'

'That's exactly what I mean.'

Alexis covered her eyes and kneaded her temples. Then she looked up at me. 'I can't believe that's what you'll find. But even if you do, is that any reason why the rest of us have to have our lives destroyed too?'

Just call me the girl who can't say no.

7

The pleasant, caring atmosphere of the Compton Clinic hit me as soon as I walked through the door. Air subtly perfumed and temperature controlled, decor more like a country house than a medical facility, bowls of fresh flowers on every surface. I could almost believe they employed the only gynaecologists in the world who warm the speculums before plunging them deep into a woman's most intimate orifice. I made a mental note to ask Alexis about it later.

The clinic was in St John Street, a little Georgian oasis off Deansgate that pretends very hard to be Harley Street. The doctors who have their private consulting rooms there obviously figure that one of the most convincing ways of doing that is to charge the most outrageous prices for their services. From what I'd heard, you could make the down payment on one of the purpose-built yuppie flats round the corner on what they'd charge you to remove an unsightly blackhead. If Helen Maitland demanded that kind of price for her treatments, I couldn't imagine there were enough dykes desperate for motherhood and sufficiently well-heeled to make it worth her while. But then, what do I know? I'm the only woman I'm aware of who's been using the pill *and* demanding a condom since she was sixteen.

The Compton Clinic was about halfway down on the righthand side, a three-storey terraced house with a plague of plaques arrayed on either side of the door. Interestingly, Helen Maitland's name didn't appear on any of them. Neither did Sarah Blackstone's. I opened the heavy front door and found myself in a short hallway with a large sign directing me left to the reception area. I noted a closed-circuit TV camera mounted above the outside door, pointing down the hall towards the door I was being encouraged to use. It was a considerable incentive not to go walkabout especially since I hadn't brought a tub of Vaseline to smear over the lens.

One of the many problems with my job is you do such a lot of different things in a day, you're seldom appropriately dressed. If I'd known what the carpet at the clinic was like, I'd have brought my snow shoes, but as it was, I just had to make do with wading through the deep pile in an ordinary pair of leather loafers. There were two other potential patients sitting a discreet distance from each other on deep, chintz-covered sofas, reading the sort of home and garden magazine the nouveaux riches need to copy to shore up their conviction that they've arrived and they belong.

A tip from the private-eye manual: magazines are one of the dead giveaways as to whether you're dealing with the NHS or the private sector. The NHS features year-old, dogeared copies of slender weeklies that feature soap stars talking about their operations and TV personalities discussing their drink problems or their diets. The private sector provides this month's copies of doorstop glossies full of best-selling authors talking about their gardens and living with Prozac, and Hollywood stars discussing their drink problems, their diets and living with Prozac.

I managed to reach the reception desk without spraining my ankle. It was pure English country-house library repro, right down to the fake tooled-leather top and the cottage-garden prints on the wall behind it. The middle-aged woman sitting at the desk had a pleasant face, the lines on it carved by comfortable optimism rather than adversity, an impression supported by her Jaeger suit and the weight of the gold chains at neck and wrist. Her eyes betrayed her, however. They were quick, sharp and assessing as they flicked over my smartest suit, the lightweight wool in grey and moss green. It felt like she was instantly appraising the likely level of my bank balance and the concomitant degree of politeness required.

'How may I help you?' she asked, her voice the perfect match for the house-and-garden images of the decor.

'I'd like to make an appointment with Dr Maitland,' I said, deliberately lowering my voice so she'd think I didn't want the other two women to overhear.

'One moment,' she said, leaning to one side to stretch down and open one of the lower drawers in the desk. If Helen Maitland really was the murdered Dr Sarah Blackstone, the news hadn't made it to the Compton Clinic yet. The woman straightened up with a black A5 desk diary in her hand. She laid it on top of the larger diary that was already sitting open in front of her, and flicked through it to the following Sunday's date. Even I could see that every half-hour appointment was already filled up. If Alexis was right, there were going to be a lot of disappointed faces on Sunday.

I watched as the receptionist flicked forward a week. Same story. On the third attempt, I could see there were a couple of vacant slots. 'The earliest I can offer you is 3.30 on the twenty-fourth,' she said. There was no apology in her voice.

'Does it have to be a Sunday?' I asked. 'Couldn't I see her before then if I come during the week?'

'I'm afraid not. Dr Maitland only consults here on a Sunday.'

'It's just that Sundays are a little awkward for me,' I said, trying the muscularly difficult but almost invariably successful combination of frown and smile. I should have known it was a waste of time. Every medical receptionist since Hippocrates has been inoculated against sympathy.

The receptionist's expression didn't alter a millimetre. 'Sunday is the only day Dr Maitland consults here. She is not a member of the Compton partnership, she merely leases our facilities and employs our services in an administrative capacity.'

'You mean, you just make appointments on her behalf?'

'Precisely. Now, would you like me to make this appointment for you, Ms . . . ?'

'Do you know where else she works? Maybe I could arrange to see her there?'

Ms Country House and Garden was too well trained to let her facade slip, but I was watching for any signs, so I spotted the slight tightening of the skin round her eyes. 'I'm afraid we have no knowledge of Dr Maitland's other commitments,' she said, her voice revealing no trace of the irritation I was sure she was starting to feel.

'I guess I'll just have to settle for the twenty-fourth, then,' I said, pursing my lips.

'And your name is?'

'Blackstone,' I said firmly. 'Sarah Blackstone.'

Not a flicker. The receptionist wrote the name in the half-past-three slot. 'And a phone number? In case of any problems?'

I gave her my home number. Somehow, I don't think she had the same problems in mind as I did.

I had time to kill before I headed over to South Manchester to pick up Debbie for our prison visit, but I didn't want to go back to the office. I hate violence and I don't like putting myself in situations where GBH seems to be the only available option. I cut down through Castlefield to the canal and walked along the bank as far as Metz, a bar and Mittel European bistro on the edges of the city's gay village. Metz is so trendy I knew the chances of being spotted by anyone I knew were nil. I bought a bottle of designer mineral water allegedly flavoured with wild Scottish raspberries and settled down in a corner to review what little I knew so far.

I'd been taken aback when Alexis had revealed that she and Chris had been consulting Helen Maitland for six months. After all, we were best buddies. I had secrets from Richard, just as Alexis had from Chris. Show me a woman who doesn't keep things from her partner, and I'll show you a relationship on the point of self-destructing. But I was pretty certain I had no secrets from Alexis, and I'd thought that was mutual. Even though I understood her motives for not telling me about something so illegal, to discover she'd been hiding something this big made me wonder what else I'd been kidding myself about.

Alexis and Chris had been told about Dr Helen Maitland – in total confidence – by a close friend of theirs, a lesbian lawyer who'd been approached very cautiously by another couple who wanted to know the legal status of what they were planning to do. Because she knew about Alexis and Chris's desire to have a child, their lawyer friend introduced them to her clients. I sincerely hoped the Law Society wasn't going to hear about this – even two years of a law degree was enough for me to realize that what was going on here wasn't just illegal, it was unethical too. And let's face it, there aren't enough lawyers around who act out of compassion and concern for the prospect of losing one of them to be anything other than bleak.

Alexis had phoned the Compton Clinic and made an appointment for her and Chris to see Dr Maitland the following Sunday. Obviously, the word had spread since then, judging by the delay I'd faced. She'd been told, as I had been, to go to the back door of the clinic, as the main part of the building was closed on Sundays. Alexis had told me that the initial consultation made interviewing bereft parents look as easy as finding a non-smoking seat on a train. Dr Maitland had offered nothing, instigated nothing. It had been Alexis and Chris who had to navigate through the minefield, to explain what they wanted and what they hoped she could do for them. According to Alexis, Helen Maitland had been as stiff and unyielding as a steel shutter.

In fact, she'd nearly thrown them out when she was taking their details and Alexis admitted to being a journalist. 'Why did you tell her?' I'd asked, amazed.

'Because I wanted her to work with us, soft girl,' Alexis had replied scornfully. 'She was obviously really paranoid about being caught doing what she was doing. That whole first consultation, it was like she was determined she wasn't going to say a word that would put her in the wrong if someone was taping the conversation. And then she was taking down all these details. Plus she insisted on leaving a three-week gap between the first and second appointments. I figured she must be checking people out. And I reckon that if what she found out didn't square with what she'd been told, you never got past that second appointment. So I had to tell her, didn't I?'

'How come she didn't throw you out then and there?'

The familiar crooked grin. 'Like I always say, KB, they don't pay me my wages for working a forty-hour week. They pay me for that five minutes a day when I persuade somebody who isn't going to talk to a living soul to talk to me. I can be very convincing when I really want something. I just told her that being a journalist didn't automatically make me a scumbag, and that I was a dyke before I was a hack. And that the best way to make sure a story never got out was to involve a journo with a bit of clout.'

I hadn't been able to argue with that, and I suspected that Helen Maitland hadn't either, especially since it would have been delivered with a hefty dollop of the Alexis Lee charm. So the doctor had agreed to work with them both to make Chris pregnant with their child. First, they each had to take courses of drugs that cost a small fortune and made both of them feel like death on legs. The drugs maximized their fertility and also controlled their ovulation so that on a particular Sunday, they'd both be at the optimum point for having their eggs harvested. Helen Maitland herself had carried out this apparently straightforward procedure. According to Alexis, who never forgets she's a journalist, the eggs were then transferred into a portable incubator which Helen Maitland could plug into the cigarette lighter of her car and transport to her lab, wherever that was. Another small detail I didn't have.

In the lab, one egg from Alexis would be stripped down to its nucleus and loaded into a micropipette one tenth the thickness of a human hair. Then one of Chris's eggs would be injected with Alexis's nucleus and hopefully the chromosomes would get it on and make a baby. This nuclear fusion was a lot less immediately spectacular than nuclear fission, but its implications for the human race were probably bigger. It was obvious why the doctor had chosen to use an alias.

I couldn't help wondering what would happen when men found out what was going on. If there was one thing that was certain, it was that sooner or later the world was going to know about this. It didn't seem possible that Helen Maitland was the only one who had worked out the practical means of making men redundant. I had this niggling feeling that all over California, women were making babies with women and doctors with fewer scruples than Helen Maitland were making a lot of money.

That was another thing that had become clear from Alexis's story. In spite of their desperation, Helen Maitland wasn't bleeding her patients dry. The prescriptions were expensive, but there was nothing she could do about that. However, her fees for the rest of the treatment seemed remarkably cheap. She was charging less per hour than I do. If the medical establishment had found out about that, she'd have been struck off a lot faster for undercharging than she ever would have been for experimenting on humans.

There was no other word for it. What she had been doing was an experiment, with all the attendant dangers. I didn't know enough about embryology to know what could go wrong, but I was damn sure that all the normal genetic risks a foetus faced would be multiplied by such an unorthodox beginning. If I'd been the praying sort, I'd have been lighting enough candles to floodlight Old Trafford on the off chance it would give Chris a better chance of bearing a healthy, normal daughter. Being the practical sort, the best thing I could do would be to find Helen Maitland's killer before the investigation led to my friends. Or worse. I couldn't rule out the possibility that someone had killed Helen Maitland because they'd discovered what she was doing and decided she had to die. Anyone with so fundamental a set of beliefs wasn't going to stop at seeing off the doctor who had set these pregnancies in motion. There was a lot to do, and the trouble was, I didn't really know where to start. All I had was an alias and a consulting room that I hadn't been able to get near.

I finished my drink and stared moodily at the dirty grey water of the canal. The city has screwed so much inner-city renewal money out of Europe that the banks of our canals are smarter than Venice these days. The water doesn't stink either. In spite of that, I figured I'd be waiting a long time before I saw a gondola pass. Probably about as long as it would take me to raise the money to buy Bill out of the partnership.

I couldn't bear the idea of just throwing in the towel, though. I'd worked bloody hard for my share of the business, and I'd learned a few devious tricks along the way. Surely I could think of *something* to get myself off the hook? Even if I could persuade the bank to lend me the money, working solo I could never generate enough money to pay off the loan and employ Shelley, never mind the nonessentials like eating and keeping a roof over my head. The obvious answer was to find a way to generate more profit. I knew I couldn't work any harder, but maybe I could do what Bill had done and employ someone young, keen and cheap. The only problem was where and how to find a junior Brannigan. I could imagine the assorted maniacs and nerds who would answer a small ad in the *Chronicle*. Being a private eye is a bit like being a politician – wanting the job should be an automatic disqualification for getting it. I mean, what kind of person *admits* they want to spend their time spying on other people, lying about their identity, taking liberties with the law, risking life and limb in the pursuit of profit, and never getting enough sleep? I didn't have time to follow the path of my own apprenticeship – I'd met Bill when I was a penniless law student and he was having a fling with one of the women I shared a house with. He needed someone to serve injunctions and bankruptcy petitions, and I needed a flexible and profitable part-time job. It took me a year to realize that I liked the people I spent my time with when I was working for Bill a lot better than I liked lawyers.

I walked out of Metz and set off across town to where I'd parked my car. On my way through Chinatown, I popped into one of the supermarkets and picked up some dried mushrooms, five spice powder and a big bottle of soy sauce. There were prawns and char siu pork in the fridge already and I'd stop off to buy some fresh vegetables later. I couldn't think of a better way to deal with my frustrations than chopping and slicing the ingredients for hot and sour soup and sing chow vermicelli.

At the till, the elderly Chinese woman on the cash register gave me a fortune cookie to sample as part of a promotion they were running. Out on the street, I broke it open, throwing the shell into the gutter for the pigeons. I straightened out the slip of paper and read it. It was hard not to believe it was an omen. 'Sometimes, beggars can be choosers,' it said.

8

As my car rolled to a halt outside Debbie and Dennis's house on a modern suburban estate, the curtains started to twitch the length of the close. Before I could get out of the car and ring the bell, the front door was open and Debbie was coming down the drive of their detached home with gleaming blonde head held high for the benefit of the neighbours. She looked like a recently retired supermodel slumming it for the day. The dignified impression was only slightly diminished by the tiny stride imposed by the tightness of her skirt and the height of her heels. Debbie folded herself into the passenger seat of my car, her long legs gleaming with Lycra, and said, 'Nosy so-and-sos. Did you see them nets? Up and down like a bride's nightie. Imagine having nothing better to do all day than spy on everybody else. That Neighbourhood Watch scheme is just a licence to poke your nose into other people's business, if you ask me. Sad bastards.'

'How you doing, Debbie?' I asked in the first pause in the tirade.

She sighed. 'You don't want to know, Kate.'

She wasn't wrong. I'd had a brief taste of seeing the man I loved behind bars, and that had been enough for me to realize how hellish it must be to lose them to prison for months or years. 'You know you can always talk to me, Debbie,' I lied.

'I know, but it does my head in just thinking about it. Talking about it'd only make it worse.' Debbie flicked open the cover of the car's ashtray with a manicured nail. Seeing it was clean and empty, she closed it again and breathed out heavily through her nose.

'It's OK to smoke if you don't mind having the window open,' I told her.

She took a pack of Dunhills out of a handbag that I knew wasn't Chanel in spite of the distinctive gilt double C on the clasp. I knew it wasn't Chanel because I had an identical one in the same burgundy leather-look plastic. It had been a passing gift from Dennis about a year before, when he'd come by a vanload of counterfeit designer accessories. It had been good gear; Richard was still using the 'Cerruti' wallet. She managed to light up without smudging her perfect lipstick, then said, 'I flaming hate seeing him in there. I really appreciate you coming today. It'll do him good to see you. He always asks Christie if she's seen you and how you're doing.'

From anyone other than Debbie, that would

have been a deliberate crack, a sideswipe aimed at triggering a major guilt trip. But given that her IQ and her dress size are near neighbours, I knew she'd meant exactly what she said, no more and no less. It didn't make any difference to me; I still got the stab of guilt. In the seven weeks Dennis had been inside, I'd only got along to see him once so far, and that had been the week after he went down. Sure, I'd been stretched at work, with Bill clearing his desk before Australia. But that was only half the story. Like Debbie, I hated seeing Dennis inside Strangeways. Unlike her, nobody was going to give me a bad time for not visiting him every week. Nobody except me.

'I'm sorry I've not managed more often,' I said lamely.

'Don't worry about it, love,' Debbie said. 'If I didn't have to go, you wouldn't catch me within a hundred miles of the place.'

I refrained from pointing out she lived only half a dozen miles from the red-brick prison walls; I like Debbie too much. 'How's he doing?'

'Not so bad now. You know how he is about drugs? Well, they've just opened this drug-free unit where you can get away from all the junkies and the dealers and he's got on it. The deal is if you stay away from drugs you get unlimited access to the gym. And if you work out daily, you get extra rations. So he's spending a lot of time on the weights. Plus the other blokes on this drug-free wing are mostly older like him, so

101

it's not like being stuck on a wing with a load of drugged-up idiots.' Debbie sighed. 'He just hates being banged up. You know he can't be doing with anybody keeping tabs on him.'

I knew only too well. It was one of the things that united the two of us, superficially so different, but underneath disturbingly similar. 'And time passes a lot faster on the outside than it does behind those walls,' I said, half to myself.

'Don't you believe it,' Debbie said bitterly.

In silence, I navigated my way through the city centre, catching every red light on Deansgate before we passed the new Nynex arena. It's an impressive sight, towering over the substantial nineteenth-century edifice of Victoria Station. Unfortunately but predictably, it opened to a chorus of problems, the main one being that the seats are so steeply raked that people sitting in the top tiers have had to leave because they were suffering from vertigo.

I swung into the visitors' car park and stared up at another impressive sight – the new round-topped wall containing Her Majesty's Prison. The prisoners who destroyed half of Strangeways in a spectacular riot a few years ago ended up doing their successors a major favour. Instead of the horrors of the old Victorian prison – three men to a cramped cell without plumbing – they now have comfortable cells with latrines and basins. For once, the authorities listened to the people who have to run prisons, who explained that the hardest prisoners to deal with are the ones on relatively short sentences. A lifer knows he's in there for a long time, and he wants to make sure that one day he sees the outside again. A man who's got a ten-year sentence knows he'll only serve five years if he keeps his nose clean, so he's got a real incentive to stay out of trouble. But to some toerag who's been handed down eighteen months, it's not the end of the world to lose remission and serve the whole sentence. The short-term prisoners also tend to be the younger lads, who don't have the maturity to get their heads down and get through it. They're angry because they're inside, and they don't know how to control their anger. When cell blocks explode into anarchy and violence, nine times out of ten, it's the short-term men who are behind it.

So Strangeways has got a gym, satellite TV and a variety of other distractions. It's the kind of regime that has the rabid right-wingers foaming at the mouth about holiday camps for villains. Me, I've never been on a holiday where they lock you in your room at night, don't let you see your friends and family whenever you want to and never let you go shopping. Whatever else Strangeways is, a holiday camp it ain't. Most of the loudmouths who complain would be screaming for their mothers within twenty-four hours of being banged up in there. Just visiting is more than enough for me, even though one of the benefits of the rebuilding programme is the Visitors' Centre. In the bad old days, visitors were treated so atrociously they felt like they were criminals too. It's no wonder that a lot of men told their wives not to bring the kids to visit. It was easier to deal with the pain of missing them than to put them through the experience.

Now, they actually treat visitors like members of the human race. Debbie and I arrived with ten minutes to spare, and there wasn't even a queue to check in. We found a couple of seats among the other visitors, mostly women and children. These days, a Visiting Order covers up to three adults, and small children don't count. With every prisoner entitled to a weekly visit, it doesn't take long for a crowd to build up. Nevertheless, we didn't have to hang around for long. Five minutes before our visit time, we were escorted into the prison proper, our bags were searched by a strapping blonde woman prison officer who looked like a Valkyrie on her day off from Wagner's Ring Cycle. Then we were led through anonymous corridors and upstairs to the Visitors' Hall, a large, clean room with views across the city from its long windows. With its off-white walls, vending machines, no-smoking rule, tables laid out across the room and tense atmosphere, it was like a church hall ready for a whist tournament.

We found Dennis sitting back in his chair, legs stretched in front of him. As we sat down, he smiled. 'Great to see you both,' he said. 'Business must be slack for you to take the afternoon off, Kate.'

'Christie's got a cross-country trial,' Debbie said. 'Kate didn't want me coming in here on my own.' There was less bitterness in her voice than there would have been in mine in the same circumstances.

'I'm sorry, doll,' Dennis said, shifting in his seat and leaning forward, elbows on the table, eyes fixed on Debbie with all the appeal of a puppy dog. But Debbie knew only too well what that cute pup had grown into, and she wasn't melting.

'Sorry doesn't make it to parents' night, does it?' Debbie said.

Dennis looked away. 'No. But you're better off than most of this lot,' he added, gesturing round the room with his thumb. 'Look at them. Scruffy kids, market-stall wardrobes, you know they're living in shitholes. Half of them are on the game or on drugs. At least I leave you with money in the bank.'

Debbie shook her head, more in sorrow than in anger. 'Haven't you got it through your thick head yet that me and the kids wouldn't mind going without as long as we'd got you in the house?'

Time for me not to be here. I stood up and took the orders for the vending machines. There were enough kids milling around for it to take me a good ten minutes to collect coffees and chocolate bars, more than long enough for Dennis and Debbie to rehash their grievances and move on. By the time I got back, they were discussing what A levels Christie was planning on taking.

'She should be sticking with her sciences,' Dennis insisted forcefully. 'She wants to get herself qualified as a doctor or a vet or a dentist. People and animals are always going to get sick, that's the only thing that's guaranteed.'

'But she wants to keep up with her sport,' Debbie said. 'Three science A levels is a lot of homework. It doesn't leave her a lot of time for herself. She could be a PE teacher no bother.'

Dennis snorted. 'A teacher? You've got to be joking! Have you seen the way other people's kids are today? You only go into teaching these days if you can't get anybody else to give you a job!'

'What does Christie want to do?' I cut in mildly as I dumped the coffees in front of us.

Dennis grinned. 'What's that got to do with it?' He was only half joking. 'Anyway, never mind all this bollocks. No point us talking to each other when we've got entertainment on tap, is there, Debs? Tell us what you've been up to, Kate.'

Debbie sighed. She'd been married to Dennis too long to be bothered arguing, but it was clear that Christie's future was occupying all of her spare synapses. As Dennis turned the headlamp glare of his sparkling eyes on me, I could sense her going off the air and retreating into herself. Suited me, heartless bastard that I am. I didn't mind that Debbie was out of the conversation. That way I could get to the point without having to explain every second sentence. So I gave Dennis a blow-by-blow account of my aborted attempt to nail the gravestone scammers as a warm-up to asking for his help.

He loved the tale, I could tell. Especially the bit where Richard walked through the door with the takeaway and the Celtic cartoon characters. It was a short step from there to outlining Dan Druff's problems with the saboteurs. Dennis sat back again, linking his hands behind his chair with the expansive air of a man who knows his supplicant has come to the right place.

'Flyposting, isn't it?' he said as if delivering a profound pronouncement.

'Well, yeah, that's one of the problems they've been having,' I said, wondering if his spell behind bars was blunting Dennis's edge. I had already explained that the Scabby Heided Bairns's posters had been covered up by other people's.

'No, that's what it's all about,' he said impatiently. 'This whole thing is about staking out territory in the flyposting game.'

'You're going to have to give me a tutorial in this one, Dennis,' I said. Ain't too proud to beg, and there are times when that's what it takes.

Happy that he'd established his superiority despite his temporary absence from the streets, Dennis filled me in. 'Illegal flyposting is mega business in Manchester. Think about it. Everywhere you go in the city, you see fly posters for bands and events. The city council just don't bother prosecuting, so it's a serious business. The way it works is that people stake out their own territory and then they do exclusive deals with particular clubs and bands. The really clever ones set up their own printing businesses and do deals with ticket promoters as well. They'll do a deal with a club whereby they'll book bands for them, arrange the publicity and organize the ticket sales at other outlets. So for a band to get on and nail down a record deal, best thing they can do is get tied in with one of the boss operators. That way, they'll get gigs at the best venues, plenty of poster coverage on prime sites and their tickets get sold by all the key players.'

'Which costs what?'

Dennis shrugged. 'A big slice, obviously. But it's worth it to get noticed.'

'And you think what's going on here is something to do with that?'

'Must be, stands to reason. Looks like your lads have picked the wrong punter to do business with. They'll have chosen him because he's cheap, silly bastards. He's probably some kid trying to break into the market and your band's getting his kicking.'

I made the circular gesture with my hand that you do in charades when you're asking the audience to expand on their guesses. 'Gimme more, Dennis, I'm not seeing daylight yet,' I said.

'He'll have been papering somebody else's sites. If the person whose site he's been nicking doesn't know which chancer is behind the pirate flyposting, he'll go for the band or the venues the chancer's promoting. So your band are getting picked on as a way of warning off their cowboy promoter that he's treading on somebody else's ground.'

I understood. 'So if they want to get out from under, they need to get themselves a new promoter?'

He nodded. 'And they want to do it fast, before somebody gets seriously hurt.'

I gave a sardonic smile. 'There's no need to go over the top, Dennis. We're talking a bit of illegal flyposting here, not the ice-cream wars.'

His genial mask slipped and he was staring straight into my eyes in full chill mode, reminding me why his enemies call him Dennis the Menace. 'You're not understanding, Kate,' he said softly. 'We're talking heavy-duty damage here. The live-music business in Manchester is worth a lot of dosh. If you've got a proper flyposting business up and running with a finger in the ticket-sales pie, then you're talking a couple of grand a week tax free for doing not a lot except keeping your foot soldiers in line. That kind of money makes for serious enforcement.'

'And that's what my clients have been getting. Skinheads on super lager breaking up their gigs, their van being set on fire,' I reminded him. 'I'm not taking this lightly.'

'You've still not got it, Kate. You remember Terry Spotto?'

I frowned. The name rang vague bells, but I couldn't put a face to it.

'Little runty guy, lived in one of the Hulme crescents? Strawberry mark down his right cheek?'

I shook my head. 'I don't know who you mean.'

'Sure you do. They found him lying on the bridge over the Medlock, just down from your office. Somebody had removed his strawberry mark with a sawn-off shotgun.'

I remembered now. It had happened about a year ago. I'd arrived at work one Tuesday morning to see yellow police tapes shutting off part of the street. Alexis had chased the story for a couple of days, but hadn't got any further than the official line that Terry Spotto had been a small-time drug dealer. 'That was about flyposting?' I asked.

'Terry was dealing crack but he decided he wanted a second profit centre,' Dennis said, reminding me how expertly today's intelligent villains have assimilated the language of business. 'He started flyposting, only he didn't have the nous to stay off other people's patches or the muscle to take territory off them. He got warned a couple of times, but he paid no never mind to it. Since he wouldn't take a telling, or a bit of a seeing to, somebody decided it was time to make an example. I don't think anybody's seriously tried to cut in since then. But it sounds like your lads have made the mistake of linking up with somebody who's too new on the block to remember Terry Spotto.'

I took a deep breath. 'Hell of a way of seeing off the competition. Dennis, I need to talk to somebody about this. Get the boys off the hook before this gets silly. Gimme a name.'

'Denzel Williams,' Dennis said. 'Garibaldi's. Mention my name.'

'Thanks.' I hadn't been to Garibaldi's, but I'd heard plenty about it. If I'd had to guess where to find someone I could talk to about so dodgy a game, that's probably the place I'd have gone for.

'Anything else?'

I shook my head. 'Not in the way of business. Not unless you know somebody with a wad of cash to invest in a private-eye business.'

Dennis's eyebrows lowered. 'What's Bill up to?'

I told him. Debbie tuned back in to the conversation and the subject kept us going for the remainder of the visit. By the time I'd dropped Debbie back at the house, I had a list of a dozen or so names that Dennis reckoned had the kind of money to hand that they could invest in the business. Somehow, I didn't think I'd be following any of them up. I'm unpopular enough with the Old Bill as it is without becoming a money laundry for the Manchester Mafia.

Come five o'clock, I was parked down the street from Sell Phones. All I needed was a name and address on this pair of con merchants and I could hand the case over to the police as I'd already agreed with my clients. We had the names and addresses of nearly a dozen complainants, some of whom were bound to be capable of picking

Will Allen or his female sidekick out of a line-up. I looked forward to handing the whole package over to Detective Chief Inspector Della Prentice, head honcho of the Regional Crime Squad's fraud task force. It wasn't exactly her bailiwick, but Della's one of the tightknit group of women I call friends, and I trusted her not to screw it up. There are coppers who hate private enterprise so much they'd let a villain walk rather than let a PI take an ounce of credit for a collar. Della isn't one of them. But before I could have the pleasure of nailing these cheap crooks, I had to attach names and addresses to them. And I was damned if they were going to defeat me two nights running.

This time I was ready for them. When Allen swung left down the hill, I was right behind him. I stayed in close touch as we threaded through back streets flanked by decaying mills half filled with struggling small businesses and vacant lots turned into car parks, across the Rochdale Road and the Oldham Road, emerging on Great Ancoats Street just south of the black glass facade of the old Daily Express Building. I slipped into the heavy traffic with just one car separating me from the silver Mazda, and stayed like that right across town, past the mail-order warehouses and through the council estates.

In Hathersage Road, the car pulled up outside a general store opposite the old Turkish Baths, closed down by the council on the grounds that it cost too much to maintain the only leisure facility within walking distance for the thousands of local inner-city residents. As one of those locals, it made me fizz with fury every time I paid an instalment of my council tax. So much for New Labour. I carried on past the parked car as the woman jumped out and headed into the shop. I pulled into a parking space further down the street, hastily adjusting my rear-view mirror so I could see what was going on. A few minutes later, she emerged carrying a copy of the *Chronicle* and a packet of cigarettes.

As the Mazda passed me and headed for the traffic lights, I hung back. The lights were on red, and I wasn't going to emerge till they changed. On green, the Mazda swung left into Anson Road, the overhanging trees turning daylight to dusk like a dimmer switch. They turned off almost immediately into a quiet street lined with large Victorian houses. About halfway down on the left, the red brick gave way to modern concrete. Filling a space equivalent to a couple of the sprawling Victorians was a four-storey block of flats in a squared-off U. The Mazda turned into the block's car park and stopped. I cruised past, then accelerated, swung the car round at the next junction and drove back in time to see Allen and the woman from Sell Phones disappear through the block's entrance door. Even from this distance, I could see the entry phone. There must have been close on fifty flats in the block.

A whole day had trickled through my fingers

and I didn't seem to be much further forward with anything. Maybe I should follow Shelley's advice and put my share of the business on the market. And not just as a ploy.

9

It was too early in the evening for me to have anything better to do, so I decided to keep an eye on the gravestone grifters. I figured that since they'd both gone indoors, the chances were that they were going to have a bite to eat and a change of clothes before heading out to hit the heart-broken, so I took fifteen minutes to shoot back to my house, pick up my copy of that night's *Chronicle* from the mat and throw together a quick sandwich of Dolcelatte and rocket that was well past its launch-by date. It was the last of the bread too, I mentally noted as I binned the wrapper. So much for a night of chopping and slicing and home-made Chinese. I tossed a can of Aqua Libra into my bag along with the film-wrapped sandwich and drove back to my observation post.

Just after seven, the woman emerged alone with one of those expensive anorexic girlie briefcases that have a shoulder strap instead of a handle. She made straight for the car. I waited until she was behind the wheel, then I started my engine and swiftly reversed into the drive of the house behind me. That way I could get on her tail no matter which direction she chose. She turned left out of the car park, and I followed her back to Anson Road and down towards the bottom end of Kingsway, past rows of between-the-wars semis where the vast assortment of what passes for family life in the nineties happened behind closed doors, a world we were completely cut off from as we drifted down the half-empty roads, sealed in our separate boxes.

Luckily we didn't have far to go, since I was acutely aware that there wasn't enough traffic around to cover me adequately. Shortly after we hit Kingsway, she hung a left at some lights and headed deep into the heart of suburban Burnage. Again, luck was on my side, a phenomenon I hadn't been experiencing much of lately. Her destination was on one of the long, wide avenues running parallel to Kingsway, rather than up one of the narrow streets or cul-de-sacs built in an era when nobody expected there would come a day when every household had at least one car. In those choked chicanes, she couldn't have avoided spotting me. When she did slow down, obviously checking out house numbers, I overtook her and parked a few hundred yards ahead, figuring she must be close to her target. I was right. She actually stopped less than twenty yards in front of me and walked straight up the path of a three-bedroomed semi with a set of flower beds so neat it was hard to imagine a dandelion with enough bottle to sprout there.

I watched her ring the bell. The door opened, but I couldn't see the person behind it. Three sentences and she was in. I flicked through my copy of that evening's *Chronicle* till I got to the death announcements and read down the column. There it was.

> *Sheridan. Angela Mary, of Burnage, suddenly on Tuesday at Manchester Royal Infirmary after a short illness. Beloved wife of Tony, mother of Becky and Richard. Service to be held at Our Lady of the Sorrows, Monday, 2 p.m., followed by committal at Stockport Crematorium at 3 p.m.*

With that information and the phone book, it wouldn't be hard to identify the right address. And you could usually tell from the names roughly what age group you were looking at. I'd have guessed that Tony and Angela were probably in their middle to late forties, their kids late teens to early twenties. Perfect targets for the con merchants. Bereft husband young enough to notice an attractive woman, whether consciously or not. Probably enough money in the pot to be able to afford a decent headstone. The thought of it made me sick.

What was worse was the knowledge that even as I was working all this out, Will Allen's accomplice was giving the shattered widower a sales pitch designed to separate him from a large chunk of his cash. I couldn't just sit there and let it happen. On the other hand, I couldn't march up the path and unmask her unless I wanted her and her sleazy sidekick to cover their tracks and leave town fast. I couldn't call the cops; I knew Della was out of town at a conference, and trying to convince some strange officer that I wasn't a nutter fast enough to get them out here in time to stop it was way beyond my capabilities. I racked my brains. There had to be a way of blowing her out without blowing my cover.

There was only one thing I could come up with. And that depended on how well the Sheridans got along with their neighbours. If they'd had years of attrition over parking, teenage stereos and footballs over fences, I'd had it. Squaring my shoulders, I walked up the path of the other half of the Sheridans' semi. The woman who answered the door looked to be in her mid-thirties, thick dark hair pulled back into a ponytail, a face all nose, teeth and chin. She wore a pair of faded jeans, supermarket trainers and a Body Shop T-shirt demanding that some part of the planet should be saved. When she registered that it was a stranger on the doorstep, her cheery grin faded to a faint frown. Clearly, I was less interesting than whoever she'd been expecting. I handed her a business card. 'I'm sorry to bother you,' I started apologetically.

'Private investigator?' she interrupted. 'You mean, like on the telly? I didn't know women did that.'

Some days, you'd kill for an original response. Still, I was just grateful not to have the door slammed in my face. I smiled, nodded and ploughed on. 'I need you help,' I said. 'How well do you know Mr Sheridan next door?'

The woman gasped. 'He's never murdered her, has he? I know it were sudden, like, and God knows they've had their ups and downs, but I can't believe he killed her!'

I closed my eyes momentarily. 'It's nothing like that. As far as I'm aware, there's nothing at all suspicious about Mrs Sheridan's death. Look, can I come in for a minute? This is a bit difficult to explain.'

She looked dubious. 'How do I know you're who you say you are?'

I spread my hands in a shrug. 'Do I look the dangerous type? Believe me, I'm trying to prevent a crime, not take part in one. Mr Sheridan is about to be robbed unless you can help me here.'

She gasped again, her hand flying to her mouth this time. 'It's just like the telly,' she said, ushering me into a narrow hallway where there was barely room for both of us and the mountain bike that hung on one wall. 'What's going on?' she demanded avidly.

'A particularly nasty team of crooks are conning bereaved families out of hundreds of pounds,' I said, dressing it up in the tabloid style she clearly relished. 'They catch them at a weak moment and persuade them to part with cash for cut-price gravestones. Now, I'm very close to completing a watertight case against them, so I don't want to alert them to the fact that their cover's blown. But I can't just sit idly by while poor Mr Sheridan gets ripped off.'

'So you want me to go and tell him there's a crook in his living room?' she asked eagerly.

'Not exactly, no. I want you to pop round in a neighbourly sort of way, just to see he's all right, and do what you can to prevent him parting with any money. Say things like, "If this is a respectable firm, they won't mind you sleeping on this and talking it over with your funeral director." Don't let on you're at all suspicious, just that you're a cautious sort of person. And that Angela wouldn't have wanted him to rush into anything without consulting other members of the family. You get the idea?'

She nodded. 'I've got you. You can count on me.' I didn't have a lot of choice, so I just smiled. 'I'll get round there right away. I was going to pop round anyway to see how Tony was doing. We got on really well, me and Angela. She was older than me, of course, but we played tenpin bowls in the same team every Wednesday. I couldn't get over it when I heard. Burst appendix. You never know the hour or the day, do you? You leave this to me, Kate,' she added, glancing at my card again.

We walked down the path together, me heading back to my car and her next door. As we parted, she promised to call me on my mobile to let me know what happened. I was on pins as I sat watching the Sheridans' house. My new sidekick was definitely a bit of a loose cannon, but I couldn't think of anything else I could have done that would have been effective without warning off Allen's partner in crime, particularly since they'd be on their guard after the earlier debacle at Richard's house. About half an hour passed, then the front door opened and my target emerged. Judging by the way she threw her briefcase into the car, she wasn't in the best of moods. I'd had my phone switched off all day to avoid communicating with the office, but I turned it back on as I pulled out behind the woman.

She was back inside the block of flats by the time my new confederate called. 'Hiya,' she greeted me. 'I think it went off all right. I don't think she was suspicious, just brassed off because I was sitting there being dead neg about the whole thing. I just kept saying to Tony he shouldn't make any decision without the kids being there, and that was all the support he needed, really. She realized she wasn't getting anywhere and I wasn't shifting, so she just took herself off.'

'You did really well. Do you know what she was calling herself?' I asked when I could get a word in.

'She had these business cards. Greenhalgh and

Edwards. Tony showed me after she'd gone. Sarah Sargent, it says her name is. Will you need us to go to court?' she asked, the phone line crackling with excitement.

'Possibly,' I hedged. 'I really appreciate your help. If the police need your evidence to support a case, I'll let them know where to find you.'

'Great! Hey, I think your job's dead exciting, you know. Any time you need a hand again, just call me, OK?'

'OK,' I said. Anything to get out from under. But she insisted on giving me her name and phone number before I could finally disengage. I wondered how glamorous she'd find the job when she had to do a fifteen-hour surveillance in a freezing van in the dead of winter with a plastic bucket to pee in and no guarantee that she'd get the pictures she needed to avoid having to do the whole thing all over again the next day.

I started my engine. I didn't think the con merchants would be having another go tonight. But I still had miles to go before I could sleep. A little burglary, perhaps, and then a visit to clubland for a nightcap. Given that I wasn't dressed for either pursuit, it seemed like a good excuse to head for home. Maybe I could even squeeze in a couple of hours kip before I had to go about my nocturnal business.

Never mind mice and men. Every time I make a plan these days it seems to go more off track than a blindfolded unicyclist. I hadn't taken more than a couple of steps towards my bungalow when I heard another car door open and I saw a figure move in my direction through the dusk. I automatically moved into position, ready for fight or flight, arms hanging at my side, shoulder bag clutched firmly, ready to swing it in a tight arc, all my weight on the balls of my feet, ready to kick, pivot or run. I waited for the figure to approach, tensed for battle.

It was just as well I'm the kind who looks before she leaps into action. I don't think Detective Constable Linda Shaw would have been too impressed with a flying kick to the abdomen. 'DC Shaw?' I said, surprised and baffled as she stepped into a pool of sodium orange.

'Ms Brannigan,' she acknowledged, looking more than a little sheepish. 'I wonder if we might have a word?' Looming up in the gloom behind her, I noticed a burly bloke with more than a passing resemblance to Mike Tyson. I sincerely hoped we weren't going to get into the 'nice cop, nasty cop' routine. I had a funny feeling I wouldn't come off best.

'Sure, come on in and have a brew,' I said.

She cleared her throat. 'Actually, we'd prefer it if you came down to the station,' she said, her embarrassment growing by the sentence.

Now I was completely bewildered. The one and only time I'd met Linda Shaw, she'd been one of Detective Inspector Cliff Jackson's gophers on a murder case I'd been hired to investigate. There was a bit of history between me and Jackson that meant every time our paths crossed, we both ended up with sore heads, but Linda Shaw had acted as the perfect buffer zone, keeping the pair of us far enough apart to ensure that the job got done without another murder being added to the case's tally. I'd liked her, not least because she was her own woman, seemingly determined not to let Jackson's abrasive bull-headedness rub off on her. What I couldn't work out was why she was trying to drag me off to a police station for questioning. For once, I wasn't doing anything that involved tap-dancing over a policeman's toes. That might change once I got properly stuck in to the investigation of Alexis's murdered doctor, but even if it did, the detectives I'd be irritating were forty miles away on the other side of the Pennines. 'Why?' I asked mildly.

'We've got some questions we'd like to ask you.' By now, Linda wasn't even pretending to meet my eye. She was pointedly staring somewhere over my left shoulder.

'So come in, have a brew and we'll see if I can answer them,' I repeated. I call it the irregular verb theory of life; I am firm, you are stubborn, he/she is a pig-headed, rigid, anally retentive stick-in-the mud.

'Like DC Shaw said, we'd like you to come down the station,' her oppo rumbled. It was like listening to Vesuvius by stethoscope. Only with a Liverpudlian accent instead of an Italian one.

I sighed. 'We can do this one of two ways. Either you can come into the house and ask me what you've got to ask me, or you can arrest me and we'll go down the station and I don't say a word until my brief arrives. You choose.' I gave the pair of them my sweetest smile, somehow choking down the anger. I knew whose hand was behind this. It had Cliff Jackson's sadistic fingerprints all over it.

Linda breathed out hard through her nose and compressed her lips into a thin line. I imagined she was thinking about the rocket Cliff Jackson was going to fire at her when she got back to base without me meekly following at her heels. That wasn't my problem, and I wasn't going to be guilt-tripped into behaving as if it was. When I made no response, Linda shrugged and said, 'We'd better have that brew, then.'

The pair of them followed me down the path and into the house. I pointed at the living room, told them they were having coffee and brewed up in the kitchen, desperately trying to figure out why Jackson had sent a team round to hassle me. I dripped a pot of coffee while I thought about it, laying milk, sugar, mugs and spoons on a tray at the same time. By the time the coffee was done, I was no nearer an answer. I was going to have to opt for the obvious and ask Linda Shaw.

I walked through the living-room door, dumped

the tray on the coffee table in front of the detectives and took the initiative. 'This had better be good, Linda,' I said. 'I have had a bitch of a week, and it's only Tuesday. Tell me why I'm sitting here talking to you instead of running myself a long hot bath.'

Linda flashed a quick look at her partner, who was enjoying himself far too much to help her out. He leaned forward and poured out three mugs of coffee. Looking like she'd bitten into a pickled lemon, Linda said, 'We've received an allegation which my inspector felt merited investigation.'

'From whom? About whom?' I demanded, best grammar on show.

She poured milk into her coffee and made a major production number out of stirring it. 'Our informant alleges that you have engaged in a campaign of threats against the life of one Richard Barclay.'

I was beyond speech. I was beyond movement. I sat with my mouth open, hand halfway towards a mug of coffee, like a Damien Hirst installation floating motionless in formaldehyde.

'The complainant alleges that this harassment has included placing false death announcements in the local press. We have verified that such an advert has appeared. And now Mr Barclay appears to have gone missing,' the male detective asserted, sitting back in his seat, legs wide apart, arm along the back of the sofa, asserting himself all over my living room.

Anger kicked in. 'And this informant. It wouldn't be an anonymous tip-off, would it?'

He looked at her, his face puzzled, hers resigned. 'You know we can't disclose that,' Linda said wearily. 'But we have been trying without success to contact Mr Barclay since nine this morning, and as my colleague says, we have confirmed that a death announcement was placed in the *Chronicle* containing false information. It does appear that you have some explaining to do, Ms Brannigan.' Any more apologetic and you could have used her voice as a doormat.

I'd had enough. 'Bollocks,' I said. 'We both know what's really happening here. You get an anonymous tip-off and your boss rubs his hands with glee. Oh goody, a borderline legitimate excuse to nip round and make Brannigan's life a misery. You've got no evidence that any crime has taken place. Even if somebody did place a bullshit ad in the *Chronicle*, and *The Times* too for all I know or care, you've got nothing to indicate it's anything other than a practical joke or that it's anything at all to do with me.' My voice rose in outrage. I knew I was on firm ground; I'd paid for the *Chronicle* announcement cash on the nail, making sure I popped in at lunch time when the classified ads department is at its busiest.

'It's our duty to investigate serious allegations,' the Tyson lookalike rumbled. 'And so far you haven't explained why anyone would want to accuse you of a serious crime like this. I mean, it's not the sort of thing most people do unless they've got a good reason for it. Like knowing about some crime you've committed, Ms Brannigan.'

I stood up. I was inches away from really giving them something to arrest me for. 'Right,' I said, furious. 'Out. Now. Never mind finishing your coffee. This is bollocks and you know it. You want to talk to Richard, sit outside on your arses and waste the taxpayers' money until he comes home. The reason you haven't been able to contact him, soft lad, is because he's a rock journalist. He doesn't answer his phone to the likes of you, and right now, he's probably sitting in some dive listening to a very bad band desperate to attract his attention. He'll be in the perfect mood to deal with this crap when he gets home. Now you,' I added, leaning forward and pointing straight between his astonished eyes, 'are new in my life, so you probably don't know there's a hidden agenda here.'

I swung round to point at Linda, who was also on her feet and edging towards the door. 'But you should know better, lady. Now walk, before I have to drag Ruth Hunter away from her favourite TV cop to slap you with a suit for harassment. Bugger off and bother some proper villains. Or don't you know any? Are you kicking your heels waiting for me to provide you with enough evidence to arrest some?'

Linda was halfway through the door by the time I'd finished my tirade. Her sidekick looked from me to her and back again before deciding that he'd better follow her and find out what the real story was here. I didn't bother seeing them out.

I couldn't believe Linda Shaw had let herself be sucked into Cliff Jackson's spiteful little game. But then, he was the boss, she had a career to think about, and women don't climb the career ladder in the police force by telling their bosses to shove their stupid vendettas where the perverts shove their gerbils. And as for their anonymous source – that cheeky, malicious little toad Will Allen was going to pay for ruining my evening. If he thought he could frighten me off with a bit of police harassment, he was in for the rudest shock of his life.

10

The front door closed on a silence so tremendous I could hear the blood beating in my brain. The last time I'd been this angry had nearly cost me my relationship with Richard, who had infuriated me to the point where violence seemed the most attractive option. This time it had been a police officer I'd nearly decked. The repercussions from that might have been less emotionally traumatic, but they would probably have cost me just as much in different ways. On the other hand, trying to sell a share in a business where the remaining partner is on bail for assault would present Bill with one or two problems . . . I nearly ran after Linda Shaw and begged her to wind me up again.

I rotated my head enthusiastically in a bid to loosen some of the knots the CID had put there and went through to the kitchen. I wasn't about to let Linda Shaw put me off the job I had planned for later that night, but I could allow myself the necessary indulgence of one stiff drink. I raked around in the freezer until I found the half-bottle of Polish lemon pepper vodka I'd been saving for a rainy day and poured the last sluggish inch into a tall slim tumbler. There was no freshly squeezed grapefruit juice in the fridge, which tells you all you need to know about the week I was having. I had to settle for a mixer bottle lurking behind the cheese. It needed the kind of shaking I'd wanted to give Linda Shaw. I'd barely swallowed the first mouthful when the silence gave up the ghost under the onslaught of the patio doors opening from the conservatory.

'Brannigan?' I heard.

Stifling a groan, I reached back into the fridge and pulled out one of the bottles Richard periodically donates from his world beer collection so he doesn't have to walk all the way back to his kitchen when he's in my bed. Staropramen from Prague, I noted irrelevantly as I grasped the bottle opener, wishing I were there. 'Kitchen,' I called.

'Hullawrerrhen,' said another voice behind me. At least, that's what I think it said. I turned to see Dan Druff grinning warily in the doorway. Silently, I handed him the Czech beer and reached for the next bottle in line. Radeberger Pilsner. I popped the top just as Richard appeared alongside Dan.

'What the hell were Pinky and Perky after?' Richard demanded after the first half of the bottle had cleared his oesophagus.

'They spoke to you?'

He nodded. 'Weird as fuck. They were just getting into their motor when we pulled up. The brick shithouse got all excited and said, "That's him," to the Chris Cagney wannabe. She looked absolutely parrot and got out of the car.'

Richard paused to swallow again and Dan took up the tale. 'She comes across to us and says to your man, "Are you Richard Barclay?" and he goes, "Yeah, who's asking?" And she goes, "Police. Have you been the victim of any death threats?" And he looks at her as if she's just dropped off the planet Demented and shakes his head.'

'So she turns round and says, "Satisfied?" to her partner. She sounds dead narked, he looks as bemused as I feel, and off the pair of them go, little trotters twinkling all the way back to their unmarked pigsty,' Richard concluded. 'Now, I might not be Mastermind, but I reckon there's a higher chance of me winning the Lottery than there is of that little encounter being completely unconnected to you.'

'I cannot tell a lie,' I said.

Richard snorted. To Dan, he said, 'Do you know the story about the two Cretans? One could only tell lies, the other could only tell the truth. Guess which one is Brannigan?'

'Hey,' I protested. 'This man is my client.'

'That's right,' Dan said. 'Gonnae no' take the mince out of her?'

At last, something Richard and I could share,

even if it was only total incomprehension. 'What?' we both chorused.

Dan looked like he was used to the reaction. 'Doesnae matter,' he sighed. 'When it does, I'll keep it simple enough for youse English, OK?'

I shooed the pair of them through to the living room and ran through my brief encounter. 'Obviously, that toerag who was here the other night decided to warn me off,' I concluded.

Richard frowned. 'But how did he know who you were? Presumably, you were just Mrs Barclay to him. How did he make the connection to Kate Brannigan? Isn't that a bit worrying?'

'It would be if you hadn't shouted "Brannigan" after me the other night when he was three steps in front of me,' I said drily.

'Which is not good news because if this guy knows your name, he's going to come after you. And then he'll be really sorry,' Dan chipped in, making a sideways chopping gesture with his hand. His faith was touching.

'I'm glad you dropped by,' I said. 'I've been making one or two inquiries about your problem. What I'm hearing as the most likely scenario is that it all comes down to flyposting. The person you're using is almost certainly invading somebody else's territory. Either by accident or deliberately.'

Dan pushed a hand through his long red fringe. He looked puzzled. 'It's kind of hard to get my head round that,' he said. 'The guy we're using isn't some new kid on the block. He's been knocking around the Manchester promotions scene for years. He did everybody when they were nobody.'

'You're sure about that?' I asked. 'He's not telling you porkies?'

Dan shook his head. 'No way. We checked him out before we came down here. Lice knows this guy that used to drive the van for the Inspiral Carpets when they were just starting out, and it was him that told us about Sean.'

'Sean?'

'Sean Costigan,' Dan said. 'The guy that does our promotions.'

'I need to talk to him. Can you give me his number?'

Dan pulled a face and looked to Richard for help. My lover was too busy building a spliff that would have spanned the Mersey to notice. 'I'm not supposed to give his number out,' Dan finally said. Embarrassment didn't sit well on his ferocious appearance.

I took a deep breath. 'I need to talk to him, Dan. I'm sure that when he told you not to hand out his number, he didn't have people like me in mind.'

'I don't know,' Dan hedged. 'I mean, he's not going to be very happy when he finds there's a private polis on the end of his mobile, is he?'

Give me strength. 'Tell him I'm the people's pig,' I said, exasperated. 'Look, if you feel bad about giving me his number, you're going to have to set up a meet between us. I can't make any more progress until I talk to Sean Costigan myself. So if you don't want to waste the money you've clocked up on my meter so far, you'd better get something sorted.' I smiled sweetly. 'More beer, anyone?'

Brannigan's second rule of burglary: when in doubt, go home. I was already breaking rule number three, which states that you never burgle offices outside working hours because some nosey parker is bound to spot a light. One look at the back of the Compton Clinic told me that if I went ahead, I was going to be breaking the second rule too. Although the ginnel the clinic backed on to was only a narrow back alley, it was well lit. Never mind the block of flats behind me; any late-night carousers walking along Deansgate who happened to glance down the lane would immediately notice anything out of the ordinary.

And whatever means I used to get inside the clinic, ordinary wasn't on the menu. I'd already seen the closed-circuit video surveillance in the hall, which ruled out going in through the rear entrance and getting to the second-floor consulting room via the main staircase. Alexis had told me that when they went for their Sunday consultations, she and Chris followed instructions to approach by climbing a fire escape which led up to a heavy door which in turn gave on to a landing between the first and second floors. The only problem with that approach was the security floodlight mounted on the back of the building which would make me as visible as a bluebottle on a kitchen worktop. And even if I got past that, the chances were strong that I wouldn't be able to make it through the fire door which wasn't going to be conveniently wedged open for me as it had been for Alexis and Chris.

There was nothing else for it. I was going to have to brazen it out and hope there were no police cars cruising the quiet midnight streets. I walked round the block till I was looking at the front door of the clinic. Like a lot of people who spend a few grand on state-of-the-art security, they had neglected to spend fifty quid on serious locks. There were two mortices and a Yale, and just glancing at them, I knew I was only looking at ten minutes max with my lock picks. I undid the middle button on Richard's baggy but lightweight indigo linen jacket that was covering the leather tradesman's apron which houses my going-equipped-to-burgle kit, and took out my set of picks. I shoved my black ski cap up a couple of inches and switched on the narrow-beamed lamp I had strapped round my head. I studied the top lock for a few seconds, then chose a slender strip of metal and started poking around. Even with the handicap of latex gloves, I had both mortices open in less than six minutes. The Yale was the work of a couple of minutes. Now for the difficult bit.

I turned the handle and pushed the door open. I heard the electronic beep of a burglar alarm about to have hysterics as I closed the door firmly behind me. I set the timing ring on the diver's watch I was wearing. Locking the mortices should be slightly easier now I knew exactly which picks to use, but I'd be lying if I didn't admit that the wailing klaxon of the burglar alarm put me off my stride. Five minutes later, I was locked in with an alarm that was louder than the front row at a heavy-metal gig. I switched off my lamp, opened the inside door but didn't step into the hall just yet. There was still the small matter of the video camera. In the darkness, I strained my eyes to see if there were any dull glimmers, indicating sensors that would flood the hall with light. Nothing. I was going to have to chance it, and hope that the camera wasn't loaded with infrared film. Somehow, I doubted it.

Cautiously, I moved forward in the pitch black. Nothing happened. No lights came on, no passive infrared sensors blossomed into red jewels recording the sequence of my journey. I was so intent on my surroundings, I misjudged the length of the hall and went sprawling over the bottom stair. Thank goodness the deep-pile carpet continued up the stairs otherwise I'd have been on the fast track to Casualty. I picked myself up and went up as fast as I could manage without breaking anything. I might be in a clinic but I didn't fancy my chances if the doctors arrived to find their burglar languishing on the stair carpet with a broken leg.

I made it round the turn of the stairs to the first floor and started to climb again. At the head of the stairs, I started groping down the hallway for door handles. The first one I came to opened and I stumbled inside. I took my heavy rubber torch out of my apron and risked a quick flash. I was in a consulting room. No hiding place. I backed out onto the landing and tried the next door. A bathroom. No hiding place apart from cubicles where any self-respecting security guard would check instantly. The third door was locked, as was the fourth, across the hall. Next came another consulting room, but this time the swift sweep of my torch revealed a kneehole desk with a solid side facing the door. I hurried round the desk and squeezed myself into the narrow space, wriggling until I was comfortable enough to stay still for a while. I checked my watch, which indicated that it had been twelve minutes since the alarm was triggered. That meant it should switch itself off automatically in eight minutes. With luck, I might still have some residual hearing left by then. I stuffed my thumbs in my ears and waited.

When the alarm stopped, it was like a physical blow, snapping my head back. Almost beyond belief, I unjammed my ears, struggling to accept that the ringing noise that remained was only inside my head. My watch said eighteen minutes had passed since the alarm had started its hideous cacophony. That meant a key holder had arrived. I felt myself sweat with nerves, clammy trickles in my armpits and down my spine. If I was caught now, there wasn't a lie in the world that was going to keep me out of a prison cell.

Trying not to think about it, I started a mental replay of every note of the six minutes of Annie Lennox's 'Downtown Lights'. I was coming to the end when I heard a low murmur of voices that definitely wasn't part of my mental soundtrack. Then the door of my shelter swung open, casting a rectangle of light on the far wall opposite me.

'And this is the last one,' a man's voice said, sounding anxious. I made out two distorted shadows, one with a familiar peaked cap, before the light snapped on.

I sensed rather than heard a body moving nearer. Then a second voice, speaking from what seemed to be a couple of feet above my head, said, 'Your alarm must be on the blink, sir. No sign of forced entry, no one on the premises.'

'It's never done this before,' the first voice said, sounding irritated this time.

'Have it serviced regular, do you?'

'I don't know, it's not my area of responsibility,' the first voice said. 'So what do we do now?'

'I suggest we reset it, sir, and hope it's just a one-off.' The light died and the door closed. I exhaled slowly and quietly. I gave it five minutes, then I stepped out cautiously onto the landing. Nothing happened. I waved my arms around in a bizarre parody of a Hollywood babe work-out video. Still nothing.

I couldn't believe it. They'd spent a small fortune

on perimeter security and a video camera, but they didn't have any internal tremblers or passive infrared detectors. And there I'd been, planning to keep setting the alarm off at five-minute intervals until they finally abandoned the building with an unset alarm. I almost felt cheated.

From what Alexis had told me, the second locked door I'd tried had been Helen Maitland's consulting room. I kneeled down in front of the door and turned on my headlamp. Interestingly, the lock on her consulting room had cost twice the total of all three front-door locks. A seven-lever deadbolt mortice. Just out of curiosity, I took a quick look at the other locked door. A straightforward three-lever lock that a ten-year-old with a Swiss Army knife could have been through in less time than it takes an expert to complete the first level of Donkey Kong. Helen Maitland hadn't been taking any chances.

It took nearly fifteen minutes of total concentration for me to get past the lock. I closed the door softly behind me and shone the torch in a slow arc round the room, like a bad movie. More wall-to-wall heavy-duty carpet in the same shade of champagne. Their carpet-cleaning bill must have been phenomenal. Curtained screen folded against the wall. Examination couch. Sink. Grey metal filing cabinet. Shredder. Printer table with an ink jet on it. Tall cupboard with drawers underneath. A leather chair with a writing surface attached to the right arm, set at an angle to a two-seater sofa covered in cream canvas. No pictures on the walls. No rugs, just basic hard-wearing, pale green, industrial-weight carpet. No desk. No computer. At least I knew it wasn't going to take me long to search. And by the look of things, nobody had been here before me.

I started on the filing cabinet. I was glad to see it was one of the old-fashioned ones that can be unlocked by tipping them back and releasing the lock bar from below. Filing-cabinet locks are a pig to pick, and I'd had enough fiddling with small pieces of metal for one night. I was doubly glad I hadn't had to pick it when I finally got to examine the contents. The bottom drawer contained photostats of articles in medical journals and offprints of published papers. A couple of the articles had Sarah Blackstone's name among the contributors, and I tucked them into the waistband of my trousers.

The next drawer up contained a couple of gynaecological textbooks and a pile of literature about artificial insemination. The drawer above that was partly filled with sealed packets of A4 printer paper. The top drawer held a kettle, three mugs, an assortment of fruit teas and a jar of honey. The cupboard held medical supplies. Metal contraptions I didn't want to be able to put a name to. Boxes of surgical gloves. Those overgrown lollipop sticks that appear whenever it's cervical smear time. The drawers underneath were empty except for a near-empty box of regular tampons. I love it when I'm snowed under with clues.

I sat back on my heels and looked around. The only sign that anyone had ever used this room was the shredder, whose bin was half full. But I knew there was no point in trying to get anything from that. Life's too short to stuff a mushroom and to reassemble shredded print-outs. But I couldn't believe that Helen Maitland had left nothing at all in her consulting room. That was turning paranoia into a fine art.

I knew from Alexis that the doctor worked with a laptop rather than a pen and paper, keying everything in as she went along. Even so, I'd have expected to find something, even if it was only a letterhead. I decided to have another look in the less obvious places. Under the examination couch: nothing except dust. Under the sofa cushions: not even biscuit crumbs.

It was taped to the underside of one of the drawers below the cupboard. A card-backed envelope containing three computer disks. I slid them out of the envelope and into the inside pocket of Richard's jacket. I checked my watch. I'd been inside the room getting on for twenty minutes and I didn't think there was anything more to learn here.

Back on the landing, I locked the door behind me. No point in telegraphing my visit to the world. I started off down the stairs, but just before I reached the first-floor landing, I realized there was a glow of light from downstairs. Cautiously, I crouched down, edged forward and peered through the bannisters. Almost directly below me, sitting on the bottom stairs was the unmistakable foreshortened figure of a police officer.

11

To be accused of one summary offence is unfortunate; to be accused of two within a twenty-four-hour period looks remarkably like carelessness. And since a reputation for carelessness doesn't bring clients to the door, I decided this wasn't a good time to attract the attention of the officer on the stairs. I shrank back from the bannisters and crept towards the upper flight of stairs. In the gloom, I noticed what I hadn't before. There actually were passive infrared sensors high in the corners of the stairwell; they were the ultra-modern ones that don't actually show a light when they're triggered. The reason nothing had happened when I'd waved my arms around on the upper landing earlier was that the alarm hadn't been switched on. Thank God for the need to impress clients with the luxury carpeting.

As I crouched at the foot of the second flight, I heard the crackle of the policeman's personal radio. I sidled forward again, trying to hear what he was saying. '. . . still here in St John Street,' I made out. '. . . burglar-alarm bloke arrives. The key holder's worried . . . Yeah, drugs, expensive equipment . . . should be here by now . . . OK, Sarge.'

Now I knew what was going on. The key holder had been nervous of leaving the building with what seemed to be a faulty alarm. Presumably, they had a maintenance contract that provided for twenty-four-hour call-out, and he'd decided to take advantage of it. It probably hadn't been difficult to pitch the Dibble into hanging around until the burglar-alarm technician arrived. It was a cold night out there, and minding a warm clinic had to be an improvement on cruising the early-morning streets with nothing more uplifting to deal with than nightclub brawls or drunken domestics.

I tiptoed back up to the top floor and considered my options. No way could I get past the copper. Once the burglar-alarm technician arrived and reset the system, I wasn't going to be able to get out without setting off the alarm again, and this time they'd realize it couldn't be a fault. OK, I'd be long gone, but with a murder investigation going on that might just lead back here, I didn't want any suspicious circumstances muddying the waters.

For all of five seconds, I considered the fire door leading off the half-landing below me. Chances were the hinges would squeak, the security lights would be on a separate system from the burglar alarm and I'd be spotlit on a fire escape with an apron full of exotica that I couldn't pretend was my knitting bag. Not to mention a pocketful of computer disks that might well tie me right into an even bigger crime. I could see only one alternative.

With a soft sigh, I got down on my knees again and started to unlock the door of Helen Maitland's consulting room.

I've slept in a lot less comfortable places than a gynaecologist's sofa. It was a bit short, even for me, but it was cosy, especially after I'd annexed the cotton cellular blanket from the examination couch and peeled off my latex gloves. I'd locked the door behind me, so I figured I was safe if anyone decided further investigations were necessary. Looking on the bright side, I'd managed to postpone a thrill-packed evening in Garibaldi's with some spaced-out rock promoter. And I'd used up every last bit of adrenaline in my system. I was too tired now to be scared. As I drifted off to sleep, I had the vague sense that I could hear electronic chirruping in the distance, but I was past caring.

I'd set my mental clock to waken me around nine. It was five to when my eyelids ungummed themselves. Six hours sleep wasn't enough, but it was as much as I usually squeezed in when I was chasing a handful of cases as packed with incident as my current load seemed to be. I unfolded my cramped body from the sofa and did some languid stretching to loosen my stiffened muscles. I peed in the sink, rinsed it out with paranoid care then splashed water over my face, dumping the used paper towels in the empty bin below. It looked like Helen Maitland had even taken her used bin liners home. Learning a lesson in caution from her, I used a paper towel to open cupboard and box and helped myself to a pair of her surgical gloves, then moved across to the door and listened. I couldn't hear a thing.

As quietly as possible, I unlocked the door. I opened it a crack and listened some more. Now I could hear the sort of noises that an occupied building gives off: distant murmurs of speech, feet moving on stairs and hallways, doors opening and closing. I didn't know how appointments were spaced at the Compton Clinic, but I reckoned that the best time to avoid coming into contact with too many other people was probably around twenty-five past the hour. I softly closed the door and checked myself over. I'd taken off the ski cap and headlamp, but I still looked a pretty unlikely private patient in my black hockey boots, leggings and polo-neck sweater. Even the fashionable bagginess of Richard's designer-label jacket didn't lift the outfit much. If anyone did see me, I'd have to hope they put me down as someone in one of those arty jobs never seen by the general public – radio producer, publisher's editor, novelist, literary critic.

I watched the second hand sweep round until it was time. Then I inched the door open. The landing was clear. I slipped out and pulled the door closed behind me, holding the handle so the catch wouldn't click into place. I carefully released it and stepped away smartly. The door was going to have to stay unlocked, but with luck, by the time it was discovered, the fault in the burglar alarm would be ancient history. I tripped down the stairs with the easy nonchalance of someone who's just been given some very good news by their gynae. I didn't see another soul. When I reached the foot of the stairs, I sketched a cheery wave at the video camera. Then I was out on the street, happily sucking in the traffic fumes of the city centre. Free and clear.

I walked up the street to the meter where I'd left the car the night before, expecting to pay the penalty for parking without payment for the first hour of the working day. This close to the traffic wardens' HQ just off Deansgate, it was practically inevitable. By some accidental miracle that the gods had obviously intended for some other mortal, I hadn't been wheel-clamped. I didn't even have a ticket.

The luck didn't last, of course. The phone was ringing as I got through the door and I made the mistake of answering it rather than letting the machine deal with the call. 'Your mobile has been switched off since this time yesterday,' Shelley stated without preamble.

'I know that,' I retorted.

'Have you lost the instruction manual? To turn it on, you depress the button marked "power".'

'I know that too.'

'Are you coming in today?'

'I doubt it,' I said briskly. 'Stuff to do. Clinkers to riddle, pots to side, cases to solve.'

'You are still working, then?' For once, Shelley's voice wasn't dripping sarcasm. It almost sounded like she was concerned about me, but that may have been my overactive imagination.

'I'm working on the gravestone scam, plus I have two other cases that are currently occupying significant amounts of my time,' I said, probably more abruptly than I intended.

'What other cases?' Shelley asked accusingly. Back to normal, thank God. Shelley as sergeant major I could cope with; Shelley as mother hen wasn't part of the deal.

'New cases. I'll let you have the paperwork just as soon as I get to it,' I said. 'Now I've got to go. There's a librarian out there waiting for me to make her day.' I cut the connection before Shelley could say anything more. I knew I was being childish about avoiding Bill, but until I could get my head straight about my future, I couldn't even bear to be in the office where we'd worked together so successfully.

I dumped my stale clothes in the laundry basket, left Richard's jacket by the door so I'd remember to take it to be dry-cleaned, and dived into the shower. Needles of water stung my flesh on the borderline of pain, stripping away my world-weariness. By the time I'd finished with the coconut shampoo, the strawberry body wash and the grapefruit body lotion, I must have smelled like a fruit salad, but at least I'd stopped feeling like chopped liver.

While I was waiting for the coffee to brew, I booted up my trusty PC and took a look at the disks I'd raided from Helen Maitland's consulting room. Each disk contained about a dozen files, all with names like SMITGRIN.DAT, FOSTHILL.DAT and EDWAJACK.DAT. When I came to one called APPLELEE.DAT my initial guess that the file names corresponded to pairs of patients was confirmed. I didn't have to be much of a detective to realize that this contained the data relating to Chris Appleton and Alexis Lee. The only problem was accessing the information. I tried various word-processing packages but whatever software Helen Maitland had used, it wasn't one that I had on my machine. So I tried cheating my way into the file, renaming it so my software would think it was a different kind of file and read it. No joy. Either these files were password protected, or the software was too specialized to give up its secrets to my rather crude methods.

I finished my coffee, copied the disks and sent Gizmo a piece of e-mail to tell him that he was about to find an envelope with three disks on his doormat and that I'd appreciate a print-out of the files contained on them. Then I went on a wardrobe mission for something that would persuade a doctor that I was a fit and proper person to talk to. Failing combat fatigues and a Kalashnikov, I settled for navy linen trousers, a navy silk tweed jacket and a lightweight cream cotton turtleneck. At least I wouldn't look like a drug rep.

I raided the cash dispenser again and stuffed some cash in an envelope with the originals of the disks and pushed the whole lot through Gizmo's letter box. I wasn't in the mood for conversation, not even Gizmo's laconic variety. Next stop was Central Ref. It was chucking it down in stair rods by then, and of course I hadn't brought an umbrella. Which made it inevitable that the nearest available parking space was on the far side of Albert Square down on Jackson's Row. With my jacket pulled over my head so that I looked like a strange, deformed creature from a Hammer Horror film, I sprinted through the rain-darkened streets to the massive circular building that manages to dominate St Peter's Square in spite of the taller buildings around it.

Under the portico, I joined the other people shaking themselves like dogs before we filed into the grand foyer with its twin staircases. I ignored the information desk and the lift and walked up to the reference room. Modelled on the British Museum reading room, the tables radiate out from the hub of a central desk like the spokes from a vast, literary wheel. Light filters down from the dome of the high ceiling, and everything is hushed, like a library ought to be. All these modern buildings with their strip lighting, antistatic carpets and individual carrels never feel like proper libraries to me. I often used to come and work in Central Ref. when I was a student. The atmosphere was more calm than the university law library, and nobody ever tried to chat you up.

Today, though, I wasn't after Halsbury's *Statutes of England*, or Michael Zander's analysis of the Police and Criminal Evidence Act. The first thing I wanted was Black's *Medical Directory*, the list of doctors licensed to practise in the UK, complete with their qualifications and their professional history. I'd used it before, so I knew where to look. Black's told me that Sarah Blackstone had qualified twelve years before. She was a graduate of Edinburgh University, a fellow of the Royal College of Obstetricians and Gynaecologists, and she had worked in Obs & Gynae in Glasgow, then one of the London teaching hospitals before winding up as a consultant at St Hilda's Infirmary in Leeds, one of the key hospitals in the north. It was clear from the information here plus the articles I'd taken from the consulting room that Dr Blackstone was an expert on sub-fertility, out there at the leading edge of an increasingly controversial field, a woman with a reputation for solid achievement. That explained in part why she'd chosen to operate under an alias.

Since the book was there in front of me, I

idly thumbed forward. There was no reason why she should have chosen to use another doctor's name as an alias, except that Alexis had told me that Sarah Blackstone had written prescriptions in the name of Helen Maitland. While it wasn't impossible that she'd used an entirely fictitious name to do this, it would have been easier and safer to steal another doctor's identity. If she'd done that, uncovering the real Helen Maitland might just take me a step or two further forward.

Impatiently I ran my finger down the twin columns, past the Madisons, the Maffertys and the Mahons, and there it was. Helen Maitland. Another Edinburgh graduate, though she'd qualified three years before Sarah Blackstone. Member of the Royal College of Physicians. She'd worked in Oxford, briefly in Belfast, as a medical registrar in Newcastle, and now, like Sarah Blackstone, she was also a consultant at St Hilda's in Leeds, with research responsibilities. According to Black's, and the indices of the medical journals I checked afterwards, Helen Maitland had nothing to do with fertility treatment. She was a specialist in cystic fibrosis, and had published extensively on recent advances in gene replacement therapy. On the surface, it might seem that there was no point of contact between the two women professionally; but the embryologist who worked on Helen Maitland's patients' offspring in vitro might well be the same one who worked with Sarah Blackstone's subfertile couples. They'd certainly work in the same lab.

Even if I had all the files on the disks I'd recovered in the night, I still needed to make some more checks. The original computer files, of which I was sure these were only back-up copies, had to be on a computer somewhere. And I needed to check out whether the real Helen Maitland was sufficiently involved in Sarah Blackstone's fertility project to be a potential threat to Alexis and Chris, or whether she was simply an innocent victim of her colleague's deception.

Before I made the inevitable trip across the Pennines, I thought I'd make the most of being in Central Ref. Replacing the medical directory, I wandered across to the shelves where the city's electoral rolls are kept. I looked up the main index and found the volume that contained the street where 'Will Allen' and his partner 'Sarah Sargent' lived. I pulled the appropriate box file from the shelf and thumbed through the wards until I got to the right one. I found them inside a minute.

It's one of the truisms of life that when people pick an alias, they go for something that is easy for them to remember, so they won't be readily caught out. They'll opt for the same initials, or a name that has some connection for them. There, in Flat 24, was living proof. Alan Williams and Sarah Constable.

If I played my cards right, maybe I could get them done for wasting police time as well as everything else. That would teach them to mess with me.

12

I used the old flower-delivery trick on the real
Helen Maitland. A quick call to St Hilda's Infirmary
had established that Dr Maitland was doing an out-
patients clinic that afternoon. A slow scan of the
phone book had revealed that her phone number
was ex-directory. Given the protective layers of
receptionists and nurses, I didn't rate my chances
of getting anywhere near her at work unless I'd
made an appointment three months in advance.
That meant fronting up at her home. The only
problem with that was that I didn't know where
she lived.

I headed for the hospital florist and looked at the
flowers on offer. There were the usual predictable,
tired arrangements of chrysanthemums and spray
carnations. Some of them wouldn't have looked
out of place sitting on top of a coffin. I suppose it saved money if your nearest and dearest
seemed to be near death's door: one lot of flowers
would do for bedside and graveside. Gave a whole

new meaning to saying it with flowers. The only exception was a basket of freesias mixed with irises. When I went to pay for it, I realized why they only bothered stocking the one. It was twice the price of the others. I got a receipt. My client would never believe flowers could cost that much otherwise. I've seen the tired garage bunches she brings home for Chris.

The price included a card, which I didn't write out until I was well clear of the florist. 'Dear Doctor, thanks for everything, Sue.' Every doctor has grateful patients; the law of averages says some of them must be called Sue. Then I toddled round to the outpatients clinic and thrust the arrangement at the receptionist. 'Flowers for Dr Maitland,' I mumbled.

The receptionist looked surprised. 'Oh, that's nice. Who are they from?'

I shrugged. 'I just deliver them. Can I leave them with you?'

'That's fine, I'll see she gets them.'

A couple of hours later, a tall, rangy woman emerged from the outpatients department with a long loping stride. Given that she was in her mid- to late forties and she'd presumably done a hard day's work, she moved with remarkable energy. She was wearing black straight-leg jeans and cowboy boots, a blue and white striped shirt under a black blazer, and a trench coat thrown casually over her shoulders to protect her from the soft Yorkshire drizzle. In one hand, she carried a pilot's case. In the other, as if it were something that might explode, the basket of flowers. If this was Dr Helen Maitland, I had no doubt she wasn't the woman Alexis and Chris had seen. There was no way anyone could have confused her with the photograph in the paper by accident. This woman had fine features in an oval face, nothing like the strong, definite square face Alexis had shown me. Her hair was totally different too. Where Sarah Blackstone had a heavy mop of dark hair in a jagged fringe, this woman had dark blonde curls rampaging over the top of her head, while the sides and back were cropped short. I started my engine. Lucky I'd been parking in a 'consultants only' slot, really. Otherwise I might have missed her.

She stopped beside an old MGB roadster in British racing green and balanced the flowers on the roof while she unlocked the car. The case was tossed in, followed by the mac, then she carefully put the flowers in the passenger foot well. She folded her long legs under the wheel and the engine started with a throaty growl. The presumed Dr Maitland reversed out of her parking space and shot forwards towards the exit with the aplomb of a woman who would know exactly what to do if her car started fishtailing on the greasy Tarmac. More cautiously, I followed. We wove through the narrow alleys between the tall Victorian brick buildings of the old part of the hospital and emerged on the main road just below the university. She turned up the hill into the early-evening traffic and together we slogged up the hill, through Hyde Park and out towards Headingley. Just as we approached the girls' grammar school, she indicated a right turn. From where I was, it was hard to see where she was going, but as she turned, I saw her destination was a narrow cobbled lane almost invisible from the main road.

I positioned myself to follow her, watching as she shot up the hill with a puff of exhaust. At the top, she turned right. Me, I was stuck on the main drag, the prisoner of traffic that wouldn't pause to let me through. A good thirty seconds passed before I could find a gap, long enough for her to have vanished without trace. Quoting extensively if repetitiously from the first few scenes of *Four Weddings and a Funeral*, I drove in her wake.

As I turned right at the top of the lane, I saw her put the key in the lock. She was standing in front of a tall, narrow Edwardian stone villa, the car tucked into a parking space that had been carved out of half of the front garden. I carried on past the house, turning the next available corner and squeezing into a parking space. A quick call to the local library to check their electoral register confirmed that Helen Maitland lived there. I always make sure these days after the time that the florist trick failed because the target was a hay-fever sufferer who passed the flowers on to her secretary.

I gave Dr Maitland ten minutes to feed the cat

and put the kettle on, then I rang the bell set in stone to the right of a front door gleaming with gloss paint the same shade of green as the car. The eyes that looked questioningly into mine when the door opened were green too, though a softer shade, like autumn leaves on the turn. 'Dr Maitland? I'm sorry to trouble you,' I started.

'I'm sorry, I don't . . . ?' Her eyebrows twitched towards each other like caterpillars in a mating dance.

'My name is Brannigan, Kate Brannigan. I'm a private investigator. I wondered if you could spare me a few minutes.'

That's the point where most people look wary. We've all got something to feel guilty about. Helen Maitland simply looked curious. 'What on earth for?' she asked mildly.

'I'd like to ask you a few questions about Sarah Blackstone.' This wasn't the time for bullshit.

'Sarah Blackstone?' She looked surprised. 'What's that got to do with me?'

'You knew her,' I said bluntly. I knew now she did; a stranger would have said something along the lines of, 'Sarah Blackstone? The doctor who was murdered?'

'We worked in the same hospital,' Dr Maitland replied swiftly. I couldn't read her at all. There was something closed off in her face. I suppose doctors have to learn how to hide what they're thinking and feeling otherwise the rest of us would run a mile every time the news was iffy.

I waited. Most people can't resist silence for long. 'What business is it of yours?' she eventually added.

'My client was a patient of hers,' I said.

'I still don't see why that should bring you to my door.' Dr Maitland's voice was still friendly, but the hand gripping the doorjamb was tightening so that her knucklebones stood out in sharp relief. I hadn't been suspicious of her a moment before, but now I was definitely intrigued.

'My client was under the mistaken impression that she was being treated by one Dr Helen Maitland,' I said. 'Sarah Blackstone was using your name as an alias. I thought you might know why.'

Her eyebrows rose, but it was surprise rather than shock I thought I read there. I had the distinct feeling I wasn't telling her anything she didn't already know. 'How very strange,' she said, and I suspected it was my knowing that was the strange thing. I'd have expected any doctor confronted with the information that a colleague had stolen their identity to be outraged and concerned. But Helen Maitland seemed to be taking it very calmly.

'You weren't aware of it?'

'It's not something we doctors generally allow,' she said drily, her face giving nothing away.

I shrugged. 'Well, if you don't know why Dr Blackstone helped herself to your name, I'll just have to keep digging until I find someone who does.'

As I spoke, the rain turned from drizzle to downpour. 'Oh Lord,' she sighed. 'Look, you'd better come in before you catch pneumonia.'

I followed her into a surprisingly light hallway. She led me past the stairs and into a dining kitchen so cluttered Richard would have felt perfectly at home. Stacks of medical journals threatened to teeter over onto haphazard piles of cookery books; newspapers virtually covered a large table, themselves obscured by strata of opened mail. The worktops and open shelves spilled over with interesting jars and bottles. I spotted olive oil with chillis, with rosemary and garlic, with thyme, oregano, sage and rosemary, olives layered in oil with what looked like basil, bottled damsons and serried rows of jams, all with neat, handwritten labels. On one shelf, in an Art-Nouveau-style silver frame there was a ten-by-eight colour photograph of Helen Maitland with an arm draped casually over the shoulders of a pale Pre-Raphaelite maiden with a mane of wavy black hair and enough dark eye make-up to pass as an extra in the *Rocky Horror Show*. On one wall was a cork board covered with snapshots of cats and people. As far as I could see, there were no pictures of Sarah Blackstone.

'Move one of the team and sit down,' Dr Maitland said, waving a hand at the pine chairs surrounding the table. I pulled one back and found a large tabby cat staring balefully up at me. I decided not to tangle with it and tried the next chair along. A black cat looked up at me with startled yellow

161

eyes, grumbled in its throat and leapt elegantly to the floor like a pint of Guinness pouring itself. I sat down hastily and looked up to find Helen Maitland watching me with a knowing smile. 'Tea?'

'Please.'

She opened a high cupboard that was stuffed with boxes. I remembered the filing-cabinet drawer in the consulting room. 'I've got apple and cinnamon, licorice, elderflower, peach and orange blossom, alpine strawberry . . .'

'Just plain tea would be fine,' I interrupted.

She shook her head. 'Sorry. I'm caffeine free. I can do you a decaff coffee?'

'No thanks. Decaff's a bit like cutting the swearing out of a Tarantino film. There's no point bothering with what's left. I'll try the alpine strawberry.'

She switched on the kettle and leaned against the worktop, looking at me over the rim of the cup she'd already made for herself. Closer, the youthful impression of her stride and her style was undercut by the tired lines around the eyes. There was not a trace of silver in her hair. Either her hairdresser was very good, or she was one of the lucky ones. 'Dr Blackstone's death came as a shock to all her colleagues,' she said.

'But you weren't really colleagues,' I pointed out. 'You worked in different departments. You're medical, she was surgical.'

She shrugged. 'Hilda's is a friendly hospital. Besides, there aren't so many women consultants that you can easily miss each other.'

The kettle clicked off, and she busied herself with tea bag, mug and water. When she slid the mug across the table to me our hands didn't touch, and I had the sense that this was deliberate. 'She must have known you reasonably well to feel comfortable about pretending to be you. She was even writing prescriptions in your name,' I tried.

'What can I say?' she replied with a shrug. 'I had no idea she was doing it, and I have no idea why she was doing it. I certainly don't know why she picked on me.'

'Were there other doctors she was more friendly with? Ones who might be able to shed some light on her actions?' I cut in. It was the threat of going elsewhere that had got me across the threshold, not the rain. Maybe repeating it would shake something loose from Helen Maitland's tree.

'I don't think she was particularly friendly with any of her colleagues,' Dr Maitland said quickly.

That was an interesting comment from someone who was acting as if she were on the same footing as all those other colleagues. 'How can you be sure who she was and wasn't friendly with? Given that you work in different departments?'

She smiled wryly. 'It's very simple. Sarah lived under my roof for a while when she first came to Leeds. She expected to sell her flat in London pretty quickly, so she didn't want to get into a formal lease on rented property. She was asking around if anyone had a spare room to rent. I remembered what that felt like, so I offered her a room here.'

'And she was here long enough for you to know that she didn't have particular friends in the hospital?' I challenged.

'In the event, yes. She was here for almost a year. Her London flat proved harder to shift than she imagined. We seemed not to get on each other's nerves, so she stayed.'

'So you must have known who her friends were?'

Dr Maitland shrugged again. 'She didn't seem to need many. When you've got a research element in your job and you have to work as hard as we do, you don't get a lot of time to build a social life. She went away a lot at weekends, various places. Bristol, Bedford, London. I didn't interrogate her about who she was visiting. I regarded it as none of my business.'

Her words might have been cool, but her voice remained warm. 'You haven't asked what she was doing with your identity,' I pointed out.

That wry smile again. 'I presumed you'd get round to that.'

There was something irritatingly provocative about Helen Maitland. It undid all my good intentions and made my interview techniques disappear. 'Did you know she was a lesbian when you offered her your spare room?' I demanded.

A small snort of laughter. 'I presumed she was. It didn't occur to me she might have changed her

164

sexuality between arriving in Leeds and moving in here.'

She was playing with me, and I didn't like it at all. 'Did she have a lover when she was living here?' I asked bluntly. Games were over for today.

'She never brought anyone back here,' Dr Maitland replied, still unruffled. 'And as far as I know, she did not spend nights in anyone else's bed, either in Leeds or elsewhere. However, as I have said, I can't claim to have exhaustive knowledge of her acquaintance.'

'Don't you mind that she was using your name to carry out medical procedures?' I demanded. 'Doesn't it worry you that she might have put you at professional risk by what she was doing?'

'Why should it? If anyone ever claimed that I had carried out inappropriate medical treatment on them, they would realize as soon as we came face to face that I had not been the doctor involved. Besides, I can't imagine Sarah would involve herself, or me, in anything unethical. I never thought of her as a risk taker.'

'Why else would she be using your identity?' I said forcefully. 'If it was all above board, she wouldn't have needed to pretend to be someone else, would she?'

Dr Maitland suddenly looked tired. 'I suppose not,' she said. 'So what exactly was she doing that was so heinous?'

'She was working with lesbian couples who

wanted children,' I said, picking my words with care. If I'd learned anything about Helen Maitland, it was that it would be impossible to tell where her loyalties lay. The last thing I wanted was to expose Alexis and Chris accidentally.

'Hardly the crime of the century,' she commented, turning to put her cup in the sink. 'Look, I'm sorry I can't help you,' she continued, facing me and running her hands through her curls, giving them fresh life. 'It's three years now since Sarah moved out of here. I don't know what she was doing or who she was seeing. I have no idea why she chose to fly under false colours in the first place, nor why she chose to impersonate me. And I really don't know what possible interest it could be to anyone. According to the newspapers, Sarah was murdered by a burglar whom she had the misfortune to interrupt trying to find something he could sell, no doubt to buy drugs. That had nothing to do with anything else in her life. I don't know what your client has hired you to do, but I suspect that he or she is wasting their money. Sarah's dead, and no amount of raking into her past is going to come up with the identity of the crackhead who killed her.'

'As a doctor, you'll appreciate the burdens of confidentiality. Even if I wanted to tell you what I've been hired to do, I couldn't. So I'll have to be the judge of whether I'm wasting my time or not,' I said, staking out the cool ground now

I'd finally raised Helen Maitland's temperature a degree or two.

'Be that as it may, you're certainly wasting mine,' she said sharply.

'When did you see Sarah last?' I asked, taking advantage of the fact that our conversation had become a subtlety-free zone.

She frowned. 'Hard to say. Two, three weeks ago? We bumped into each other in the lab.'

'You didn't see each other socially?'

'Not often,' she said, biting the words off abruptly.

'What? She shared your house for the best part of a year because the two of you got along just fine, then she moves out and the only time you see each other is when you bump into each other in hospital corridors? What happened? You have a row or what?'

Helen Maitland glowered at me. 'I never said we were friends,' she said, enunciating each word carefully. 'All I said was that we didn't get on each other's nerves. After she moved out, we didn't stay in close touch. But even if we had fallen out, it would still have nothing to do with the fact that Sarah Blackstone was murdered by some junkie burglar.'

I smiled sweetly as I got to my feet. 'You'll get no argument from me on that score,' I said. 'What it might explain, though, is why Sarah Blackstone was hiding behind your name to commit her crimes.'

I started for the door. 'What crimes?' I heard.

Half turning, I said, 'Obviously nothing to do with you, Dr Maitland, since you had nothing to do with her. Thanks for the tea.'

She didn't follow me down the hall. I opened the door and nearly walked into a key stabbing towards me at eye height. I jumped backwards and so did the woman wielding the key. She was the original of the photograph in the kitchen. With her cascade of dark hair, skin pale as marble and a long cape-shouldered coat, she looked as extreme as a character in an Angela Carter story. 'God, I'm sorry,' she gasped. 'You look like you've seen a ghost!'

No, just an extra from Francis Ford Coppola's *Dracula*, I thought but didn't say. 'You startled me,' I said, putting a hand on my pounding heart.

'Me too!' she exclaimed.

From behind me, I heard Helen Maitland's voice. 'Ms Brannigan was just leaving.'

The other woman and I skirted round each other, swapping places. 'Bye,' I said brightly as the door closed behind me. Trotting down the stone steps leading to the garden, I told myself off for being childish enough to give away my secrets to Helen Maitland just to score a cheap point because she'd made her way under my skin. It was hard to resist the conclusion that she had learned more from our interview than I had.

I didn't think she had lied to me. Not in so many words. Over the years, I've developed a bullshit detector that usually picks up on outright porkies. But I was fairly sure she wasn't telling me anything like the whole story. Whether any of it was relevant to my inquiries, I had no idea. But I had an idea where I might find some of the facts lurking behind her smoke screen of half-truths. When I got back to the car, I switched on my mobile and left a message for Shelley on the office answering machine. An urgent letter needed to go off to the Land Registry first thing in the morning. The reply would take a few days, but when it came, I had a sneaky feeling I'd have some bigger guns in my armoury to go after Helen Maitland with.

13

In these days of political correctness, it's probably an indictable offence to say it, but Sean Costigan didn't have to open his mouth to reveal he was Irish. I only had to look at him, even in the sweaty laser-split gloom of the nightclub. He had dark hair with the sort of kink in it that guarantees a bad hair life, no matter how much he spent on expensive stylists. His eyes were dark blue, his complexion fair and smooth, his raw bones giving him a youthful, unformed look that his watchful expression and the deep lines from his nostrils to the corners of his mouth denied.

I'd got home around nine after fish and chips in Leeds's legendary Bryan's, making the mistake I always do of thinking I'm hungry enough for a jumbo haddock. Feeling more tightly stuffed than a Burns Night haggis, I'd driven back with the prospect of an early night all that was keeping me going. I should have known better, really. Among the several messages on my machine – Alexis, Bill,

Gizmo and Richard, just for a kickoff – there was one I couldn't ignore. Dan Druff had called to say he'd set up a meet at midnight in Paradise. Why does nobody keep office hours any more?

I've never been able to catnap. I always wake up with a thick head and a mouth that feels like it's lined with sheep-skin. I don't mean the sanitized stuff they put in slippers – I mean the stuff you find in the wild, still attached to its smelly owner. I rang Alexis, but she didn't want to talk in front of Chris, whom she was keeping in the dark about Sarah Blackstone's murder on account of her delicate condition. Richard was out – his message had been to tell me he wouldn't be home until late. We'd probably meet on the doorstep as we both staggered home in the small hours. Bill I still wasn't talking to, and Gizmo doesn't do conversation. So I booted up the computer and settled down for a serious session with my football team. Not many people know this, but I'm the most successful manager in the history of the football league. In just five seasons, I've taken struggling Halifax Town from the bottom of the Conference League up through the divisions to the Premier League. In our first season there, we even won the Cup. This game, Premier Manager 3, is one of my darkest secrets. Even Richard doesn't know about my hidden nights of passion with my first-team squad. He wouldn't understand that it's just fantasy; he'd see it as an excuse to buy me a Manchester United season ticket for my

171

next birthday so I could sit next to him in the stands every other week and perish from cold and boredom. He'd never comprehend that while watching football sends me catatonic, developing the strategies it takes to run a successful team is my idea of a really good time. So I always make sure he's out when I sit down with my squad.

Around half past eleven, I told the boys to take an early bath and grabbed my leather jacket. When I stepped outside the door, I discovered the rain had stopped, so I decided to leave the car and walk to the Paradise. It's only fifteen minutes on foot, and the streets of central Manchester are still fairly safe to walk around late at night. Especially if you're a Thai boxer. Besides, I figured it wouldn't do me any harm to limber up for looking chilled out.

The Paradise Factory considers itself Manchester's coolest nightclub. The brick building is on the corner of Princess Street and Charles Street, near Chinatown and the casinos, slightly off the beaten track of clubland. It used to house Factory Records, the famous indie label that was home to Joy Division and lots of other bands less talented but definitely more joyful. When Factory failed, a casualty to the recession, an astute local business-woman took over the building and turned it into a poser's heaven. Officially, it's supposed to be an eclectic mix of gay and hetero, camp and straight, but it's the only club where I've been asked on the door to verify that I'm not a gender tourist by listing other Manchester gay and lesbian venues where I've drunk and danced.

As soon as I went through the door, I was hit by a bass rhythm that pounded stronger in my body than my heart ever had. It was hard to move without keeping the beat. I found Dan and Lice propped against a wall near the first bar I came to as I walked into the three-storey building. The guy I knew without asking was Sean Costigan stood slightly to one side, his wiry body dwarfed by his fellow Celts. His eyes were restless, constantly checking out the room. He let me buy the drinks. Both rounds. That wasn't the only way he made it plain he was there on sufferance. The sneer was another dead giveaway. It stayed firmly in place long after the formal introductions were over and he'd given me the kind of appraising look that's more about the labels and the price tags on the clothes than the body inside them.

'I don't know what the boys have been saying to you, but I want to make one thing absolutely plain,' he told me in a hard-edged Belfast whine. 'We are the victims here, not the villains.' He sounded like every self-justifying Northern Irish politician I'd ever heard. Only this one was leaning over me, bellowing in my ear, as opposed to on a TV screen I could silence with one blast of the remote control.

'So how do you see what's been happening?' I asked.

'I've been in this game a very long time,' he

173

shouted over the insistent techno beat. 'I was the one put Morrissey on the map, you know. And the Mondays. All the big boys, I've had them all through my hands. You're talking to a very experienced operator here,' he added, wetting his whistle with a swig of the large dark rum and Coke he'd asked for. Dan and Lice nodded sagely, backing up their man. Funny how quickly clients forget whose side you're on.

I waited, sipping my extremely average vodka and bottled grapefruit juice. Costigan lit a Marlboro Light and let me share the plume of smoke from his nostrils. Sometimes I wonder if being a lawyer would really have been such a bad choice. 'And I have not been trespassing,' he said, stabbing my right shoulder with the fingers that held the cigarette. 'I am the one trespassed against.'

'You're telling me that you haven't been sticking up posters on someone else's ground?' I asked sceptically.

'That's exactly what I'm telling you. Like I said, we're the victims here. It's my ground that's getting invaded. More times than I can count in the past few weeks, I've had my legitimate poster sites covered up by cowboys.'

'So you've been taking revenge on the guilty men?'

'I have not,' he yelled indignantly. 'I don't even know who's behind it. This city's always been well regulated, you know what I mean? Everybody knows what's what and nobody gets hurt if they

174

stick to their own patch. I've been doing this too long to fuck with the opposition. So if you're trying to lay the boys' trouble at my door, you can forget it, OK?'

'Is there any kind of pattern to the cowboy flyposting?' I asked.

'What do you mean, a pattern?'

'Is it always the same sites where they're taking liberties? Or is it random? Are you the only one who's being hit, or is it a general thing?'

He shrugged. 'It's all over, as far as I can tell. It's not the sort of thing you talk about, d'you understand? Nobody wants the opposition to think they're weak, you know? But the word on the street is that I'm not the only one suffering.'

'But none of the other bands are getting the kind of shit we're getting,' Dan interjected. God knows how he managed to follow the conversation. He must have trained as a lip-reader. 'I've been asking around. Plenty other people have had some of their posters covered up, but nobody's had the aggravation we've had.'

'Yeah, well, it's nothing to do with me, OK?' Costigan retorted aggressively.

There didn't seem to be anything else to say. I told Dan and Lice I'd be in touch, drained my drink and walked home staring at every poster I passed, wondering what the hell was going on.

I dragged my feet up the stairs to the office just after quarter past nine the next morning. I felt like I was fourteen again, Monday morning before double Latin. I'd lain staring at the ceiling, trying to think of good excuses for not going in, but none of the ones that presented themselves convinced either me or Richard, which gave them no chance against Shelley or Bill.

I needn't have worried. There was news waiting that took Bill off the front page for a while. I walked in to find Josh Gilbert perched on the edge of Shelley's desk, one elegantly trousered leg crossed casually over the other. I could have paid my mortgage for a couple of months easily with what the suit had cost. Throw in the shirt, tie and shoes and we'd be looking at the utility bills too. Josh is a financial consultant who has managed to surf every wave and trough of the volatile economy and somehow come out so far ahead of the field that I keep expecting the Serious Fraud Office to feel his collar. Josh and I have a deal: he gives me information, I buy him expensive dinners. In these days of computerization, it would be cheaper to pay Gizmo for the same stuff, but a lot less entertaining. Computers don't gossip. Yet.

Shelley was looking up at Josh with that mixture of wariness and amusement she reserves for born womanizers. When he saw me, he broke off the tale he was in the middle of and jumped to his feet. 'Kate!' he exclaimed, stepping forward and sweeping me into a chaste embrace.

I air-kissed each cheek and stepped clear. The older he got, the more his resemblance to Robert

Redford seemed to grow. It was disconcerting, as if Hollywood had invaded reality. Even his eyes seemed bluer. You didn't have to be a private eye to suspect tinted contacts. 'I don't mean to sound rude,' I said, 'but what are you doing here at this time of the morning? Shouldn't you be blinding some poor innocent with science about the latest fluctuations of the Nikkei? Or persuading some lucky Lottery winner that their money is safe in your hands?'

'Those days are behind me,' he said.

'Meaning?'

'I am thirty-nine years and fifty weeks old today.'

I wasn't sure whether to laugh or cry. Ever since I've known him Josh has boasted of his intention to retire to some tax haven when he was forty. Part of me had always taken this with a pinch of salt. I don't move in the sort of circles where people amass the kind of readies to make that a realistic possibility. I should have realized he meant it; Josh will bullshit till the end of time about women, but he's never less than one hundred per cent serious about money. 'Ah,' I said.

'Josh has come to invite us to his fortieth birthday and retirement party.' Shelley confirmed my bleak fear with a sympathetic look.

'Selling up and selling out, eh?' I said.

'Not as such,' Josh said languidly, returning to his perch on Shelley's desk. 'I'm not actually selling the consultancy. Julia's learned enough from me

177

to run the business, and I'm not abandoning her entirely. I might be going to live on Grand Cayman, but with fax machines and e-mail, she'll feel as though I've only moved a few miles away.'

'Only if you don't have conversations about the weather,' I said. 'You'll get bored, Josh. Nothing to do all day but play.'

The smile crinkled the skin round his eyes, and he gave me the look Redford reserves for Debra Winger in *Legal Eagles*. 'How could I be bored when there are still beautiful women on the planet I haven't met?'

I heard the door open behind me and Bill's voice said, 'Are we using "met" in the biblical sense here?'

Bill and Josh gave each other the usual once-over, a bit like dogs who have to sniff each other's bollocks before they decide a fight isn't worth the bother. They'd never been friends, probably because they'd thought they were competitors for women. Neither had ever realized how wrong they were; Bill could never have bedded a woman without brains, and Josh never bedded one with an IQ greater than her age except by accident. Shelley had her pet theories on their respective motivations, but life's too short to rerun that seminar.

'So it's all change then,' Bill said once Josh had brought him up to speed on his reasons for visiting. 'You off to Grand Cayman, me off to Australia.'

'I thought you'd only just come back,' Josh said.

'I'm planning to move out there permanently. I'm marrying an Australian businesswoman.'

'Is she pregnant?' Josh blurted out without thinking. Seeing my face, he gave an apologetic smile and shrug.

'No. And she's not a rich widow either,' Bill replied, not in the least put out. 'I'm exercising free will here, Josh.'

I swear Josh actually changed colour. The thought of a man as dedicated as he was to a turbo-charged love life finally settling down, and from choice, was like suddenly discovering his body was harbouring a secret cancer. 'So because of this woman, you're going to get married and live in *Australia*? My God, Bill, that's worse than moving to Birmingham. And what about the business? You can keep a finger on the financial pulse from anywhere you can plug in a PC, but you can't run an investigation agency from the other side of the globe.'

'The game plan is that I'll sell my share of the agency here and start up again in Australia.'

Josh's eyebrows rose. 'At your age? Bill, you're only a couple of years younger than me. You're really planning to start from ground zero in a foreign country where you don't even speak the language? God, that sounds too much like hard work to me. And what about Kate?'

I'd had enough. 'Kate's gotta go,' I said brusquely. 'People to be, places to see. Thanks for the invite, Josh. I wouldn't miss it for the world.' I wheeled round and headed back out of the door. I wasn't sure where I was going, and I didn't care. I knew I was behaving like a brat, but I didn't care about that either. I stood on the corner outside the office, not even caring about the vicious northeasterly wind that was exfoliating every bit of exposed skin. A giggling flurry of young women in leg warmers and tights accompanied by a couple of well-muscled men enveloped me, waiting for the lights to change as they headed for rehearsals at the new dance theatre up the street, one of the handful of tangible benefits we got from being UK City of Drama for a year. Their energy and sense of direction shamed me, so I followed briskly in their wake and collected my car from the meter where I'd left it less than twenty minutes before. Given that I'd planned to be in the office for a couple of hours, somebody was going to get lucky.

One quick phone call and fifteen minutes later, I was walking round the big Regent Road Sainsbury's with Detective Chief Inspector Della Prentice. When I'd called and asked her if she could spare half an hour, she'd suggested the supermarket. Her fridge was in the same dire straits as mine, and this way we could both stock up on groceries while we did the business. We took turns pushing the trolley, using our packs of toilet rolls as a convenient Maginot line between our separate purchases. I filled her in on the headstone scam in the fruit and veg. department, handing over a list of victims who should be able to pick out Williams and Constable in an identity parade. She promised to pass it on to one of her bright young things.

The outrageous tale of Cliff Jackson's waste of police time kept us going as far as the chill cabinets. By the time we hit the breakfast cereals, I'd moved on to the problems at Mortensen and Brannigan, which lasted right up to hosiery and tampons. Della tried an emerald green ruffle against her copper hair. I nodded agreement. 'I can see why Shelley suggested you putting your share of the business on the market too,' Della said. 'But that could present you with a different set of problems.'

'I know,' I sighed. 'But what else can I do?'

'You could talk to Josh,' she said. Sometimes I forget the pair of them were at Cambridge together, they're such different types. It's true that they were both fascinated by money but while Josh wanted to make as much of it as possible, Della wanted to stop people like him doing it illegally. She was too bright for him to fancy, so he gave her his respect instead, and a few years ago he did me the biggest favour he's ever managed when he introduced us.

'What good would that do? Josh deals with multinational conglomerates, not backstreet detective agencies. I can't believe he knows anyone with investigative skills and enough money to buy Bill out that he hasn't already introduced me to. Besides, investigative skills never seem to go hand in hand with the acquisition of hard cash. You should know that.'

181

Della reached for a tin of black olives then turned her direct green eyes on me. 'You'd be surprised at what Josh knows about,' she said, giving a deliberate stage wink.

'I'm not even going to ask if the Fraud task force is about to lose its major inside source,' I said. 'Besides, Josh is too busy extricating himself from business right now. He's not about to get involved in setting up a whole new partnership for me. Did you know he's retiring in a couple of weeks?'

Della nodded, looking depressed. 'He's been saying he was going to retire at forty since he was nineteen.'

'I wouldn't worry about it, Della. He'll never retire. Not properly. He'll die of boredom in a week if he's not spreading fear and loathing in global financial institutions. He'll always have fingers in enough pies to keep you busy.'

Whatever I'd said, it seemed to have deepened Della's gloom. Then I twigged. If Josh was about to hit the big four zero, it couldn't be far off for Della. And she wasn't a multimillionaire with the world her oyster. She was a hardworking, ferociously bright woman in what was still a man's world, a woman whose career commitment left her no space for relationships other than a few close friendships. I stopped the trolley by the spirits and liqueurs, put a hand on her arm and said, 'He might have made the money, but you've made the difference.'

'Yeah, and everything at the agency is going to

work out for the best,' she said grimly. We looked at each other, registering the self-pitying misery that was absorbing each of us. Then, suddenly and simultaneously, we burst out laughing. Nobody could get near the gin, but we didn't give a damn. Like the song says, girls just wanna have fun.

14

If you think it's embarrassing to get a hysterical fit of the giggles with one of your best friends in Sainsbury's wines and spirits department, try having your mobile phone ring in the middle of it. Now that's *really* excruciating. At least when it's someone as laconic as Gizmo, you don't have to destroy your street cred totally by having a conversation. A series of grunts signifying 'yes' and 'no' will do just fine. I gathered he'd got the stuff I wanted and he was about to stuff it through my letter box unless I had any serious objections. I didn't. Even if it was Police Harassment Week and Linda Shaw and her sidekick were back on my doorstep, they could hardly arrest Gizmo for impersonating a postman.

Being midweek and mid-morning, we were through the checkouts in less time than it takes to buy a newspaper in our local corner shop. Della and I hugged farewell in the car park and went our separate ways, each intent on making some criminal's life a misery. 'Talk to Josh,' were her final words.

Gizmo had done me proud. Not only had he translated the files into a format I could easily read on my computer, but he'd also printed out hard copies for me. As far as her patient notes were concerned, Sarah Blackstone's passion for secrecy had been superseded by a medical training that had instilled the principle of always leaving clear notes that another doctor could follow through should you be murdered by a burglar between treatments. I flicked through until I found the file relating to Alexis and Chris. Not only were their names correct on the print-out, but so also were their phone numbers at home and work, address and dates of birth. Which meant the chances were high that all the other patients' details were accurate. If ever I needed to interview any of them, I knew where to start looking.

At one level, the job Alexis had hired me to do was now complete. I had checked out the consulting rooms and removed any evidence that might lead back to Sarah Blackstone's patients. But what I had were only backup copies. The originals were still out there somewhere, presumably sitting on the hard drive of the laptop that the doctor had used throughout her consultations. If Gizmo had cracked their file protection, it was always possible that the police had someone who could do the same thing. It was also possible that whoever had killed Sarah Blackstone had stolen her computer and was sitting on the best black-mail source since Marilyn Monroe's address book. Women who could afford this treatment could afford payoffs too. The game was a long way from being over.

What I needed now was more information. I understood very little of the patient notes sitting in front of me and I understood even less of the fertility technology that I was dealing with here. I needed to know what technical backup Sarah Blackstone had needed, and just how difficult it was to achieve what she had done. I also needed to know if this was something she could do alone, or if she'd have had to involve someone else. Time to beg another favour from someone I already owed one to. Dr Beth Taylor is one of the legion of women who have been out with Bill Mortensen without managing to accomplish what an Australian boutique bimbo had pulled off. Beth works part time in an inner-city group practice where nobody's had to pay a prescription charge in living memory. The rest of the time she lectures on ethics to medical students who think that's a county in the south of England. If she feels like a bit of light relief, she does the odd bit of freelance work for us when we're investigating medical insurance claims.

I tracked Beth down at the surgery. I didn't tell her about Bill's planned move. It wasn't that I thought it would hurt her feelings; I just couldn't bear to run through it yet again. Once we'd got the social niceties out of the way, I said, 'Test-tube babies.'

She snorted. 'You've been reading too many tabloids. IVF, that's what you call it when you want a bit of respect from the medical profession. Subfertility treatment, when you want to impress us with your state-of-the-art consciousness. What are you after? Treatment or information?'

'Behave,' I said scathingly.

'I know someone at St Mary's. He used to be a research gynaecologist, now he works part time in the subfertility unit. I bring him in to do a seminar on my course on the ethics of interference with human fertility.'

'Would he talk to me?' I asked.

'Probably. He likes to show off what a new man he is. Nothing he loves more than the chance to demonstrate to a woman how sensitive he is to our reproductive urges. What is it you want to know, and why?'

'I need the five-minute crash course in IVF for beginners and a quick rundown on where the leading edge is right now. What can and can't be done. I'm not asking for anything that isn't readily available in the literature, I just need it in bite-sized pieces that a lay person can understand.'

'Gus is your man, then. You didn't mention why this sudden interest?'

'That's right, I didn't. Is he going to want a reason?'

Beth thought for a moment. 'I think it might

be as well if you were a journalist. Maybe looking for nonattributable background for a piece
you're doing following women's experiences of
being treated for subfertility?'

'Fine. How soon can you fix it?'

'How soon do you need it?'

'I'm free for lunch today,' I said. The devil finds
work for idle hands; if you can't manage any other
exercise, you can always push your luck.

'So I'll lie. I'll tell him you're young, gorgeous
and single. Gus Walters, that's his name. I'll get
him to call you.'

Ten minutes later, my phone rang. It was Gus
Walters. Young, gorgeous and single must have
worked. I hoped he wouldn't be too disappointed.
Two out of three might not be bad, but none
ain't good. 'Thanks for getting back to me so
quickly,' I said.

'No problem. Besides, I owe Beth a favour.'

'Are you free for lunch today? I know it's short
notice . . .'

'If you can meet me at half past twelve at the
front entrance, I can give you an hour and you
can buy me a curry,' he said.

'Deal. How will I know you?' I asked.

'Oh, I think I'll know you,' he said, voice all dark
brown smoothness. Definitely a doctor.

It's a constant source of amazement to me that the
staff at Manchester's major hospital complex don't
all have serious weight problems. They're only five

minutes' walk from the Rusholme curry parade, as serious a selection of Asian restaurants as you'll find anywhere in the world. If I worked that close to food that good, cheap and fast, I couldn't resist stuffing my face at least twice a day. Richard might be convinced that the Chinese are the only nation on earth with any claim to culinary excellence, but for me, it's a dead heat with the chefs of the subcontinent. Frankly, as soon as I had sat down at a window table with a menu in front of me, I was a lot more interested in the range of pakoras than in anything Gus Walters could possibly tell me.

He was one of the non-rugby-playing medics: medium height, slim build, shoulders obviously narrow inside the disguise of a heavy, well-cut tweed jacket. His hands were long and slender, so pale they looked as if they were already encased in latex. Facially, he had a disturbing resemblance to Brains, the *Thunderbirds* puppet. Given that he'd opted for the identical haircut and very similar large-framed glasses, I wondered if he had enough sense of irony to have adopted them deliberately. Then I remembered he was a doctor and dismissed the idea. He probably thought he looked like Elvis Costello.

On the short walk to the nearest curry house we'd done the social chitchat about how long we'd lived in Manchester and what we liked most and least about the city. Now I wanted to get the ordering done with so we could cut to the chase. I settled for chicken pakora followed by karahi gosht with a garlic nan. Gus opted for onion bhajis and chicken rogan josh. He grinned across the table at me and said, 'The orifice I get closest to doesn't bother about garlic breath.' It rolled out with the smoothness of a line that never gets the chance to go rusty.

I smiled politely. 'So tell me about IVF,' I said. 'For a start, what kind of technology do you need to make it work?'

'It's all very low tech, I'm afraid,' he replied, his mouth turning down at the corners. 'No million-pound scanners or radioactive isotopes. The main thing you need is what's called a Class II containment lab which you need to keep the bugs out. Clean ducted air, laminar flow, temperature stages that keep things at body temperature, an incubator, culture media. The only really specialized stuff is the glassware – micropipettes and micromanipulating equipment and of course a microscope. Also, when you're collecting the eggs, you need a transvaginal ultrasound scanner, which gives you a picture of the ovary.'

He was off and running. All I needed to do was provide the odd prompt. I was glad I wasn't his partner; I could just imagine how erotic his bedroom conversation would be. 'So what are the mechanics of carrying out an IVF procedure?' I asked.

'OK. Normally, women release one egg a month. But our patients are put on a course of drugs which gives us an optimum month when they'll produce five or six eggs. The eggs are in individual sacs we call follicles. You pass a very fine needle through the top of the vagina and puncture each follicle in turn and draw out the contents, which is about a teaspoonful of fluid. The egg is floating within that. You stick the fluid on the heated stage of the microscope, find the egg, and strip off some of the surrounding cells, which makes it easier to fertilize. Then you put it in an individual glass Petri dish with a squirt of sperm and culture medium made of salts and sugars and amino acids – the kind of soup that would normally be around in the body to nourish an embryo. Then you leave them overnight in a warm dark incubator and hope they'll do what opposite genders usually do in warm dark places at night.' He grinned. 'It's very straightforward.'

The food arrived and we both attacked. 'But it doesn't always work, does it?' I asked. 'Sometimes they don't do what comes naturally, do they?'

'That's right. Some sperm are lazy. They don't swim well and they give up the ghost before they've made it through to the nucleus of the egg. For quite a few years, when we were dealing with men with lazy sperm, there wasn't a lot we could do and we mostly ended up having to use donor sperm. But that wasn't very satisfactory because most men couldn't get over the feeling that the baby was a cuckoo in the nest.' He gave a smile that was meant to be self-deprecating but failed. Try as he might, you didn't have to

191

go far below the surface before Old Man re-asserted itself.

'So what do you do now?' I asked.

But he wasn't to be diverted. He'd started so he was going to finish. 'First they developed a technique where they made a slit in the "shell" of the harvested egg,' he said, waggling his fingers either side of his head to indicate he was using inverted commas because he was unable to use technical terms to a mere mortal. 'That made it easier. Twenty-five per cent success rate. But it wasn't enough for some real dead-leg sperm. So they came up with SUZI.' He paused expectantly. I raised my eyebrows in a question. It wasn't enough. Clearly I was supposed to ask who Suzie was.

Disappointed, he carried on regardless as the impassive waiter delivered our main courses. 'That involves passing a very fine microneedle through the "shell" and depositing two or three sperm inside, in what you could call the egg white if you were comparing it to a bird's egg. And still some sperm just won't make the trip to the nucleus of the egg. Twenty-two per cent success rate is the best we've managed so far. So now, clinics like ours out on the leading edge have started to use a procedure called ICSI.'

'ICSI?' I thought I'd better play this time. Even puppies need a bit of encouragement.

'Intracytoplasmic Sperm Injection,' he said portentously. 'One step beyond.'

I wished I hadn't bothered. 'Translation?'

'You take a single sperm and strip away its tail and all the surrounding gunge until you're left with the nucleus. Then the embryologist takes a needle about a tenth the thickness of a human hair and pushes that through the "shell", through the equivalent of the egg white right into the very nucleus of the egg itself, the "yolk". Then the nucleus of the sperm is injected into the heart of the egg.'

'Wow,' I said. It seemed to be what was expected. 'So is it you, the doctor, who does all this fiddling around?'

He smiled indulgently. 'No, no, the micro-manipulation is done by the embryologist. My job is to harvest the eggs and then to transfer the resulting embryo into the waiting mother. Of course, we keep a close eye on what the embryologist does, but they're essentially glorified lab technicians. I've no doubt I could do what they do in a pinch. God knows, I've watched them often enough. See one, do one, teach one.' It's hard to preen yourself while you're scoffing curry, but he managed.

'So, does the lab have to be on twenty-four-hour stand-by so you're ready to roll the minute a woman ovulates?' I'd been presuming that Sarah Blackstone did her fiddling with eggs and microscopes in the watches of the night when the place was deserted, but I needed to check that hypothesis.

'We don't just leave it to chance,' Gus protested. 'We control the very hour of ovulation with drugs. But big labs like ours do offer seven days a week, round-the-clock service so we can fit in with the lives of our patients. There's always a full team on call: embryologist, doctor and nurse.'

'But not constantly in the lab?'

'No, in the hospital. With their pagers.'

'So anybody could walk into the lab in the middle of the night and wreak havoc?' I asked.

He frowned. 'What kind of article are you researching here? Are you trying to terrify people?'

Furious with myself for forgetting I wasn't supposed to be a hard-nosed detective, I gave him a high-watt smile. 'I'm sorry, I get carried away. I read too much detective fiction. I'm sure people's embryos are as safe as houses.' And we all know how safe that is in 1990s Britain.

'You're right. The lab's always locked, even when we're working inside. No one gets in without the right combination.' His smile was the smug one of those who never consider the enemy within.

'I suppose you have to be careful because you've got to account to the Human Fertilisation and Embryology Authority,' I said.

'You're not kidding. Every treatment cycle we do has to be documented and reported to the HFEA. Screw up your paperwork and you can lose your licence. This whole area of IVF and embryo experimentation is such a hot potato with the God squad and the politically paranoid that we all have to be squeaky clean. Even the faintest suggestion that we were doing any research that was outside the scope of our licence could have us shut down temporarily while our lords and masters investigated. And it's not just losing the clinic licence that's the only danger. If you did mess around doing unauthorized stuff with the embryos that we don't transfer, you'd be looking at being struck off and never practising medicine again. Not to mention facing criminal charges.'

I tore off another lump of nan bread and scooped up a tender lump of lamb, desperately trying not to react to his words. 'That must put quite a bit of pressure on your team, if you're always having to look over your shoulder at what the others are doing,' I said.

Gus gave me a patronizing smile. 'Not really. The kind of people employed in units like ours aren't mad scientists, you know. They're responsible medical professionals who care about helping people fulfil their destiny. No Dr Frankensteins in our labs.'

I don't know how I kept my curry down. Probably the thought of being tended by the responsible medical professional opposite me. Either that or the fact that I wasn't paying much attention because I was still getting my head round what he'd said just before. If I was short of a motive for terminating Dr Sarah Blackstone, Gus Walters had just handed me one on a plate.

15

A few days before, I'd have reckoned that as
motives for murder go, the prospect of losing
your livelihood was a pretty thin one. That had
been before Bill's bombshell. Since then, I'd been
harbouring plenty of murderous thoughts, not
just against a business partner who'd been one
of my best friends for years, but also against a
blameless Australian woman I'd barely met. For
all I knew, Sheila could be Sydney's answer to
Mother Teresa. Somehow, I doubted it, but I'd been
more than ready to include her in the homicidal
fantasies that kept slipping into my mind. Like
unwanted junk mail, I always intended to throw
them straight in the bin, but every time I found
myself attracted by some little detail that sucked
me in. If a well-adjusted crime fighter like me felt
the desire to kill the people I saw as stealing my
dream, how easy it would be for someone who was
borderline psychotic to be pushed over the edge by
the prospect of losing their professional life. What

Gus Walters told me handed motive on a plate to everyone Sarah Blackstone had worked with at St Hilda's, from the professor who supervised the department to the secretary who maintained the files.

There was nothing I could do now about pursuing that line of inquiry. By the time I'd got home and driven to Leeds, it would be the end of the medical working day. I made a mental note to follow it up, which freed my brain to gnaw away at the problem which had been uppermost there since Bill's return. Never mind murderers, never mind rock saboteurs, what I wanted the answer to was what to do about Mortensen and Brannigan. The one thing I was sure about was that I didn't intend to roll over and die, waiting for Bill to find the buyer of his choice. As I walked back through the red-brick streets dotted with grass-filled vacant sites that lie between Rusholme and my home, I was plagued by the question of whether I could find a way to generate enough income to pay off a loan big enough to buy Bill out while managing to remain personally solvent.

The key to that was to find a way to make the agency work more profitably. There was one obvious avenue that might prove lucrative, but I'd need an extra pair of hands. Back when I'd started working for Bill, I'd done bread-and-butter process-serving. Every week, I'd abandon the law library and turn up at the office where Shelley would hand me a bundle of court papers that had to be served a.s.a.p. Domestic-violence injunctions, writs and a whole range of documents relating to debt. My job was to track down the individuals concerned and make sure they were legally served with the court documents. Sometimes that was as straightforward as cycling to the address on the papers, ringing the doorbell and handing over the relevant bumf. Mostly, it wasn't. Mostly, it involved a lot of nosing about, asking questions of former colleagues, neighbours, drinking cronies and lovers. Sometimes it got heavy, especially when I was trying to serve injunctions on men who had been persistently violent to wives who took out injunctions one week and were terrorized, bullied, sweet-talked or guilt-tripped into taking their battering men back the next. The sort of men who see women as sexually available punchbags don't usually take kindly to being served papers by a teenager who barely comes up to their elbow.

In spite of the aggravation, I'd really got into the work. I'd loved the challenge of tracking down people who didn't want to be found. I'd enjoyed outwitting men who thought that because they were bigger and stronger than me, they weren't going to accept service. I can't say I took any pleasure slapping some of the debtors with bankruptcy papers when all they were guilty of was believing the propaganda of the Thatcher years, but even that was instructive. It gave me a far sharper awareness of real life than any of my fellow law students. So I'd quit to work for Bill full time as soon as the opportunity arose.

But I hadn't joined the agency to be a process-server. In the medium to long term, Bill wanted a partner and he was prepared to train me to do everything he could do. I learned about surveillance, working undercover, doing things with computers that I didn't know were possible, security systems, white-collar crime, industrial sabotage and espionage, and subterfuge. I learned how to use a video camera and how to bug, how to uncover bugs and how to take photographs in extreme conditions. I'd also picked up a few things that weren't on the syllabus, like kick boxing and lock picking.

Of course, as my skills grew, the range of jobs Bill was prepared to let me loose on expanded too. The end result of that was that we'd been content to let most of the process-serving fall into the laps of other agencies in the city. Maybe the time had come to snatch back that work for ourselves.

What I needed was a strategy and a body to serve the papers.

Shelley sipped her glass of white wine suspiciously, as if she were checking it for drugs, and glanced around her with the concentration of a bailiff taking an inventory. She had only been in my house a couple of times before, since we tended to do our socializing on the neutral ground of bars and restaurants. That way, when Richard reached screaming point we could make our excuses and leave. It's not that he doesn't like Shelley's partner Ted, a former client who opted for a date with her instead of a discount for cash and ended up moving in. It's just that Ted has the conversational repertoire of a three-toed sloth and is about as quick on the uptake. Nice bloke, but . . .

'You can't stay out of the office forever,' she said. A woman who's never been afraid to state the obvious, is Shelley.

'Call it preventative medicine. I'm trying to get a plan in place before I have to confront Bill,' I said. 'At the moment, every time I'm within three yards of him, I feel an overwhelming desire to cave his head in, and I don't fancy spending the next twenty years in prison. Besides, I do have some cases that I'm working on.' I picked up the microcassette recorder on the table and flipped the cassette out of it. 'I dictated some reports this afternoon. That brings me up to date. I've included the new client details.'

Shelley leaned across and picked up the tape. 'So why am I here? I don't guess it's because you couldn't go without my company for a whole day.'

I explained my idea about generating more income by reclaiming process-serving work. Shelley listened, a frown pulling her eyebrows closer together. 'How are you going to get the business? All the solicitors who used to put the work our way have switched to somebody else, and presumably they're satisfied with the service they're getting.'

This was the bit I was slightly embarrassed about. I leaned back and looked at the ceiling. 'I thought I could do a Charlie's Angel and try some personal visits.'

I risked a look. Shelley had a face like thunder. Jasper Charles runs one of the city's biggest firms of criminal solicitors. The primary qualification for employment as a clerk or legal executive there is having terrific tits and long legs. The key role of these women, known in legal circles as Charlie's Angels, is to generate more business for the firm. Every day, one or more of the Angels will visit remand clients in prison, often for the slenderest of reasons. They'll get the business out of the way then sit and chat to the prisoner for another half-hour or so. All the other prisoners who are having visits from their briefs see these gorgeous women fawning all over their mates, and a significant proportion of them sack their current lawyers and shift their business to Jasper Charles. Every woman brief in Manchester hates them. 'You've done some cheesy things in your time, Kate, but this is about as low as it gets,' she eventually said.

'I know. But it'll work. That's the depressing thing.'

'So you go out and prostitute yourself and you snatch back all this business. How you going to find the time to do it?'

'I'm not.'

Shelley's head tipped to one side. Unconsciously, she drew herself in and away from me. 'Oh no,' she said, shaking her head vigorously. 'Oh no.'

'Why not? You'd be great. You're the biggest no-shit I know.'

'Absolutely not. There isn't enough money printed yet to make me want to do that. Know what you're good at and stick to it, that's my motto, and what I'm good at is running that office and keeping you in line.' She slammed her drink down on the table so hard that the wine lurched in the glass like the contents of a drunk's stomach.

So far, it was going just like I'd expected it to. 'OK,' I said with a small sigh. 'I just thought I'd give you first refusal. So you won't mind me hiring someone else to do it?'

'Can we afford it?' was her only concern.

'We can if we do it on piecework, same as Bill did with me.'

Shelley nodded slowly and picked up her glass again. 'Plenty of students out there hungry for a bit extra.'

'Tell me about it,' I said. 'Actually, I've got someone provisionally lined up.'

'You never did hang about,' Shelley said drily. 'How did you find somebody so fast? How d'you know they're going to be able to cut it?'

I couldn't keep the grin from my face. Any minute now, there was going to be the kind of explosion that Saddam could have used to win the Gulf War if there had been a way of harnessing it. 'I think he'll fit in just fine,' I told her. 'You know how wary I am of involving strangers in the business, but this guy is almost like one of the family.' I got up and opened the door into the hall. 'You can come through now,' I called in the direction of the spare room that doubles as my home office.

He had to stoop slightly to clear the lintel. Six feet and three inches of lithe muscle, the kind you get not from pumping iron but from actually exercising. Lycra cycling trousers that revealed a lunchbox like Linford's and quads to match, topped with a baggy plaid shirt. He moved lightly down the hall, his Air Nikes barely making a sound. I stepped back to let him precede me into the living room and put my fingers in my ears.

'Donovan? What you doing here?' Shelley's thunderous roar penetrated my defences, no messing. The volume she can produce from her slight frame is a direct contradiction of the laws of physics. Don half turned towards me, his face pleading for help.

'I've hired him to do our process-serving, as and when we need him. We pay him a flat fee of –'

'No way,' Shelley yelled. 'This boy has a career in front of him. He is going to be an engineer. Not a private eye. No child of mine. No way.'

'I quite agree, Shelley. He's not going to be a private eye –'

'You're damn right he's not,' she interrupted.

'He's not going to be a private eye, any more

than students who work in Burger King three nights a week are going to be stuffing Whoppers for the rest of their working lives. All he's doing is a bit of work on the side to relieve the financial pressures on his hard-working single mother. Because that's the kind of lad he is,' I said quietly.

'She's right, Mam,' Don rumbled. 'I don't wanna do what she does. I just wanna make some readies, right? I don't wanna ponce off you all the time, OK?' He looked as if he was going to burst into tears. So much for muscle man. Forget valets; no man is a hero to his mother.

'He's not a kid any more,' I said gently. For a long moment, mother and son stared at each other. Hardest thing in the world, letting kids go. This was worse than the first day at school, though. There was nothing familiar or safe about the world she was releasing him into.

Shelley pursed her lips. 'About time you started acting like a man and took some of the responsibility for putting food on the table,' she said, trying to disguise the pain of loss with sternness. 'And if it stops you wasting your time with that band of no-good losers that call themselves musicians, so much the better. But all you do is serve papers, you hear me, Donovan?'

Don nodded. 'I hear you, Mam. Like I said, I don't want to do what she does, right?'

'And you don't neglect your studies either, you hear?'

'I won't. I *want* to be an engineer, OK?'

'Why don't you two discuss the details on the way home?' I inserted tactfully. I had the feeling it was going to take a while for the pair of them to be reconciled at any level beyond the purely superficial, and I had a life to get on with.

When I said 'life', I'd been using the term loosely, I decided as I tagged on to the tail end of a bunch of girl Goths and scowled my way past the door security. If this was life, it only had a marginal edge on the alternative. Garibaldi's was currently the boss night spot in Manchester. According to the *Evening Chronicle*'s yoof correspondent, it had just edged past the Hacienda in the trendiness stakes with the acquisition of Shabba Pilot, the hottest DJ in the north. In keeping with its status, the door crew were all wearing headsets with radio mikes. They're supposed to make them look high tech and in control; I can never see them without remembering all those old black-and-white movies where little old dears ran old-fashioned telephone exchanges and eavesdropped on all the calls.

I'd dressed for the occasion. I couldn't manage the paper white, hollow-eyed *Interview with the Vampire* look adopted by the serious fashion victims, not without a minor concussion. So I'd opted for the hard-case pretentious-philosopher image. Timberland boots, blue jeans, unbleached cotton T-shirt that told the world that Manchester was the Ur-city, and a leather jacket with the collar turned up. Plus, of course, a pair of fake Ray-Bans, courtesy of Dennis's brother Nick. The look got me past the door no bother and didn't earn me a second glance as I walked into the main part of the club.

Garibaldi's belongs to a guy called Devlin. I've never met anybody who knows what his other name is. Just Devlin. He materialized in Manchester in the late seventies with a Cumbrian accent and more money than even the resident gangsters dared question. He started small, buying a couple of clubs that had less life in them than the average geriatric ward. He spent enough on the interior, the music and the celebs who could be bought for a case of champagne to turn the clubs into money machines. Since when Devlin has bought up every ailing joint that's come on the market. Now he owns half a dozen pubs, a couple of restaurants known more for their clientele than their cuisine, and four city-centre clubs.

Garibaldi's was the latest. The building used to be a warehouse. It sat right on the canal, directly opposite the railway arches that raise Deansgate Station high above street level. When Devlin bought it, the interior was pretty bare. Devlin hired a designer who took Beaubourg as his inspiration. An inside-out Beaubourg. Big, multi-coloured drainage pipes curved and wove throughout the building, iron stairs like fire escapes led to iron galleries and walkways suspended above the dancers and drinkers. The joys of post-modernism.

I climbed up steps that vibrated to the beat of unidentifiable, repetitive dance music. At the second level, I made my way along a gallery that seemed to sway under my feet like a suspension footbridge. It was still early, so there weren't too many people around swigging designer beers from the bottle and dabbing whizz on their tongues. At the far end of the gallery, a rectangular structure jutted out thirty feet above the dance floor. It looked like a Portakabin on cantilevers. According to Dennis, this was the 'office' of Denzel Williams, music promoter and, nominally, assistant manager of Garibaldi's.

I couldn't see much point in knocking, so I simply stuck my head round the door. I was looking at an anteroom that contained a pair of battered scarlet leather sofas and a scarred black ash dining table pushed against the wall with a couple of metal mesh chairs set at obviously accidental angles to it. The walls were papered with gig posters. In the far wall, there was another door. I let the door close behind me and instantly the noise level dropped enough for me to decide to knock on the inner door.

'Who is it?' I heard.

I pushed the door open. The noise of the music dropped further, and so did the temperature, thanks to an air-conditioning unit that grunted in the side wall. The man behind the cheap wood-grain desk stared at me with no great interest. 'Who are you?' he demanded, the strong Welsh vowels immediately obvious. Call me a racist, but when it comes to the Welsh, I immediately summon my irregular verb theory of life. In this instance, it goes, 'I have considered opinions; you are prejudiced; he/she is a raging bigot.' And in my considered opinion, the Welsh are a humourless, clannish bunch whose contribution to the sum total of human happiness is on the negative side of the ledger. The last time I said that to a Welshman, he replied, 'But what about Max Boyce?' QED.

I had the feeling just by looking at him that Denzel Williams wasn't going to redeem my opinion of his fellow countrymen. He was in his middle thirties, and none of the deep lines that scored his narrow face had been put there by laughter. His curly brown hair was fast losing the battle with his forehead and the moustache he'd carefully spread across as much of his face as possible couldn't hide a narrow-lipped mouth that clamped meanly shut between sentences. 'Do I know you?' he said when I failed to reply before sitting in one of the creaky wicker chairs that faced his desk.

'I'm a friend of Dennis O'Brien's,' I said. 'He suggested I talk to you.'

He snorted. 'Anybody could say that right now.'

'You mean because he's inside and it's not easy to check me out? You're right. So either I am a genuine friend of Dennis's or else I'm a fake who knows enough to mention the right name. You choose.'

He looked at me uncertainly, slate-grey eyes narrowing as he weighed up the odds. If I was telling the truth and he booted me out, then when Dennis came out, Williams might be eating through a straw for a few weeks. Hedging his bets, he finally said, 'So what is it you want? I may as well tell you now, if you're fronting a band, you're about ten years too old.'

I'd already had a very bad week. And if there's one thing that really winds me up, it's bad manners. I looked around the shabby room. The money he'd spent on that mandarin-collared linen suit would probably have bought the office furnishings three times over. The only thing that looked remotely valuable in any sense was the big tank of tropical fish facing Williams. I stood up and felt in my pocket for my Swiss Army knife. As I turned away from him and appeared to be making for the door, I flipped the big blade open, side-stepped and picked up the loose loop of flex that fed power to the tank. Without a heater and oxygenation, the fish wouldn't last too long. Tipped on to the floor, they'd have an even shorter life span.

I turned and gave him my nastiest grin. 'One wrong move and the fish get it,' I snarled, loving every terrible B-movie moment of it. I saw his hand twitch towards the underside of his desk and grinned even wider. 'Go on, punk,' I said, all bonsai Clint Eastwood. 'Hit the panic button. Make my day.'

16

I wouldn't have hurt the fish. I knew that, but Denzel Williams didn't. 'For fuck's sake!' he yelled, starting up from his seat.

'Sit down and chill out,' I growled. 'I only wanted to ask you a couple of questions, but you had to get smart, didn't you?'

He subsided into his chair and scowled at me. 'Who the fuck are you? Who sent you here?'

'Nobody sent me. Nobody *ever* sends me anywhere,' I said. I was beginning to enjoy playing the bastard. I couldn't remember the last time I'd had so much fun. No point in lying, though. He could find out who I was easily enough if he cared enough to make trouble later. 'The name's Brannigan. Kate Brannigan. I'm a private eye.'

He looked shaken but not stirred. 'And what do you think you're going to see here?' he sneered.

I shook my head wonderingly. 'I can't believe Dennis said you were worth talking to. I've met coppers with better manners.'

The reminder of who had recommended Williams to me worked wonders. He swallowed his surliness and said, 'OK, OK, ask your questions, but don't piss about. I've got some people coming shortly, see?'

I saw only too well. Threatening the fish might hold Williams at bay, but it would cut no ice with his sidekicks. He'd also be very unhappy at anybody else witnessing his humiliation. Held to ransom by a midget with a Swiss Army knife. Regretfully I waved my posturing farewell and cut to the chase. 'Flyposting,' I said. 'My client's been having some problems. Obviously nobody likes admitting they're being had over, but somebody is definitely taking liberties. All I'm trying to do is to check out whether this is a personal vendetta or if everybody in the business is feeling the same pain.'

'Who's your client, then?'

'Dream on, Denzel. Just a simple yes or no. Has anybody been papering over your fly posters? Has anybody been fucking with your venues? Has anybody been screwing up gigs for your bands?'

'What if they have?' he demanded.

'If they have, Denzel, you just got lucky, because you will reap the benefit of the work I'm doing without having to part with a single shilling. All I'm concerned about is finding out who is pouring sugar in the petrol tank of my client's business, and getting them to stop. Now, level with me before I decide to have sushi for dinner. Have you been getting agg?'

'There's been one or two incidents,' he grudgingly admitted.

'Like?'

He shrugged. 'Yeah, some of my posters have been papered over.' He took a deep breath. He'd obviously decided that since he'd started talking, he might as well spill the lot. Funny how the ones that seem the hardest often turn out the gobbiest. 'The fresh paperwork has always been promoting out-of-town bands, so I'm pretty sure it's a stranger who doesn't know the way things work here. We've had one or two problems with tickets too. Some of the agents that sell tickets for our gigs have had phone calls saying the gig's a sellout, not to sell any more tickets. We've even had some scumbag pretending to be me ringing up and saying the gig was cancelled. It's got to be somebody from out of town. Nobody else would dare to mess with me.' His tone of voice left me in no doubt that when he got his hands on the new kid in town, the guy would be sorry he'd been born.

'Where specifically?'

He rattled of a list of names and venues. I hoped I'd be able to remember them later, because I didn't have a spare hand for note taking. 'Any ideas who's behind it?' I asked.

He gave me the look I suspected he normally reserved for traffic wardens who thought that giving him a ticket would discourage him from parking on double yellow lines. 'If I had any ideas, do you think he'd still be out there walking around?'

Ignoring the sarcasm, I persisted. 'Anybody else been hit that you know of?'

'Nobody's boasting about it. But I know Sean Costigan's taken worse shit than I have. The Crumpsall firm's been hit, so has Parrot Finnegan. And Joey di Salvo.'

'Collar di Salvo's lad?' I asked, surprised. I hadn't known the family of the local godfather were involved in flyposting. Whoever was muscling in on the patch was treading on the kind of toes that hand out a proper kicking.

'That's right.'

'That's serious.'

'We're talking war,' Williams said. He wasn't exaggerating. People who deprive the di Salvos of what they regard as their legitimate sources of income have an unfortunate habit of winding up silenced with extreme prejudice.

'So are you all supposed to take your bats and balls and go home? Does the new team expect everybody to back down so they can pick up the business?'

Williams shrugged. 'Who knows? But some of the boys that put the nod-and-a-wink record-company business our way are starting to get a bit cheesed off, see? They pay us to do a job and they're not too happy when their fancy posters get covered up the night after they've appeared. And one or two of the bigger managers are starting to mutter too. You're not the only one wanting to put a stop to this.'

Before I could ask more, I heard the telltale sequence of sounds that revealed the outer door to the anteroom opening and closing. I dropped the electric cable and opened the office door. As I walked swiftly past a trio of sharp-suited youths who looked like flyweight boxers, I heard Williams shouting, 'Fucking stop her.'

By the time they got their brains to connect with their legs, I was out the door and sprinting down the gallery, head down, tanking past the bodies leaning over the railings and surveying the dancers down below. I could feel the rhythmic thud of the pursuing feet cutting across the beat as I swung onto the stairs and hurtled down as fast as I could go.

I had the advantage. I was small enough to weave through the bodies on the stairs and landings. My pursuers had to shove curious people out of the way. By ground level, I was hidden from my followers by the turn of the stair. I slid into the press of bodies on the dance floor, pulling off my shades and my jacket. I squirmed through the dancers till I was at the heart of the movement, imitating their blank-eyed stares and twitching movements. I couldn't even glimpse the three toughs who had come after me. That meant they probably couldn't see me either. That was just the way I wanted to keep it.

*   *   *

There was one salt-and-pepper chicken wing left. My heart said yes, my head said no. It would be a lot easier to enlist Richard's help if he wasn't harbouring a grudge. 'There you go,' I said, shoving the foil container towards him. There was none of that false politesse about Richard. No, 'Oh no, I couldn't possibly.' I filled my bowl with spicy vermicelli and added a crab cake wrapped in sesame seeds and a couple of Szechuan king prawns. 'I was at Garibaldi's earlier on,' I said casually.

Richard's teeth stopped their efficient stripping job. 'For fun?' he asked incredulously.

'What do you think?'

'Not,' he said with a grin.

'You'd be right. You know Denzel Williams?'

He went back to his chicken wing, sucking it noisily as he nodded. 'I know the Weasel,' he said eventually. 'So called because of his ability to worm his way out of any deal going. Doesn't matter how tight you think you've got him tied up. Doesn't even matter if you've got your lawyer to draw up the paperwork. If Weasel Williams wants out, he'll get out.'

'Does he do the business for his bands?'

Richard shrugged noncommittally, filling his bowl again. 'I've not heard many complaints. He seems to have a deal going with Devlin – he does the flyposting for all of the man's venues, and he has a ticket agency going on the side as well. He bought a jobbing printer's last year, so now he prints all his own posters and a lot of the band merchandising as well. T-shirts, posters, programmes, flyers. And, of course, he manages bands as well. He's one of the serious players.'

'He's been having a taste of the same agg as Dan and the boys.'

Richard looked surprised. 'Weasel has? You must be looking at some operator, then. With Devlin's muscle to call on, I can't see the Weasel taking it from some street punk.'

'That's what I figured. I need to find out who is behind it, and I don't think Denzel Williams knows. But somebody must.' There was a short silence while we ate and digested what we'd been saying. 'I need your help, Richard,' I said.

He stopped eating. He actually stopped eating to look at me and consider what I'd just said. When Richard and I first got together, we'd both been wary, like experimental mice who have learned that certain activities result in pain and damage. Somehow, we'd managed to build a relationship that felt equal. We gave each other space, neither preventing the other from doing the things we felt were important. It had taken real strength from both of us not to interfere with the other's life when we felt we knew better, but mostly we'd managed it. Then a year before, I'd had to call in every favour anybody ever owed me to get him out of jail. He'd been stripped of power, reliant on me, my skills and my contacts. Since then, our relationship had been off balance. His last attempt to square things between us had nearly cost us the relationship and driven me into someone else's arms. Maybe I finally had a real opportunity to let him take the first step towards evening the scores. 'What is it you think I can do for you?' he asked, his voice giving nothing away.

'You know everybody in the rock business in this town. Half of them must owe you. I need you to call in a couple of favours and get me some kind of a lead into who's pulling the strings here.'

He shrugged and started eating again. 'If the Weasel doesn't know, I don't know who will. He's got the best grapevine in town.'

'I can't believe it's better than yours,' I said, meaning it. 'Besides, there must be people who wouldn't lose any sleep at the thought of Devlin and the Weasel getting a hard time. They might be keeping their mouths shut out of pure *Schadenfreude*.'

'Or fear,' Richard pointed out.

'Or fear. But they're not necessarily going to be afraid of talking to you off the record, are they? If they trust you as much as you seem to think, they'll have slipped you unattributable stuff before without any comebacks. So they know in advance that you're not going to drop them in the shit with the Weasel or with Devlin himself.'

Richard ran a hand along his jaw and I heard the faint rasp of the day's stubble. Normally, it's a sound I find irresistibly erotic, but for once it had no effect. There was too much going on under the surface of this conversation.

'Sure, I've covered their backs before. But I've

never asked questions like this before. It's a bit different from getting the latest goss on who's signing deals with whom. Nosing into stuff like this is your business, not mine. If I put the word around that I'm looking for info on the cowboy fly posters, I'm the one the finger will point at when you clear up the shit. I need to keep people's confidence or I don't get the exclusive stories and if I don't get the stories, I don't eat.'

'You think I don't understand about keeping contacts cultivated? Look, based on what I've dug up so far, I've drawn up a list of places and people who have been hit. You must know somebody on the list who trusts you enough to tell you what they know about who's behind this business.' I took the paper out of my pocket, unfolded it and proffered it across the table. It was so tense between us that if a car had backfired outside, we'd both have hit the deck.

Without taking it from me, Richard read the list. He tapped one name with a chopstick. 'Manassas. I've known the manager there for years. We were muckers in London together before we both came up here. Yeah, I could talk to him. He knows I won't drop him in it.' He took a deep breath and let it out in a slow sigh. 'OK, Brannigan, I'll talk to him tomorrow.'

'I'll come along.'

He scowled. 'Don't you trust me? He's not going to open up if I've got company, you know.'

'Of course I trust you. But I need to hear what he's got to say for myself. Like you said, these are my kind of questions, not yours. Treat me like a bimbo all you want, but you have to take me with you.'

Richard looked at me for a long minute, then he nodded gravely. 'OK. I'll be happy to help.' He grinned and the tension dissipated so suddenly it was hard to believe how wound up we'd both been moments earlier.

'I appreciate it.' I put down my bowl and chopsticks and leaned forward to kiss him deeply, running my hands up the insides of his thighs. For an unheard of second time in the same Chinese meal, Richard lost interest in food. This time, for rather longer.

Later, we lay, too comfortable to move from the sofa. I reached over and pulled the throw over our sweaty bodies so we wouldn't get chilled too soon. My head in the crook between Richard's strong shoulder and his jaw, I told him about my decision to hire Don and claw back enough process-serving business to keep him busy. I didn't mention the Charlie's Angels ploy; the moment was too sweet for that, and besides, one lecture a day is more than enough for me.

'Will that be enough?' Richard asked dubiously.

'No,' I said. Sometimes I wish I didn't have such a strong streak of realism. There are times when it would be a blessing to be afflicted with blind optimism.

'So what are you going to do?' he asked, gently stroking my back to show there was nothing aggressive in the question.

'I'm not entirely sure yet,' I admitted. 'Hiring Don is just a starting point. What I'm really worried about is if Bill goes we're going to lose a lot of the computer-security business. He's spent a lot of time and energy playing games with the big boys to establish his credentials in the field of computer security. Now, when it comes to making your system secure in the first place, or tracking down the creeps who are trying to steal your secrets or your money via your computer, Mortensen and Brannigan is right up there alongside some of the really big companies,' I said proudly.

'And that's all tied in to Bill's name, right?' Richard chipped in, shoving me back on track.

'Give the boy a coconut,' I said. 'Most of the people Bill deals with don't even know who Brannigan is. They're fully paid up members of the laddish tendency. Not the sort of men who are going to be convinced that a woman knows her RAM from her ROM.'

'Least of all a cute redhead with the best legs in Manchester,' Richard said, reaching round me to check the accuracy of his comment with the hand that wasn't holding me.

'So the problem is twofold,' I continued, trying to ignore the sensations his touch was triggering off. 'First, I don't have the credibility. Secondly, if I'm being brutally honest –'

'Be brutal, be brutal,' Richard interrupted with a mock moan.

'– I don't have the expertise either,' I said firmly, wriggling away from his wandering fingers.

'You could learn,' he murmured, refusing to be evaded. 'You're a very quick learner.'

'Only when I'm motivated,' I said sternly, squirming down and away. 'I can't get excited enough to put in the hours it takes to develop the skills. And I haven't got the patience to devote days to finding a leak and plugging it.'

'So don't. Do what you've done with Don. GSI.'

'GSI?'

'Get somebody in.'

'Like who?' I asked sarcastically. 'People with those kind of skills don't grow on trees. If they're straight, they're already earning far more than I could afford to pay them. And if they're dark-side hackers, they don't want to do anything as straight as work for me.'

'Set a thief to catch a thief, isn't that what they say? Didn't you mention that Telecom had just given Gizmo the "Dear John" note?'

I could have kissed him. But frankly, he didn't need the encouragement.

17

Private eyes should have the same motto as boy scouts: 'Be Prepared'. If I had to pass on one secret to any aspiring PI, that's what it would be. With that in mind, I settled down in my half of the conservatory with breakfast and the printed version of Sarah Blackstone's case notes. I needed to look more closely at the idea of her former colleagues having a motive for murder. If I was going to grip them by the lapels of their lab coats, thrust them against the wall and apply the red-hot pincers to treasured parts of their anatomy, I wanted to be sure I was asking the right questions.

Armed with the background information I'd picked up from the boy wonder of St Mary's, this time I was able to make a lot more sense of what I was reading. And it was the kind of sense that made the hairs on the back of my neck stand up. I flicked back through the pages to check that I wasn't misunderstanding what I saw in front of me. But there was no mistake. If I'd been short of motives for Sarah Blackstone's murder before, I was awash with them now.

Women tend to assume that it's only male doctors who are sufficiently arrogant, overbearing and insensitive to ride roughshod over their patients' lives. Wrong. Overexposure to these charming traits during training obviously rubs off on a lot of the women who go the distance too. However pleasant, supportive and discreet Dr Blackstone might have appeared to the women who consulted her, it seemed they hadn't so much been patients as the subjects of her experiments. That was the message that came through loud and clear from her notes.

It wasn't enough for her that she'd been breaking new ground by performing miracles that women had never had the chance to experience before; she wanted a different kind of immortality. What her notes told me was that she'd been playing a kind of Russian roulette to achieve it. She had been harvesting her own eggs for as long as she'd been treating other women. The notes were there. She'd persuaded one of her colleagues to do the egg collection, on the basis that Sarah was going to donate the eggs to women who couldn't produce fertile ones of their own. I knew now from my own research that because of the courses of fertility drugs involved in producing half a dozen eggs at once, she'd only have been able to harvest her own eggs two or three times a year. But that had been enough. Although she couldn't use her own eggs exclusively in the mix, she had been including one of her own eggs with each couple's batch. She'd have been growing on four or five embryos for each couple, and returning three of them to the womb. For every woman she'd successfully impregnated, there was a one-in-four or-five chance that the baby was not the child of the mother and her partner. Instead, it would be the result of a genetic mixture from the mother and Sarah Blackstone. And Chris was pregnant.

It was a nightmare, and one that I absolutely couldn't share with my client. And if I couldn't tell my best friend, there was nobody else I could dump on either. Certainly not Richard. After the recent rockiness of our road, the last thing he needed to hear about was a testosterone-free tomorrow. But it wasn't just the implications for Chris's pregnancy that bothered me. It was the long-term dangers within the gene pool. Judging by what I knew from Alexis, a lot of lesbian mothers in Manchester formed a close-knit social group, for obvious reasons. Their kids played together, visited each other's houses, grew up together. Chances were by the time they were adults, two women making babies together would be accepted medical practice, not some hole-in-the-corner criminal activity. What would happen if a couple of those girls fell in love, decided they wanted to make babies and they were half-sisters because they'd both come from Sarah Blackstone's eggs? Either they'd find out in preliminary genetic tests. Or even worse, they'd start a cycle of inbreeding whose consequences could poison the future for children not yet imagined, never mind conceived. It was a terrifying thought. But it didn't surprise me that it was a possibility on the horizon. When society sets things up so that the only way people can achieve their dreams is to go outside the law, it automatically loses any opportunity to control the chain reaction.

It was also an experiment that wasn't hard to unravel. Any of the couples who were looking at a child who didn't look a bit like either of them but had a striking resemblance to their doctor wasn't likely to be handing out the benefit of the doubt. It's not hard to have private DNA testing done these days, and at around five hundred pounds, not particularly expensive either, compared to the cost of IVF treatment and the expense of actually having a child. A few weeks and the couple would have their answer. And if the mother's partner wasn't the biological coparent, you wouldn't have to be a contender on *Mastermind* to work out that the chances were that the other egg had come from the person most concerned with the procedure.

The more I found out, the more the idea of a random burglar sounded as likely as Barry Manilow duetting with Snoop Doggy Dog. Forget her colleagues in Leeds. They'd still be there tomorrow. Right now, I needed to check whether there was a murderer on my own doorstep.

*　　*　　*

Lesley Hilton was Sarah Blackstone's first experimental mother. According to the files, she lived with her partner on the edge of the Saddleworth moors, where the red-brick terraced slopes of Oldham yield to the Yorkshire stone villas built by those of the Victorians who managed to get rich on the backs of the ones toiling in the humid spinning mills. It was far from the nearest address to me, but Lesley's daughter Coriander must be around eighteen months old by now, and if she was Blackstone's baby, it might be obvious. It was as good a place to start as any, and better than most.

The house was one of a group of three cottages set at the foot of a steep field where sheep did the job I'd have cheerfully paid a gardener to do. Anything's preferable to having a herd of wild animals at the back door. The original tawny colour of the stone was smudged with more than a century's worth of grime. So much for the clean country air. I yanked an old-fashioned bell pull and heard a disproportionately small tinkle.

The woman who opened the door looked like a social worker in her fisherman's smock, loose cotton trousers and the kind of sensible leather sandals that make Clarks Startrite look positively dashing. She was short and squarely built, with dark blonde hair cut spiky on top. She peered at me through granny glasses, her chubby face smiling tentatively. 'Yes?' she said.

I'd been working on a decent cover story all the

way out along the Oldham Road. What I had was pitifully thin, but it was going to have to do. 'I wonder if you could spare me a few minutes?' I started. 'This isn't easy to talk about on the doorstep, but it concerns a Dr Sarah Blackstone.'

Either Lesley Hilton had never heard the name before, or she had more acting skills than a family outing of Redgraves. She looked blank and frowned. 'Are you sure you've got the right house?'

'You are Lesley Hilton?'

She nodded, her head cocked in what I recognized as the classic pose of a mother listening for a toddler who is probably dismantling the TV set as we speak.

'I think you probably knew Dr Blackstone as Dr Helen Maitland,' I said.

This time the name got a reaction. Her cheekbones bloomed scarlet and she stepped back involuntarily, the door starting to close. 'I think you'd better go,' she said.

'I'm no threat to you and Coriander. I'm not from the authorities, I swear,' I pleaded, fishing out a card that simply said 'Kate Brannigan, Confidential Consultant', with the office address and phone number. I gave her the card. 'Look, it's important that we talk. Dr Blackstone or Dr Maitland, whatever you prefer to call her, is dead and I'm trying to –'

The door closed, shutting off the expression of panic that had gripped Lesley Hilton's features. Cursing myself for my clumsiness, I walked back to my car. At least I hadn't blown it with someone who knew that Dr Helen Maitland was really Sarah Blackstone. I'd have put money on that. And if she wasn't aware of that, chances were she hadn't killed her.

I fared better with Jude Webster, another of the early births. According to the files, she'd been a self-employed PR copywriter when she became pregnant. Judging by the word processor whose screen glowed on the table next to the pack of disposable nappies, she was still trying to earn some money that way. She had glossy chestnut hair which, considering the depth of the lines round her eyes, owed more to the bottle than to nature. Even though little Leonie was at the child minder, the buttons on Jude's cardigan had been done up in a hurry and didn't match the appropriate buttonholes, but I didn't feel it would help our rapport if I pointed that out.

The news of Sarah Blackstone's real identity and her death had got me across the threshold. I hadn't even needed a business card. Maybe she assumed I was another of the lesbian mothers come to bring the bad news. 'I'm sorry,' she now said, settling me down with the best cup of tea I'd had in weeks. 'I didn't catch your connection to Dr Maitland . . . Dr Blackstone, I mean.'

Time for the likeliest story since Mary told Joseph it was God's. 'As you know,' I started, 'Sarah was a real pioneer in her field. I'm representing women who are concerned that her death doesn't mean the end of her work. What we're trying to do is to put together a sort of case book that those who follow in her footsteps will be able to refer to. But we want it to be more than just her case notes. It's an important piece of lesbian history. The experience of the women who led the way mustn't be lost.'

Jude was nodding sympathetically. She was going for it, all the way. Pity she had acted totally blankly when I'd first mentioned the name Sarah Blackstone. 'You're so right,' she said earnestly. 'So much of women's achievements and contributions just get buried because the books are written by men. It's vital that we reclaim our history. But –'

'I know, you're concerned about confidentiality,' I cut in. 'And let me tell you, I can fully appreciate why. Obviously, the last thing my clients want is for people's privacy to be compromised, especially in circumstances like these. It wouldn't serve anyone's interests for that to happen. But I can assure you that there will be nothing in the finished material to identify any of the mothers or the children.'

We danced around the issue of confidentiality for a bit, then she capitulated. My Granny Brannigan always remarked that I had an honest face. She said it made up for my devious soul. Within an hour, Jude had told me everything there was to tell about the consultations that she and her partner Sue had had with Dr Blackstone. And it was all a complete waste of time. The first two minutes with the photograph album revealed a child that was the image of Sue, right down to an irrepressible cowlick above the right eye that wouldn't lie down and die. This time, Sarah Blackstone had missed.

By late afternoon, I knew the laws of probability had been on the doctor's side. But then, aren't they always? Ask anybody who's ever tried to sue a surgeon. At least two of the kids I'd seen bore more than a passing resemblance to the dead doctor. I was astonished the parents didn't seem to notice. I suppose people have always looked at their children and seen what they wanted to see. Otherwise there would be even more divorces than there are already.

At ten to five, I decided to hit one more and then call it a day. Jan Parrish and Mary Delaney lived less than a mile away from me in a red-brick semi on what had once been one of the city's smarter council housing estates. When the Tories had introduced a right-to-buy scheme so loaded with inducements that anyone in employment would have had to be crazy to say no, this estate had fallen like a line of dominoes. Now finding a resident who still paid rent to the council was harder than finding food in Richard's fridge.

Porches, car ports and new front doors had sprouted rampantly with no regard to any of their neighbours, each excrescence an indicator of private ownership, like a dog pissing on its own gatepost. Jan and Mary were among the more restrained; their porch was a simple red-brick and glass affair that actually looked as if it were part of the house rather than bolted on as a sad afterthought. I rang the bell and waited.

The woman who answered the door had an unruly mop of flaming red hair. It matched perfectly the small girl wrestling for freedom on her hip. I went through the familiar routine. When I got to the part where I revealed the doctor's real identity, Jan Parrish looked appalled. 'Oh my God,' she breathed. 'Oh my God.'

It was the first time I'd struck anything other than cracked plastic with that line. And that was even before I'd told her Sarah Blackstone was dead. 'It doesn't get any better,' I said, not sure quite how to capitalize on her state. 'I'm afraid she's dead. Murdered, in fact.'

I thought she was going to drop the baby. The child took the opportunity to abseil down her mother's body and stumble uncertainly towards me. I moved in front of her, legs together and bent at the knees like a hockey goalkeeper and blocked her escape route. Jan picked her up without seeming to be aware of it and stepped back. 'You'd better come in,' she said.

The living room was chaos. If I'd ever considered motherhood for more than the duration of a movie, that living room would have put me off for life. It made Richard's mess look structured. And this woman was a qualified librarian, according to her medical record. Worrying. I shoved a pile of unironed washing to one end of a sofa and perched gingerly, carefully avoiding a damp patch that I didn't want to think too closely about. Jan deposited the child on the carpet and sat down heavily on a dining chair with a towel thrown over it. I was confused; I couldn't work out what Jan Parrish's excessive reaction to my exposure of her doctor's real identity meant. It didn't fit my expectation of how a killer would react. I couldn't see Jan Parrish as a killer, either. She didn't seem nearly organized enough. But she had been horrified and panicked by what I'd said and I needed to find out why. Playing for time, I gave her the rigmarole about lesbian history. She was too distracted to pay much attention. 'I'm sorry it's been such a shock,' I said finally, trying to get the conversation back on track.

'What? Oh yes, her being murdered. Yes, that's a shock, but it's the other thing that's thrown me. Her not being who she said she was. Oh my God, what have I done?'

That's exactly what I was wondering too. It wasn't that I was too polite to say so, only too cautious. 'Whatever it was, I'm sure it had nothing to do with her death,' I said soothingly.

Jan looked at me as if I was from the planet Out To Lunch. 'Of course it didn't,' she said, frowning in puzzlement. 'I'm talking about blowing her cover with the letter.'

I knew the meaning of every word, but the sentence failed to send messages from my ears to my brain. 'I'm sorry . . . ?'

Jan Parrish shook her head as if it had just dawned on her that she had done something so stupid that even a drunken child of two and a half would have held fire. 'We were all paranoid about security, for obvious reasons. Dr Maitland always impressed on us the importance of that. She told us never to write to her at the clinic, because she was afraid someone might open the letter by mistake. She said if we needed to contact her again, we should make an appointment through the clinic. But we were so thrilled about Siobhan. When she had her first birthday, we both decided we wanted Dr Maitland to know how successful she'd been. I'm a librarian, I'm back at work part time, so I looked her up in Black's. The *Medical Directory*, you know? And it said she was a consultant at St Hilda's in Leeds, so we sent her a letter with a photograph of Siobhan with the two of us and a lock of her hair, just as a sort of keepsake. But now you're telling me she wasn't Dr Maitland at all? That means I've exposed us all to a terrible risk!' Her voice rose in a wail and I thought she was going to burst into tears.

'When was this?' I asked.

'About three months ago,' she said, momentarily distracted by Siobhan's sudden desire to commune with the mains electricity supply via a plug socket. She leapt to her feet and scooped up her daughter, returning her to the carpet but facing in the opposite direction. Showing all the stubbornness of toddlers everywhere, Siobhan immediately did a five-point turn and crawled back towards the skirting board. This time, I took a better look at her face. The hair might be Jan Parrish's but the shape of her face was unmistakable. I wondered whether Helen Maitland had also noticed.

'Well, if you haven't heard anything by now, I'd think you're all safe,' I reassured her. 'What did the letter actually say?'

She frowned. 'I can't remember the exact wording, but something like, "We'll never be able to thank you enough for Siobhan. You made a dream come true for us, that we could really share our own child." Something along those lines.'

'I wouldn't worry about it,' I said. 'That could mean anything. It certainly wouldn't make anyone jump to the conclusion that something so revolutionary was going on. And it doesn't give any clue as to who was actually treating you, does it? Unless the real Helen Maitland knew Sarah Blackstone was using her name, she's got no way of guessing. And if she did know, then presumably she was in on the secret too. I really don't think you should worry about it, honestly,' I lied. I wanted to grab her by the shoulders and shake her for her stupidity. With a secret that held so much threat for her and her daughter, she should never have taken such an outrageous risk. Given that her mother faced a lifetime of discretion, I didn't rate little Siobhan's chances of making it to adulthood without being taken into care and treated like an experimental animal in a lab. Instead, I made my excuses and left.

I hadn't found a serious suspect yet among the women who had been Sarah Blackstone's patients. I hoped I'd still be able to say that when I'd finished interviewing them. I cared far too much for Alexis and Chris to want to take responsibility for the hurricane of official and media attention that would sweep through their lives if I had to open that particular corner of Sarah Blackstone's life to public scrutiny.

Sometimes I think Alexis is psychic. I'd driven home thinking about her, and there she was on my doorstep. But it only took one glimpse of her face to realize she hadn't popped round to say how gratified she was at my concern for her. If looks could kill, I'd have been hanging in some psychopath's dungeon praying for the merciful end that death would bring.

18

Ask people what they think of when they hear the name 'Liverpool' and they'll tell you first about the Scouse sense of humour, then about the city's violent image. Tonight, Alexis definitely wasn't seeing the funny side. I'd barely got out of my car before she was in my face, the three inches she has on me suddenly seeming a lot more. Her tempestuous bush of black hair rose round her head like Medusa on a bad hair day and her dark eyes stared angrily at me from under the lowering ledges of her brows. 'What in the name of God are you playing at?' she demanded.

'Alexis, please stop shouting at me,' I said quietly but firmly. 'You know how it winds me up.'

'Winds you up? Winds *you* up? You put me and Chris in jeopardy and you expect me to care about winding you up?' She was so close now I could feel the warmth of her breath on my mouth.

'We'll talk about it inside,' I said. 'And I mean talk, not shout.' I ducked under the hand that was moving towards my shoulder, swivelled on the balls of my feet and walked smartly up the path. It was follow me or lose me.

Alexis was right behind me as I opened the inside door and marched into the kitchen. Mercifully, she was silent. Without asking, I headed for the fridge freezer and made us both stiff drinks. I pushed hers down the worktop towards her and after a long moment, she picked it up and took a deep swallow. 'Can we start again?' I asked.

'I hired you to make some discreet inquiries and cover our backs, not stir up a hornet's nest,' Alexis said, normal volume resumed.

'My professional opinion is that talking to other women in the same position as you is not exposing you to any danger, particularly since I have not identified you as my client to any of the women I have spoken to,' I said formally, trying to take the heat out of the situation. I knew it was fear not fury that really lay behind her display. In her stressed-out place, I'd probably have behaved in exactly the same way, best friend or not. 'I had a perfectly credible cover story.'

'Yeah, I heard that load of toffee about lesbian history,' Alexis said derisively, lighting a cigarette. She knows I hate smoking in my kitchen, but she clearly reckoned this was one time she was going to get away with it. 'No flaming wonder you set off more alarm bells than all the burglars in Greater Manchester. It's not on, girl. I asked you to make sure we weren't going to be exposed because of

Sarah Blackstone's murder. I didn't expect you to go round putting the fear of God into half the lesbian mothers in Manchester. What the hell did you think you were playing at?'

It was a good question, and one I didn't have an answer for yet. The one thing I knew for sure was that this wasn't the right time to tell Alexis that Sarah Blackstone had added her mystery ingredient to the primordial soup. I was far from certain there was ever going to be a right time, but I know a wrong one when I see it. 'Who told you anyway?' I stalled.

'Jude Webster rang me. She assumed that because you had the names and addresses of all the women involved that you were kosher. But she thought she'd better warn me in case I didn't want Chris bothered in her condition. So what's the game?'

Inspiration had provided me with an attempt at an answer. 'I wanted to make sure none of them knew Blackstone's real identity,' I said. 'If they had, they might have contacted her at her home under her real name, and there could be a record of that. A letter, an entry in an address book. I need to be certain that there isn't a chink in the armour that could lead the police back to this group of women if they get suspicious about the burglar theory and start routine background inquiries.' I spread my hands in front of me and tried for wide-eyed innocence.

Alexis looked doubtful. 'But they're not going to, are they? I've been keeping an eye on the local papers, and there's no sign the police are even thinking it might have been anything more than a burglary that went wrong. What makes you think it was?'

I shrugged. 'If anybody she worked with had found out what she was up to, they had a great motive for getting rid of her. A scandal like this associated with the IVF unit at St Hilda's would have the place closed down overnight.' This was thinner than Kate Moss, but given what I couldn't tell Alexis, it was the best I could do.

'Hey, I know it's hard getting a decent job these days, but I can't get my head round the idea of somebody knocking off a doctor just to avoid signing on,' Alexis protested. Her anger had evaporated now I had anaesthetized her fears and her sense of humour had kicked in.

'Heat of the moment? She's arguing with somebody? They grab a knife?'

'I suppose,' Alexis conceded. 'OK, I accept you did what you did with the best of motives. Only it stops here, all right? No more terrorizing poor innocent women, all right?'

That's the trouble when friends become clients. You lose the power to ignore them.

Midnight, and we were arranged tastefully round the outer office of Mortensen and Brannigan. As soon as Richard had mentioned the f-word to Tony Tambo, the manager of Manassas had insisted that we meet somewhere nobody from clubland could possibly see him talking to a woman who'd already been publicly asking questions on the subject. Otherwise, flyposting was definitely off the agenda. He'd vetoed a rendezvous in a Chinese restaurant, a casino, an all-night caff in the industrial zone over in Trafford Park and the motorway services area. Richard's house was off limits because it was next door to mine. But the office was OK. I couldn't work out the logic in that until Richard explained.

'Now they've converted the neighbouring building into a student hall of residence, if anybody sees Tony coming out of your building, they'll assume he's been having a leg-over with some teenage raver,' he said.

'And I bet he wouldn't mind that,' I said drily.

'Show me a man over thirty who'd object to people making that assumption and I'll show you a liar,' Richard replied wistfully.

So we were sitting with the blinds drawn, the only light coming from the standard lamp in the corner and Shelley's desk lamp. Tony Tambo was hunched into one corner of the sofa, somehow managing to make his six feet of muscles look half their usual size. Although it was cold enough in the office for me to have kept my jacket on, the slanting light revealed a sheen of sweat on skin the colour of a cooked chestnut that covered Tony's shaved skull. He was wearing immaculate taupe chinos, black Wannabes, a black silk T-shirt that seemed moulded to his pectorals and a beige jacket whose soft folds revealed it was made of some mixture of natural materials like silk and cashmere.

It's a mystery to me, silk. For centuries it was a rare, exotic fabric, worn only by the seriously rich. Then, almost overnight, somewhere around 1992, it was everywhere. From Marks and Spencer to market stalls, you couldn't get away from the stuff. Kids on council estates living on benefits were suddenly wearing silk shirts. What I want to know is where it all came from. Were the Chinese giving silkworms fertility drugs? Had they been stockpiling it since the Boxer rebellion? Or is there some deeper, darker secret lurking behind the silk explosion? And why does nobody know the answer? One of these days, I'm going to drive over to Macclesfield, grip the curator of the Silk Museum by the throat and demand an answer.

I was sitting in an armchair at right angles to the opposite end of the sofa from Tony. Richard was in Shelley's chair, his feet on the desk. The pool of light illuminated him to somewhere around mid-thigh, then he disappeared into darkness. The whole scenario looked like a straight lift from a bad French cop movie. I decided pretty quickly that there weren't going to be any subtitles to help me out. The questions were down to me.

'I really appreciate you talking to me, Tony,' I said.

'Yeah, well,' he mumbled. 'I ain't said nothing yet. It's edgy out there right now, you know?

Stability's gone, know what I mean? It's not a good time to stick your head above the parapet, people are too twitchy.'

'Anything you tell me, nobody's going to know it came from you,' I tried.

He snorted. 'So you say. But if some bruiser's got you up against the wall, how do I know you ain't going to give him me?'

'You don't know for sure.' I gestured round the office, which we've spent enough on to impress corporate clients. 'But I didn't get a gaff like this by dropping people in the shit. Anyway, in my experience, if some bruiser's got you up against the wall, he's going to do what he's going to do. So there's not a lot of point in giving him any more bodies. It doesn't save you any grief.'

He gave me a long, slow, head-to-toe look. 'What's your interest?' he eventually said.

'I'm working for Dan Druff and the Scabby Heided Bairns.' Sometimes you need to give a bit to get a lot.

'They got well unlucky,' Tony observed.

'How do you mean? What have they done to deserve what they're getting?'

'Nothing. Like I said, they just got unlucky. Any war of attrition, somebody always has to be made an example of. To keep the rest in line. Dan and the Bairns just drew the short straw, that's all. Nothing personal. Least, I don't think it is. I haven't heard anything that says it is.'

'So who's making the example of the boys?'

Tony took a packet of Camels out of his pocket and lit up without asking permission. I said nothing, but walked through into my office, took the saucer out from under a mother-in-law's tongue that wasn't ever going to dish out any more lip and pointedly slid it down the coffee table so it was in front of Tony. Richard took that as a sign and straightened up in the chair, using the desk top to roll a joint. Shelley was going to be well pleased in the morning to find tobacco shreds all over her paperwork. 'So what's happening in the music business?' I asked, getting bored with all this mannered posturing we were playing at. 'Who's making a bid for a piece of the action?'

'I don't think it's a piece of the action they want,' Tony said in a sigh of smoke. 'I think they want the lion's share.'

'Tell me about it,' I said.

'It started a couple of months ago. There was a wave of cowboy flyposting. Nobody seemed to know who was behind it. It wasn't the usual small-time gangsters trying to muscle in. So one or two of the major players decided to have a go at the bands and the venues who were having their posters put up by the cowboys. The intention was to find out who was behind it, but also to put the frighteners on the bands and the venues, so they'd come back to heel and abandon this new team.'

Tony paused, staring into the middle distance. 'So what happened?' I asked.

'They got a coating,' he said simply.

243

'What happened?'

'They sent a team of enforcers along to one of the gigs. They found themselves staring down the barrels of half a dozen sawn-off shotguns. Not the kind of thing you argue with. So they went off to get tooled up themselves. By the time they came back, the Old Bill were waiting and the whole vanload got a nicking. And not a one of the door crew got lifted.' Tony shook his head, as if he still couldn't quite comprehend it.

I was taken aback. I couldn't remember a time when Manchester villains had ever called the police in to sort out an internal matter. Whoever was trying for a takeover bid was so far outside the rules it must be impossible for the resident villains to know what the hell was coming round the next corner. 'So what happened?' I asked.

'There were a lot of unhappy people around. I don't have to draw pictures, do I? So they decided they'd go down one of the venues mob-handed. Out of working hours, so the door crew wouldn't be around. They figured a good wrecking job would sort things out. They'd hardly got the door broken down when the Old Bill arrived even more mob-handed and nicked the fucking lot of them. They couldn't believe it. I mean, you're talking people who've got coppers on their teams. Where do you think they get the extra door muscle on Friday and Saturday nights? But there they were being faced down by a fucking busload of coppers in riot gear. You can't get that kind of a turnout when it all goes off in the Moss on a hot summer's night!' Tony crushed out his cigarette and pulled another one out of the pack.

'So, whoever is behind all of this has got a bit of pull?' It was more of a statement than a question.

'You could say that.'

'Who is it, Tony?' I asked.

A drift of smoke from Richard's joint hid Tony's face for a moment. When it passed, his dark eyes met mine. I could see worry, but also a kind of calculation. I felt like I was being weighed in the balance. I'd wondered why Tony had agreed to talk to me. It hadn't seemed enough that he was an old mate of Richard's. Now I realized what the hidden agenda was. Like his buddies, Tony had been comfortable with the way things were run in the city. Like a lot of other people, he wasn't comfortable with what was happening now. They'd tried to sort it out themselves in the conventional ways, and that hadn't worked. Now Tony was wondering if he'd found a cleaner way of getting the new team off the patch. 'Somebody came to see me a couple of weeks ago,' he said obliquely. 'A pair of somebodies, to be precise. Very heavy-duty somebodies. They told me that if I wanted Manassas to carry on being a successful club, I should hand my promotions over to them. I told them I didn't negotiate with messengers and that if they wanted my business, the boss man had better get off his butt and talk face to face.'

I nodded. I liked his style. It was a gamble, but he was on his own turf, so it wasn't likely to have been too expensive. 'And?'

'They went away. Two nights later, I was walking from my car to my front door when three guys jumped me. They put a sack over my head and threw me in the back of a van. They drove me around for a while. Felt like we were going in circles. Then they tipped me out in a warehouse. And I met the boss.'

'Who is it, Tony?' I asked softly. He wasn't talking to me any more. He was talking to himself.

'Peter Lovell. Detective Inspector Peter Lovell. Of the Vice Squad. He's due to retire next year. So he's setting himself up in business now to make sure he can replace all his backhanders with a nice little earner.'

There was a long pause. Then eventually I said, 'What's he like, this Lovell?'

'You ask the plod, they'll probably tell you he's a model copper. He's got commendations, the lot. The top brass don't want to know the truth, do they? Long as their cleanup rate looks OK to the police committee, everything's hunky-dory. But this Lovell, he's a real bastard. He's on the pad with all the serious teams that really run the vice in this city. The faces behind the class-act brothels, the boss porn men, the mucky-movie boys, they're all paying Lovell's wages. But he makes it look good by picking up plenty of the small fry. Street girls, rent boys, any small-time operators that think they can live off the crumbs from the top lads' tables. Whenever Lovell needs a good body, they're his for the taking, there to make him look like a hero in the *Chronicle*. But he never touches anybody serious.' Tony's voice was bitter with contempt.

'What about his private life? He married?'

'Divorced. No kids.'

'Girlfriend?'

Tony shook his head, his mouth twisting in a grimace. 'Word is, he likes fresh meat. And his paymasters know it. Soon as they get some nice new recruit who's managed to avoid being raped, they give her to Lovell to break her in. Not too young, though. Not below about fourteen. He wouldn't like people to think he was a pervert.' He spat out the word as if it tasted as unpleasant as Lovell himself.

I took a deep breath. It was going to be a real pleasure to nail this bastard. 'How many people know he's the face behind the flyposting invasion?'

'Not many,' Tony said. 'It's not common knowledge, take it from me. One or two of the big players on the music scene, not more than that. That's the only reason there's not a war on the streets right now. They're keeping the lid on it, because as long as Lovell's still on the force, he can screw us all one way or another. But somebody's got to put a stop to him. Or else there's going to be blood and teeth on the floor.'

I stood up. 'I'm going to have to think about this, Tony,' was all I said. We all knew what I meant.

He lit his cigarette and jammed it into the corner of his mouth. 'Yeah,' he muttered, unfolding his body from the sofa and making for the door.

'I'll be in touch,' I said.

He jerked to a stop and half turned. 'No way,' he said. 'You want to talk, get Richard to call me and we'll set something up. I don't want you anywhere near Manassas, you hear?'

I heard. He walked out the door and I moved over to the window, snapping the standard lamp off as I went. I pulled the blind back a couple of inches and gazed down three storeys to the shiny wet street below. A taxi sat at the traffic lights, its diesel ticking noisily above the background hum of the city. The lights changed and the taxi juddered off.

'I've never worked for gangsters before,' I remarked as I watched Tony dodge out of the front door and double back past the student residence.

'It can't be that different. Some of your other clients have been just as dodgy, only they were wearing suits.'

'There's one crucial difference,' I said. 'With straight clients, if you succeed, they pay. With gangsters, unless you succeed, *you* pay. I'm not sure I can afford the price.'

Richard put an arm round my shoulders. 'Better not fail then, Brannigan.'

19

Even I don't know many people whose doors I can knock on just after one in the morning in the absolute certainty I won't be waking them up. But I didn't have any qualms about this particular door. I pressed the bell and waited, leaning up against the doorjamb to shelter from the persistent night rain.

After Tony had sloped off into the groovy world of nightclub Manchester, I'd felt too wired to go home to bed. Richard had tried to talk me into a Chinese followed by cool jazz in some Whalley Range cellar known only to a handful of the true faith. It hadn't been hard to say no. I've always thought jazz was for anoraks who think they're too intellectual for train spotting, and my stomach already felt like it had been stir-fried. Besides, I knew exactly how I could profitably fill the time till sleep ambushed me.

The door opened suddenly and, caught unawares, I tipped forward. I almost fell into Gizmo's arms. I don't know which of us was more appalled by the prospect, but we both jumped back like a pair of fifties teenagers doing the Bunny Hop. 'You don't believe in office hours, do you?' Gizmo demanded belligerently.

'No more than you do. You going to let me in? It's pissing it down out here,' I complained.

I followed him back upstairs to the computer room, where screens glowed softly in the dim interior and REM reminded me that night swimming deserves a quiet night. 'Tell me about it,' I muttered, shaking the raindrops from my head well out of range of any hardware.

'Gimme a minute,' he said. There were only two chairs in the room, both of them leather desk chairs. I sat in the one Gizmo wasn't occupying and waited patiently while he finished whatever he'd been in the middle of doing. After ten minutes, I began to wish I'd brought my own games software with me. I cleared my throat. 'Be right there,' he said. 'This is crucial.'

A few more minutes passed and I watched the headlights on Stockport Road sneak round the edge of the blinds and send slender beams across the ceiling, an activity that could give counting sheep a run for its money. Then Gizmo hit a bunch of keys, pushed his chair away from the desk and swivelled round to face me. He was wearing an elderly plaid dressing gown over jeans that were ripped from age not fashion and an unironed granddad shirt. Eat your heart out, corporate man. 'Got some work for me, then?' he asked.

'Depends. You found another job yet?'

He snorted. 'Come round to take the piss, have you? Like I said, Kate, I'm too old to be a wunderkind any more. Nobody believes in you if you're old enough to vote and shave unless your name's Bill Gates. No, I haven't got another job yet.'

I took a deep breath. 'You make a bit of money on the side, don't you? Doing bits and pieces for people like me?'

'Yeah, but not enough to support a habit like this,' he said wryly, waving a hand round at the computers and their associated software and peripherals.

'But you're good at finding the weak points in systems and worming your way in, aren't you?'

He nodded. 'You know I'm the best.'

'How do you fancy working the other side of the street?'

He frowned suspiciously. 'Meaning what, exactly?'

'Meaning going straight. At least in normal working hours. Meaning, coming to work for me.'

'Thought you had a partner who did all the legit security stuff?' he demanded. 'I don't want charity, you know. I either want a proper job or nothing.'

'My partner is taking early retirement due to ill health,' I said grimly.

'What's the matter with him?'

'Delusional psychosis. He thinks he's in love and wants to live in Australia.'

251

Gizmo grinned. 'Sounds like an accurate diagnosis to me. So what's the job description?'

'We do a lot of corporate computer security work, liaising with their software engineers and consultants to make their systems as unbeatable as we can get them. We also work with people whose systems have been breached, both plugging the holes and trying to track what's been raided and where it's gone. We've done a little bit of work with banks and insurance companies tracking money that's been stolen by breaching Electronic Fund Transfers. I know enough about it to pitch for the business, but not enough to do the work. That's where I'm going to need to replace Bill. Interested?'

He spun round on his chair a couple of times. 'I think I might be,' he said. 'Are you talking a full-time job or ad hoc consultancy?'

'I'll be honest, Giz. Right now, I can't afford to take you on full time. Initially, it would have to be as and when I can bring the work in. But if you're as good as you say you are, we'll generate a lot of word-of-mouth business.'

He nodded noncommittally. 'When would you want me to start?'

'Mutually agreed date in the not-too-distant?'

'Dosh?'

'Fifty per cent of the net? Per job?'

'Gross.'

I shook my head. 'Net. I'm not a charity. Shelley has to put the pitch document together and she has

252

to do all the admin. Her time comes off the fee. Plus phone expenses, faxes, photocopying. Most jobs, it's not big bucks. But sometimes it starts to run into money. Net or nothing.'

'I can live with it. Net it is. Six-month trial, see how we both go on?'

'Suits me. There is one thing though, Giz . . . ?' His red-rimmed eyes narrowed in suspicion. 'Well, two things,' I continued. 'A haircut and a smart suit.' I held a hand up to stem the protest I knew was coming. 'I know it breaks your heart to spend money on a suit that could be better spent on a new genlock adapter. And I know you think that anything more sophisticated than a number one all over once a year is for girlies, but these are deal breakers. If you like, I'll even come with you and make the process as painless as possible, but it's got to be done.'

Gizmo breathed out heavily through his nose. 'Fuck it, who do you think you are? I've managed to avoid that kind of shit working for Telecom, why should I do it for you?'

'Telecom have just fired you, Giz. Maybe corporate image had something to do with it, maybe not. Bottom line is, Telecom were a necessary evil for you. Working for me is going to be fun, and you know it. So get the haircut, get the suit.'

He scowled like a small boy who's been told to wash behind his ears. 'Yeah, well,' he growled, scuffing his heels on the floor. 'You drive a hard bargain.'

I smiled sweetly. 'You'll thank me for it one day. Let me know when you want to shop till you drop.'

I walked downstairs alone, leaving Gizmo staring at a screen. I still didn't know where the money was going to come from to buy Bill out. But at least I was starting to feel like it might be possible for the agency to earn enough to pay it back.

Rasul and Lal's sandwich bar is one of Manchester's best kept secrets. Nestled under the railway arches at the trendy rather than the glossy end of Deansgate, it produces some of the finest butties in town. They like to name sandwiches after their regular customers, and I'm proud to reveal there's a Brannigan Butty up there on the board – tuna and spring onion in mayo with black olives and tomatoes in crusty French bread. Strictly speaking, it's a takeaway, but in the room behind the shop some of us get to perch and munch. I'm not sure of the criteria Rasul and Lal apply for admission to the back shop, but I've found myself sharing the privileged space with doctors, lawyers, Equal Opportunities Commission executives and TV technicians. The one thing we all have in common is that we're refugees, hiding from our lives for as long as it takes to scoff a sandwich and swallow a coffee.

When I arrived in the back shop the following morning, Della was already there. She'd opted for an egg mayonnaise sandwich. I was feeling less traditional, going for a paratha with a spicy omelette on top. There was no one else around apart from the brothers. There seldom is around ten, which was why I'd chosen it for our meeting. This was one time I absolutely didn't want to be seen publicly with Della.

We gave each other as much of a hug and kiss as our breakfasts would allow. She looked like she'd had more sleep than me, her skin glowing, her green eyes clear, copper hair pulled back into the kind of chignon that never stayed neat for more than five minutes on me when I had the hair for it. On Della, there wasn't a stray hair to be seen. I couldn't quite work out why, but Della was getting better looking with every passing year. Maybe it had something to do with cheekbones her whole body seemed to hang from. 'Mysterious morning call,' she remarked as we cosied up in the corner between the fridge and the back door.

'You'll understand why when I tell you what I've got for you.'

'Goodies?' she inquired enthusiastically.

'Not so's you'd notice.' I bit into my sandwich. Anything to postpone the moment when I delivered the bad news.

Realizing I needed to work up to this one, Della said, 'We lifted your headstone con artists yesterday morning before their eyes were open. We'd fixed up an ID parade with some of the names you gave us, and we got enough positive identifications to persuade them that they might as well put their hands up and admit to the lot. Turns out they'd pulled the same routine in Birmingham and Plymouth before they turned up here. Nice work, Kate.'

'Thanks. By the way, on the subject of those two, something occurred to me which you've probably thought of already.'

'Mmm?'

'I was thinking about the business they're in. Mobile phones. I just wondered how straight the company is that they're working for. Given how many ways there are to make an illegal buck out of mobies, and given that this pair are cool as Ben and Jerry's in the way they operate, I wondered if it might be worth a poke about at Sell Phones.'

'You know, that might not be such a bad idea. I was so busy with my own team this week, I never gave it a thought. But Allen and Sargent's arrest gives me the perfect excuse to get a search warrant on Sell Phones. Thanks for the thought,' Della said, looking slightly embarrassed that she hadn't worked it out for herself. I knew just how she felt; I've been there too many times myself.

'No problem. However I don't think you're going to be quite as thrilled about today's bulletin, some-how.'

'Come on, get it over with. It can't be as bad as all that. The only news that deserves a face like yours is that Josh is a serial killer.'

'What about a bent DI?' I said gloomily.

The smile vanished from Della's eyes. 'I don't have to ask if you're sure, do I?'

'It's possible somebody's setting me up, but I don't think so. It fits the facts too well.'

Della's mouth tightened into a grim line and she looked past me into the middle distance. 'I absolutely hate corrupt police officers,' she said bitterly. 'They've always got some pathetic piece of self-justification, and it never ever justifies the damage they do. So, who are we talking about here? Just tell me it's not one of mine.'

'It really isn't one of yours,' I said, knowing it was pretty bleak as reassurances go. 'It's a DI in Vice. Peter Lovell? Heard of him?'

Della's answer had to wait. Rasul came through to the fridge for another tray of sliced ham. 'All right?' he asked cheerfully, far too polite to indicate that the expressions on our faces showed the exact opposite.

'Fine,' we chorused.

When he'd left, Della said, 'I know who you mean. I've never had anything to do with him directly, never met him socially, but I have heard the name. He's supposed to be a good copper. High body count, keeps his patch clean. What's the story?'

'I'm not too sure of the exact wording on the charge sheet, but it goes something like threatening behaviour, assault, illegal possession of firearms, conspiracy, incitement to cause an affray, obtaining money with menaces, improper use of police resources . . . Oh, and illegal billposting.'

'If I didn't know you better, I'd say you were winding me up,' Della said wearily. She looked at her half-eaten sandwich. 'I just lost my appetite.' She was about to bin it, but I stopped her. For some reason I was ravenous this morning. I had the last mouthful of my paratha and started on her leftovers. Ignoring every environmental health regulation from Brussels to Baltimore, Della pulled out her cigarettes and Zippo and sucked on a Silk Cut. 'Details, then,' she said.

Lal stuck his head round the door into the shop. 'Can you crack the window if you're smoking, Del?' he asked. I was astonished. I'd never heard anyone contract Della's name and live. Not only did she ignore his liberty-taking, she even opened the window a couple of inches. Either Della was in a state of shock or there was something going on between her and Lal that I knew nothing about.

'It all started when Richard came home with Dan Druff and the Scabby Heided Bairns,' I began. By the time I'd finished, Della looked like she was about to have a second close encounter with the half-sandwich she'd already eaten. 'So right now, Lovell's winning,' I finished up. 'He's got the muscle to get what he wants, and the gangsters can't beat him the usual way because every time they make a move, their shock troops end up behind bars.'

'I can't believe he'd be so stupid,' she said. 'He must be looking at having his thirty in when he retires. That's a good pension, and he's young enough to pull something decent in private security. And he's risking the lot.'

I helped myself to a Kit Kat from an open box on a shelf behind me. 'He's risking a hell of a lot more than that,' I pointed out as I stripped the wrapper off. 'He's risking his life. The people he's dealing with can't afford to lose that much face. If the normal ways of warning someone off aren't working with Lovell, somebody is going to shell out the requisite five grand.'

'And then there *will* be a war. It doesn't matter how bent a bobby is, when he's dead, he's a hero. And when we lose one of our own, the police service doesn't stop till somebody has paid the price.'

'I think they realize that,' I said quietly. 'They'll have to be desperate before they go for a hit. But every week that goes by where money goes into Lovell's pocket instead of theirs is a week when the ratchet gets screwed a notch tighter. I don't know how far away desperation is for the likes of Collar di Salvo's lad, but I know some of the other players are really hurting.'

Della thumbed another cigarette out of the packet. 'So Greater Manchester Police has to put a stop to Lovell on humanitarian grounds? Is that what you're saying?'

'Something like that. But I'm not talking GMP,

I'm talking DCI Della Prentice and a small hand-picked team. If Lovell's been on the force this long, he must have a fair few in his corner, and I don't see how you can be sure who they all are. You need outsiders like you've got in the Regional Crime Squad.'

Della did the time-wasting thing that smokers do to buy some space: fiddling with the cigarette, rolling the lighter round in her hand, examining the filter for holes. 'So what do you suggest?' she asked.

'An undercover operation?'

'Nice of you to volunteer.'

I shook my head. 'No way. I'm not sticking my head above the trench on this one. Remember, I'm the one who doesn't believe in private health insurance, and the waiting list for key organ transplants is too long for my liking.'

Della took another hit of nicotine then said, 'Bottle gone?'

'Cheeky bastard,' I growled. 'My bottle's as sound as it's ever been.'

'Really?' she drawled. God, I hate Oxbridge graduates. They learn that sarcastic drawl at their first tutorial and they never forget it. Those of us who grew up in the backstreets shadowed by the dreaming spires never got past the snarl.

'Yeah, really,' I snarled. 'You're the police, it's your job to catch criminals, remember?'

'Problem is, you're not bringing me any hard evidence,' Della said.

'So mount your own undercover operation. Leave me out of it.'

'It's hard for us, Kate. We don't have any way into an undercover. We haven't got some tame club manager who's going to roll over and help us. And from what you've said, your contacts are not going to welcome Officer Dibble with open arms. They might well think it's better to deal with the devil they know. Whereas you . . .'

'Call yourself my friend, and you want me to go up against an animal like Lovell with his army of hard cases?'

Della shrugged. 'You know you'll have all the back-up you need. Besides, from what you tell me, there's been a lot of mouth but not a lot of serious action. Nobody's been killed, nobody's even had a serious going-over. Mr Lovell's merry men seem to specialize in violence against property. When it comes to sorting people out, he seems to go for remarkably law-abiding means. He calls the police. I think you'd be perfectly safe.'

'Gee thanks,' I said.

Della put a hand on my arm. Her eyes were serious. 'I'm not asking you to do anything I wouldn't do myself. I'll handpick the back-up team.'

'You think that makes me feel any better? Everybody knows you're an even madder bastard than I am!' I pointed out bitterly, knowing I was beaten.

'So you'll do it?'

'I'll call you when I've got the setup sorted,' I

said resignedly. 'I'm not a happy camper, I want you to know that.'

'You won't regret this,' Della said, pulling me into a hug.

'I better not.'

Della paid for the Kit Kat on the way out.

I thought it was about time I showed my face in the office lest Bill got to thinking he could start the revolution without me. With luck, he would still be busy showing Sheila the delights of the NorthWest.

I don't know why I indulged myself with the notion that luck might be on my side. It had been out of my life so long I was beginning to think it had run off to sea. When I walked in Bill was sitting on Shelley's desk, going through a file with her. Given that I wasn't speaking to Bill and Shelley wasn't speaking to me, it looked like an interesting conversation might be on the cards. 'Kate,' Bill greeted me with a cheerful boom. 'Great to see you.' And I am Marie of Romania.

'Hi,' I said to no one in particular. 'Has anything come for me from the Land Registry?'

'If you checked your in-tray occasionally, you'd know, wouldn't you?' Shelley said acidly. It probably wasn't the time to tell her I'd gone through it at one that morning. Not if I wanted to keep my office manager.

'Have you thought any more about the implications of my move?' Bill asked anxiously.

I stopped midway to my office door, threw my hands up in mock amazement and said, 'Oh dearie me, I *knew* there was something I was supposed to be thinking about. Silly me! It just slipped my mind.' I cast my eyes up to the ceiling and marched into my office. 'Of course I've bloody thought about it,' I shouted as I closed the door firmly behind me. People who ask asinine questions should expect rude answers.

The letter from the Land Registry was sitting right on top of my in-tray. Their speed these days never ceases to amaze me. What I can't work out is why it still takes solicitors two months to convey a house from one owner to another. I flipped through the photocopied sheets of information that came with the covering letter. It confirmed the suspicion that had jumped up and down shouting, 'See me, Mum, I'm dancing!' when I'd interviewed Helen Maitland.

I might have been warned off talking to Sarah Blackstone's former patients. But Alexis hadn't said anything about her former lover.

20

I'd gone into my first interview with the real Dr Helen Maitland without enough background information. I wasn't about to make the same mistake twice. After a late lunch in a Bradford curry café that cost less than a trip to McDonald's, I parked up in a street of back-to-back terraced houses that spilled down a hill on the fringe of the city centre. Half a dozen Asian lads and a couple of white ones were playing cricket on a scrap of waste ground where one of the houses had been demolished. When I didn't get out of the car at once, they stopped playing and stared curiously at me. I wasn't interesting enough to hold their attention for long, and they soon returned to their game.

I sat staring at a house halfway down the street. It looked well kempt, its garden free of weeds and its paintwork intact. It was a door I hadn't knocked on for a few years, and I had no idea what kind of welcome I'd get. Even so, it still felt like a more appealing prospect than quizzing Sarah

Blackstone's medical colleagues. I'd first come here in search of a missing person. Not long after I'd found her, she ended up murdered, with her girlfriend the prime suspect. My inquiries had cleared the girlfriend, but in the process, I'd opened a lot of wounds. I hadn't spoken to Maggie Rossiter, the girlfriend, since the trial. But she was still on the office Christmas card list. Not because I ever expected her to put work our way, but because I'd liked her and hadn't been able to come up with a better way of saying so.

Maggie was a social worker and a volunteer worker at a local drug rehab unit, though you wouldn't suspect either role on first encounter. She could be prickly, sharp tongued and fierce. But I'd seen the other side. I'd seen her tenderness and her grief. Not everyone can forgive that sort of knowledge. I hoped Maggie was one who could.

I sat for the best part of an hour, listening to the rolling news programme on Radio Five Live to fight the boredom. Then an elderly blue Ford Escort with a red offside front wing drew up outside Maggie's house. As the car door opened, a small calico cat leapt from the garden to the wall to the pavement and wove itself round the legs of the woman who emerged. Maggie had had her curly salt-and-pepper hair cropped short at the back and sides, but otherwise she looked pretty much the same as when I'd seen her last, right down to the extra few pounds round the middle. She bent to scoop up the cat, draped it over her shoulder and took a briefcase and an armful of files out of the car. I watched her struggle into the house and gave it five more minutes.

One of my rules of private investigation is, always try to leave an interviewee happy enough that they'll talk to you a second time. I was about to find out how well I'd practised what I preached. When the door opened, hostility replaced interested curiosity so fast on Maggie's face that I wondered whether I'd imagined the first expression. 'Well, well, well,' she said. 'If it isn't Kate Brannigan, girl detective. And whose life are you buggering up this week?'

'Hello, Maggie,' I said. 'I don't suppose you'd believe me if I said I was just passing?'

'Correct,' she said sarcastically. 'I'd also tell you that next time you're passing, just pass.'

'I know you blame me for Moira's death . . .'

'Correct again. You going for three in a row?'

'If I hadn't brought her back, he'd just have hired somebody else. Probably somebody with even fewer scruples.'

'It's hard to believe people with fewer scruples than you exist,' Maggie said.

'Don't you ever listen to *Yesterday in Parliament*?'

In spite of herself, Maggie couldn't help cracking a smile. 'Give me one good reason why I shouldn't close the door,' she said.

'Lesbians will suffer?' I tried, a half-grin quirking my mouth.

'I don't think so,' she sighed. The door started to close.

'I'm not joking, Maggie,' I said desperately. 'My client's a lesbian who could be facing worse than a murder charge if I don't get to the bottom of the case.'

The door stopped moving. I'd hooked her, but she wasn't letting me reel her in too easily. 'Worse than a murder charge?' she asked, her face suspicious.

'I'm talking about losing her child. And not for any of the conventional reasons.'

Maggie shook her head and swung the door open. 'This had better be good,' she warned me.

I followed her indoors and aimed for a rocking chair that hadn't been there the last time I'd visited. The shelves of books, records and tapes looked the same. But she'd replaced the big Klimt with a blue-and-white print from Matisse's *Jazz* sequence. It made the room cooler and brighter. 'I know I've got a cheek asking you for help, but I don't care how much I have to humiliate myself to do the business for my clients.' I tried for the self-effacing look.

'Ain't too proud to beg, huh?' Maggie said sardonically.

'I'm hoping you won't make me. But I am going to have to ask you to promise me one thing.'

'Which is?' she asked, sitting on the arm of the sofa, one foot on the seat, the other still on the floor.

'That you'll treat what I have to tell you with the same degree of confidence you'd offer to one of your own clients.'

'If you want confidentiality, you can afford to pay a therapist for it. My clients don't have that option. But if that's the price for hearing this tale of yours, consider it paid. Nothing you tell me goes beyond these four walls, unless I think people are going to come to harm if I keep silence. Is that fair enough?'

'That'll do me. Did you know a doctor called Sarah Blackstone?'

The way her face closed down gave me the answer. 'Tell me your tale. Then we'll see about questions,' Maggie said, her voice harsh.

Time to rearrange the truth into a well-known phrase or saying. 'My client and her partner were patients of Dr Blackstone. She was using them as human guinea pigs in an experiment to see if it's possible to make babies from two women. It is. And my client's partner is currently a couple of months pregnant.' Maggie's attitude had melted like snow on a ceramic hob. She was staring at me with the amazement of a child who's just had Christmas explained to her. Then she remembered.

'But Sarah Blackstone's just been murdered,' she breathed. 'Oh my God.'

'Exactly. Publicly, the police are saying she was killed by a burglar she disturbed. It's only a matter of time before the words "drug-crazed" start showing up in their press briefings. My client is concerned that they have uncovered what Dr Blackstone was really doing, but they're keeping quiet about it while they carry out their investigations.'

'So why are you here?'

Good question. This time, I'd had plenty of time to think about the interview so I had my lies ready. 'I'm trying to get as much background on Sarah Blackstone as I possibly can. If there was more to her killing than meets the eye, I want to find out who was behind it. That way, I can hand the information to the police on a plate, which might stop any kind of investigation into what Sarah was really up to.'

'Sounds plausible. But then, you always did,' Maggie commented. She didn't appear to be over-whelmed with the desire to help me out.

'I don't have any contacts on the lesbian scene this side of the Pennines except you,' I said. 'Believe me, if there had been any other way of getting into this, I'd have gone for it. Being here under these circumstances probably thrills me about as much as it does you. But I need help, Maggie. If what Sarah Blackstone was doing gets into the public domain, there's going to be more than just an outcry. There's going to be a witch-hunt.'

Maggie wasn't meeting my eyes. She looked like she was giving the matter serious thought and she didn't want to be distracted by any more passion from me. Eventually, she glanced across at me and said, 'I might be able to help you with some aspects of your inquiry.'

'Did you know Sarah Blackstone?'

Maggie shrugged. 'Not well. We met through Women's Aid. I'm involved with the refuge in Leeds as well as the one here. Sarah used to run an informal clinic at the refuge in Leeds. She was also one of the doctors they call out to provide medical evidence when they get emergency admissions of women and children who have been badly beaten. We were both on the management committee up until a couple of years ago when Sarah resigned. She said she didn't have the time to give it the energy it demanded.'

'What was she like?'

A smile ghosted on Maggie's face. 'She was exhausting. One of those women who's always full of bounce, never doing anything by halves. Ambitious, clever, committed. She gave up a lot of her time for the causes she believed in. Passionate about the women she dealt with professionally. A great sense of humour. She could be a real clown sometimes.'

'You make her sound like Mother Teresa.'

Maggie gave a bark of laughter. 'Sarah Blackstone? God, no. She had the faults to match her virtues. Like every doctor I've ever met, she was convinced she knew better than God. She was stubborn, arrogant and sometimes flippant about things that are never funny. And when she got a bee in her bonnet about something, she wouldn't leave it alone until everybody had agreed to go along with her ideas.'

'Did you see much of her socially?'

'A bit. We'd end up at the same parties, barbecues, benefits, you know the sort of thing.'

Only by reputation, thank God. 'Was she involved with anyone when she died?' I asked. If Maggie was going to block me, this was where it would start.

'I don't think so,' Maggie said. She appeared to be sincere. 'The last relationship she was in ended round about the end of last summer. The woman she was seeing, Diana, moved to Exeter to start a new job, and there wasn't enough between them for the relationship to survive. They'd been knocking around together for the best part of a year, but not in a committed kind of way. There was always something a bit aloof about Sarah, as if she didn't want to let anyone too close.'

'Did that include Helen Maitland?'

Maggie's eyebrows shot up. 'That's been over for years. How did you hear about Helen and Sarah?'

'Sarah used Helen's name as an alias. I wasn't sure whether the connection between them went deeper than colleagues.' All perfectly truthful, as far as it went. There really wasn't any need to tell Maggie that my suspicions had been confirmed by the Land Registry. Before Helen Maitland's house had been registered in her sole name, it had been jointly owned by Dr Maitland and Dr

Sarah Blackstone. I don't know many people who buy houses with anyone other than their lover.

Maggie's mouth twisted into a rueful grimace. 'And I just told you it did, didn't I?'

'Well, I had my suspicions,' I said. 'What was the score there?'

'Oh well, in for a penny . . . Let me see now . . . It must be six or seven years ago that they first got together. Helen was already in Leeds when Sarah arrived, and it was one of those thunderbolt things. I remember the night they met – it was at a Lesbian Line benefit. Somebody introduced them and they looked at each other like they both had concussion. They moved in together within a couple of weeks, and eventually bought a house together. Then it all fell apart.'

'Why?'

Maggie squeezed the bridge of her nose between her thumb and forefinger, like a woman who's suddenly discovered she's got a sinus headache. 'I had a lot on my mind,' she said quietly. 'It was around three years ago. Not a good time for me.'

I stayed silent, remembering. It had been hard enough for me to accept Moira's death. For Maggie, it must have been a waking nightmare. I waited without impatience for her to fast forward from the worst days of her life. Some things even I'm sensitive to. After a few moments, she stopped massaging her forehead and tuned back in to the here and now. 'I don't know if I ever knew the exact details, but I certainly don't remember them now. I've got a feeling it had something to do with Helen wanting kids and Sarah not. Whatever it was, it was serious. As far as I know, they never spoke again after the bust-up except through their lawyers. A mate of mine acted for Sarah and she said she'd never seen anything like it. It was as if they went from total love to total hatred overnight.'

'That's interesting,' I said, my brain working overtime. My first thought was that she'd got the bit about the kids the wrong way round. Then I thought about what it would mean if she hadn't.

Before I could pursue that line, Maggie shook her head wonderingly and said, 'Oh, so that's what this is about, is it? Looking for a suitable dyke to replace your client on the suspect list?'

'You know I don't work like that. If I did, I'd have told the police about a certain incident three years ago . . .'

Her embarrassment was obvious even if it didn't stretch to an apology. 'Yeah, well,' she said. 'Helen's not the type. Believe me, I know her. She went out with my best mate for about a year not long after she came to Leeds. Anyway, Helen's had stuff to deal with in the last year that must have seemed a hell of a lot more significant to her than whatever Sarah Blackstone was up to.'

'Like what?'

'Like cervical cancer. She had to have a complete hysterectomy. She's only been back at work for about three months.'

I felt like a fruit machine with two lemons up and a fistful of nudges. 'And has she been involved with anyone since Sarah?' I thought I knew the answer, but it's always worth checking.

'Oh yes,' Maggie said. 'She's got a girlfriend in York. Flora. A librarian at the university. Masses of black hair, like one of those Victorian maidens in distress.'

'I think I've met her. Looks like she'd break if you spoke too loud?'

'You'd think so to see her doing that vulnerable innocent routine. But when you watch her in action, you soon see she's tough as old boots. If St George had rescued her from a dragon, he'd not have had her home long before he realized he'd spared the wrong one. And when it comes to Helen Maitland, that Flora's besotted. You could see from early on. Flora had Helen in her sights, and she was going to have her. A ruthless charm offensive, that's what it was. You never get the chance to get Helen on her own these days. Flora's never more than a heartbeat away.'

'How long have they been together?'

Maggie frowned, trying to recall. 'It's been a while now. Since before Helen was diagnosed. Mind I get the impression that if it hadn't been for the cancer and the fact that she needed the emotional support, Helen would have dumped Flora a long time ago. You often see it in relationships – you get the one who worships and the one who's not much more than fond. Well,

Helen's not the worshipper here. But she definitely wasn't hankering after Sarah, if that's what you're thinking. That relationship was dead and buried well before Sarah died,' she added definitely.

Before I could say more, the front door opened and a tall woman in her twenties wearing an ambulance paramedic's uniform walked in. 'Hi, hon,' she said to Maggie, moving into the room and kissing the top of her head. She grinned at me. 'Hi. We've not met.'

'This is Amanda. She's the one who burns your Christmas cards,' Maggie said drily.

The tall woman's face darkened in a scowl. 'You're Kate Brannigan?' she demanded.

'That's me.'

'My God,' she said. 'You've got a nerve. How dare you come round here hassling us! Haven't you done enough?' She took an involuntary step towards me.

I got to my feet. 'It's probably time I was going,' I said.

'You're not wrong,' the paramedic snapped.

'It's all right, Mand,' Maggie said, reaching out and touching her partner lightly on the hip. 'I'll walk you to your car, Kate.'

Amanda stood on the step watching us down the path. 'She thinks you're the one who broke my heart,' Maggie said as we walked up the hill towards my car. 'I thought so too for a while. It took me about a year to realize I'd been idealizing Moira. She was a wonderful woman, but she wasn't really the fabulous creature I had constructed in my mind. If I'm brutally honest, I have to admit we'd never have gone the distance. There were too many things that separated us. But Amanda . . . With her, I do feel like I've got a future. So on the rare occasions when I remember you're on the planet, I don't think of you with anger. I think of you as the person who probably kept me out of prison so that I was free to meet Amanda.'

We had reached my car. I held out a hand and we shook. 'Thanks,' I said.

'That's us quits now.'

I watched her walk back down the pavement. She took the steps to her front door at a run and fell into the kind of hug that would have got her arrested twenty years before. I hoped I'd still be off her hate list by the end of this case.

I walked up the wide path and stopped by the Egyptian temple, sitting down on a stone plinth between the paws of a sphinx. Over to one side, I could just see the columns of a Graeco-Roman temple, complete with enough angels for a barbershop quartet, if not a full heavenly choir. I leaned back and contemplated a Gothic spire like a scaled down version of Edinburgh's Scott Monument. The watery spring sunshine greened the grass up in sharp contrast to the granite and millstone grit. There's nothing quite like a Victorian cemetery for contemplation.

I didn't have to be back in Manchester until eight, and I needed a bit of space to think about the fragmented pieces of information I'd picked up about Sarah Blackstone's life and death. I'd persuaded myself without too much difficulty that I didn't really have enough time to nip over to Leeds and start interrogating the IVF-unit staff. Instead, Undercliffe Cemetery, out on the Otley Road, seemed the perfect answer, with its views across Bradford and its reminders of mortality. Surrounded by obelisks, crosses, giant urns, elaborately carved headstones and mock temples, thinking about death seemed the most natural thing in the world.

According to Alexis, the burglar who had allegedly been disturbed by Sarah Blackstone hadn't actually stolen anything. The only thing missing from the scene was the murder weapon, believed to be a kitchen knife. I found it hard to get my head around that. Even if he'd only just broken in when she walked in on him, there should have been some sign that a theft was in progress, even if it was only a gathering together of small, portable valuables. The other thing was the knife. If the murder weapon came from the kitchen, the reasonable burglar's response would be to drop it or even to leave it in the wound. That's because a burglar would be gloved up. A proper burglar wouldn't need to take the knife with him in case he'd left any forensic traces. Even the drug-crazed junkie burglar would have the sense to realize that taking the knife was a hell of a risk. It's harder to lose good-quality knives than most people think. They've got a way of getting themselves found sooner or later.

So if it wasn't a bona fide burglar, who was it? I shivered as a cold blast of moorland wind caught the back of my neck. I turned my collar up and hunched into the lee of the sphinx. Sarah Blackstone posed a risk to the future of her colleagues, there was no denying that. But the more I thought about it, the less likely it seemed that she'd been killed for that. Even if her secret had been discovered, presumably no one else was directly implicated. In spite of the truism that mud sticks, in my experience it dries pretty quickly and once it's been whitewashed over, nobody remembers it was ever there in the first place. So I could probably strike the angry/frightened colleagues.

There was no doubt in my mind that some of the babies Sarah Blackstone had made owed more to the doctor than the exercise of her skills. Her eggs had gone into the mix, and I had the evidence of my own eyes that she had cruelly duped some of her patients. Even though I'm a woman who'd rather breed ferrets than babies, I can imagine how devastating it would be to discover that a child you thought came equipped with half your genes was in fact the offspring of an egomaniac. I could imagine how Alexis would react if the child Chris was carrying was the result of so wicked a deception. It would be as well for Sarah Blackstone that she was already dead. So there was a group of women out there who, if they'd managed to put two and two together and unravel Sarah Blackstone's real identity, had an excellent motive for murder.

And then there was Helen Maitland.

21

The hardest part had been getting Tony Tambo to play. Briefing me was as far as he had wanted to go. Tony and his friends didn't mind pitting me against DI Lovell and his thugs, but they drew the line at taking too many risks themselves. I knew there was no point in simply phoning him and asking him to cooperate in a sting. What I needed was a pressure point. That's why I'd taken a trip to a certain Italian espresso bar before I'd gone to Bradford.

Every morning between eleven and twelve, Collar di Salvo sits in a booth at the rear of Carpaccio, just round the corner from the Crown Court building. Collar likes to think of himself as the Godfather of Manchester. In reality, the old man's probably got closer links to the media than the Mafia. Even though he was born in the old Tripe Colony in Miles Platting, Collar affects an Italian accent. He has legitimate businesses, but his real income comes from the wrong side of the law. Nothing

280

heavy duty for Collar; a bit of what Manchester calls taxing and other, less subtle, cities call protection rackets; counterfeit leisurewear, mock auctions and ringing stolen cars are what keeps Mrs di Salvo in genuine Cartier jewellery and Marina Rinaldi clothes. And definitely no drugs.

The story goes that Collar got his nickname from his method of persuading rival taxation teams to find another way of earning a living. He'd put a dog collar round their neck, attach a leash to it and loop the leash over an overhead beam in his warehouse. Then a couple of his strong-arm boys would take the dog for a walk . . . History tells us that the competition took up alternative occupations in droves.

In recent years, with the rise of the drug lords, Collar's style of management and range of crimes has started to look like pretty small potatoes. But his is still a name that provokes second thoughts for anybody on the fringes of legality in Manchester. Given that young Joey, the heir apparent, was supposedly involved in the flyposting business, Collar seemed the obvious person to talk to. We'd never met and we owed each other no favours; but equally, I couldn't think of any reason why Collar wouldn't listen.

I walked confidently down the coffee bar and stopped opposite the old man's booth. 'I'd like to buy you a coffee, Mr di Salvo,' I said. He likes everyone around him to act like they're in a movie. It made me feel like an idiot, but that's not an unusual sensation in this job.

His large head was like the ruin of one of those Roman busts you see in museums, right down to the broken nose. Dark, liquid eyes like a spaniel with conjunctivitis looked me up and down. 'Is-a my pleasure, Signorina Brannigan,' he said with a stately nod. That he knew who I was simply confirmed everything I'd ever heard about him. The thug sitting opposite him slid out of the booth and moved to a table a few feet away.

I sat down. 'Life treating you well?'

He shrugged like he was auditioning for Scorsese. 'Apart from the tax man and the VAT man, I have no complaints.'

'The family well?'

'Cosi, cosa.'

Two double espressos arrived on the table, one in front of each of us. Never mind that I'd really wanted a cappuccino and a chunk of panettone. Fuelled by this much caffeine, I'd be flying to Bradford. 'The matter I wanted to discuss with you concerns Joey,' I said, reaching for the sugar bowl to compound the felony.

His head tilted to one side, revealing a fold of wrinkled chicken skin between his silk cravat and his shirt collar. 'Go on,' he said softly.

Joey was Collar's grandson and the apple of his beady eye. His father Marco had died in a high-speed car chase a dozen years ago. Now Joey was twenty, trying and failing to live up to the old man's expectations. The trouble with Joey was that temperamentally he took after his mother, a gentle Irish woman who had never quite recovered from the shock of discovering that the man she had agreed to marry was a gangster rather than a respectable second-hand car salesman. Joey had none of the di Salvo ruthlessness and all the Costello kindness. He was never going to make it as a villain, but his grandfather would have to be six feet under before Joey got the chance to find out what his real métier was. Until then, Collar was going to be faced with people like me bringing him the bad news.

'His flyposting business is suffering. I won't insult your intelligence by outlining the problem. I'm sure you know all about Detective Inspector Lovell. I'm sure you also know that conventional means of dealing with the problem are proving ineffective because of Lovell's access to law enforcement. Joey's difficulty happens to coincide with that of my client, and I'm offering to provide a solution that will make this whole thing go away.' I stopped talking and took a sip of the lethal brew in my cup. My mouth felt sulphurous and dark, like the pits of hell.

'Very commendable,' he said, one liver-spotted hand reaching inside his jacket and emerging with a cigar that could have done service as a pit prop, always supposing there were any pits left.

'I need your help to make it work,' I continued as he chopped the end off his cigar and sucked indecently on it. 'I need Tony Tambo's cooperation,

283

and I don't have sufficient powers of persuasion to secure it.'

'And you hope' – puff – 'that in exchange' – puff – 'for you getting Joey off the hook' – puff – 'I will persuade Tony to help?'

'That's exactly right, Mr di Salvo.'

'Why you want Tambo?'

'DI Lovell has been keeping a low profile. Not a lot of people know he's behind these attempts to take over the turf. But Tony's already had a face-to-face with him, so the man's got nothing to lose by coming in to a meeting. All Tony has to do is set it up. I'll do the rest. It's my head on the block, nobody else's.'

Collar nodded. He closed his eyes momentarily. That didn't stop him abusing my air space with his cigar. His eyes opened and he stared into mine. Any more ham and he could have opened a deli counter. 'You got it,' he said. 'Unless you hear otherwise, the meet will be at Tambo's club, half past eight, tonight. OK?'

'OK.' I didn't want to ask how he was going to get it sorted that fast. To be honest, I didn't want to know. I stood up and was about to thank him when he said menacingly, 'You don't like your coffee?'

I'd had enough of playing games. 'It looks like sump oil and tastes worse,' I said.

I thought he was going to bite the end off his cigar. Then he smiled, like a python who finds a dancing mouse too entertaining to eat. I paid for both coffees on the way out, though. I'm not that daft.

Eight o'clock and Della Prentice had her hand down the front of my most audacious underwired bra. We were in an interview room at Bootle Street nick, and Della was making sure the radio mike was firmly anchored to the infrastructure of my cleavage. If Lovell paid the kind of attention to breasts that most Vice cops are prone to, I didn't want anything showing that shouldn't be. Nipples were one thing, radio mikes another altogether.

'Right,' said Della. 'He's not going to spot that unless things get rather more out of hand than we're anticipating.' She stepped back and gave me the once-over. I'd gone for a shiny gun-metal lycra leotard over black leggings and the black hockey boots I normally reserved for a bit of cat burglary. Draped over the leotard was an old denim jacket with slashed sleeves that revealed the temporary tattoos I'd got stencilled on both biceps. The make-up aimed for the recovering-junkie look; the hair was gelled into a glossy helmet. 'Very tasteful,' she commented.

'You can talk,' I muttered. Della wore a white shirt with the collar turned up and the buttons undone almost as far as her navel. The shirt tucked into a black lycra skirt a little wider than the average weightlifter's belt. Her legs were bare, her feet sensibly shod in flat-soled pumps. From her vantage point washing glasses behind the bar, no one would see more than the tarty top half and immediately dismiss her. With her hair loose and enough make-up to change the shape of eyes and mouth, Lovell was never going to recognize a woman DCI who might have been pointed out to him a couple of times across a crowded canteen. 'Did you manage to pick up anything on the grapevine about Lovell?' I asked.

She pulled a face. 'Not a lot. I didn't want word getting back to him that I was interested. I heard his wife divorced him because he was too handy with his fists, but that's hardly exceptional in the Job. What I did find out, though, was that he claims to have a couple of weeks' time-share in a villa in Lanzarote. Very tasteful property up in the hills, swimming pool, terraced garden, half a dozen *en suite* bedrooms. A little bit of poking around and the calling in of a couple of favours reveals that the holding company that owns the villa is in turn wholly owned by Peter Lovell. Since the property's worth the thick end of quarter of a million, it does raise one or two questions about DI Lovell's finances.'

'Nice one, Della,' I said.

'That's not quite the end of it,' she said as we walked up to the waiting car. 'An old school friend of mine is married to a chap who manages one of the vineyards there, so I gave her a call. Her husband knows Lovell. Clothes by Versace, car by Ferrari, part owner of a restaurant, a bar and two discos in Puerto del Carmen,' she said, her voice tight with anger.

'Obviously not the kind of life style one could sustain on a police pension.'

'Quite. And about bloody time his gravy train hit the buffers. Let's go and make it happen.'

The plan was simple enough. Della would be inside the club watching what was going down. Three of her most trusted lieutenants would be hidden within yards of the main bar where the meeting was scheduled for – two in the ladies' loo, one behind the DJ's setup. Another four hand-picked officers would be stationed outside the club, listening to the transmission from my radio mike. When they had enough on tape to hang Lovell out to dry, they would move in and relieve him of his liberty. A classic sting.

Considering Tony had only had eight hours to sort everything out, he'd come up with a credible cover story for me. I was the keyboard player in a new all-female band. We'd allegedly got together in Germany and we'd been touring in Europe, so successfully that we already had a recording contract with a small indie label in Hamburg. But we wanted more, so we'd come back to Britain to make a full-frontal assault on the music scene in a bid to get a major label contract. Because we were already fairly established, we didn't want to piss around. We wanted promotion, we wanted exposure. We wanted it fast and we wanted it top quality. And we'd told Tony Tambo we wanted to talk to the top man because we weren't going to waste time or money. Now I just had to pray that Lovell would give us enough to pull him on, or I was going to owe so many favours the only solution would be to leave town.

Thinking of favours reminded me of my grave robbers. 'Did you turn over Sell Phones?' I asked.

Della nodded. 'We sent a team in this morning. The shop was clean, but one of my bright boys noticed there was a trap door for a cellar. And lo and behold, there was a phone room down below.'

'A phone room?'

Della raised her eyebrows. 'You mean I've finally found a scam you haven't heard about?'

'Try me.'

'OK. There's a little electronic box you can buy that allows you to eavesdrop on mobile phone calls. What it also tells you is the phone number of the mobile phone that's being used, and its electronic code number. With that information, you can reprogram the silicon chip in a stolen phone and turn it into a clone of a legitimate phone. You can then use that phone to call all over the world until the cellphone company cottons on and cuts you off. Normally, you can get a few hours' worth of calls, but if you're making international calls, sometimes they cut you off within the hour. So if you're cloning phones, you set aside a room with a dozen or so cloned phones in it, and hire the room out for, say, £20 per person per hour, and as soon as one phone gets cut off, the hirer just moves on to the next phone on the table. The hirer gets their calls dirt cheap and untraceable. And the crook's got virtually no outlay once they've got the original scanner and stolen phones.'

'And you found one of these at Sell Phones?'

'We did.'

'So I'm flavour of the month?'

'Let's see how tonight goes down.'

At ten past eight, Della and I descended into the club via the fire escape, as I'd prearranged with Tony. He was waiting for us, nervously toking on his Camel. 'Your friends got here,' he said, his unease and resentment obvious.

'Where are we going to do this?' I asked.

Tony pointed to a small circular table in the far corner, surrounded on three sides by a banquette. 'That's my table, everybody knows that. Anywhere else and he's going to be even more suspicious than he is already.'

I followed him across the room while Della made for the bar and the dirty glasses stacked ready for her. The lights were up, stripping Manassas bare of any pretensions to glamour or cool. In the harsh light, the carpet looked stained and tacky, the furnishings cheap and chipped, the colours garish and grotesque. It was like seeing a torch singer in the harsh dressing-room lights before she's applied her stage make-up. The air smelled of stale sweat, smoke and spilled drink overlaid with a chemically floral fragrance that caught the throat like the rasp of cheap spirit.

Tony gestured for me to precede him into the booth. I shook my head. There was no way I was going to be sandwiched between him and Lovell. It wasn't beyond the bounds of possibility that I was about to become the victim of a classic double-cross, and if Tony Tambo had decided to hitch his wagon to the rising star rather than the comet starting to dip below the horizon, I wasn't about to make it any easier for him. 'You go in first,' I told him.

He scowled and muttered under his breath, but he did what he was told, slipping over upholstery cloth made smooth by hundreds of sliding buttocks. I perched right on the end of the seat, so Lovell wasn't going to be able to corner me without making a big issue of it. Tony pulled the heavy glass ashtray towards him. 'I hope you know what you're doing,' he said.

'So do I. Or we're all up shit creek.'

'I fuckin' hate you women with the smart mouths, acting like you've got balls when all you've got is bullshit,' he said bitterly, crushing out the remains of the cigarette with the sort of venom most people reserve for ex-lovers.

'You think I like hanging out with gangstas? Get real, Tony. It'll all be over soon, anyway.'

He snorted. 'So you say. Me, I think this'll be rumbling round for a long while yet.' He leaned forward and shouted in Della's direction. 'Hey, you!' Della looked up from the glass she was polishing. 'Do something useful and bring me a fuckin' big Southern Comfort and lemonade.'

Della's look would have shrivelled Priapus, but Tony was too tense to care. 'You want the usual, Kate?' she asked me. I nodded.

The door at the far end of the club crashed open with the force that only a boot can produce. All three of us swung round, startled. In the doorway stood a tall, thin man dressed in the kind of warm-up suit top tennis players wear when arriving at Wimbledon. He was flanked by two men who could have played line backer in an American football team without bothering with the body padding. Their shoulders were so wide they'd have had to enter my house sideways. They looked like they were built, not born, complete with suits cut so boxy they could have been constructed out of Lego.

The trio moved across the room at a measured pace and I had the chance to take a proper look at Peter Lovell. He had a narrow head with the regular features of a fifties matinée idol, an image nurtured by a head of thick brown hair swept straight back like Peter Firth's. It was an impression that crumbled at closer range, when skin wrecked by teenage acne became impossible to disguise or to deflect attention from. He stopped a few feet away from me, his minders closing ranks behind him. His eyes were like two granite pebbles, cold and grey as the North Sea in January. 'Segue,' he said contemptuously, his voice like hard soles on gravel. 'What kind of a name is that?'

'It's Italian,' I said. 'It means "it follows". Which means my band is the next big thing, yeah?'

'That depends. And you're Cory?'

'That's right. Tony says you're the business when it comes to getting a band on the map.'

Lovell slipped into the seat opposite me. 'A brandy, Tony,' he said. 'Best you've got, there's a good lad.'

'A large Hennessy over here, girl,' Tony shouted. 'What's keeping you?'

I didn't even glance at Della. 'So what can you do for us, Mr . . . ?'

'My company's called Big Promo. You can call me Mr Big or Mr Promo, depending how friendly you want to be,' he said without a hint of irony.

I acted like I was deeply unimpressed. 'The question stands,' I said. 'We're really cooking in Europe, but this is where the serious deals get made. We want to be noticed, and we don't want to hang around. We don't want to be pissed about by somebody who doesn't really know what they're doing, who isn't up to playing with the big boys.'

Something approaching a smile cracked his face. 'Attitude, eh? Well, Cory, attitude is no bad thing in its place.' Then he leaned forward and the smile died faster than a fly hitting a windscreen at ninety. 'This is not the place. I'm not in the habit of dealing directly with people. It wastes time I could be using to make money. So the least, the very least, I demand from you is respect.'

'Fine by me,' I said. 'So can we stop wasting your time? What can you do for us that makes you the one we should do business with?'

'Why don't you have a manager?' he demanded.

'We never found anybody we trusted enough. Believe it or not, I'm a qualified accountant. I can tell a good deal from a bad one.'

'Then we're not going to have any problems. I'm offering the only good deal in town. This is my city. In exchange for forty per cent of your earnings, including any record deals you sign, I can place you in the key venues. I can make sure your tickets get sold, I can get you media coverage and I can paper the whole city with your tits.' Lovell leaned back as Della approached with our drinks on a tray. Sensibly, she served Lovell first, then me, then Tony. As she walked away, Lovell said, 'Since when did you start employing pensioners?'

'All she does is sort the glasses and stock the bar. She's out of here before the punters start coming in. The girlfriend's auntie,' Tony said dismissively.

'I hear on the grapevine that there's been a bit of bother lately. Posters getting covered up, bands having their gigs wrecked, that kind of shit. What's to stop that happening to us?' I asked.

Lovell drummed his fingers on his brandy bowl. 'Signing with us, that's what. You stupid cow, who do you think has been handing out the aggravation? I told you, this is my city. Anybody who thinks different has to take what's coming to them. You stick with me and nothing bad will happen to you. Ask Tony. He pays his taxes like a good 'un. You never have any bother, do you, Tone?'

'No,' Tony said tonelessly, reaching for his cigarettes and lighting up. 'No bother.'

'Let me get this straight, then. You're saying if we pay you forty per cent of everything we make, you'll sort it for us. But if we choose somebody whose prices are more in line with the rest of the planet, we'll live to regret it? Is that what you're saying?'

Lovell picked up his glass and wasted the brandy in one swallow. 'Sixty per cent of something's a lot better than a hundred per cent of fuck all. There's a lot of things can go wrong for a band trying to make a break in this town. Posters that never make it onto walls. Tickets that mysteriously don't sell. Riots at the few crappy gigs they manage to pick up. Vans full of gear burning up for no obvious reason.'

'You saying that could happen to us if we don't sign up with you?'

He replaced the glass on the table with infinite care. 'Not could. Will. It was you asked for this meeting,' he reminded me, stabbing his finger towards the centre of my chest. 'You need what I can do for you. Otherwise you might as well fuck off back to Germany.'

I jerked back from his finger. I could relax now.

Lovell had just nailed himself to the wall. 'OK, OK,' I said. 'No reason why we can't do business. I was just checking.'

Lovell got to his feet. 'Well, you've done your checking and now you know what the score is. You don't ever get smart with me, bitch, you hear? I tell your poxy band where they play and when; you do no deals without consulting me first.' He put a hand in his pocket and tossed a small mobile phone on the table. 'Keep it on you. My number's programmed in at number one. That's the only number you call, you hear? I get any bills that say otherwise and you pay a service charge I guarantee you won't like. You can buy a charger unit anywhere that sells phones. I'll let you know when your first gig is.'

Whatever he was going to say next was lost. The door to the club crashed open again and two men piled in, shouting, 'Police. Don't move.' The door to the ladies' toilet opened and the other two rushed into the room, heading for the minders. A fifth cop jumped over the DJ's turntables as Della ran out from behind the bar towards Lovell. Everybody was screaming, 'Police. Don't move.' The acoustics of the club had a strange effect on their voices, almost swallowing them in the vastness of the space.

Lovell's face went deep red from the neck up, like a glass filling with coloured liquid. 'Fucking bitch,' he yelled. 'Let's get the fuck out of here.'

But before he could go anywhere Della's sergeant, a rugby prop forward from Yorkshire, misjudged his run from the DJ's platform and cannoned into him. Seeing their boss floored and themselves outnumbered, the muscle decided that the game that had been keeping them in made-to-measure suits was over. Lovell was dead in the water. But that didn't mean Tweedledum and Tweedledee had to sink with him. In perfect sync, two right hands disappeared inside their jackets and emerged holding a matching pair of semiautomatic pistols.

Suddenly, everything went quiet.

22

It's not just the immediate prospect of being hanged that concentrates the mind wonderfully. Staring down the barrel of a gun does the trick just as well. For a long minute, nobody moved or said a word. Then Tweedledum gestured with his pistol towards Della. 'You, bitch. Over here.'

At first she didn't move. I knew what she was thinking. The more spread out we were, the harder it would be to keep us all covered. 'I said, over here,' the gunman screamed, dropping the nose of his pistol and firing. A chunk of wood from the dance floor leapt into the air inches from Della's feet and frisbeed away across the room. 'Fucking do it,' he shrieked. I've never understood why it is that the guys with the guns always sound more scared than those of us without them.

Slowly, cautiously, Della moved towards him. As soon as she came within reach, he pulled her to him by the hair, back against his chest, gun muzzle jammed into her neck. I knew then that these guys were the real thing. The neck is the professional's option. Much more sensible than holding it to the temple. The muzzle buries itself in the flesh of the neck rather than sliding on bone covered by sweating skin. Guns to temples are amateur city, a mark of someone who's watched more movies than they've committed crimes.

The man holding Della turned so that he and his companion were almost back to back. 'Nobody fucking move,' the other one screamed.

'Get this fucker off me,' Lovell yelled.

'I said *nobody* fucking move, and that means you.'

'You fucking *work* for me, shithead,' Lovell screeched, his face purpling now with sheer rage.

'We just handed in our notice, OK?' the gun-man shouted, his gun pointing at Lovell and the cop still sprawled on top of him. 'OK, Let's go.' He took a step backwards as his buddy moved forwards. Awkwardly they made their way over to the fire exit. Given that only two cops had burst in the main door, I guessed that the remaining two men were outside the fire door. I sincerely hoped neither of them was the heroic type.

The gunmen had nearly made it to the fire door when Tony Tambo suddenly erupted into action. I don't know if he was playing at knights in shining armour or if it was just sheer rage at seeing his club abused like this, but he jumped up on the seat, ran straight across the table, leapt to the floor and went for the heavies. The one facing us didn't

298

even pause for breath. He just let off two shots. The first caught Tony in the thigh, his leg bursting into shattered fragments of flesh and bone in a spray of blood. The second caught him in the abdomen as he fell, the exit wound bursting out of his back like someone had used a morphing program on his suit. His scream was like every nightmare you hope you'll never have. The groans that followed it weren't a whole lot better.

'I fucking warned you,' the gunman shrieked, sounding like he was about to burst into tears. 'Let's get the fuck out,' he added.

His companion kicked the bar on the fire exit, which sprang open. I could just see the corner of the basement stairs that led up to the street. Then he shouted, 'Get the fuck down here now, or the bitch gets it, you hear?' He stepped back, yanking Della with him. Nothing happened, so he sidestepped her, still holding her hair, leaned into the doorway and fired. I heard the singing whine of a ricochet against the stone walls of the stairway. Then he hauled Della in close again. 'Get them down here,' he snarled.

'Come down quietly,' Della shouted. 'That's an order.'

By now, Tony had stopped groaning, so I was able to hear the sound of heavy feet on the steps. Two men edged through the door into the club. They followed the gestures of the man with Della and the gun and moved round the walls until they were almost parallel to Lovell and Della's sergeant.

'OK. Nobody follow, you hear? Or the bitch dies,' he screamed, rushing the door, followed by his companion.

As they disappeared, Lovell made a superhuman effort that caught the sergeant unawares. Suddenly he was wriggling free. I jumped onto the table and launched myself in a flying kick that would have got me suspended for life in any legitimate Thai boxing club. I hit Lovell in the side, and as we crashed to the ground together, I heard the satisfying crunch of snapping ribs and his simultaneous squeal of pain before the wind was completely knocked out of him. I rolled free and left him to Della's sergeant. I ran for the fire exit, along with one of the cops. The others were already out of the main door and heading for the street in a desperate bid to cut off the gunmen.

We reached the door at about the same moment the gunmen, slowed by an uncooperative Della, reached the street. With a roar that King Kong wouldn't have been ashamed of, the one trying to control her picked her up bodily and threw her down the flight of narrow stairs.

No amount of training in how to fall drills you for that sort of experience. Della tumbled down the steps in a loose ball, head defended by her forearms, bouncing off the walls. The cop and I stepped forward to break her fall. It was probably the worst thing we could have done. As she hit us, her leg shot out and snagged the wall. I heard the crack as bone snapped. Then we were a tumble of limbs. We settled with her face a couple of inches from mine. 'What a fuck-up,' she breathed. Then she fainted. I managed to free one arm from under her in spite of the excruciating pain that ran like a flame up to my shoulder. When I saw the tattered sleeve of my jacket drenched in blood I fainted too.

It had been a quiet night in Casualty until we hit the infirmary. Tony Tambo was on the critical list, having blood pumped into him and hanging onto life by sheer willpower, according to the nurse strapping up the wrist I'd merely sprained in the crush at the foot of the fire stairs. The blood had been Tony's. I'd landed in it when I'd rolled free of Lovell. Mr Big Promo was under arrest with four broken ribs and a collapsed lung, and I was half expecting one of Della's zealots to charge me with assault. Della herself had been sent down to the plaster room to have her ankle set and immobilized. The cop whom we'd both landed on was being kept in for observation with a double concussion, two unlovely black eyes and a missing front tooth. You couldn't get near the coffee machine in Reception for uniformed cops.

When the nurse had finished with the bandages, I walked down to the plaster room, taking it slowly to avoid jolting any part of my protesting body. I'd only just pushed the swing doors open when I heard a familiar Scouse accent. Alexis's cheerful raucousness was to my headache what Agent

Orange is to house plants. Della's head swung round with all the belligerence of a punch-drunk boxer who's gone one round too many and we chorused, 'Go *away*.'

'Well, that's a charming way to greet your friends. Soon as the newsdesk hears there's a bit of a fracas involving DCI Prentice and a private eye called Brannigan, I say to them, "I'll take care of this, the girls need to see a friendly face,"' Alexis said self-righteously.

'If you're here as a journalist, go away, Alexis,' I said wearily. 'If I said this has not been a good night, it would be the understatement of my life. Things have gone so wrong in the last hour that I'm desperate to hit somebody. Now, we might be in the right place for the aftermath of that sort of thing, but I really don't want it to happen to you.'

'Me, I'd just settle for somebody to arrest,' Della said, her voice sounding as emotionally exhausted as she had every right to feel. 'So, as Kate said, Alexis the journalist can take a hike. Alexis the friend, however, is welcome to stay provided she has a set of wheels that can take us all home after this little fiasco has run its course.'

'I'm sorry,' I said.

Della shook her head. 'It really wasn't your fault. I should have had the sense to realize he'd be walking around with armed minders. We should have let them all walk out of there then picked Lovell up in the middle of the night when he was on his own. I misjudged it.'

That should have made me feel better. Instead, I felt infinitely worse. Della was on the point of being promoted to superintendent and an operation like this that could be painted as a screw-up wasn't going to help. Add to that the pariah status automatically granted to any police officer who puts other cops away, and it looked like my bright idea might have put Della's next promotion into cold storage. 'You'd better come back and stay with me,' I offered as the first stage in what was going to be a long apology. 'You won't be able to manage the stairs at your place for a few days.'

She nodded. 'You're probably right. Won't Richard mind?'

'Only if you try to arrest him for possession.'

Della managed a tired smile. 'I think I can manage to restrain myself.'

'So what actually happened?' Alexis chipped in, unable to restrain herself indefinitely.

'Gun battle in Manchester's clubland,' I said. 'Police officer held hostage. Man helping police with inquiries, two gunmen sought. Club owner seriously injured, two police officers with minor injuries. One private investigator who wasn't there.'

Alexis grinned. 'I hate it when you come home with half a tale.'

Later, a lot later, when Della was asleep in my bed and Richard in his, I sat in the dark in the conservatory with a strong mixture of Smirnoff Black Label and freshly squeezed grapefruit juice and contemplated the capital D of the moon. Tony Tambo hadn't made it; one of Della's colleagues had rung to tell her not ten minutes after we got home. I sipped my drink and thought about how far reality had diverged from the simple little sting I'd envisaged. I'd gone in all gung ho and full of myself, and now a man was dead. He'd had a girlfriend and an ex-wife and a little daughter who was the apple of his eye, according to Richard. He wasn't supposed to behave like a hero, but then, I hadn't imagined there was going to be any need for heroics.

If my life was like the movies, my character would be planning vengeance, putting the word out in the underworld that she wanted those guys so bad she could taste it. And they would be delivered to her in such a way that she could decide their fate. But my life isn't like the movies. I knew I'd be doing nothing to discover the identities of the gunmen, where they hung out or who they ran with. That was the police's job, and I couldn't do it without placing more lives in danger. After what had happened to Tony Tambo, I was through with setting myself up against the major players.

I took a long cool swallow and tried not to think about Tony's daughter. Tried not to despise myself too much. Tried desperately to remember why I'd been working so hard to find a way to stay in this destructive game.

I woke around half past seven, just as the sun climbed over my back fence and hit the end of the wicker settee where I'd finally lost consciousness. I was still wearing the T-shirt and jogging pants I'd put on after the shower I'd needed to get the last of Tony Tambo's blood off me. If there's a female equivalent of unshaven, I felt it. I rubbed the grit out of my eyes, wincing at the arrow of pain in my left wrist, and stumbled through to the kitchen. I was just filling the coffee maker with water when I heard Della call me. 'Be right there,' I said, finishing the job.

Della was propped up on my pillows looking ten years older than she had done the day before. According to my wardrobe mirror, that still gave her a few on me. 'How are you feeling?' I asked.

'You see it all.'

'That bad? Shit, I'd better take your shoelaces and belt then.'

Della reached out and limply patted my hand. 'Do I smell coffee?'

'You do. Life-support systems will be available shortly.'

Ten minutes later, we were sharing the first pot of coffee of the day. I even relaxed the house rules enough to let her smoke in my bed. 'What have you got on today?' she asked.

I shrugged. 'I thought I might go down to the university and see if I can sign up to finish my law degree this autumn.'

Della was suddenly alert. 'Part time?' she said suspiciously.

'Full time.'

'Tony Tambo's death was not your fault,' she said firmly.

'I know that. I just don't know if I want to do this job any more. I didn't think it was going to be like this. Come to that, it didn't use to be like this. I don't know if it's the world that's turning nastier or if it's just that I've had a run of cheesy luck, but some days I feel like there should be a task force of counsellors, undertakers and paramedics in the car behind me.'

Della shook her head, exasperated. 'My God, you are feeling sorry for yourself this morning, aren't you? Listen, I'm the one who screwed up royally last night. A man died, and other people could have. The only way I could feel worse than I do now is if it had been you lying there on the mortuary slab. I've also probably kissed goodbye to my next promotion. But I'm not about to hand in my resignation. Even though I make mistakes, the police service needs people like me more than I need to gratify my guilt. I don't have to tell you about the dozens of sleazy, creepy exploitative PIs there are out there. Your business needs you, just like the police needs me. What about all the times when you've changed people's lives for the better? You got Richard out of jail, didn't you?'

'Yeah, but if it hadn't been for me, he wouldn't have been there in the first place,' I reminded her.

'You've saved businesses from going down the tube because you've identified the people who were stealing their money and their ideas. You've done work that has helped to clear up major drug syndicates.'

'Oh yeah? And that's really made a difference to the amount of drugs rattling around the streets of Manchester.'

'What about that case you were working when I first met you? The land fraud? If it hadn't been for your work, Alexis and Chris would have been comprehensively ripped off and they wouldn't be living in their dream home now. You've made a real difference in their lives,' Della insisted.

Her mention of Alexis and Chris reminded me forcibly of one job I still had to finish. Even if I was going to throw the towel in and sell my share of the business along with Bill, I couldn't walk away from Sarah Blackstone's murder.

When I failed to respond to Della, she gave my arm a gentle punch. 'You see? It breaks my little police heart to say it, but this city needs people who don't carry a warrant card.'

I swallowed my coffee. 'You sound like Commissioner Gordon,' I said acidly. 'Della, I'm not Batman and this isn't Gotham City. Maybe I could make just as much difference as a lawyer. Maybe Ruth would take me on.'

Della snorted. 'Listen to yourself. You want to go from cutting the feet from under the villains to defending them? You couldn't be a criminal lawyer. It's not possible only to defend the innocent, and you know it.'

'I sure as hell couldn't be a Crown Prosecutor either,' I growled.

'I know you couldn't. It's just as impossible only to prosecute the guilty. The trouble with you, Kate, is you understand the moral ambiguity of real life. And you're lucky, because the job you do lets you exercise that. You decide who your clients will be. You decide to defend the innocent and nail the guilty. You're too moral to be a lawyer. You're a natural maverick. Exploit it, don't ignore it.'

I sighed. Now I knew why Philip Marlowe didn't bother with buddies.

23

I'd got as far as Leeds before my determination ran
out. It wasn't entirely my fault. Sherpa Tensing
would have a job unravelling the roads in the
centre of Leeds fast enough to take the right turning for the police admin building where I'd find
the press officer I needed. Since I found myself
inevitably heading for Skipton, I pulled off at Hyde
Park Corner and killed some time with a decadent
fruit shake in the radical chic Hepzi-bahz café while
I reviewed where I was up to on the case that stood
between me and a new life.

The more I looked at Sarah Blackstone, the
more I grew convinced that this murder was about
the personal, not the accidental or even the professional. Sure, one of her patients might have
her suspicions about the biological co-parent of
her daughter, but to confirm even that much
wouldn't be easy for a lay person. And even if
it were confirmed, it was still a long way from
there to murder, given that her patients didn't

even know her real name. Logically, if a patient had killed her, the body should have been in the Manchester clinic, not the Leeds house.

That thrust Helen Maitland into the position of front runner. I knew now that she had wanted a child but that Sarah Blackstone had refused her. God only knew why, given what she'd been doing for two of the three years since they split up. But since that separation, Helen had lost the capability to have children. If I'd learned one thing from Chris's relentless drive towards pregnancy, it was the overwhelming, obsessive power of a childless woman's desire for motherhood. Chris once described the feeling as possession. 'It's there as soon as you wake up, and it's there until you go back to sleep,' she'd explained. 'Some nights, it even invades your dreams. Nothing matters except being pregnant. And it stops as soon as your body realizes it's pregnant. Like a weight lifting from your brain. Liberation.'

If Helen Maitland had been feeling like that before her cancer was diagnosed, the arrival of a card from Jan Parrish with a photograph of a baby girl and a lock of silky hair must have seemed a grotesque gift, cruel and gratuitous and, at first glance, bewildering. But when she'd examined it more closely, she couldn't have failed to see the child's undoubted resemblance to Sarah Blackstone. Helen was nobody's fool. She must have known Sarah's work was at the leading edge of human fertility treatment. Seeing a photograph of a baby who looked so like Sarah must have set her wondering what her lover had done now, especially coming so soon after the final dashing of her own hopes.

For a doctor involved in research, tenacity is as necessary a virtue as it is in my job. Faced with a puzzle, Helen would not simply have shelved it any more than I would. Given her specialism in the area of cystic fibrosis, she would have routine access to DNA testing and to researchers working in the field. I knew it wasn't standard practice to obtain DNA from hair shafts – it's difficult, technically demanding and often a waste of time because the DNA it yields is too poor in quality to be meaningful. But I knew that it was possible. It was the sort of thing some eager-beaver researcher would doubtless be happy to do as a favour for a consultant. Having met Helen Maitland, I didn't doubt she could be both charming and terrifying enough to get it done.

Getting a comparison sample of Sarah's DNA wouldn't have been so difficult either – a couple of hairs from the collar of her lab coat would be enough, and probably easier than cut hair, since they would have the roots still attached. Checking the two DNA profiles against each other would tell Helen a truth that for her in particular was a stab to the heart.

Given her probably fragile state, who knew how she might react? She could easily have stormed round to Sarah's, determined to have it out with her ex-lover. It didn't take much to imagine a scenario ending in Sarah's heart pumping her blood out on to the kitchen floor instead of round her arterial system. Now I had two problems. The first was proving it.

The second was what I did with that proof.

When the Yorkshire TV crowd started to pile in for lunch, the women in striped men's shirts and tailored jackets, the men in unstructured linen and silk, I decided it was time to go. I still had no idea how to deal with the second question, but it was academic if I couldn't answer the first.

This time, I decided to abandon the car in the Holiday Inn car park and make for the police station on foot. I hoped I wasn't going to be there long enough to be clamped. Just in case, I stuck my head into the restaurant, spotted a table where the half-dozen business lunchers included a couple of women. Then if I came back and the car was clamped, I could pitch the hotel into setting me free on the basis that I'd just had lunch, that table over there, no I didn't have the receipt because one of the others had paid for me. Usually works.

After I'd left Hepzi-bahz, I'd called ahead to warn the press officer I wanted to see not to go to lunch until I got there. At the front desk, I presented my official press card to the officer on duty, who gave it a cursory glance. It was, of course, a complete fake, based on a colour photocopy of Alexis's card plus a passport photograph of me, all shoved through the office laminating machine. Must have taken me all of ten minutes to cobble it together, and it would take close comparison with the real thing to tell the difference. I'd never try to get away with it in a police station in Manchester, where my face is too familiar to too many coppers, but over the Pennines it seemed a chance worth taking.

Ten minutes later, Jimmy Collier and I were nursing glasses in a busy pub which was a rarity in northern city centres in that it preferred customers to hear the sound of their voices rather than loud music. Jimmy was a dapper little man who could have been any age between thirty and fifty and dressed like he thought men's magazines had to have dirty pictures in them. He looked a bit like a penguin and walked like a duck, but there was nothing birdlike about the appetite with which he was attacking a cheese and onion barm that was approximately the size of a traditional Yorkshire flat cap. Along with his lunch, I fed him a story he swallowed as easily as the sandwich.

I told him I was working for one of the women's weekly magazines on a feature about burglary and home invasions. 'What we want to do is give them a "what you should do" guide, using real-life cases as an indicator of what you should and shouldn't do.' I smiled brightly. 'I thought the Sarah Blackstone murder was a perfect example of what you don't want the outcome to be,' I added, letting the smile drop.

Collier nodded and mumbled something indecipherable. He swallowed, washed his mouthful down with a draught of Tetley, then said, 'You're not kidding.' It hardly seemed worth the wait.

'So . . . what can you tell me about this case?' I asked.

He wiped his mouth on the back of his hand. 'Sarah Blackstone had been working late in the IVF laboratory at St Hilda's Infirmary. As far as we can ascertain, she left the hospital at around half past nine. At 10.27, we got a treble niner from a call box on the corner of her street. A woman who didn't give her name said she'd just been nearly knocked down by a black youth with what looked like a knife in his hand. He'd come running out of a house, leaving the door wide open. We took it seriously, because let's face it, between you and me, you don't get a lot of blacks living in a street like Pargeter Grove. We got there at 10.40, four minutes after the ambulance. Dr Blackstone was already dead. The knife had gone straight under her ribs and into her heart.'

I took notes as he spoke. 'And you reckon she disturbed a burglar?' I asked.

'That's right. A pane of glass in the back door was smashed. The key was in the lock. That's something to remind your readers about. Unbelievably stupid, but you'd be surprised how many people do that.'

'I read that nothing appeared to have been stolen,' I said.

'That's right. We reckon he'd just walked in the back door when she walked in the front. She were still wearing her mac. He didn't have time to do anything except strike out at her. I doubt he even had time to think about what he were doing, he just lunged at her. She was really unlucky. Not many stab wounds kill you as fast as that. When he saw what he'd done, he legged it empty-handed.'

'Wasn't the house alarmed?'

'No, it was just a bit nervous!' He guffawed. I'd heard the riposte too many times to find it funny any more, but I smiled nevertheless. 'She did have an alarm fitted,' he continued. 'But like a lot of people, I suppose she just left it switched off. People never think it's going to happen to them. You should stress that to your readers. If you've got an alarm fitted, never leave the house without setting it.'

'Good point,' I said appreciatively. He wasn't to know, after all, that Sarah Blackstone was so security conscious it bordered on the paranoid, and with good reason. Another argument against the random burglar. There was no way Sarah Blackstone would leave the alarm switched off. 'This woman that phoned in – wasn't it a bit funny that she didn't give her name?' I asked.

He shook his head. 'More often than not, they don't, around there,' I deciphered through a mouthful of barm cake. 'They don't want to get

315

involved. Even when they're the only proper witness we've got. They don't want to have to miss work to come to court to give evidence, they're frightened that if they stick their necks out, it'll be their house the bad boys come to next. Far as they're concerned, their civic duty stops with the 999 call.'

'That's your middle classes for you,' I said.

'You're not wrong. Especially after the riots down Hyde Park. They're terrified of repercussions. We tell them they're safe to give evidence, but they don't believe us.'

Neither did I. I'd heard too much about West Yorkshire Police. I know a woman whose house was being broken into by three teenagers with a sledgehammer in broad daylight. The next-door neighbour dialled 999 and the police arrived a full half-hour later, protesting that there wasn't a lot they could do since the burglars had already gone. I flicked back through my notes. 'Fascinating case, this one. No forensic, I take it?'

'There are some indicators that the forensic team are working with,' he said guardedly. 'But they won't even tell me what they've got. All I know is that it's a bit of a struggle to make it look like one of the usual suspects.' He winked.

'She took her time coming home from St Hilda's,' I commented. 'Can't be more than fifteen minutes' drive at that time of night.'

'She'll have stopped off on her way home for a drink or fish and chips,' he said confidently.

'Or popped round to see somebody who turned out not to be in,' I suggested. 'So you've no other eye witnesses except for the mystery caller?'

'That's right. It was chucking it down, so the usual dog walkers and drunks would have been head down and hurrying, that time of night. We were a bit surprised that no one saw him going over the back wall on his way in, since it's over-looked by the student residences, but we've not had a lot of luck all round with this one. Something else to tell your readers – set up a Neighbourhood Watch scheme if you want to cut down the risk of violent burglary in your street. It really works, according to our Community Security team.'

'Community Security?'

He had the grace to look embarrassed. 'What used to be called Crime Prevention,' he admitted sheepishly.

Only it didn't. So in the same way that 'closing hospital beds' became 'care in the community', a quick name change had been necessary. I asked a few anodyne questions, bought Collier a second pint, then made my excuses and left before I had to watch him demolish a slice of Black Forest gateau about the same size as its namesake.

I sat on the top floor of the city art gallery under the huge Frank Brangwen panels representing the horny-handed sons of toil of the industrial revolution, their bodies suspiciously like those of the desk-bound Stallone wannabes you see down every designer gym in the country. Today, though, I wasn't thinking about social change. I was staring at *The Rolling Mill* without seeing it. All I could see was the picture in my mind's eye of Helen Maitland's face, ugly with anger and pain as she lashed out at the woman she had once loved and who had deprived her of her dream of motherhood.

I had a pretty clear idea now what had happened. The results of DNA testing would have confirmed Helen's guess at what Sarah had been doing. This wasn't an experiment that had come out of nowhere; I could imagine the conversations as the lovers had snuggled together under the duvet, Sarah fantasizing about the day the technology would be there to make babies from two women, Helen dreaming of what it would mean to them, to her. But Sarah had refused, for whatever reason. And the refusal had driven a wedge so deeply between them that it was impossible to continue their relationship.

The scenario was as vivid as film to me. When she realized the truth, Helen must have gone round to confront Sarah. But Sarah hadn't been home. She'd been working late. I could picture Helen sitting in her car, impotent rage building like a bonfire. When Sarah had eventually arrived, Helen had probably been beyond rational conversation. She had insisted on being admitted and the two women had gone through to the kitchen. There, the argument had raged before Helen had snapped, seized a knife and thrust it deep into Sarah's body.

The act of murder must have sobered her. She'd had the sense to go to the back door and make it look like someone had broken in. If they'd had drinks, she had cleared glasses or cups. Then, making sure she was hidden by darkness, she'd slipped out of the house, back to her car, and driven to the phone box where she'd made the spurious 999 call.

It accounted for the awkward facts that spoke against it being a burglar. It covered the time gap between Sarah leaving the hospital and being found dead. It explained why the killer had taken the knife; she wouldn't have been wearing gloves and for her there was less risk in taking it home, sterilizing it and dumping it in her own cutlery drawer. She'd probably been bloodstained, but it had been raining that night and she'd likely been wearing a mac or raincoat that she could simply take off and dispose of later.

Helen Maitland had done a good job of covering her tracks. Lucky for her that West Yorkshire Police are crap. But if the police did start to take a serious interest in her rather than doggedly chasing their mystery burglar, there would be proof for the taking. A voice print of the 999 tape would match hers. A new mac would be another circumstantial nail in her coffin. And, of course, she'd have no alibi. They might be short on motive, but if they started to push Helen Maitland, the truth might pour out. If that happened, it was only a matter of time before they started knocking on Alexis and Chris's door. And that was what I'd been hired to prevent.

I sighed. It must have been louder than I thought, because the middle-aged attendant strolled casually into my line of vision, concern producing a pair of tram tracks between her eyebrows. 'You all right, lovey?' she asked.

I nodded. 'I'm fine. Just something I'm trying to work out.'

She inclined her head. Now she understood. 'We get a lot of that,' she said. 'Especially since Alan Bennett did that TV programme about the gallery.'

Like a character in one of Bennett's screenplays, she walked on, nodding to herself, her shampoo-and-set hair as rigid as one of the Epstein busts next door. I roused myself and looked at my watch. Just gone four. Time to head for another confrontation. At least this time I could be fairly sure that I wouldn't end up staring down the barrel of a gun.

I parked about fifty metres down the street from Helen Maitland's house and settled back to wait. By six o'clock, I knew the news headlines better than the newsreaders. Seven o'clock and I was expecting Godot along any minute. As the numbers on the clock headed towards 20:00 I decided I'd had enough. I needed to eat, and Bryan's was frying a haddock with my name on it not five minutes' drive away.

When I returned nearly an hour later, there were lights showing in Helen Maitland's house. When she opened the door to see me on her doorstep, she looked momentarily annoyed, then resigned. 'The return of Sherlock Holmes,' she said wryly.

'I have things to say you should listen to,' I said.

Her eyebrows quirked. 'And they say etiquette's dead. You'd better come in. Ms Branagh, wasn't it?'

'Brannigan,' I corrected her as I followed her indoors. 'Branagh's the actor. I do it for real.' Sometimes I hear myself and think if I was a punter I'd laugh at me.

'Sorry, Ms *Brannigan*,' Helen Maitland said. 'Have a seat,' she added as we arrived in the kitchen. I ignored her. She leaned against the worktop, facing me, one hand absently stroking a tortoise-shell cat sprawled on the draining board. 'Well, you have my undivided attention. I presume this is to do with Sarah?'

'I know you were lovers,' I said bluntly. 'I know you wanted children and she refused to go along with you. But after you split up, the technology was perfected that allowed Sarah to build babies from the eggs of two women rather than using sperm. But the immortality of being the first to do it wasn't enough for Sarah. She wanted her genes to carry on too. So she started mixing her own harvested eggs in with the patients'. And one of those patients was so grateful that she broke the injunction of secrecy and sent a photograph with a lock of hair to the doctor who'd helped her make her dream come true. To nice Dr Helen Maitland. How am I doing so far?'

Her face had remained impassive, but the hand stroking the cat had stopped, fur clenched between her fingers. She tried a smile that came out more like a snarl. 'Badly. I don't have the faintest idea what you're talking about.'

'Somewhere there will be a record of the DNA tests you ran on that lock of hair and on Sarah's DNA. You can't lose something like that. The police would have no trouble finding it. A lot of legwork, perhaps, but they'll get there in the end.'

Her eyes were cautious now, watching me like a hawk's, hardly blinking. 'I'm sorry, I must have missed a turning somewhere. How did we get to the police?'

'Don't, Dr Maitland. Neither of us is stupid, so stop acting like we both are. I can imagine how distressed you were when you discovered what Sarah was doing, especially after she had denied you the chance to be the first to try the treatment. Even more so since your own operation. You went round to see her, to confront her with the outrage she'd perpetrated against you. And she dismissed you, didn't she? She didn't take your emotions

322

seriously, just like before when she'd dismissed your desires for motherhood.'

Helen Maitland shook her head slowly from side to side. 'I thought you said you were for real, Ms Brannigan. Sounds to me like you need treatment.'

'I don't think so. I think you're the one with the problem, Dr Maitland. You might give the impression of being cool, smart and in control, and God knows, you're good at it. But then you'd have to be, to kill your ex-lover and get away with it.'

She pushed off from the worktop and stood bristling at me, like one of her cats finding a strange tom on the front step. 'You've gone too far. It's time you were leaving,' she said, her voice low and thick with anger.

'I knew there was a temper lurking in there. It's the same temper that flared when you confronted Sarah and she dismissed your pain. It's the same temper that made you grab the nearest knife and thrust it under Sarah's ribs right into her heart.'

'Get out,' she said, anger and incredulity fighting in her. 'I don't have to take this from you.' She took a step towards me.

'You can't get away with it, Helen,' I said, my hands coming up automatically, palms facing her. 'Once the police start looking at you, they'll find the evidence. It's all there, once you accept that Sarah wasn't killed by a burglar. As soon as they match your voice against that 999 call, you're right there in the frame.'

'That's not going to happen.' The voice wasn't Helen Maitland's. It came from behind my right shoulder. I whirled round, straight into fighting stance, poised on the balls of my feet.

It was Flora. And in her hand was a shiny long-barrelled revolver.

24

Her small pale hands looked too fragile to wield a big cannon like that, but the barrel wasn't trembling. Whatever was driving Flora, it was powerful stuff. 'Flora,' Helen said calmly.

'It's all right, Helen,' Flora said, not taking her eyes off me.

Not with me it wasn't. I'd had enough of people waving guns at me. And frankly, I didn't think Flora was in the same league as Peter Lovell's gunmen. I glanced over at Helen Maitland and let my jaw go slack.

'My God!' I exclaimed.

Out of the corner of my eye, I saw Flora's hand jerk as her eyes swivelled towards Helen. On the instant, I launched myself, right leg jabbing up and out at shoulder height, my own voice roaring in my ears like Bruce Willis on heat. Everything suddenly seemed to be in slo-mo: my foot connecting with her shoulder, Flora toppling towards the floor, her gun arm flying out to one side, her finger tightening on the trigger as I landed on top of her, my body tensing against the expected blast of the gunshot.

A tongue of flame spurted from the gun barrel, then died as Flora released her pressure on the trigger.

I'd been scared shitless by a cigarette lighter.

I'd been scared, no two ways about it. But now I was really, really cross. When I'd walked through the door, I'd been feeling sympathetic. My instincts had all been to find a way out of this situation that didn't mean Helen Maitland spending the rest of her useful life behind bars. Now I wasn't so sure that was what I wanted.

'That was really silly, Flo,' Helen remarked in an offhand tone I'd never have been able to manage in the circumstances.

I disentangled myself from Flora's hair and limbs and pushed myself back to my feet. 'It was a lot more than silly,' I said. 'For fuck's sake, I could have really hurt you, you pillock.'

Flora threw the gun across the room. It clattered into the kitchen unit next to Helen. Then she curled up into a ball and burst into tears.

Helen picked up the lighter and laid it on the kitchen table, then moved to Flora's side. She crouched down and put her arms around her. It felt like Flora wept for a very long time, but it was less than five minutes by the kitchen clock. I didn't mind. It gave my heart time to return to its normal speed and rhythm.

Eventually Helen steered Flora into a kitchen chair and sat down beside her. 'Even a real gun wouldn't stop the police running those voice comparisons,' I said. 'I'm not daft enough to embark on a confrontation like this without leaving a bit of insurance behind in case some idiot pulls some brainless stunt where I actually do get hurt.'

'Then it's all over,' Flora said dully.

'How can you say that?' Helen demanded, pulling away. 'How can you think that I . . . That's crazy.'

'It's not crazy, actually.' Flora's voice was shaky. 'You see, if the police did start to run comparisons on that 999 tape, they would find a match.'

'Look, Flora, I don't know where you've got this idea from. I didn't kill Sarah,' Helen protested. 'I'm appalled you could think so.'

'I *don't* think so. No one knows the truth better than me.'

There was a silence as Helen and I digested the implications of Flora's words. Then the enormity of my second screw-up in two days hit me. I'd been right about the obsessive power of love being responsible for Sarah Blackstone's death. But I'd picked the wrong candidate for the killer. I'd been so convinced that Helen was the killer I hadn't even paid attention to Flora.

'Are you saying what I think you're saying?' Helen asked. There was an edge of horror in her voice.

'It was you, wasn't it?' I asked. Flora said

327

nothing. She didn't have to. We both knew the truth now. 'So tell me. Was I close? The scenario I painted? Was I on the right lines?'

Flora pushed her hair back with her free hand. 'Why are you so keen to know the details? So you can run to the nearest police station and turn me in?'

I sighed. 'The reason I became a private investigator was because I like to know the reasons why things happen. I understand the difference between the law and justice. I know that handing people over to the police isn't always the best way of ending things. If you want to prevent me going to the police, you've got more chance talking to me than you have trying to terrorize me. I have a client who has an interest in Sarah Blackstone's death. She has her own, very pressing, reasons for wanting to know the truth here.'

While I had been speaking, Helen Maitland had been rummaging through a drawer in the kitchen table. As I got to the end of a speech that owed more to the British commanding officer in *The Great Escape* than any innate nobility of spirit, she pulled out a bashed packet of Silk Cut. 'I knew there was a packet in here somewhere.' She ripped the cellophane off, flipped the top up, tore out the silver paper, shoved a cigarette up with her thumb and drew it out with her lips. She picked up the gun and lit the cigarette. Pure bathos.

'I think we're in deep shit here, Flora,' she said through a sigh of smoke, 'but from what I've seen of Ms Brannigan, it seems to me she's the person who can best deal with that. I think you should tell us what happened.'

Flora started crying again. I still wasn't impressed. 'I didn't *mean* to kill her,' she said through a veil of hair and tears.

'I know that,' Helen soothed in her practical, no-nonsense way. There was going to be a reckoning between these two, I could see that in her eyes. But Helen Maitland had the sense to realize this wasn't the time or the place. 'It's not your style, Flo.'

Flora did a bit more weeping, and Helen just sat there smoking, her eyes never leaving her lover. It was impossible even to guess at what was going on behind that blank stare. Finally Flora sat back, pushed her hair away from her face and scrubbed her eyes with her small hands, like a child who's been crying from tiredness. She took a deep breath, gave Helen a pleading look, then turned to face me. 'I really didn't mean to kill her,' she said. 'I didn't go there with that intention.'

'Tell me about it,' I said. Helen only crushed out one cigarette and lit a second.

Flora breathed out heavily through her nose. 'This isn't easy,' she complained.

'Easier than killing someone,' I remarked.

'Not really,' Flora said tremulously. 'That happened in the heat of the moment. Before I even knew I had the knife in my hand, she was dead. Telling you is a lot harder, you have to believe that, Helen.'

Helen nodded curtly. 'So what happened, Flora? I want to know just as badly as Ms Brannigan does.'

Flora pushed her hair back from her face and adopted a beseeching expression. I couldn't get a handle on this woman at all. The image she projected was of a fairly timid, vulnerable innocent. Then I'd get a flash from those dark eyes and I'd feel like an entire brigade of dark, supernatural nasties were dancing on my grave. I realized exactly what Maggie had meant about the dragon and the maiden. I could see that it might be a powerful erotic mixture, but it left me feeling pathetically grateful that the gun hadn't been for real. Flora was a woman who could easily have pulled the trigger then pulled the same 'I didn't mean it' routine over me that she was giving us now over Sarah Blackstone.

'Can't it wait till we're alone?' Flora pleaded.

'Ms Brannigan already knows too much for us to throw her out now,' Helen said. Somehow her words didn't scare me like Flora did. 'I suspect that telling her the whole story is the best chance we've got of salvaging something from this mess.' I couldn't have put it better myself.

Flora looked as if she was about to protest, then she registered the determination in her lover's face. 'It all started when Helen was diagnosed with cervical cancer,' she said.

'I know about that,' I interrupted her, not wanting to let her get into a flow of pathos too early in her narrative. 'It resulted in a complete hysterectomy What had that to do with the murder of Sarah Blackstone?'

Flora darted me a look of pure malice. It wasn't lost on Helen Maitland. This time, when she spoke, her voice was more brisk. 'Helen was desperate to have a child, and as soon as she was diagnosed, she got a gynaecologist friend of hers, not Sarah, to harvest her eggs for the next three months.'

'Why?' I asked.

Helen stared at the table and spoke rapidly. 'Part of me hoped that a full hysterectomy wouldn't be necessary, that even if I couldn't produce fertile eggs any more, I might just be able to have a child by artificial insemination, or even surrogacy. You know, get someone else to carry my child. So we took what eggs we could harvest before my surgery and froze them. It's dodgy, freezing eggs; nobody really knows yet how successful it is. But I had this crazy idea that even if I couldn't have a child myself, at least my genes might continue. And if all else had failed, at least I could have made an egg donation to someone who needed it.'

Not for the first time in the past few days, the desperate nature of the need to reproduce hit me between the eyes. I said a small prayer to the goddess of infertility that it would continue to avoid taking up residence in my soul. 'Right,' I said, determined to move this along and keep the emotional level as low key as possible. 'So

Helen had her eggs frozen. How does that get us to murder?'

'One morning a couple of months ago, Helen had a really strange letter in the post. It was from Manchester –'

'I know about that too,' I interrupted, partly to maintain control over events, partly to impress both of them with how much I'd already found out. 'It contained a baby's photograph and a lock of hair and a message of thanks.'

Helen's composure showed a crack for the first time. 'The baby was the spitting image of Sarah at the same age. I couldn't believe the similarity. I'd heard Sarah talking about the technical possibility of making babies from two women's eggs, and I realized that's what she was probably doing. I work with cystics, so I have access to DNA-testing facilities.'

'They were able to get DNA from the cut hairs?' I asked.

There are always researchers who love a challenge and one of the women at St Hilda's relished the chance to extract viable DNA from the hair shafts. I bribed one of my students to get a blood sample from Sarah. He told her it was for random testing in some experiment he was doing into some obscure aspect of blood chemistry, and she let him take it. The DNA test was very clear. Sarah was one of the parents of the child.' She was smoking now like she'd made it her lifelong ambition to be a forty-a-day woman.

This time, it was Flora who reached out, gripping Helen's free hand tightly. Helen continued, almost talking to herself. 'It was all the more bitter because that was the issue that split us up. I wanted a child desperately, but Sarah didn't. I knew subfertility treatment was close to the stage where it would be possible to make a child from two women. And she refused point-blank to do it with us. She said she wasn't prepared to experiment with my body. That if the experiment produced a monster, or even a handicapped child, she wouldn't be able to live with herself. Me, I thought it probably had more to do with the fact that she absolutely didn't want to share her life with a child. I eventually came to the conclusion I'd rather have the possibility of a child than the certainty of life with her. You can imagine the kind of rows . . .' Her voice tailed off into a quiet exhalation of smoke.

'You must have been devastated to discover she was experimenting with other women,' I said in the crass mode of television news reports.

Helen pulled a face. 'I think if she had been in front of me when I got the DNA results through from the lab, I might have killed her. But the more I thought about it, the more I realized that I was actually glad that I hadn't had her child. That I didn't want a daughter of mine to consist of half Sarah's genes. Distance doesn't lend enchantment, you know. It allows you to put things in perspective. I hadn't stopped wanting a child, but I'd stopped caring about Sarah. I didn't even hate her any more. Despised her, yes, because there wasn't anything in her life she wouldn't betray. So I didn't actually want to kill her for very long.'

'Long enough to tell Flora?' I asked softly.

Flora turned on me then, eyes wide and angry. 'Don't try and blame Helen. She said nothing of the sort to me. It was my idea to go and see Sarah. Helen didn't even know I was going.'

'So why did you go, if it wasn't to confront Sarah with her double-cross?'

'Yes,' Helen said. 'Why did you go to see her?'

Flora gave a weary smile. 'I went to try to persuade her to do for us what she'd done for those other women. My eggs and yours. So we could share a child.'

There was a long silence, Helen's eyes raking Flora's face as if she was trying to scour any falsehood from her words by reading her features. Then her head dropped into her hands. She didn't cry. After a few moments, she looked up, dry-eyed, and said, 'That is an extraordinary thing to say.'

'It's the truth,' Flora said. 'Why else would I have gone to see her?'

'I had no idea you felt like that.'

'What? That I loved you that much, or that I wanted a child that much?' Flora challenged, chin up.

'Either or both,' Helen said, her voice tired. 'What did Sarah say?'

Flora looked away, her face clouding over. I was starting to feel seriously redundant here. 'She laughed in my face. She said she wasn't going to give a baby to a brainless bimbo and a compulsive obsessive. So I told her that if she wouldn't co-operate, I'd go to the authorities and tell them exactly what she was doing.'

'Not a clever move,' Helen said, reaching for another cigarette. 'Sarah and threats were never a comfortable mix.' Her cool irony was starting to get to me. Sooner or later, an explosion was going to come. The longer she kept the lid on, the worse it was going to be. I hoped I'd be well out of the fallout zone when it did.

'How did she react to your threat?' I asked.

'She grabbed me by the lapels and shoved me up against the kitchen counter,' Flora said, still incredulous that someone in her world would do such a thing. 'She kept banging me against the counter, telling me I was a dirty blackmailing bitch and that she knew a lot of women who'd happily kill to keep the children she'd given them. I was terrified. She kept twisting her hand in my coat, it was so tight it was strangling me. I was desperate. I groped about on the worktop behind me and my hand touched a knife. I just grabbed it and thrust it up into her. I wasn't thinking, I just did it. And she sort of fell back onto the floor. I was standing there, holding the knife, watching her die. And I couldn't do a thing about it.'

'You could have called an ambulance,' Helen said, her voice cold.

'I did. I went straight to the phone box down the street and called an ambulance.'

'Not then, you didn't,' I said. 'You did one or two other things first. You cleared up any signs of a struggle. You unlocked the back door, leaving the key in the lock, went outside and smashed a pane of glass to make it look like a burglary. You took off your bloodstained mac and checked nobody was about, then you walked calmly out of the front door and up to the phone box on the corner. And then you phoned 999 and told the operator you'd just seen a black man running out of an open door on that street with a bloodstained knife. By which time Sarah Blackstone was dead.'

'It wouldn't have made any difference if I'd phoned straightaway,' Flora said desperately. 'She died so quickly. Honestly, Helen, she was dead in seconds.'

'Not that quickly,' I said coldly. 'She can't have been dead for long otherwise the ambulance crew would have told the police there was a discrepancy between the time of death and the time of the call-out.'

The way Flora looked at me, I was glad there wasn't a knife handy. 'Let's face it, Flora, you couldn't really allow her to live, could you?' Helen said bleakly. 'Not after what you'd done. No wonder you said to me the next day that you'd give me an alibi if the police came asking. You wanted to make sure you had one, didn't you? Just don't you dare ever say you did it for me.'

336

Flora said nothing. Helen faced me. 'I suspect there's a tape recorder whirring away in your handbag.'

My jacket pocket, actually, but I wasn't about to tell them that in case either of them got any clever ideas. 'Technology's got a bit smarter than that these days. I wouldn't still be alive if I didn't believe in insurance,' I said.

'So now you go to the police, is that it?'

'Helen!' Flora wailed. 'I can't go to jail!'

'I don't think that's necessary,' I said. 'The way Flora tells it, it sounds pretty much like self-defence that got out of hand. I don't think she's a risk to anyone else. I don't see a need for this to come out into the open.'

A cynical smile curled Flora's lip. 'You mean you don't want the world to know what that bitch Sarah was doing. I bet your client's one of those women she gave a baby to. She won't want that can of worms opened, will she?'

'Don't push your luck, Flora,' Helen said. 'Ms Brannigan holds your freedom in her hand. Or wherever she has her tape recorder stashed.'

I nodded. 'There are conditions to my silence,' I said. 'If anyone else is charged with Sarah's murder, I can't stand idly by. And if Sarah's secret work becomes public knowledge and I think it's anything to do with you, the tape goes to the police. Is that a deal?'

Epilogue

The cops picked up Peter Lovell's thugs a couple of weeks later in a routine raid on an after-hours shebeen in Bradford. They charged them with Tony's murder. The Crown Prosecution Service, who love bent coppers about as much as the police do, also added murder to Lovell's list of charges under the 'joint enterprise' principle. According to Della, who was on the point of giving up the elbow crutches and moving back into her house, it looks like they're all going to go down for a very long time. Oh, and Dan Druff and the Scabby Heided Bairns signed a deal with an indie record company on the strength of their first Nazi-free gig. They've promised me the first pressing of the first single to roll off the production line. I can hardly wait. It'll look great framed on my office wall. Not.

The law on fraud being what it is, Alan Williams and Sarah Constable probably thought they were unlucky to do any time at all. But the police did a good job, tying them into ripping off the bereaved in Birmingham, Durham and Plymouth. They each got eighteen months, which they'll do easy time in an open prison. It probably won't stop them dreaming up another nasty little scam when they come out, but at least it's got them off the streets for a few months. Their boss at Sell Phones did a bit better; all they could get him on was obtaining phone calls by deception, on account of the laws in this country affecting telecommunications are so archaic it's hard to nail anybody on anything to do with cellular phones. And since nobody much likes phone companies, he only got a suspended sentence. He lost the business, though, which is a kind of rough justice.

I also got round to talking to Josh. He gave me a load of toffee about how he wanted to devote some of his capital to working with small businesses, and I told him to cut the crap and get to the horses. The deal we worked out meant he bought Bill's share of the business, but in recognition of my sole contribution to the profits, my stake in the partnership was upgraded to fifty-five per cent. So I got an extra twenty per cent for nothing except running the agency and doing all the hard graft . . . Josh also promised me that when I can afford it, I can buy him out for what he'd paid plus the rate of inflation. I know a good deal when I see it. I nearly bit his hand off. The best part about it was that overnight I stopped wanting to rip Bill's arm off and hit him with the wet end. That Sheila's a really good laugh when you get to know her.

Alexis was happy with the way I sorted things out with Helen and Flora. With the single-mindedness of all parents-to-be, she didn't much mind who'd killed Sarah as long as it wasn't going to bounce back and wreck her happy little idyll. I never did tell her about Sarah Blackstone's nasty little trick of dropping her own eggs into the mix. I couldn't bring myself to say anything that would poison Alexis's happiness.

It's just as well I didn't. When Chris gave birth six months later, there was no mistaking the genetic source of Jay Appleton Lee's shock of jet black spikes. I swear the child cries with a Scouse accent.

I wish I could close the account there. Everything in credit, almost a happy ending. It's never been that neat in my experience. About two months after the showdown in her kitchen, Helen Maitland turned up at my office one afternoon around close of business. I left Shelley in charge and took her up to the café at the Cornerhouse for a herbal tea and a flapjack. Sometimes it's dead handy having an art cinema so close to the office.

Over a cup of wild strawberry she told me that Flora had just got a job in a university library in Wyoming. 'I didn't know they had universities in Wyoming,' I said. Cheap, I know, but I never claimed to be otherwise.

'Me neither,' Helen said, smiling with the half of her mouth that wasn't clamped around a cigarette.

340

'You looking for jobs, then?'

'You mean am I going with her?'

I nodded. 'I wondered if this was goodbye, don't worry, we're out of your life.'

'I suppose it is, in a way. Flora won't be back, and the one thing I'd pray for if I had any religion left is to be allowed to forget the whole sorry mess. So you can rest assured you won't be hearing any more of this from me. And Flora . . . well, she has too much to lose. The police never arrested anyone, never even seriously questioned them. The case is going to die now, just like Sarah did.'

'Better that way,' I said.

'Better all round,' she agreed. Her green eyes looked distantly over my shoulder. 'I'm not going to join Flora, though. Ever since she told us what had happened, I've scarcely been able to tolerate being in the same room as her. I may have stopped loving or hating Sarah, but I never wanted her to die, not even in our most terrible fights. And I hate the thought that I was the instrument of her death.'

'Don't be daft,' I protested. 'It was Flora who knifed her, not you. You didn't even know she was going to see her. You certainly didn't suggest it, that much was obvious from your reaction to Flora's confession.'

'Maybe not overtly. But she'd never have dreamed up the idea if my obsession hadn't planted it. If I hadn't told her the meaning of the photograph and the lock of hair, she'd never have gone near

Sarah. I may not have held the knife, but I carry the guilt.'

I could tell there was no point in trying to get her to change her mind about that. We finished our drinks, talking about anything except Sarah and Flora. Then she excused herself, saying she had someone to meet. I sat by the first-floor window and watched her stepping out across Oxford Road, dodging cars and buses. I watched her long stride as far as the corner of Princess Street, where she turned left and disappeared.

The story was in the next night's *Chronicle*. DOC-TOR DIES IN HOTEL PLUNGE. She'd taken a room on the top floor of the Piccadilly Hotel. She'd even brought a club hammer in her overnight bag in case the window didn't open far enough. At the inquest, they read out a note where she'd quoted that bit from Keats about ceasing on the midnight with no pain.

Some nights, I dream of Helen Maitland falling through the air, morphing into a bird and suddenly soaring just before she hits the ground. I hope someone somewhere is making babies with her eggs.

Clean Break

ACKNOWLEDGEMENTS

The usual gang all let me pick their brains to make this a better and more accurate book than it would otherwise have been – Coop, Uncle Lee, BB, Paula, Jai, Brother Brian, Lisanne and Jane, and Julia. I also scrounged assistance from Frankie Hegarty, Fairy Baillie and Diana Muir. Don't blame them if you spot any mistakes. To anyone who recognizes where we went on our holidays – my heartfelt sympathies.

To Chelsea fans everywhere,
in deepest sympathy;
God knows, you need something to
cheer you up.

1

I don't know much about art, but I know what I don't like. I don't like paintings that go walkabout after I've set up the security system. I especially don't like them when I've packed my business partner off to the Antipodes for two months with the calm assurance that I can handle things while he's gone.

The painting in question was a small Monet. When I say small, I mean in size, not in value. It would barely cover the hole my lover Richard punched in the wall of his living room in a moment of drunken ecstasy when Eric Cantona clinched the double for Manchester United, but it was worth a good dozen times as much as both our adjoining bungalows put together. Which, incidentally, they never will be. The painting depicted an apple tree in blossom and not a lot else. You could tell it was an apple tree; according to our office manager Shelley, that's because it was painted quite early on in Monet's career, before his eyesight

1

began to go and his whole world started to look like an Impressionist painting. Imagine, a whole artistic movement emanating from one bloke's duff eyesight. Amazing what you can learn from the Open University. Shelley started a degree course last year, and what she doesn't know about the history of art I'm certainly not qualified to uncover. It's not one of the course options in Teach Yourself Private Dicking.

The Monet in question, called, imaginatively enough, *Apple Tree in Blossom*, belonged to Henry Naismith, Lord of the Manor of Birchfield with Polver. Henry to his friends, and, thanks to John Major's classless society, to mere tradespeople like me. There were no airs and graces with Henry, but that didn't mean he didn't hide his thoughts and feelings behind his charming façade. That's how I knew it was serious when I picked up the phone to his perfect vowels that September morning. 'Kate? Henry Naismith,' he started. I leaned back in my chair, expecting the usual cheery chat about his recent exploits before we got down to the nuts and bolts. Not today. 'Can you come over to the house?' he asked.

I straightened up. This sounded like the kind of start to a Monday morning that makes me wish I'd stayed in bed. 'When did you have in mind, Henry?'

'As soon as you can. We ah . . . we had a burglary in the night and a chap from the police is popping round for more details. He'll want to know things

2

about the security system that I probably won't be able to answer, and I'd be awfully grateful if you could take a run over.' All this barely pausing for breath, never mind giving me the opportunity to ask questions.

I didn't have to check the diary to know that I had nothing more pressing than routine inquiries into the whereabouts of a company chairman whose directors were rather eager to ask him some questions about the balance sheet. 'No problem,' I said. 'What's missing?' I prayed it was going to be the TV and the video.

No such luck. There was silence on the end of the phone. I thought I could hear Henry drawing in a deep breath. 'The Monet,' he said tersely.

My stomach clenched. Birchfield Place was the first security system I'd designed and watched installed. My partner Bill Mortensen is the security expert, and he'd checked my work, but it was still down to me. 'I'm leaving now,' I said.

I drove out through the southern suburbs to the motorway on automatic pilot. Even the inevitable, ubiquitous roadworks didn't impinge. I was too busy reviewing Mortensen and Brannigan's involvement with Henry Naismith. When I'd seen his original appointment in the office diary, I'd thought Shelley was at the wind-up, especially since I'd been having one of my periodic anti-monarchy rants only the day before, triggered by the heir to the throne asserting that what was wrong with the country was not enough

3

Shakespeare and smacking of small children. Once I realized the appointment was for real, I'd expected some chinless wonder with the sort of inbred stupidity that's only found among the aristocracy and the population of isolated mountain villages. I couldn't have been more wrong, on both counts.

Henry Naismith was in his late twenties, built like an Australian lifeguard with the blonde hair to match and with more than enough chin to provide a boxer with a target. According to *Who's Who*, his only listed recreations were sailing and ocean yacht racing, something I could have guessed for myself the first time I saw him. He had sailor's eyes, always looking beyond me to some distant horizon only he could see. His face was burnished a ruddy brown by wind and sun, apart from the white creases round those dark blue eyes. He'd been educated at Marlborough and New College, Oxford. Even though I'd grown up there, I didn't think his city of dreaming spires and mine of car factories would give us much in common to reminisce about. He had the same clipped accent as Prince Charles, but in spite of that and everything else, I liked him. I liked anybody who was prepared to get off their backsides and graft. And Henry could graft, no messing. Anyone who tells you yacht racing is a holiday doesn't know an anchor from a wanker.

The newspaper archive database that we use had coloured in the outline. Henry had inherited his title, a black and white Tudor manor house in

4

Cheshire, a clutch of valuable paintings and not a lot of readies a couple of years before when his parents had been caught in an avalanche in some chic Alpine resort. Henry had been sailing in the Caribbean at the time. Life's a bitch, and then you marry one. Only Henry hadn't. Married, that is. He was right up there in the gossip columnists' lists of eligible bachelors. Maybe not in the top twenty, on account of the lack of dosh, but the good looks and the tasty gaff put him in the running nevertheless.

Henry had come to us precisely because of the serious deficiencies in the cashflow area. Because his father hadn't anticipated dying at the age of forty-seven, he hadn't got round to the sort of arrangements the landed gentry usually make to avoid the Exchequer getting their mitts on the widow's mite. Having done his sums, Henry realized the only way he was going to be able to hang on to the house and the art collection and still spend half the year at the helm of a racing yacht was to bite the bullet and open Birchfield Place to the day-trippers.

The great British public are notoriously sticky-fingered on the stately home circuit. You wouldn't think it to look at the coach-loads of little old ladies that roll up on bank holidays, but they'll walk off with anything that isn't actually nailed down, and one or two things that are. This makes insurance companies even more twitchy than usual when it comes to providing cover, which in turn makes

5

the security business a nice little earner for private investigation agencies like us. These days, security makes up about a quarter of our annual turnover, which is why Bill and I had decided I needed to learn that side of the business.

It's impossible to make any building impregnable, unless you brick up the doors and windows, which makes it hard to get a decent light to do your petit point. The best you can do is make it obvious that you've made it as hard as possible to get in, so the prospective burglar goes away discouraged and turns over the next manor down the road. To make sure I got it right, as well as picking Bill's brains I'd consulted my old friend Dennis, himself a recovering burglar. 'You know the one deterrent, Brannigan?' Dennis had demanded.

'Heat-seeking thermonuclear missiles?' I'd hazarded.

'A dog. You get a big Alsatian, give him the run of the place and your professional thief doesn't want to know. When I was at it, there wasn't an alarm system in the world that I wouldn't have a pop at. But dogs? Forget it.'

Unfortunately, clients aren't too keen on having Rottweilers running around on their priceless Oriental carpets. They're too worried about finding dog hairs – or worse – on the Hepplewhite. So Birchfield Place had relied, like most stately homes, on a state-of-the-art mix of hard-wired detectors on doors and windows, passive infrared detectors at all key points and pressure-activated alert pads in front of any items of significance. Given the fail-safes I'd put in place, I couldn't for the life of me see how anyone could have got through my system undetected without setting off enough bells to drive Quasimodo completely round the twist.

I turned off the motorway and headed into the depths of the leafy Cheshire stockbroker, soap star and football player belt. As usual, I almost missed the gap in the tall hedgerow that marked the end of Birchfield Place's drive. The trippers' entrance was round the back, but I had no intention of parking in a field half a mile from the house. I yanked the wheel round just in time and turned on to a narrow ribbon of road curling between fields where placid sheep didn't even glance up from their chewing as I passed. I always feel slightly edgy out in the country; I don't know the names of anything and very quickly develop anxiety about where my next meal is coming from. Give me an urban landscape where no sensible sheep would think for even a fleeting moment it might safely graze. The field gave way to thick coppices of assorted trees that looked like they'd been on the planet longer than my Granny Brannigan. Then, suddenly, the drive took a sharp right-hand bend and I shot out of the trees to a full frontal view of Birchfield Place.

Built by some distant Naismith who had done some unmentionable service to his monarch, the house looked as if it should be on a postcard or a jigsaw. The passage of time had skewed its black beams and white panels just enough to make sure no self-respecting building society would grant you a mortgage on it. It never looked real to me.

I pulled up beside an anonymous Ford which I assumed belonged to the police on account of the radio. A peacock screamed in the distance, more shattering to my composure than any amount of midnight sirens. I only knew it was a peacock because Henry had told me the first time one had made me jump out of my skin. Before I could reach out for the ancient bell-pull, the door swung open and Henry smiled apologetically at me. 'I really appreciate this, Kate,' he said.

'All part of the service,' I said reassuringly. 'The police here?'

'An Inspector Mellor from the Art Squad,' Henry said as he led the way across the inner courtyard to the Great Hall, where the Impressionist paintings hung incongruously. 'He doesn't say much.'

We passed through the Hall Porch, whose solid oak door looked like it had taken a few blows from a heavy sledge-hammer. At the door of the Great Hall, I put out a hand to delay Henry. 'So what exactly happened?'

Henry rubbed his jaw. 'The alarm woke me. Just before three, according to the clock. I checked the main panel. It said Hall Porch, Great Hall door, Great Hall and pressure pads. I phoned the police to confirm it wasn't a false alarm, and ran downstairs. When I got to the hall, there was nobody in sight and the Monet was gone. They must have been in and out again in less than five minutes.' He sighed. 'They obviously knew what they were looking for.'

'Didn't the beeper on the courtyard security lights waken you?' I asked, puzzled.

Henry looked sheepish. 'I turned the beeper off. We've been having a bit of a problem with foxes, and I got fed up with being wakened up night after night.' I said nothing. I hoped the look on my face said it for me. 'I know, I know,' Henry said. 'I don't think Inspector Mellor's overly impressed either. Shall we?'

I followed him into the hall. It was a surprisingly bright room for the period. It was two storeys high, with a whitewashed vaulted roof and gallery for Blondel unplugged. The wall that gave on to the inner courtyard had a couple of feet of wood panelling above floor level, then it was hundreds of tiny leaded panes of glass to a height of about eight feet. The outer wall's panelling was about four feet high before it gave way to more windows. I didn't envy the window cleaner. At the far end was a raised dais where Henry's distant ancestors had sat and lorded it over the plebs and railed against the iniquities of the window tax. It was around the dais that the paintings hung. A tall, thin man was stooped like a crane over the space where the Monet used to be. As we entered, he turned towards us and fixed me with a glum stare.

Henry performed the introductions while Inspector Mellor and I weighed each other up. He looked more patrician than Henry, with a high forehead over a beaky nose and a small, cupid's bow mouth. At his request, I ran him through the security arrangements. He nodded noncommittally as he listened, then said, 'Not a lot more you could have done, short of having CCTV.'

'Professional job, yeah?' I said.

'No doubt about it. They obviously chose their target, cased the place thoroughly, then did a quick in and out. No identifiable forensic traces, according to my colleagues who turned up after the event.' Mellor looked as depressed as I felt.

'Does it put you in mind of anyone in particular?' I asked.

Mellor shrugged. 'I've seen jobs like this, but we haven't managed an arrest on any of them yet.'

Henry closed his eyes and sighed. 'Is there any chance of getting my Monet back?' he asked wearily.

'If I'm honest, sir, not a lot. Thieves like this only take what they've already got a market for,' Mellor said. 'Sooner or later, we'll get a lucky break and we'll nail them. It could be on this case. What I'd like to do is send a couple of my lads over when your staff are next in. These thieves will have been round the house more than once. It's just possible one of your attendants noticed repeat visitors.'

'They'll be in at half past nine on Thursday,' Henry said. 'The house is closed to the public on Mondays, Tuesdays and Wednesdays, excepting bank holidays.'

Mellor turned away and spent a few minutes

studying the Boudin, the Renoir and the two Pissarros that flanked the space where the Monet had been. 'Personally,' he said softly, 'I'd have gone for the Boudin.'

Not me. The Monet would have looked much better with my colour scheme. But maybe Inspector Mellor's living room was blue-based rather than green, cream and peach. While Henry escorted Mellor off the premises, I mooched around the hall, wondering what to do next. Mellor's plan to interrogate the staff had disposed of the only idea I had for pursuing any kind of investigation. I slumped in the attendant's chair by the door and stared down the hall at the wires sticking out of the ancient panelling where the Monet had been attached to the alarm system and the wall. Inspiration failed to strike; but then, nothing does in this country any more.

When Henry came back, I forced myself upright and said brightly, 'Well, Henry, Mellor didn't sound too optimistic about what the forces of law and order can achieve. Looks like it's down to me to get your Monet back.'

Henry tugged at the lobe of his ear and looked uncomfortable. 'Is there much point, Kate?' he asked. 'I mean, if the specialists don't know where to start looking, how can you expect to succeed?'

'People have a tendency to tell me things they don't necessarily want to share with the police. And that includes insurance companies. I also have more unorthodox sources of information.

I'm sure I can develop leads the police will never encounter.' It was all true. Well, all except the last sentence.

'I don't know, Kate. These are professional thieves. Looking at the state of the porch door, they're clearly quite comfortable with a considerable degree of violence. I'm not sure I'm entirely happy about you pursuing them,' he said dubiously.

'Henry, I might only be five foot three, but I can look after myself,' I said, trying not to think about the last occasion where I'd told the men in my life the same damn lie. The scar on my head was just a distant twinge when I brushed my hair now, but the scar inside went a lot deeper. I hadn't exactly lost my bottle; I'd just acquired an overdose of wariness.

'Besides,' I carried on, seeing his look of frank disbelief, 'you're entitled to the first thirty hours of my time for free, according to your contract.'

'Ah. Yes. Of course.' His reserve was nailed firmly in place again, the eyes locked on the middle distance.

'Apart from anything else, me nosing around will convince your insurance company that you're not trying it on,' I added.

His eyes narrowed, like a man who's seen a bloody great wave heading straight for his bows. 'Why should they think that?' he said sharply.

'It wouldn't be the first time somebody's set up their own burglary for the insurance,' I said. 'It

12

happens all the time round where I live.' A frown flickered across Henry's face. 'There's nothing you want to tell me, Henry, is there?' I added apprehensively.

'There's no earthly reason why I should arrange this,' he said stiffly. 'The police and the insurance company are welcome to check the books. We're making a profit here. House admissions are up on last year, the gift shop has increased its turnover by twenty-five per cent and the Great Hall is booked for banquets almost every Saturday between now and February. The only thing I'm concerned about is that I'm due to leave for Australia in three weeks and I'd like the matter resolved by then.'

'I'd better get weaving, in that case,' I said mildly.

I drove back to Manchester with a lot on my mind. I don't like secrets. It's one of the reasons I became a private eye in the first place. I especially don't like them when they're ones my client is keeping from me.

2

The atrium of Fortissimus Insurance told me all I needed to know about where Henry's massive premiums were going. The company had relocated in Manchester from the City, doubtless tempted by the wodges of cash being handed out by various inner city initiative programmes. They'd opted for a site five minutes' walk down Oxford Road from the rather less palatial offices of Mortensen and Brannigan. Handy, we'd thought, if they ever needed any freelance investigating, though if they had done, it hadn't been our door they'd come knocking on. They probably preferred firms with the same steel-and-glass taste in interior decor, and prices to match.

Like a lot of new office complexes in Manchester, Fortissimus had smacked a brand new modern building behind a grandiose Victorian façade. In their case, they'd acquired the front of what had been a rather grand hotel, its marble and granite buffed to a shine more sparkling than its native century had ever seen. The entrance hall retained some of the original character, but the glassed-in atrium beyond the security desk was one hundred per cent *fin de* quite another *siècle*. The pair of receptionists had clearly absorbed their customer care course. Their grooming was immaculate, their smiles would have made a crocodile proud, and the mid-Atlantic twang in their 'Good morning, how may I help you?' stopped short of making my ears bleed. Needless to say, they were as misleading as the building's façade. After I'd given them my card, asked for Michael Haroun and told them his department, I still had to kick my heels for ten minutes while they ran their debriefing on the weekend's romantic encounters, rang Mr Haroun, filled out a visitor's pass and told me Mr Haroun would be waiting for me at the lift.

I emerged on the fifth floor to find they'd been economical with the truth. There was no Mr Haroun, and no one behind the desk marked 'Claims Inquiries' either. Before I could decide which direction to head in, a door down the hallway opened and someone backed out, saying, 'And I want to compare those other cases. Karen, dig out the files, there's a love.'

He swivelled round on the balls of his feet and *déjà vu* swept over me. Confused, I just stood and stared as he walked towards me. When he got closer, he held out his hand and said, 'Ms Brannigan? Michael Haroun.'

For a moment, I was speechless and paralysed.

I must have been gawping like a starving goldfish, for he frowned and said, 'You are Ms Brannigan?' Then, suspicion appeared in his liquid sloe eyes. 'What's the matter? Am I not what you expected? I can assure you, I am head of the claims division.'

Power returned to my muscles and I hurriedly reached out and shook his hand. 'Sorry,' I stammered. 'Yes, I . . . Sorry, you're the spitting image of . . . somebody,' I stumbled on. 'I was just taken aback, that's all.'

He gave me a look that told me he'd already decided I was either a racist pig or I didn't have all my chairs at home. His smile was strained as he said, 'I didn't realize I had a doppelgänger. Shall we go through to my office and talk?'

Wordlessly, I nodded and followed his broad shoulders back down the hall. He moved like a man who played a lot of sport. It wasn't hard to imagine him in the same role as I'd first seen his likeness.

When I was about fourteen, we'd gone on a school trip to the British Museum. I'd been so engrossed in the Rosetta Stone, I'd got separated from the rest of the group and wandered round for ages looking for them. That's how I stumbled on the Assyrian bas-reliefs. As soon as I saw them, I understood for the first time in my life that it wasn't entirely bullshit when critics said that great art speaks directly to us. These enormous carvings of the lion hunt didn't so much speak as resonate inside my chest like the bass note of an organ. I fell in love with the archers and the charioteers, their shoulder-length hair curled as tight as poodle fur, their profiles keen as sparrowhawks. I must have spent an hour there that day. Every time I went to London on shopping trips after that, I always found an excuse to slip away from my mates as they trawled Oxford Street so I could nip to the museum for a quick tryst with King Ashurbanipal. If Aslan had come along and breathed life into the carving of the Assyrian king, he would have walked off the wall looking just like Michael Haroun, his glowing skin the colour of perfect roast potatoes. OK, so he'd swapped the tunic for a Paul Smith shirt, Italian silk tie and chinos, but you don't make much progress up the corporate ladder wearing a mini-skirt unless you're a woman. Just one look at Michael Haroun and I was an adoring adolescent all over again, Richard a distant memory.

I followed Haroun meekly into his office. The opulence of the atrium hadn't quite made it this high. The furniture was functional rather than designed to impress. At least he overlooked the recently renovated Rochdale Canal (European funding), though the view of the Canal Café must have been a depressing reminder of the rest of the world enjoying itself while he was working. We settled down on the L-shaped sofa at right angles to each other, my adolescent urge to jump on him held in check by the low coffee table between us. Haroun dumped the file he'd been carrying on the table. 'I hear good things about your agency, Ms Brannigan,' he said. From his tone, I gathered he

17

couldn't quite square what he'd heard with my moonstruck gaze.

I forced myself to get a grip and remember I was twice the age of that romantic teenager. 'You've obviously been talking to the clients who haven't been burgled,' I said in something approaching my normal voice.

'No security system is burglar-proof,' he said gloomily.

'But some are better than others. And ours are better than most.'

'That's certainly how it looked when we first agreed the premium. It's one of the factors we consider when we set the rate. That and how high-risk the area is.'

'You don't have to tell me. My postcode is M13,' I complained.

He pulled a face and sucked his breath in sharply, the way plumbers are trained to do when they look at your central heating system. 'And I thought you security consultants made a good living.'

'It's not all a hellhole,' I said sharply.

He held his hands up and grinned. I felt the years slide away again and struggled to stay in the present. 'Henry Naismith called to say you'd be coming in. He faxed me a preliminary claim,' he said.

'I'm investigating the theft on Henry's behalf, and he thought it might be helpful if we had a chat,' I said briskly.

'My pleasure,' he said. 'Of course, one of our staff investigators will also be looking into it, but I see no reason why we can't talk to you as well. Can you run it past me?'

I went through everything I'd learned from Henry and Inspector Mellor. Haroun took notes. 'Just as a matter of interest,' I finished up, 'Inspector Mellor mentioned they'd had other burglaries with a similar style. Were any of them insured with you?'

Haroun nodded. 'Yes, unfortunately. Off the top of my head, I'd say three others in the last nine months. And that's where we have a problem.'

'We as in you and me, or we as in Fortissimus?'

'We as in Mr Naismith and Fortissimus.'

'Does that mean you're not going to tell me about it?'

Haroun stared down at the file. 'Client confidentiality. You should understand that.'

'I wouldn't be here if Henry didn't trust me. Why don't you give him a call and confirm that you can tell me anything you would tell him? That way, I get it from the horse's mouth rather than via Chinese whispers.'

His straight brows twitched. 'Even if he agreed, it wouldn't be fair of me to have the conversation with you before I have it with him.'

'So get Henry over. I don't mind waiting.' As long as I can keep looking at you, I added mentally.

Haroun inclined his head, conceding. 'I'll call him,' he said.

He was gone for the best part of ten minutes. Instead of fishing a computer magazine out of my shoulder bag, or dictating a report into my micro-cassette recorder, I daydreamed. What about is nobody's business but mine.

When Haroun came back, he looked serious. 'I've explained the situation to Mr Naismith, and he was quite insistent that I should discuss the ramifications with you.'

I was too well brought up to say, 'I told you so,' but according to Richard I've cornered the market in smug smiles. I hoped I wasn't displaying one of them right then. 'So, tell me about it,' I said, locking eyes.

Haroun held my gaze for a long few seconds before turning back to his file. 'As I said, we've had other incidents very similar to this. These thefts have all been from similar properties – medium-sized period properties that are open to the public. In each case, the thieves have broken in as near to the target as they could get. In a couple of cases, they've smashed through a window, but in a property like Birchfield Place, that obviously wasn't appropriate. They ignore the alarms, go straight to the object they're after, whip it off the wall or out of its case and get out. We estimate the longest they've been inside a property is five minutes. In most cases, that's barely enough time to alert the police or the security guards, never mind get anyone to the site.'

'Very professional,' I commented. 'And?'

'We're very unhappy about it. It's costing us a lot of money. Normally, we'd simply have to bite the bullet and increase premiums accordingly.'

'I hear the sound of a "but" straining at the leash,' I said.

'You have very acute hearing, Ms Brannigan.'

'Kate,' I smiled.

'Well, Kate,' he said, echoing the smile, 'here comes the "but". The first of our clients to be robbed in this way was targeted again three months later. Following that, my bosses took a policy decision that in future, after stately homes had been robbed once, we would refuse to reinsure unless and until their security was increased to an acceptable level.'

He might have looked like an ancient Assyrian, but Michael Haroun sounded exactly like a twentieth-century insurance man. We won't make a drama out of a crisis; we'll make a full-scale tragic grand opera. Pay your spiralling premiums for ten years good as gold, and then when you really need us, we'll be gone like thieves in the night. Nothing like it for killing adolescent fantasies stone dead. 'And what exactly is your definition of "an acceptable level"?' I asked, hoping he was receiving the cold sarcasm I was sending.

'Obviously, it varies from case to case.'

'In Henry's case then?'

Haroun shrugged. 'I'd have to get one of our assessors out there to make an accurate judgement.'

'Go on, stick your neck out. I know that comes as easy to an insurance man as it does to an ostrich, but give it a go.' I kept my voice light with an effort. This was my security system he was damning.

He scowled, obviously needled. 'Based on past

experience, I would suggest a security guard on a 24-hour basis in the rooms where the most valuable items are sited.'

I shook my head in disbelief. 'You really believe in getting shut of clients who have the temerity to get robbed, don't you?'

'On the contrary. We want to ensure that neither we nor our clients are exposed to unacceptable losses,' he said defensively.

'The cost of that kind of security could make the difference between profit and loss to an operation the size of Henry's. You must know that.'

Haroun spread his hands out and shrugged. 'He can always put up the admission charges if it's that crucial to the economics of running the place.'

'So you're saying that as of now Birchfield Place is uninsured?'

'No, no, you misunderstand me. But we will retain a portion of the payout on the stolen property until the security levels are rendered acceptable. Kate, we do care about our clients, but we have a business to run too, you must see that.' His eyes pleaded, and my fury melted. This was bad for my business, so I forced myself to my feet.

'We'll keep in touch,' I said.

'I'd like that,' he said, getting to his feet and nailing me with the sincerity in his voice.

As we walked back to the lift, my brain checked in again. 'One more thing,' I said. 'How come I haven't been reading about these raids in the papers?'

Haroun smiled the thin smile of a lizard. 'We like

to keep things like this as low profile as possible,' he said. 'It does our clients' business no good at all if the public gain the impression that the choicest exhibits in their collections are no longer there. The thefts have been quite widely scattered, and the policy has been only to release the information to local press, and even then to keep it very low key. You know the sort of thing: "Thieves broke in to Bloggs Manor last night, but were disturbed before they could remove the Manor's priceless collection of bottle tops."'

'You just omit to mention that they had it away on their toes with the Constable,' I said cynically.

'Something like that,' he agreed. The lift pinged and I stepped inside as the doors opened. 'Nice talking to you, Kate.'

'We must do it again some time,' I said before the doors cut him off from me. The day was looking up. Not only had I met Michael Haroun, but I knew where to go next.

I'm convinced that the security staff at the *Manchester Evening Chronicle* think I work there. Maybe it's because I know the door combination. Or maybe it's because I'm in and out of the building with a confident wave several times a week. Either way, it's handy to be able to stroll in and out at will. Their canteen is cheap and cheerful, a convenient place to refuel when I'm at the opposite end of town from the office. That day, though, I wasn't after a bacon butty and a mug of tea. My target was Alexis Lee, the

Chronicle's crime correspondent and my best buddy.

I walked briskly down the newsroom, no one paying any attention. I could probably walk off with the entire computer network before anyone would notice or try to stop me. Mind you, if I'd laid a finger on the newsdesk TV, I'd have been lynched before I'd got five yards.

I knew Alexis was at her desk. I couldn't actually see her through the wall of luxuriant foliage that surrounds her corner of the office. But the spiral of smoke climbing towards the air-conditioning vent was a clear indicator that she was there. When they installed the computer terminals at the *Chronicle*, the management tried to make the newsroom a no-smoking zone. The policy lasted about five minutes. Separating journalists from nicotine is about as easy as separating a philandering government minister from his job.

I stuck my head round the screen of variegated green stuff. Alexis was leaning back in her seat, feet propped up on the rim of her wastepaper bin, dabbing her cigarette vaguely at her mouth as she frowned at her terminal. I checked out her anarchic black hair. Its degree of chaos is a fairly accurate barometer of her stress levels. The more uptight she gets, the more she runs her hands through it. Today, it looked like I could risk interrupting her without getting a rich gobful of Scouse abuse.

'I thought they paid you to work,' I said, moving through the gap in the leaves into her jungle cubbyhole.

She swung round and grinned. 'All right, KB?' she rasped in her whisky-and-cigarettes voice.

'I think I'm in love, but apart from that, I'm fine.' I pulled up the other chair.

Alexis snorted and went into Marlene Dietrich growl. *'Falling in love again, never wanted to,'* she groaned. *'Though I'm ninety-two, I can't help it.* I've told you before, it's about time you got shut of the wimp.' She and Richard maintain this pretence of hostility. He's always giving her a bad time for being a siren chaser, and she pretends to despise him for devoting his life to the trivia of rock journalism. But underneath, I know there's a lot of affection and respect.

'Who said anything about Richard?' I asked innocently.

'And there's me thinking you two were getting things sorted out between you,' she sighed. 'So who's the lucky man? I mean, I'm assuming that you haven't seen the light, and it is a fella.'

'His name's Michael Haroun. But don't worry, it's only lust. It'll pass as soon as I have a cold shower.'

'So what does he do, this sex object?'

I pulled a face. 'You're going to laugh,' I said.

'Probably,' Alexis agreed. 'So you might as well get it over with.'

'He's in insurance.'

I'd been right. She did laugh, a deep, throaty guffaw that shook the leaves. I half expected an Amazonian parrot to fly out from among the undergrowth and join in. 'You really know how to pick them, don't you?' Alexis wheezed.

'You don't pick sex objects, they just happen,' I said frostily. 'Anyway, nothing's going to happen, so it's all academic anyway. Things between me and Richard might have seen better days, but it's nothing we can't fix.'

'So you don't want me to call Chris and get her to build a brick wall across the conservatory?'

Alexis's girlfriend Chris is the architect who designed the conservatory that runs along the back of the two houses Richard and I live in, linking them yet allowing us our own space. It had been the perfect solution for two people who want to be together but whose lifestyles are about as compatible as Burton and Taylor. 'Restrain yourself, Alexis. I'm not about to let my hormones club my brain into submission.'

'Is that it, then? You come in here, interrupting the creative process, just to tell me nothing's happening?'

'No, I only gave you the gossip so you wouldn't complain that I was only here to exploit you,' I said.

Alexis blew out a cloud of smoke and a sigh. 'All right, what do you want to know?'

'Is that any way to speak to a valued contact who's brought you a story?' I asked innocently.

Alexis tipped forward in her seat and crushed out her cigarette in an already brimming ashtray. 'Why do I have the feeling that this is the kind of gift that takes more assembling than an Airfix kit?'

3

I left Alexis to hassle the police of six counties in search of the story we both knew was lurking somewhere and headed back to Mortensen and Brannigan. Shelley was busy on the phone, so I went straight through to my office. I stopped in my tracks on the threshold. I heard Shelley finish her call and swung round to glare at her. 'What exactly is that?' I demanded.

She didn't look up from the note she was writing. 'What does it look like? It's a weeping fig.'

'It's fake,' I said through gritted teeth.

'Silk,' she corrected me absently.

'And that makes it OK?'

Shelley finally looked up. 'Every six weeks you buy a healthy, thriving, living plant. Five weeks later, it looks like locust heaven. The weeping fig will have paid for itself within six months, and even you can't kill a silk plant,' she said in matter-of-fact tones that made my fingers itch to get round her throat.

'If I wanted a schneid plant, I'd have bought one,' I said.

'You sound . . .'

' "Like one of my kids",' I finished, mimicking her calm voice. 'You don't understand, do you? It's the challenge. One day, I'm going to find a plant that runs riot for me.'

'By which time the planet will be a desert,' Shelley said, tossing her head so that the beads she had plaited into her hair jangled like a bag of marbles.

I didn't dignify that with a reply. I simply marched into my office, picked up the weeping fig and dropped it next to her desk. 'You like it so much, you live with it,' I said, stomping back to my office. If she was going to treat me like one of her teenage kids, I might as well enjoy the tantrum. I pulled the brownish remains of the asparagus fern out of the bin and defiantly dumped it on the windowsill.

Before I could do anything more, my phone rang. 'What now?' I barked at Shelley.

'Call for you. A gentleman who refuses to give his name.'

'Did you tell him we don't do matrimonials?'

'Of course I did. I'm not the one who's pre-menstrual.'

I bit back a snarl as Shelley put the call through. 'Kate Brannigan,' I said. 'How can I help you?'

'I need your help, Ms Brannigan. It's an extremely confidential matter. Brian Chalmers from PharmAce recommended you.'

'We're noted for our client confidentiality,' I reeled off. 'As you doubtless know if you've spoken to Brian. But I do need to know who I'm talking to.'

There was a moment's hesitation, long enough for me to hear sufficient background noise to realize my caller was speaking from a bar. 'My name's Trevor Kerr. I think the company I run is being blackmailed, and I need to talk to you about it.'

'Fine,' I said. 'Why don't I come round to your office this afternoon and have a chat about it?'

'Christ, no,' Kerr said, clearly alarmed. 'The last thing I want is for the blackmailers to find out I'm talking to a private detective.'

One of the ones that watches too many movies. That was all I needed to make my day. 'No problem. You come to me.'

'I don't think that's a good idea. You see, I think they're watching me.'

Just when you thought it was safe to pick up the phone . . . 'I know how disturbing threats can be when you're not accustomed to being on the receiving end,' I tried. 'Perhaps we could meet on neutral ground. Say in the lounge of the Midland?'

The reassuring tone hadn't worked. 'No,' Kerr said urgently. 'Not in public. It's got to look completely normal. Have you got a boyfriend, Ms Brannigan?'

*   *   *

I should have put the phone down then and there, I realized four hours later as I tried to explain to Richard that a crumpled cream linen suit might be fine for going on the razz with Mick Hucknall, but there was no way it would help him to pass as a member of the Round Table. 'Bloody hell, Brannigan,' he grumbled. 'I'm old enough to dress myself.'

I ignored him and raked through his wardrobe, coming up with a fairly sober double-breasted Italian suit in dark navy. 'This is more like it,' I said.

Richard scowled. 'I only wear that to funerals.'

I threw it on the bed. 'Not true. You wore it to your cousin's wedding.'

'You forgotten her husband already? Anyway, I don't see why you're making me get dressed up like a tailor's dummy. After the last time I helped you out, you swore you'd never let me near your work again,' he whinged as he shrugged out of the linen jacket.

'Believe me, if Bill wasn't out of the country, I wouldn't be asking you,' I said grimly. 'Besides, not even you can turn a Round Table treasure hunt and potluck supper into a life-threatening situation.'

Richard froze. 'That's a bit below the belt, Brannigan,' he said bitterly.

'Yeah, well, I'm going next door to find something suitably naff in my own wardrobe. Come through when you're ready.'

I walked down Richard's hall and cut through his living room to the conservatory. Back in my own house, I allowed myself a few moments of deep breathing to regain my equilibrium. A few months before, I had enlisted Richard's help in what should have been a straightforward case of car fraud. Only, as they say in all the worst police dramas, it all went pear-shaped. Spectacularly so. Richard ended up behind bars, his life in jeopardy, and I nearly got myself killed tracking down the real villains. As if that hadn't been enough, I'd also been landed with looking after his eight-year-old son Davy. And me with the maternal instincts of a Liquorice Allsort.

The physical scars had healed pretty quickly, but the real damage was to our relationship. You'd think he'd have been grateful that I sorted everything out. Instead, he'd been distant, sarcastic and out a lot. It hadn't been grim all the time, of course. If it had been, I'd have knocked it on the head weeks earlier. We still managed to have fun together, and sometimes for nearly a week things would be just like they used to be; lots of laughs, a few nights out, communal Chinese takeaways and spectacular sex. Then the clouds would descend, usually when I was up to the eyeballs in some demanding job.

This was the first time since our run-in with the drug warlords that I'd asked Richard to do anything connected with work. I'd argued with Trevor Kerr that there must be a less complicated way for us to meet, but Clever Trevor was convinced that he was right to take precautions. I nearly asked him why he was hiring a dog and still barking himself, but I bit my tongue. Business hadn't been so great lately that I could afford to antagonize new clients before they were actually signed up.

With a sigh, I walked into my own bedroom and considered the options. Richard says I don't have a wardrobe, just a collection of disguises. Looking at the array of clothes in front of me, I was tempted to agree with him. I pulled out a simple tailored dress in rough russet silk with a matching bolero jacket. I'd bought it while I'd been bodyguarding a Hollywood actress who was over here for a week to record an episode in a Granada drama series. She'd taken one look at the little black number I'd turned up in on the first evening and silently written me a cheque for five hundred pounds to go and buy 'something a little more chic, hon'. I'm not proud; I took the money and shopped. Alexis and I hadn't had so much fun in years.

I stepped into the dress and reached round to zip it up. Richard got there before me. He leaned forward and kissed me behind the ear. I turned to gooseflesh and shivered. 'Sorry,' he said. 'Bad day. Let's go and see how the other half lives.'

The address Trevor Kerr had given me was in Whitefield, a suburb of mostly semis just beyond the perennial roadworks on the M62. It's an area that's largely a colony of the upwardly mobile but not strictly Orthodox Jews who make up a significant proportion of Manchester's population. Beyond the streets of identical between-the-wars semis lay our destination, one of a handful of architect-designed developments where the serious money has gravitated. My plumber got the contract for one of them, and he told me about a conversation with one of his customers. My plumber thought the architect had made a mistake, because the plans showed plumbing for four dishwashers – two in the kitchen and two in the utility room. When he queried it, the customer looked at him as if he was thick as a yard of four-by-two and said, 'We keep kosher and we entertain a lot.' There's nothing you can say to that.

The house I'd been directed to looked more Frankenstein than Frank Lloyd Wright. It had more turrets and crenellations than Windsor Castle, all in bright red Accrington brick. 'Sometimes it's nice to be potless,' Richard remarked as we parked. It had a triple garage and hard-standing for half a dozen cars, but tonight was clearly party night. Richard's hot pink Volkswagen Beetle convertible looked as out of place as Cinderella at a minute past midnight. When the hostess opened the door, I smiled. 'Good evening,' I said. 'We're with Trevor Kerr,' I added.

The frosting on her immaculate coiffure spilled over on to the hostess's smile. 'Do come in,' she said.

The man who'd been hovering in the hall behind her stepped forward and said, 'I'm Trevor Kerr.' He signalled with his eyebrows towards the stairs and we followed him up into a den that looked like it had been bought clock, stock and panel from a country house. The only incongruity was the computer and fax machine smack in the middle of the desk. 'We won't be disturbed here,' he said. 'It'll be at least half an hour before the host distributes the clues and we move off. Perhaps your friend would like to go downstairs and help himself to the buffet?'

I could hear Richard's hackles rising. 'Mr Barclay is a valued associate of Mortensen and Brannigan. Anything you say is safe with him,' I said stiffly. I dreaded to think how many people Richard could upset at a Round Table potluck buffet.

'That's right,' he drawled. 'I'm not just scenery.'

Kerr looked uncomfortable but he wasn't really in a position to argue. As he settled himself in an armchair, we studied each other. Not even a hand-stitched suit could hide a body gone ruinously to seed. I was tempted to offer some fashion advice, but I didn't think he'd welcome the news that this year bellies are being worn inside the trousers. He couldn't have been much more than forty, but his eyes would have been the envy of any self-respecting bloodhound and his jowls would have set a bulldog a-quiver. The only attractive feature the man possessed was a head of thick, wavy brown hair with a faint silvering at the temples.

'Well, Mr Kerr?' I said.

He cleared his throat and said, 'I run Kerrchem. You probably haven't heard of us, but we're quite a large concern. We've got a big plant out at

Farnworth. We manufacture industrial cleaning materials, and we do one or two domestic products for supermarket own-brands. We pride ourselves on being a family business. Anyway, about a month ago, I got a letter in the post at home. As far as I can remember, it said I could avoid Kerrchem ending up with the same reputation as Tylenol for a very modest sum of money.'

'Product tampering,' Richard said sagely.

Kerr nodded. 'That's what I took it to mean.'

'You said: "as far as I can remember",' I remarked. 'Does that mean you haven't got the note?'

Kerr scowled. 'That's right. I thought it was some crank. It looked ridiculous, all those letters cut out of a newspaper and Sellotaped down. I binned it. You can't blame me for that,' he whined.

'No one's blaming you, Mr Kerr. It's just a pity you didn't keep the note. Has something happened since then to make you think they were serious?'

Kerr looked away and pulled a fat cigar from his inside pocket. As he went through the performance of lighting it, Richard leaned forward in his seat. 'A man has died since then, hasn't he, Mr Kerr?' I was impressed. I didn't know what the hell he was talking about, but I was impressed.

A plume of acrid blue smoke obscured Kerr's eyes as he said, 'Technically, yes. But there's no evidence that there's any connection.'

'A man dies after opening a sealed container of your products, you've had a blackmail note and you don't believe there's a connection?' Richard asked, with only mild incredulity.

I could see mischief dancing behind his glasses, so I thought I'd better head this off at the pass. Any minute now, Richard would decide to start enjoying himself, completely oblivious to the fact that not everyone has the blithe disregard for human life that characterizes journalists. 'Suppose you give me your version of events, Mr Kerr?'

He puffed on the cigar and I tried not to cough. 'Like I said, I thought this note was some crank. Then, last week, we had a phone call from the police. They said a publican had dropped down dead at work. It seemed he'd just opened a fresh container of KerrSter. That's a universal cleanser that we produce. One of our biggest sellers to the trade. Anyway, according to the postmortem, this man had died from breathing in cyanide, which is ridiculous, because cyanide doesn't go anywhere near the KerrSter process. Nobody at our place could work out how him dying could have had anything to do with the KerrSter,' he said defensively. 'We weren't looking forward to the inquest, I'll be honest, but we didn't see how we could be held to blame.'

'And?' I prompted him.

Kerr shifted in his seat, moving his weight from one buttock to the other in a movement I hadn't seen since *Dumbo*. 'I swear I never connected it with the note I'd had. It'd completely slipped my mind. And then this morning, this came.' His pudgy hand slid into his inside pocket again and emerged with a folded sheet of paper. He held it out towards me.

'Has anyone apart from you touched this?' I asked, not reaching for it.

He shook his head. 'No. It came to the house, just like the other one.'

'Put it down on the desk,' I said, raking in my bag for a pen and my Swiss Army knife. I took the eyebrow tweezers out of their compartment on the knife and gingerly unfolded the note. It was a sheet from a glue-top A4 pad, hole-punched, narrow feint and margin. Across it, in straggling newsprint letters Sellotaped down, I read, 'Bet you wish you'd done what you were told. We'll be in touch. No cops. We're watching you.' The letters were a mixture of upper and lower case, and I recognized the familiar fonts of the *Manchester Evening Chronicle*. Well, that narrowed it down to a few million bodies.

I looked up and sighed. 'On the face of it, it looks like your correspondent carried out his threat. Why haven't you taken this to the police, Mr Kerr? Murder and blackmail, that's what they're there for.'

Kerr looked uncomfortable. 'I didn't think they'd believe me,' he said awkwardly. 'Look at it from their point of view. My company's products have been implicated in a major tampering scandal. A man's dead. Can you imagine how much it's going to cost me to get out from under the lawsuits that are going to be flying around? There's nothing to show I didn't cobble this together myself to try and get off the hook. I bet mine are the only fingerprints on that note, and you can bet your bottom dollar that the police aren't going to waste their time hunting for industrial saboteurs they won't even believe exist. Anyway, the note says "No cops".'

'So you want me to find your saboteurs for you?' I asked resignedly.

'Can you?' Kerr asked eagerly.

I shrugged. 'I can try.'

Before we could discuss it further, there was a knock at the door and our hostess's head appeared. 'Sorry to interrupt, Trevor, but we're about to distribute the treasure-hunt clues, and I know you'd hate to start at a disadvantage.' She didn't invite us to join in, I noticed. Clearly my suit didn't come up to scratch.

'Be right with you, Charmian,' Trevor said, hauling himself out of his chair. 'My office, half past eight tomorrow morning?' he asked.

I had a lot more questions for Trevor Kerr, but they could wait. 'I thought you were worried about me coming to the office?' I reminded him.

He barely paused on his way out the door. 'I'll tell my secretary you're from the Health and Safety Executive,' he said. 'Those nosey bastards are always poking around where they're not wanted.'

I shook my head in despair as he departed. Some clients are like that. Before you've agreed to work for them, they're practically on their knees. Soon as you come on board, they treat you like something nasty on their Gucci loafers. 'And I thought heavy metal bands were arseholes,' Richard mused.

'They are,' I said. 'And while we're on the subject, how come you knew about the KerrSter death?'

Richard winked and produced one of those smiles that got me tangled up with him in the first place. 'Not much point in having the *Chronicle* delivered if you don't bother reading it, is there?' he asked sweetly.

'Some of us have more important things to do than laze around smoking joints and reading the papers,' I snarled.

Richard pretended to look huffed. At least, I think he was pretending. 'Oh well, if that's the way things are, you won't be wanting me to take you to dinner, will you?' he said airily.

'Try me,' I said. There are few things in life that don't look better after aromatic crispy duck. How was I to know Trevor Kerr would be one of them?

4

As I waited for the security guard in charge of the barrier at Kerrchem's car park to check that I wasn't some devious industrial spy trying to sneak in to steal their secrets, I stared across at the sprawling factory, its red brick smudged black by years of industrial pollution. Somewhere inside there I'd find the end of the ball of string that would unravel to reveal a killer.

Eventually, he let me in and directed me to the administration offices. Trevor Kerr's secretary was already at her desk when I walked in at twenty-five past eight. Unfortunately, her boss wasn't. I introduced myself. 'Mr Kerr's expecting me,' I added.

She'd clearly been hired for her efficiency rather than her charm. 'Health and Safety Executive,' she said in the same tone of voice I'd have used for the VAT inspector. 'Take a seat. Mr Kerr will be here soon.' She returned to her word processor, attacking the keys with the ferocity of someone playing Mortal Kombat.

I looked around. Neither of the two chairs looked as if it had been chosen for comfort. The only available reading material was some trade journal that I wouldn't have picked up even on a twelve-hour flight with a Sylvester Stallone film as the in-flight movie. 'Maybe I could make a start on the documents I need to see?' I said. 'To save wasting time.'

'Only Mr Kerr can authorize the release of company information to a third party,' she said coldly. 'He knows you're coming. I'm sure he won't keep you waiting for long.'

I wished I shared her conviction. I tried to make myself comfortable and used the time to review the limited information I'd gleaned so far. After Richard and I had stuffed ourselves in a small Chinese restaurant in Whitefield, where we'd both felt seriously overdressed, I'd sat down with the previous weeks' papers and brought myself up to speed. Richard, meanwhile, had changed and gone off to some dive in Longsight to hear a local techno band who'd just landed a record deal. Frankly, I felt I'd got the best end of the bargain.

On my way through the stuttering early rush-hour traffic, I'd stopped by the office to fax my local friendly financial services expert. I needed some background on Trevor Kerr and his company, and if there was dirt to be dug, Josh Gilbert was the man. Josh and I have an arrangement: he supplies me with financial information and I buy him expensive dinners. The fact that Josh wouldn't know a scruple if it took him out to the Savoy is fine by me; I don't have to think about that, just reap the rewards.

The financial data would fill one gap in my knowledge. I hoped it would be more comprehensive than the newspaper accounts. When Joey Morton died, the media responded with ghoulish swiftness. For once, there were no government scandals to divert them, and all the papers had given the Stockport publican's death a good show. At first, I couldn't figure out how I'd missed the hue and cry, till I remembered that on the day in question I'd been out all day tracking down a key defence witness for Ruth Hunter, my favourite criminal solicitor. I'd barely had time for a sandwich on the hoof, never mind a browse through the dailies.

Joey Morton was thirty-eight, a former Third Division footballer turned publican. He and his wife Marina ran the Cob and Pen pub on the banks of the infant Mersey. Joey had gone down to the cellar to clean the beer pipes, taking a new container of KerrSter. Joey was proud of his real ale, and he never let anyone else near the cellarage. When he hadn't reappeared by opening time, Marina had sent one of the bar staff down to fetch him. The barman found his boss in a crumpled heap on the floor, the KerrSter sitting open beside him. The police had revealed that the postmortem indicated Joey had died as a result of inhaling hydrogen cyanide gas.

The pathologist's job had been made easier by the barman, who reported he'd smelt bitter almonds as soon as he'd entered the cramped cellar. Kerrchem had immediately denied that their product could possibly have caused the death, and the police had informed a waiting world that they were treating Joey's death as suspicious. Since then, the story seemed to have died, as always happens when there's a dearth of shocking revelations.

It didn't seem likely that Joey Morton could have died as a result of some ghastly error inside the Kerrchem factory. The obvious conclusion was industrial sabotage. The key questions were when and by whom. Was it an inside job? Was it a disgruntled former employee? Was it an outsider looking for blackmail money? Or was it a rival trying to annex Trevor Kerr's market? Killing people seemed a bit extreme, but as I know from bitter experience, the trouble with hiring outside help to do your dirty work is that things often get dangerously out of hand.

It was ten to nine when Trevor Kerr barged in. His eyes looked like the only treasure he'd found the night before had been in the bottom of a bottle. 'You Miss Brannigan, then?' he greeted me. If he was harbouring dreams of an acting career, I could only hope that Kerrchem wasn't going to fold. I followed him into his office, catching an unappealing whiff of Scotch revisited blended with Polo before we moved into the aroma of stale cigars and lemon furniture polish. Clearly, the Spartan motif didn't extend beyond the outer office. Trevor Kerr had spared no expense to make his office comfortable. That is, if you find gentlemen's clubs comfortable. Leather wing armchairs surrounded a low table buffed to a mirror sheen. Trevor's desk was repro, but what it lacked in class, it made up for in size. All they'd need to stage the world snooker championships on it would be a bit of green baize. That and clear the clutter. The walls were hung with old golfing prints. If his bulk was anything to go by, golf was something Trevor Kerr honoured more in the breach than the observance.

He dumped his briefcase by the desk and settled in behind it. I chose the armchair nearest him. I figured if I waited till I was invited, I'd be past my sell-by date. 'So, what do you need from me?' he demanded.

Before I could reply, the secretary came in with a steaming mug of coffee. The mug said 'World's Greatest Bullshitter'. I wasn't about to disagree. I wouldn't have minded a cup myself, but clearly the hired help around Kerrchem wasn't deemed worthy of that. If I'd really been from the HSE, the lack of courtesy would have had me sharpening my knives for Trevor Kerr's well-cushioned ribs. I waited for the secretary to withdraw, then I said, 'Have you recalled the rest of the batch?'

He nodded impatiently. 'Of course. We got on to all the wholesalers, and we've placed an ad in the national press as well as the trade. We've already had a load of stuff back, and there's more due in today.'

'Good,' I said. 'I'll want to see that, as well as the dispatch paperwork relating to that batch. I take it that won't be a problem?'

'No problem. I'll get Sheila to sort it out for you.' He made a note on a pad on his desk. 'Next?'

'Do you use cyanide in any of your processes?'

'No way,' he said belligerently. 'It has industrial uses, but mainly in the plastics industry and electroplating. There's nothing we produce that we'd need it for.'

'OK. Going back to the original blackmail note. Did it include any instructions about the amount of money they were after, or how you were to contact them?'

He took a cigar out of a humidor the size of a small greenhouse and rolled it between his fingers. 'They didn't put a figure on it, no. There was a phone number, and the note said it was the number of one of the public phones at Piccadilly Station. I was supposed to be there at nine o'clock on the Friday night. I didn't go, of course.'

'Pity you didn't call us then,' I said.

'I told you, I thought it was a crank. Some nutter trying to wind me up. No way was I going to give him the satisfaction.'

'Or her,' I added. 'The thing that bothers me, Mr Kerr, is that killing people is a pretty extreme thing for a blackmailer to do. The usual analysis of blackmailers is that they are on the cowardly side.

45

The crimes they commit are at arm's-length, and usually don't put life at risk. I would have expected the blackmailer in this case to have done something a lot more low key, certainly initially. You know, dumped caustic soda in washing-up liquid, that sort of thing.'

'Maybe they didn't intend to kill anybody, just to give people a nasty turn,' he said. He lit the cigar, exhaling a cloud of smoke that gave me a nasty turn so early in the day.

I shrugged. 'In that case, cyanide's a strange choice. The fatal dose is pretty small. Also, you couldn't just stick it in the drum and wait for someone to open it up. There must have been some kind of device rigged up inside it. To produce the lethal gas, cyanide pellets need to react with something else. So they'd have had to be released into the liquid somehow. That's a lot of trouble to go to when you could achieve an unpleasant warning with dozens of other chemical mixtures. If it was me, I'd have filled a few drums either with something that smelled disgusting, or something that would destroy surfaces rather than clean them, just to persuade you that they were capable of making your life hell. Then, I'd have followed it up with a second note saying something like: "Next time, it'll be cyanide."'

'So maybe we're dealing with a complete nutter,' he said bitterly. 'Great.'

'Or maybe it's someone who wants to destroy you rather than blackmail you,' I said simply.

46

Kerr took his cigar out of his mouth, which remained in a perfect 'O'. Finally, he said, 'You've got to be kidding.'

'It's something you should consider. In relation to both your professional and your personal life.' He was having a lot of trouble getting his head round the idea, I could see. If he'd been a bit nicer to me, I'd have been gentler. But I figure you shouldn't dish it out unless you can take it. 'What about business rivals? Is anybody snapping at your heels? Is anybody going under because you've brought out new products or developed new sales strategies?'

'You don't murder people in business,' he protested. 'Not in my line of business, you don't.'

'Murder might not have been what was planned,' I told him flatly. 'If they wanted to sabotage you and stay at arm's-length, they might have hired someone to do the dirty. And they in turn might have hired someone else. And somewhere along the line, the Chinese whispers took over. So is there any other firm that might have a particular reason for wanting Kerrchem to go down the tubes?'

He frowned. 'The last few years have been tough, there's no denying that. Firms go bust, so there's not as much industrial cleaning to be done. Businesses cut their cleaners down from five days to three, so the commercial cleaners cut back on their purchases. We've kept our heads above water, but it's been a struggle. We've had a couple of rounds of redundancies, we've been a bit slower bringing in some new processes, and we've had to market ourselves more aggressively, but that's the story across the industry. One of our main competitors went bust about nine months ago, but that wasn't because we were squeezing them. It was more because they were based in Basingstoke and they had higher labour costs than us. I haven't heard that anybody else is on the edge, and it's a small world. To be honest, we're one of the smaller fishes. Most of our rivals are big multinationals. If they wanted to take us out, they'd come to the family and make us an offer we couldn't refuse.'

That disposed of the easy option. Time to move on. 'Has anybody left under a cloud? Any unfair dismissal claims pending?'

He shook his head. 'Not that I know of. As far as I know, and believe me, I would know, the only people who have gone are the ones we cleared out under the redundancy deals. I suppose some of them might have been a bit disgruntled, but if any of them had made any threats, I would have heard about it. Like I said, we pride ourselves on being a family firm, and the department head and production foremen all know not to keep problems to themselves.'

We were going nowhere fast, which only left the sticky bit. 'OK,' I said. 'I don't want you to take this the wrong way, Mr Kerr, but I have to ask these things. You've said that Kerrchem is a family firm. Is there any possibility that another member of the family wants to discredit you? To

48

make it look like the company's not safe in your hands?'

Suddenly I was looking at Trevor Kerr's future. Written all over his scarlet face was the not-so-distant early warning of the heart attack that was lurking in his silted arteries. His mouth opened and closed a couple of times, then he roared, 'Bollocks. Pure, absolute bollocks.'

'Think about it,' I said, smiling sweetly. That'll teach him to deprive me of a caffeine fix. 'The other thing is more personal, I'm afraid. Are you married, Mr Kerr?'

''Course I am. Three children.' He jerked his thumb towards a photograph frame on the desk. I leaned forward and turned it round. Standard studio shot of a woman groomed to within an inch of her life, two sulky-looking boys with their father's features, and a girl who'd had the dental work but still looked disturbingly like a rabbit. 'Been married to the same woman for sixteen years.'

'So there're no ex-wives or ex-girlfriends lurking around with an axe to grind?' I asked.

His eyes drifted away from mine to a point elsewhere on the far wall. 'Don't be ridiculous,' he said abruptly. Then, in an effort to win me round, he gave a bark of laughter and said, 'Bloody hell, Kate, it's me that hired you, not the wife.'

So now I knew he had, or had had, a mistress. That was the long shot I'd have to keep in the back of my mind. Before I could explore this avenue further, the intercom on his desk buzzed.

He pressed a button and said, 'What is it, Sheila?'

'Reg Unsworth is here, Mr Kerr. He says he needs to talk to you.'

'I'm in a meeting, Sheila,' he said irritably.

There were muffled sounds of conversation, then Sheila said, 'He says it's urgent, Mr Kerr. He says you'll want to know immediately. It's to do with the recalled product, he says.'

'Why didn't you say so? Send him in.'

A burly man in a brown warehouseman's coat with a head bald as a boiled egg and approximately the same shape walked in. 'Sorry to bother you, Mr Kerr. It's about the KerrSter recall.'

'Well, Reg, spit it out,' Kerr said impatiently.

Unsworth gave me a worried look. 'It's a bit confidential, like.'

'It's all right. Miss Brannigan here's from the Health and Safety Executive. She's here to help us sort this mess out.'

Unsworth still looked uncertain. 'I checked the records before the returns started coming in. We sent out a total of four hundred and eighty-three gallon containers with the same batch number as the one that there was the problem with. Only . . . so far, we've had six hundred and twenty-seven back.'

5

Kerr looked gobsmacked. 'You must have made a mistake,' he blustered.

'I double-checked,' Unsworth said. His jaw set in a line as obstinate as his boss's. 'Then I went back down to production and checked again. There's no doubt about it. We've had back one hundred and forty-four containers more than we sent out. And that's not even taking into account the one that the dead man opened, or ones that have already been used, or people who haven't even heard about the recall yet.'

'There's got to be some mistake,' Kerr repeated. 'What about the batch coding machine? Has anybody checked that it's working OK?'

'I checked with the line foreman myself,' Unsworth said. 'They've had no problems with it, and I've seen quality control's sheets. There's no two ways about it. We only sent out four hundred and eighty-three. There's a gross of gallon drums of KerrSter that we can't account for sitting in the loading bay. Come and see for yourself if you don't believe me,' he added in an aggrieved tone.

'Let's do just that,' Kerr said, heaving himself to his feet. 'Come on, Miss Brannigan. Come and see how the workers earn a living.'

I followed Kerr out of the room. Unsworth hung back, holding the door open and falling in beside me as we strode down the covered walkway that linked the administration offices with the factory. 'It's a real mystery,' he offered.

I had my own ideas about what was going on, but for the time being I decided to keep them to myself. 'The drums that have been returned,' I said, 'are they all sealed, or have some of them already been opened?'

'Some of them have been started on,' he said. 'The batch went out into the warehouse the Tuesday before last. They'll probably have started taking it out on the Thursday or Friday, going by our normal stockpile levels, so there's been plenty of time for people to use them.'

'And no one else has reported any adverse effect?'

Unsworth looked uncomfortable. 'Not as such,' he said.

Kerr half turned to catch my reply. 'But?' I asked.

Unsworth glanced at Kerr, who nodded impatiently. 'Well, a couple of the wholesalers and one or two of the reps had already had containers from that batch returned,' Unsworth admitted.

'Do you know why that was?' I asked.

'Customers complained the goods weren't up to us usual standard,' he said grudgingly.

'What sort of complaints?' Kerr demanded indignantly. 'Why wasn't I told about this?'

'It's only just come to light, Mr Kerr. They said the KerrSter wasn't right. One of them claimed it had stripped the finish off the flooring in his office toilets.'

Kerr snorted. 'He should tell his bloody workforce to stick with Boddingtons. They'll have been pissing that foreign lager all over the bloody tiles.'

'Have you had the chance to analyse any of the containers that have come back?' I butted in.

Unsworth nodded. 'The lads in the lab worked through the night on samples from some of the drums. There wasn't a trace of cyanide in any of them.'

Kerr shouldered open a pair of double doors. As I caught one on the backswing, the smell hit me. It was a curious amalgam of pine, lemon, and soap suds, but pervaded throughout with sharp chemical smells that bit my nose and throat. It was a bit like driving past the chemical works at Ellesmere Port with one of those ersatz air fresheners in the car. The ones that make you feel that a rotting polecat under the driver's seat would be preferable. Right after the smell came the noise of machinery, overlaid with the bubbling and gurgling of liquid. Kerr climbed a flight of narrow iron stairs, and I followed him along a high-level walkway that travelled the length of the factory floor. It was unpleasantly humid. I felt like a damp wash that's just been dumped in the tumble dryer.

Beneath us, vats seethed, nozzles squirted liquid into plastic containers, and surprisingly few people moved around. 'Not many bodies,' I said loudly over my shoulder to Unsworth.

'Computer controlled,' he said succinctly.

Another avenue to pursue. If the sabotage was internal, perhaps the culprit was simply sending the wrong instructions to the plant. I'd thought this was going to be a straightforward case of industrial sabotage, but my head was beginning to hurt with the permutations it was throwing up.

A couple of hundred yards along the walkway, we descended and cut through a heavy door into a warehouse. Now I know how the Finns feel when they walk into the snow from the sauna. I could feel my pores snapping shut in shock. Here, the air smelled of oil and diesel. The only sound came from fork-lift trucks shunting pallets on and off shelves. 'This is the warehouse,' Kerr said. I'd never have worked that one out all by myself. 'The full containers go through from the factory to packing, where the machines label them, stamp them with batch numbers and seal-wrap them in dozens. Then they come through here on conveyor belts and they're shelved or loaded.' He turned to Unsworth. 'Where have you stacked the recalls?'

Before Unsworth could reply, my mobile started ringing. 'Excuse me,' I said, moving away a few yards and pulling the phone out. 'Kate Brannigan,' I announced.

'Tell me,' an amused voice said. 'Is Alexis Lee a real person, or is it just your pen name?'

I recognized the voice at once. I moved further away from Kerr's curious stare and turned my back so he couldn't see that my ears had gone bright red. 'She's real all right, Mr Haroun,' I said. 'Why do you ask?'

'Oh, I think it had better be Michael. Otherwise I'd start to suspect you were being unfriendly. I've just been handed the early edition of the *Evening Chronicle*.'

'And what does it say?'

'Do you really need me to tell you?' he asked, still sounding amused.

'I forgot to bring my crystal ball with me. If you want to hang on, I'll see if I can find a chicken to disembowel so I can check out the entrails.'

He laughed. It was a sound I could easily get used to. 'It'd be a lot simpler to pop into a newsagent.'

'You're not going to tell me?'

'Oh no, I'd hate to spoil the surprise. Tell me, Kate . . . Do you fancy dinner some evening?'

'Michael, it may not look like it, but I fancy dinner every evening.' I couldn't believe myself – I'd read better lines than that in teenage romances.

Bless him, he laughed again. I like a man who doesn't seize on the first sign of weakness. 'Are you free this evening?'

I pretended to think. Let's face it, I'd have turned down Mel Gibson, Sean Bean, Lynford Christie and Daniel Day-Lewis for dinner with Michael Haroun. I didn't pretend for too long, in case he lost interest. 'I can be. As long as it's after seven.'

'Great. Shall I pick you up?'

That was a harder decision. I didn't want to let myself forget that this was a business dinner. On the other hand, it wouldn't hurt to give Richard something to think about. I gave Michael the address and we agreed on half past seven. Unlike everybody on TV who uses a mobile phone, I hit the 'end' button with a flourish, then turned back to a scowling Trevor Kerr.

'Sorry about that,' I lied. 'Somebody I've been trying to get hold of on another investigation. Now, Mr Unsworth, you were going to show us these recalled containers.'

The next half-hour was one of the more boring ones in my life, made doubly so by the fact that I was itching to get my hands on the *Chronicle*. I finally escaped at half past eleven, leaving Trevor Kerr with the suggestion that his chemists should analyse the contents of a random sample of the containers. Only this time, they wouldn't just be looking for cyanide. They'd be checking to see whether the KerrSter in the drums was the real thing. Or something quite different and a whole lot nastier.

*   *   *

By the third newsagent's, I'd confirmed what I'd always suspected about Farnworth. It's a depressing little dump that civilization forgot. Nobody had the *Chronicle*. They wouldn't have it till some time in the afternoon. They all looked deeply offended and incredulous when I explained that no, the *Bolton Evening News* just wouldn't be the same. I had to possess my soul in patience till I hit the East Lancs. Road. I sat on a garage forecourt reading the results of Alexis's research. She'd done me proud.

CULTURAL HERITAGE VANISHES

A series of spectacular robberies has been hushed up by police and stately home owners.

Now fears are growing that a gang of professional thieves are stripping Britain of valuable artworks that form a key part of the nation's heritage. Among the stolen pieces are paintings by French Impressionists Monet and Cézanne, and a bronze bust by the Italian Baroque master Bernini. Also missing is a collection of Elizabethan miniature paintings by Nicholas Hilliard. Together, the thieves' haul is estimated at nearly £10 million.

The cover-up campaign was a joint decision made by several police forces and the owners of the stately homes in question. Police did not want publicity because they were following up leads and did not want the thieves to know that they had realized one gang was behind the thefts.

And the owners were reluctant to admit the jewels of their collections had gone missing in case public attendance figures at their homes dropped off as a result.

Some owners have even resorted to hanging replicas of the missing masterpieces in a bid to fool the public.

The latest victim of the audacious robbers is the owner of a Cheshire manor house. Police have refused to reveal his identity, but will only say that a nineteenth-century French painting has been stolen.

The cheeky thieves have adopted the techniques of the pair who caused outrage at the Lillehammer Olympics when they stole Edward Munch's *The Scream*.

They break in through the nearest door or window, go straight to the one item they have selected and make their getaway. Often they are in the house or gallery for no more than a minute.

A police source said last night, 'There's no doubt that we are dealing with professionals who may well steal to order. There are obviously a limited number of outlets for their loot, and we are making inquiries in the art world.'

One of the robbed aristos, who was only prepared to talk anonymously, said, 'It's not just the heritage of this country that is at stake. It's our businesses. We employ a lot of people and if the public stop coming because our most famous exhibits have gone, it will have repercussions.

'We do our best to maintain tight security, but you can never keep the professional out.'

There was some more whingeing in the same vein, but nothing startling. Call me nit-picking, but I've never understood how the art of several European cultures has come to be a key part of our British heritage, unless it symbolizes the brigand spirit that made the Empire great. That aside, I reckoned Alexis's story would achieve what I hoped for. With a bit of luck, the nationals would pick the story up the next morning, and the jungle drums would start beating. Soon it would be time for a chat with my friend Dennis. If he ever decides to go completely straight, he could make a living as a journalist. I've never known anybody absorb or disseminate so much criminal intelligence. I'm just grateful some of it comes my way when I need it.

For the time being, I headed back to the office, stopping to pick up a couple of pizzas on the way. I knew Shelley would be waiting behind the door with a pile of paperwork that would cause more concussion than a rolling pin. At least a pizza offering might reduce the aggro to a minimum.

I was halfway through the painful process of signing cheques when Josh arrived. I pretended astonishment. 'Josh!' I exclaimed. 'It's between the hours of one and three and you're not in a restaurant! What's happened? Has the stock market collapsed?'

His sharp blue eyes crinkled in the smile that he's practised to maximize his resemblance to Robert Redford. Frankly, I'm surprised the light brown hair hasn't been bleached to perfect it, since Josh is a man whose energies are devoted to only two things – making lots of money and women. His track record with the latter is dismal; luckily he's a lot more successful with the former, which is how he's ended up as the senior partner of one of the city's most successful master brokerages. Shelley developed a theory about Josh and women after she did her A level psychology. She reckons that behind the confident façade there lurks a well of low self-esteem. So when it comes to women, his subconscious decides that any woman with half a brain and a shred of personality wouldn't spend more than five minutes with him. The logical extension of that is that any woman who sticks around for more than six weeks must by definition be a boring bimbo, and thus he shouldn't be seen dead with her.

Me, I think he just likes having fun. He swears he plans to retire when he turns forty, and that's early enough to think about settling down. I like him because he's always treated me as an equal, never as a potential conquest. I'm glad about that; I'd hate to lose my fast track into the bowels of the financial world. Believe me, the Nikkei Index doesn't burp without Josh knowing exactly what it had for dinner.

Josh flicked an imaginary speck of dust off one of the clients' chairs and sat down, crossing his elegantly suited legs. 'Things are changing in the big bad world of money, you know,' he said. 'The days of the three-hour lunch are over. Except when it's you that's buying, of course.' He tossed a file on to my desk.

'You've stopped doing lunch?' I waited for the world to stop turning.

'Today, I had a Marks and Spencer prawn sandwich in the office of one of my principal clients. Washed down with a rather piquant sparkling mineral water from the Welsh valleys. An interesting diversification from coal mining, don't you think?'

I picked up the file. 'Kerrchem?'

'The same. Want the gossip since I'm here?'

I gave him my best suspicious frown. 'Is this going to cost me?'

He pouted. 'Maybe an extra glass of XO?'

'It's worth it,' I decided. 'Tell me about it.'

'OK. Kerrchem is a family firm. Started in 1934 by Josiah Kerr, the grandfather of the present chairman, chief executive and managing director Trevor Kerr. They made soap. They were no Lever Brothers, though they've always provided a reasonable living for the family. Trevor's father Hartley was a clever chap, by all accounts, had a chemistry degree, and he made certain they spent enough on R & D to keep ahead of the game. He moved them into the industrial cleaning market.' All this off the top of his head. One of the secrets of Josh's success is a virtually photographic memory for facts and figures. Figures of the balance sheet variety, that is.

'Hartley Kerr was an only child,' he continued. 'He had three kids: Trevor, Margaret and Elizabeth. Trevor, although the youngest, owns forty-nine per cent of the shares, Margaret and Elizabeth own twenty per cent each. The remaining eleven per cent is held by Hartley Kerr's widow, Elaine Kerr. Elaine is in her early seventies, in full possession of her marbles, lives in Bermuda, and takes little part in things except for voting against Trevor at every opportunity. Trevor's sons are still at school, but he has three nephews who work at Kerrchem. John Hardy works in R & D, his brother Paul is in accounts and Margaret's son Will Tomasiuk is in sales. Trevor is by all accounts a complete and utter shit, but against all the odds, he appears to run the company well. Never been a history of industrial problems. Financially and fiscally all seems above board. Frankly, Kate, if Kerrchem were going public, they're exactly the kind of company I'd advise you to put your money in if you wanted to keep it unspectacularly safe. Before people started dying, that is.'

'I suppose that rules out an insurance job, then. Is everybody in the family happy with Trevor's stewardship? No young bucks snapping at his heels?'

Josh shook his head. 'That's not the word on the exchange floor. The old lady only votes against Trevor because she thinks he's not a patch on his old man and she wants to make a point. And the nephews have all learned the business from the bottom up, but they're climbing the greasy pole at an impressive rate. So, no, that kite won't fly, Kate.' He glanced at a watch so slim it looked anorexic and uncrossed his legs.

'You're a star, Josh. I owe you a meal.'

'Fix up a date with Julia, would you? I don't have my diary with me.' He stood up and I came round the desk to swap kisses on both cheeks. I watched five hundred pounds worth of immaculate tailoring walk out the door. Not even that amount of dosh to spend on clothes could make me spend my days talking about pension funds and unit trusts.

On the other hand, all it took to get me salivating at the thought of an evening's conversation about insurance was a profile from an ancient carving. Maybe I wasn't such a smart cookie after all.

6

I'd almost forgotten there are restaurants that don't serve dim sum. For as long as I've known Richard, he's maintained that if you don't use chopsticks on it, it ain't food. And Josh has recently taken to extracting his payment in kind in Manchester's clutch of excellent Thai restaurants. I'm not sure if that's down to the food or the subservient waitresses. Either way, I'd entirely lost touch with anything that didn't come out of a wok. Which made Michael Haroun a refreshing change in more ways than one.

He'd arrived promptly at twenty-nine minutes past seven. I'd grown so used to Richard's flexible idea of time that I was still applying eye pencil when the doorbell rang. I nearly poked my eye out in shock, and had to answer the door with a tissue covering the damage. Eat your heart out, Cindy Crawford. Michael lounged against the door frame, looking drop-dead gorgeous in blue jeans, navy silk blouson and an off-white collarless linen shirt that sure as hell hadn't come from Marks and Spencer. My stomach churned, and I don't think it was hunger. 'Long John Silver, I presume,' he said.

'Watch it, or I'll set the parrot on you,' I replied, stepping back and waving him in.

He shrugged away from the door and followed me down the hall. I gestured towards the living room and said, 'Give me a minute.'

Back in the bathroom, I repaired the damage and surveyed myself in the full-length mirror. Navy linen trousers, russet knitted silk T-shirt, navy silk tweed jacket. I looked like I'd taken a bit of trouble, without actually departing from the businesslike image. Michael wasn't to know this was my newest, smartest outfit. Besides, I'd told Richard my evening engagement was a business meeting, and I wasn't entirely ready for him to get any other ideas if he saw me leave.

I rubbed a smudge of gel over my fingers and thrust them through my hair, which I'd kept fairly short since I was shorn without consultation earlier in the year. My right eye still looked a bit red, but this was as good as it was going to get. A quick squirt of Richard's Eternity by Calvin Klein and I was ready.

I walked down the hall and stood in the doorway. Michael obviously hadn't heard me. He was deep in a computer gaming magazine. Bonus points for the boy. I cleared my throat. 'Ready when you are,' I said.

He looked up and smiled appreciatively. 'I don't want to sound disablist,' he said, 'but I have to admit I prefer the two-eyed look.' He closed the magazine and stood up. 'Shall we go?'

He drove a top-of-the-range Citroën. 'Company car?' I asked, looking forward to the prospect of being driven for a change.

'Yeah, but they let me choose. I've always had a soft spot for Citroën. I think the DS was one of the most beautiful cars ever built,' he said as he did a neat three-point turn to get out of the parking area outside my bungalow. 'My father always used to drive one.'

That told me Michael Haroun hadn't grown up on a council estate with the arse hanging out of his trousers. 'Lucky you,' I said with feeling. 'My dad works for Rover, so my childhood was spent in the back of a Mini. That's how I ended up only five foot three. The British equivalent of binding the feet.'

Michael laughed as he hit a button on the CD player and Bonnie Raitt filled the car. Richard would have giggled helplessly at something so middle of the road. Me, I was just glad of something that didn't feature crashing guitars or that insistent zippy beat that sounds just like a fly hitting an incinerator. We turned out of the small 'single professionals' development where I live and into the council estate. To my surprise, instead of heading down Upper Brook Street towards town, he turned left. As we headed down Stockport Road, my heart sank. I prayed this wasn't going to be one of those twenty-mile drives to some pretentious bistro in the sticks with compulsory spinach pancakes and only one choice of vodka.

'You into computer games, then?' I asked. Time to check out just how much I had in common with this breathtaking profile.

'I have a 486 multi-media system in my spare room. Does that answer the question?'

'It's not what you've got, it's what you do with it that counts,' I replied. As soon as I'd spoken, I wished I was on a five-second delay loop, like radio phone-ins.

He grinned and listed his current favourites. We were still arguing the relative merits of submarine simulations when he pulled up outside a snooker supplies shop in an unpromising part of Stockport Road. A short walk down the pavement brought us to That Café, an unpretentious restaurant done out in Thirties style. I'd heard plenty of good reports about it, but I'd never quite made it across the door before. The locale had put me off for one thing. Call me fussy, but I like to be sure that my car's still going to be waiting for me after I've finished dinner.

The interior looked like flea market meets Irish country pub, but the menu had me salivating. The waitress, dressed in jeans, a Deacon Blue T-shirt, big fuck-off Doc Marten boots and a long white French waiter's apron, showed us to a quiet corner table next to a blazing fire. OK, they only had one vodka, but at least it wasn't some locally distilled garbage with a phoney Russian name.

As our starters arrived, I said ruefully, 'I wish finding Henry Naismith's Monet was as easy as a computer game.'

'Yeah. At least with games, there's always a bulletin board you can access for hints. I suppose you're out on your own with this,' Michael said.

'Not entirely on my own,' I corrected him. 'I do have one or two contacts.'

He swallowed his mouthful of food and looked slightly pained. 'Is that why you agreed to have dinner with me?' he asked.

'Only partly.'

'What was the other part?' he asked, obviously fishing.

'I enjoy a good scoff, and I like interesting conversation with it.' I was back in control of myself, the adolescent firmly stuffed back into the box marked 'not wanted on voyage'.

'And you thought I'd be an interesting conversationalist, did you?'

'Bound to be,' I said sweetly. 'You're an insurance man, and right now insurance claims are one of my principal interests.'

We ate in silence for a few moments, then he said, 'I take it you were behind the story in the *Chronicle*?'

I shrugged. 'I like to stir the pot. That way, the scum rises to the surface.'

'You certainly stirred things around our office,' Michael said drily.

'The people have a right to know,' I said, self-righteously quoting Alexis.

'Cheers,' Michael said, clinking his glass against mine. 'Here's to a profitable relationship.'

'Oh, you mean Fortissimus are going to hire Mortensen and Brannigan?' I asked innocently.

He grinned again. 'I think I'll pass on that one. I simply meant that with luck, you might track down Henry Naismith's Monet.'

'Speaking of which,' I said, 'I spoke to Henry this afternoon. He says your assessor was there this afternoon.'

'That's right,' Michael said cagily.

'Henry says your man put a very interesting suggestion to him. Purely in confidence. Now, would that be the kind of confidence you're already privy to?'

Michael carefully placed his fork and knife together on the plate and mopped his lips with the napkin. 'It might be,' he said cautiously. 'But if it were, I wouldn't be inclined to discuss it with someone who has a hotline to the front page of the *Chronicle*.'

'Not even if I promised it would go no further?'

'You expect me to believe that after today's performance?' he demanded.

I smiled. 'There's a crucial difference. I was acting in my client's best interests by setting the cat among the pigeons with Alexis's story. I didn't breach my client's confidentiality, and I didn't tell Alexis anything that wasn't already in the public domain. She just put the bits together. However, if Henry acted on your colleague's suggestion and I leaked that to the press, it would seriously damage his business. And I don't do that to the people who pay my mortgage. Trust me, Michael. It won't go any further.'

The arrival of the waitress gave him a moment's breathing space. She removed the debris. 'So this would be strictly off the record?'

'Information only,' I agreed.

The waitress returned with a cheerful smile and two huge plates. I stared down at mine, where enough rabbit to account for half the population of Watership Down sat in a pool of creamy sauce. '*Nouvelle cuisine* obviously passed this place by,' I said faintly.

'I suspect we Mancunians are too canny to pay half a week's wages for a sliver of meat surrounded by three baby carrots, two mangetouts, one baby sweetcorn and an artistically carved radish,' he said wryly.

'And is it that Mancunian canniness that underlies your assessor's underhand suggestion?' I asked innocently.

'Nothing regional about it,' Michael said. 'You have to have a degree in bloody-minded caution before you get the job.'

'So you think it's OK to ask your clients to hang fakes on the wall?'

'It's a very effective safety precaution,' he said carefully.

'That's what your assessor told Henry. He said you'd be prepared not to increase his premium by the equivalent of the gross national product of a small African nation if he had copies made of his remaining masterpieces and hung them on the walls instead of the real thing,' I said conversationally.

'That's about the size of it,' Michael admitted. At least he had the decency to look uncomfortable about it.

'And is this a general policy these days?'

Slicing up his vegetables gave Michael an excuse for not meeting my eyes. 'Quite a few of our clients have opted for it as a solution to their security problems,' he said. 'It makes sense, Kate. We agreed this morning that there isn't a security system that can't be breached. If having a guard physically on site twenty-four hours a day isn't practical because of the expense or because the policyholder doesn't want that sort of presence in what is, after all, his home, then it avoids sky-high premiums.'

'It's not just about money, though,' I protested. 'It's like Henry says. He knows those paintings. He's lived with them most of his life. You get a buzz from the real thing that a fake just doesn't provide.'

'Not one member of the public has noticed the substitutions,' Michael said.

'Maybe not so far,' I conceded. 'But according to my understanding, the trouble with fakes is that they don't stand the test of time.' Thanking Shelley silently for my art tutorial that afternoon, I launched myself into my spiel. 'Look at Van Meegeren's fake Vermeers. At the time, all the experts were convinced they were the real thing. But you look at them now, and they wouldn't even fool a philistine like me. The difference between schneid and kosher is that fakes date, but the really great paintings don't. They're timeless.'

He frowned. 'Even if you're right, which I don't concede for a moment, that's not a bridge that our clients will have to cross for a long time yet.'

I wasn't about to give up that easily. 'Even so, don't you think it's a bit of a con to pull on the public? A bit of a swizz to spend your bank holiday Monday in a traffic jam just so you can ogle a Constable that's more phoney than a plastic Rolex? Aren't you in danger of breaching the Trades Descriptions Act?' I asked.

'Our clients may be,' Michael said carelessly. 'We're not.'

The brazen effrontery of it gobsmacked me. 'I can't believe I'm hearing this,' I said. 'You work in a business that must spend hundreds of thousands a year trying to catch its customers out in fraud, and yet you're happily suggesting to another bunch of clients that they go off and commit a fraud?'

'That's not how we see it,' he said stiffly. 'Besides, it works,' he said. 'In at least two cases that I know about personally, customers who have been

72

burgled have only lost copies. Surely that proves it's worthwhile.'

In spite of the blazing fire, I felt a chill on the back of my neck. Only a man with no personal knowledge of the strung-out world of crime could have made that pronouncement with such self-satisfaction. It doesn't take much imagination to picture the scene when an overwrought burglar turns up at his fence's gaff with something he thinks is an old master, only to be told it's Rembrandt by numbers. Scenario number one is that the burglar thinks the fence is trying to have him over so he takes the appropriate steps. Scenario number two is that the fence thinks the burglar is trying to have him over, and takes the appropriate steps. Either way, somebody ends up in casualty. And that's looking on the bright side. Doubtless law-abiding citizens like Michael think they've got what they deserve, but even villains have wives and kids who don't want to spend their spare time visiting hospital beds or graves.

My silence clearly spelled out defeat to Michael, since he leaned over and squeezed my hand. 'Trust me, Kate. Our way, everybody's happy,' he said.

I pretended to push my chair back and look frantically for the door. 'I'm out of here,' I said. 'Soon as an insurance man says "trust me", you know you should be in the next county.'

He grinned. 'I promise I'll never try to sell you insurance.'

'OK. But I won't promise I'll never try to pitch you into using Mortensen and Brannigan.'

'Speaking of which, how did you get into the private eye business?' Michael said.

I couldn't decide whether it was an attempt to change the subject or a deliberate shift away from the professional towards the personal. Either way, I was happy to go along with him. I didn't think I was going to get any more useful information out of him, and I only had to look across the table to remember that when I'd agreed to this dinner, my motives hadn't been entirely selfless. By the time we'd moved on to coffee and Armagnac, he knew all about my aborted law degree, abandoned after two years because the part-time job I'd got doing bread-and-butter process serving for Bill Mortensen was a damn sight more interesting than the finer points of jurisprudence.

'So tell me about your most interesting case,' he coaxed me.

'Maybe later,' I said. 'It's your turn now. How did you get into insurance?'

'It's the family business,' he said, looking faintly embarrassed.

'So you followed in Daddy's footsteps,' I said. I felt disappointed. I couldn't put my finger on why, exactly. Maybe I expected him to live up to that profile with a suitably buccaneering past.

'Eventually,' he said. 'I read Arabic at university, then I worked for the BBC World Service for a while. But the money was dire and there were no prospects. My father had the sense to see that sales had never interested me, but he persuaded me to take a shot at working in claims.' Michael raised his shoulders and held out his hands in an expressive shrug. 'What can I say? I really enjoy it.'

All of a sudden, I remembered one of the key reasons I like being with Richard. He lives an interesting life: music journalist, football fan and Sunday morning player, part-time father. I was sure if I hung around with Michael Haroun, I'd learn a lot of invaluable stuff. But not even the most brilliant raconteur can make insurance interesting for ever. With Richard, no two days are the same. With Michael, I suspected variety might not be the spice of life.

Now I'd established that I didn't want to spend the rest of my life with the man, I felt a sense of release. I could take what I needed from the encounter, and that would be that. My life wasn't about to be turned on its head because I'd fallen in love with a profile when I was fourteen.

With that comforting thought in the front of my mind, I had no hesitation about inviting him back for more coffee. The fact that I'd forgotten to mention Richard to him somehow didn't seem too important at the time.

7

Richard's car wasn't home when we got there. I wasn't sure whether to be pleased or not. On the one hand, I wanted him to see me with Michael Haroun. If it took a bit of the green-eyed monster to make Richard start thinking about where our relationship was headed, so be it. On the other hand, the last thing I wanted was for him to throw a jealous wobbler in front of someone who was potentially a useful source, if not a prospective client.

'You live alone, then?' Michael asked casually as we walked up the path.

'Yes and no,' I said. 'I have a relationship with the man next door, but we don't actually live together.' I unlocked the door, switched off the burglar alarm and led him through the living room into the conservatory that links both houses. 'This is the common ground,' I said. 'We each reserve the right to lock the door into the conservatory.' I wasn't sure why I was telling Michael all this.

Maybe there was still a smidgen of lust running through my hormones.

Michael followed me back into the living room, closing the patio doors behind him. 'Coffee?' I asked. 'Or would you prefer a drink?'

He smiled mischievously. 'That depends.'

'Oh, you'll be driving,' I told him. Even if I'd been young, free and single, he'd have been driving, I told myself firmly.

He pulled a rueful face and said, 'It had better be coffee then.'

I'd just finished grinding the beans when I heard the clattering of Richard's engine. I glanced out of the window and watched the hot pink, customized Volkswagen Beetle convertible nose into the space between Michael's car and my Leo Gemini turbo super coupé, a trophy from the case which had put our relationship on the line in the first place. I kept meaning to trade it in for something more suited to surveillance work, the coupé being about as unobtrusive as Chatsworth on a council estate. But it was such a pleasure to drive, I hadn't got round to it yet.

Back in the living room, Michael clearly wasn't brooding on his rebuff. He was absorbed in the computer games reviews again. 'Coffee won't be long,' I said.

He closed the magazine and replaced it in the rack. Either he had very good manners, or he was as obsessively tidy as I was. Richard calls it anal retentive, but I don't see why you have to live

77

in a tip just to prove you're laid back. Before we could get back into computer games, I heard the patio doors on the far side of the conservatory open. Richard's yell of greeting penetrated even my closed doors. 'Brannigan, I'm home,' he called.

Seconds later, he appeared at my doors, brandishing the unmistakable carrier bag of a Chinese takeaway. He pulled the door back, took in Michael and grinned. 'Hi,' he said expansively. I estimated three joints. 'You two still working?'

'We finished ages ago,' I said. 'Michael came back for coffee.'

'Right,' said Richard, oblivious to the implication I was thrusting under his nose. 'You won't mind if I join you then?'

Without waiting for an answer, he plonked himself down on the sofa opposite Michael and unpacked his takeaway. 'I'm Richard Barclay, by the way,' he said, extending a hand across the table to Michael. 'You wait for Brannigan to remember her manners, you could be dead.'

'Michael Haroun,' he said, shaking Richard's hand. 'Pleased to meet you.' Yes, an insurance man born and bred. Only an estate agent could have lied more convincingly.

Richard jumped to his feet and headed for the door. 'Chopsticks and bowls for three?' he asked. 'Sorry, Mike, I wasn't expecting company, but there's probably enough to go around.'

'We've just had dinner, Richard,' I said. 'I did leave you a message.'

'Yeah, I know,' he grinned. 'But I've never known you refuse a salt and pepper rib, Brannigan.'

'Sorry about that,' I said as he left.

Michael winked. 'Gives me a chance to suss out the competition.'

I didn't like the idea that I was some kind of prize, even if it was gratifying to know that he was interested in more than recovering Henry Naismith's Monet. And he didn't even have the excuse of a previous encounter in the British Museum. 'What makes you think there's a competition?' I asked sweetly.

Michael leaned back against the sofa and stretched his legs out. 'I thought you were the detective? Kate, if you two were as happy as pigs, you'd have left me sitting in the car wondering where exactly I'd made the wrong move.'

Before I could reply, Richard was back. 'I'll get the coffee,' I said, annoyed with myself for my transparency. By the time I got back, Richard and Michael were getting to know each other. And they say women are bitches.

'So, what do you do when you're not chipping a oner off people's car theft claims because your assessor spoke to the next-door neighbour who revealed that the ashtray was full?' Richard asked through a mouthful of shiu mai.

As I sat down next to him, Michael smiled at me and said, 'I play computer games. Like Kate.'

I poured the coffee in silence and let the boys

play. 'All a bit sedentary,' Richard remarked, loading his bowl with fried rice and what looked like a chicken hoi nam.

'Oh, I work out down the gym,' Michael said. I believed him. I could feel the hard muscles in the arm pressed against mine.

Richard nodded, as if confirming a guess. 'Thought as much,' he said. 'Bit too pointless for me, all that humping metal around. I prefer something a bit more social for keeping in shape. But then, I suppose it can't be easy finding people who want to play with you when you're an insurance claims manager,' he added, almost as an afterthought. 'Bit like being a VAT man.'

'I've never had any problems finding people to play with,' Michael drawled. I had no trouble believing that. 'What exactly is it that you do to keep fit, Richard? Squash? Real tennis? Polo? Or do you prefer raves?'

Richard almost choked on his food. Neither of us rushed to perform the Heimlich manoeuvre. Recovering, he swallowed hard and said, 'I'm a footie man myself. Local league. Every Sunday morning, never mind the weather.'

Michael smiled. Remember that poem? 'The Assyrian came down like the wolf on the fold'? 'I've never been much into mud myself,' he said.

'Had a good evening?' I chipped in before things got out of hand.

Richard nodded. 'Been down the Academy listening to East European grunge bands. Some good sounds.' He gave me one of his perfect smiles. 'How's your workload progressing?'

I shrugged. 'Slowly,' I said. 'Michael's been giving me some background on the art front, and I've got Alexis to chuck a few bricks into the pond. It's a question of waiting to see what floats to the surface.'

'And we all know what floats,' Richard said drily, glancing at Michael.

Michael decided enough was enough. He drained his mug and put it down on the coffee table. 'I'd better be on my way,' he said. 'Busy day tomorrow.'

We both stood up. 'I'll see you out,' I said.

'Nice to meet you, Richard,' Michael said politely on his way out the door.

'Feeling's entirely mutual,' Richard said ironically.

On the doorstep, I thanked Michael for dinner. 'It was a pleasant change,' I said.

'I can see that,' Michael said. 'Maybe we could do it again some time.'

I only hesitated for a moment. 'That'd be nice,' I admitted.

'Let me know how your investigation progresses,' he said. 'Stay in touch.' He leaned forward and brushed my cheek with his lips. He smelled of warm, clean animal, the last traces of his aftershave lingering muskily underneath. The hairs on the back of my neck stood on end as my body tingled.

I turned my head and met his lips in a swift,

breathless kiss. Before it could turn into anything more, I stepped back. 'Drive safely,' I said.

I watched him walk to his car, enjoying the light bounce of his step. Then I took a deep breath and walked back indoors.

After Michael had gone, Richard polished off the remains of his Chinese, making no comment on my choice of company for the evening. He asked if I wanted to see a movie the following evening and we bickered companionably about what we'd go to see, me holding out for *Blade Runner: The Director's Cut*, revisiting the Cornerhouse for the umpteenth time. 'No way,' Richard had said emphatically. 'I'm not going to the Cornerhouse. I'm getting too old for art houses. They're full of politically correct wankers trying to pretend they understand the articles in the *Modern Review*. You can't move for people rabbiting about semiotics and Foucault and deconstruction.' He paused, then got to the real reason. 'Besides, they don't sell popcorn or Häagen-Dazs. You can't call that a night out at the movies.'

I gave in gracefully. Satisfied that I'd made the concession, Richard announced he had to write an article about the post-Communist rockers for some American West Coast magazine, and he wanted to get it written and faxed before he went to bed. He swept the remains of his takeaway into the carrier bag and gave me a swift hug. 'I love you, Brannigan,' he muttered gruffly into my ear.

I fell asleep with the words of Dean Friedman's 'Love is not Enough' swirling round my head like a mantra. I woke up alone the next morning, and not particularly surprised by that. I felt strangely deflated, as if something I'd been anticipating hadn't happened. I wasn't sure if that was to do with Michael or Richard. Either way, I didn't like the feeling that my state of mind was dependent on anyone else. I stood in the shower for a long time, letting the water pour down. A friend of mine who's into all that New Age stuff reckons a shower cleanses your aura. I don't know about that, but it always helps me put things into perspective.

By the time I walked through the office door, I was feeling in control of my life again. That might have had something to do with the miracle of finding a parking meter that was nearer the office than my house. Parking in this city gets worse by the day. I've been seriously wondering how much it would cost to bribe the security men at the BBC building across the road to let me park my car inside their compound. Probably more than I earn.

Shelley was on the phone, so I headed straight for the coffee maker, a shiny chrome cappuccino machine that my partner, the gadget king of the Northwest, bought us for a treat after a grateful client gave us a bonus because we'd done the job faster than Speedy Gonzales. Somehow, I couldn't see either of our current employers rewarding my swiftness. I was beginning to feel like I was wading through cement on both cases.

Before I could fill the scoop with coffee, I heard Shelley say, 'Hang on, she's just walked in.'

I turned to see her waving the phone at me. 'Alexis,' Shelley said.

I headed for my office. 'Coffee?' It was a try-on, I admit it. Mortensen and Brannigan adopts a firm 'you want it, you make it' policy on coffee. But every now and again, Shelley takes pity on me.

I guess I didn't look needy enough, for there were no signs of her crossing the office after she'd switched the call through. I sighed and picked up the phone. ''Morning,' I said.

'Don't sound so enthusiastic,' the familiar Liverpudlian voice rasped. 'Here am I, bringing you tidings from the front line and you greet me with all the eager anticipation of a woman expecting bad news from her dentist.'

'It's your own fault. Never come between a woman and her cappuccino,' I retorted crisply.

I heard the sound of smoke being inhaled, then a husky chuckle. 'Some of us don't need coffee this late in the day. Some of us have already done half a day's work, KB.'

'Self-righteousness doesn't become you,' I snarled. 'Did you call for a reason, or did you just want to be told there's something clever about having a job that starts in the middle of the night?'

'There's gratitude for you,' Alexis said cheerfully. 'I call you up to pass on vital information, and what thanks do I get?'

I took a deep breath. 'Thank you, O bountiful

84

one,' I grovelled. 'So what's this vital piece of information?'

'What have you got to swap for it?'

I thought for a moment. 'You can borrow my leather jacket for a week.'

'Too tight under the armpits. What's the matter, KB? Got no gossip to trade? What's happening with the insurance man?'

If the *Chronicle*'s editor ever decides he needs to pacify the anti-smoking lobby and fire Alexis, she'll never starve. She could set up tomorrow in a booth on Blackpool pier. She wouldn't even have to change her name. Gypsy Alexis Lee sounds just fine to me. 'We had dinner last night,' I said abruptly.

'And?'

'And nothing. Dinner at That Café, he came in for coffee, Richard barged in waving a Chinese, they squabbled like two dogs over a bone, he went home.'

'Alone?'

'Of course alone, what do you take me for? On second thoughts, don't answer that. Trust me, Alexis, nothing's happening with the insurance man. You'll be the first to know if and when there is. Now, cut the crap and tell me what you rang for.'

'OK. The jungle drums have obviously been beating after that piece I did yesterday on the robberies.'

Nothing warms the cockles of the heart like the

smug self-satisfaction of being right. 'So what's the word on the street?'

'I don't know about the street. I'm working the stately home circuit these days,' Alexis replied disdainfully. 'I've just come off the blower with a punter called Lord Ballantrae.'

'Who's he?'

'I'm not entirely sure of all the titles, since I've not looked him up in Debrett yet, but he's some sort of Scotch baron.'

'You mean he's in the whisky trade?'

'No, soft girl, he's a baron and he comes from Scotland, though you'd never know to hear him talk.'

'So has he been burgled too?'

'Yeah, but that's not why he rang. Apparently, after he got turned over, he had a chat with some of his blue-blood buddies and found there was a lot of it about, so they got together in a sort of semi-informal network to pool their info and help other rich bastards to avoid the same happening to them. One of them spotted the story I did and told him about it, so he rang me for a chat. I'm doing a news feature on him and his gang, about how they're banding together to foil the robbers. And get this. They call themselves the Nottingham Group.' She paused, expectantly.

I took the bait. It was a small price to pay to keep the wheels of friendship oiled. 'Go on, tell me. I know you're dying to. Why the Nottingham Group?'

'After the Sheriff of Nottingham. On account of their goal is to stop these robbin' hoods from ripping off their wealth for redistribution to the selected poor.'

'Nice one,' I said. 'You going to give me his number?' I copied down Alexis's information and stuck the Post-it note on my phone. 'Thanks.'

'Is that it? What about "I owe you one"?'

Nobody's ever accused Alexis of being a shrinking violet. 'I don't. You're paying me back for your exclusive last night.'

'OK. You free for lunch?'

'Doubt it, somehow. What about tonight? Richard and I are going to the multi-screen. Do you two want to join us?'

'Sorry, we've already booked for *Blade Runner* at the Cornerhouse.'

Typical. 'Don't forget your Foucault,' I said.

I was halfway out of my chair, destination coffee machine, when the phone rang again. Suppressing a growl, I grabbed it and injected a bit of warmth into my voice. 'Good morning, Kate Brannigan speaking.'

'It's Trevor Kerr here.'

I wished I hadn't bothered with the warmth. 'Hello, Mr Kerr. What news?'

'I could ask you the same thing, since I'm paying you to investigate this business,' he grumbled. 'I'm ringing to let you know that my lab people have come up with some results from the analysis I asked them to carry out.'

Not a man to give credit where it's due, our Mr Kerr. I stifled a sigh and said, 'What did they discover?'

'A bloody nightmare, that's what. About half the samples they tested aren't bloody KerrSter.'

'Cyanide?' I asked, suddenly anxious.

'No, nothing like that. Just a mixture of chemicals that wouldn't clean anything. Not only would they not clean things, there are certain surfaces they'd ruin. Anything with a sealed finish like floor tiles or worktops. Bastards!' Kerr spat.

'Are these common chemicals, or what?'

'Ever heard of caustic soda? That's how bloody common we're talking here.'

'So cheap as well as common?' I asked.

'A lot bloody cheaper than what we put in KerrSter, let me tell you. So what are you going to do about it?' he demanded pugnaciously.

'Your killer's a counterfeiter,' I said, ignoring his belligerence. 'Either they're trying to wreck your business or else they're simply after a quick buck.'

'Even I'd got that far,' he said sarcastically. 'What I want you to do is find these buggers while I've still got a business left. You hear what I'm saying, Miss Brannigan? Find these bastards, or there won't be a pot left to pay you out of.'

8

Sometimes I wonder how clients managed to go to the bathroom before they hired us. Trevor Kerr was clearly one of those who think once they've hired you, you're responsible for everything up to and including emptying the wastepaper bins at night. He was adamant that it was down to me to go and see the detectives investigating the death of Joey Morton, the Stockport publican, to inform them that the person who was sabotaging Kerrchem's products was probably the one they should be beating up with rubber hoses. Incidentally, never believe the politicians and top coppers who tell you that sort of thing can't happen now all interviews are tape recorded. There are no tape recorders in police cars or vans, and I've heard of cases where it's taken three hours for a police car to travel two inner city miles.

I wasn't relishing telling some overworked and overstressed police officer how to run an inquiry. If there's one thing your average cop hates more than becoming the middle man in a domestic, it's being put on the right track by a private eye. I was even less thrilled when Kerr told me who the investigating officer was. Detective Inspector Cliff Jackson and I were old sparring partners. The first time one of my cases ended in murder, he was running the show. He hadn't exactly covered himself in glory, twice arresting the wrong person before the real killer had eventually ended up behind bars, largely as a result of some judicious tampering by Mortensen and Brannigan. You'd think he'd have been grateful. Think again.

I drove out to the incident room in Stockport. The one time I'd have welcomed being stuck in traffic, I cruised down Stockport Road without encountering a single red light. My luck was still out to lunch when I arrived at the police station. Jackson was in. I didn't even have to kick my heels while he pretended to be too busy to slot me in right away.

He didn't get up when I was shown into his office. He hadn't changed much; still slim, hair still dark and barbered to within an inch of its life, eyes still hidden behind a pair of tinted prescription lenses. His dress sense hadn't improved any. He wore a white shirt with a heavy emerald green stripe, the sleeves rolled up over his bony elbows. His tie was shiny polyester, in a shade of green that screamed for mercy against the shirt. 'I wasn't expecting to see you again,' he greeted me ungraciously.

'Nice to see you too, inspector,' I said pleasantly. 'But let's not waste our time on pleasantries. I wanted to talk to you about Joey Morton's death.'

'I see,' he said. 'Go on, then, talk.'

I told him all he needed to know. 'So you see,' I concluded, 'it looks like someone had got it in for Kerrchem, and Joey Morton just got in the way.'

He rubbed the bridge of his nose in a familiar gesture. It didn't erase the frown he'd had since I first walked through the door. 'Very interesting, Miss Brannigan,' he said. 'I take it you're planning to pursue your own inquiries along these lines?'

'It's what I'm paid to do,' I said.

'This is a possible murder inquiry,' he said sententiously. 'There's no place for you poking around in it.'

'Inspector, in case you've forgotten, it was me that came to you. I'm trying to be helpful,' I said, forcing my jaw to unclench.

'And your "help" is duly noted,' he said. 'It's our job now. If you interfere with this investigation like you did the last time, I'll have no hesitation in arresting you. Is that clear?'

I stood up. I know five foot three isn't exactly intimidating, but it made me feel better. 'I'll do my job, Inspector. And when I've done it, I'll tell you where you can find your killer.'

I tried to slam the door behind me, but it had one of those hydraulic arms. Instead of a satisfying crash, I ended up with a twisted wrist. I was still fizzing when I got back to the car, so I decided to kill two birds with one stone. Down the Thai boxing gym I could work out my rage and frustration and, with a bit of luck, acquire some information too.

I like the gym. It's a no-frills establishment, which means I tend not to run into clients there. As well as the boxing gym, it's got a weights room and basic changing facilities. The only drawback is that there are never enough showers at busy times. Judging by the number of open lockers, that wasn't going to be a problem today. I emerged from the women's changing room in the breeze-block drill hall to find my mate Dennis O'Brien lounging in a director's chair in his sweats. He was reading the *Chronicle*, his mobile phone, cigarettes and a mug of tea strategically placed on the floor by his feet. Dennis used to be a serious burglar, the kind who turn over the vulgar suburban houses of the nouveau riche. But it all came on top for him when a young lad he'd brought in to help him with a big job managed to drop the safe on Dennis's leg as they were making their getaway. He left Dennis lying on the drive with a broken ankle. By the time the cops arrived, he'd crawled half a mile. When he got out of prison three years later, he swore he was never going to do anything that would get him taken away from his kids again. As far as I know, he's kept his word, with one exception. The lad who abandoned him still walks with a limp.

It was Dennis who got me into Thai boxing. He believes all women should have self-defence skills, and when he discovered I'd been relying on nothing more than charm and a reasonable turn of speed, he'd dragged me down to the gym. His daughter's been a finalist in the national championships for the last three years running, and he lets her beat me up on a regular basis, just to remind me that there are people out there who could cause me serious damage. As if I need reminding after some of the crap I've been through in recent years.

Now he's out of major league villainy and into 'a bit of this, a bit of that, a bit of ducking and diving', Dennis has taken to using the gym as his corporate headquarters. I don't suppose the management mind. All the locals know Dennis's Draconian views on drugs so his presence keeps the gym clear of steroid abuse. And there are never any fights outside the ring. He's not known in South Manchester as Dennis the Menace for nothing.

I checked out a couple of black lads working the heavy bags at the far end of the room. They were too far away to overhear. 'Your backside will start looking like Richard's car if you carry on like that,' I said, smiling over the top of his paper.

'At last, someone worth sparring with,' Dennis said, bouncing to his feet. 'How's it hanging, kid?'

'By a fingernail,' I said, bending over to start my warm-up exercises. 'What do you know?' I glanced over at Dennis, who was mirroring my movements.

He looked glum. 'Tell you the truth, Kate, I'm in the shit,' he said.

'Want to tell me about it?'

'Remember that nice little earner I told you about a while back? My crime prevention scheme?'

How could I forget? Dennis's latest scam involved parting villains from large wads of money by persuading them they were buying a truckload of stolen merchandise from him. Dennis would show them a sample of the goods (bought or shoplifted from one of the dozens of wholesalers down Strangeways) and arrange a handover the following day in a motorway service area. Only, once the punters had swapped their stash for the keys to the alleged wagonload and Dennis's car was a distant puff of exhaust, the crooks would discover that the keys he'd handed them didn't open a single truck on the lorry park. Crime prevention? Well, if Dennis was taking their money off them, they wouldn't be inciting anyone else to steal something for them to buy, now would they?

'Somebody catch up with you?' I gasped between sit-ups.

'Worse than that,' he said gloomily. 'I set up a meet at Anderton Services on the 61. Ten grand for a wagon of Levis. Everything's going sweet as a Sunday morning shag when it all comes on top. All of a sudden, there's more bizzies than you get on crowd control at a United/City match. I legged it over the footbridge and dived into the ladies' toilet. Sat there for two hours. I went back over just in time to see the dibble loading my Audi on to a tow truck. I couldn't fucking believe it, could

I?' Dennis grunted as he did a handful of squat thrusts.

'Somebody tip them off about you?' I asked, fastening a body protector over my front.

'You kidding me? This wasn't regular Old Bill, this was the Drugs Squad. They'd only been staking the place out because they'd had a tip a big crack deal was going down. They see somebody handing over a wad of cash, and they jump to the wrong conclusion.'

'So what's happening?' I asked, pulling the ropes apart and climbing into the ring.

Dennis followed me and we began to circle each other cautiously. 'They lifted my punter and accused him of being a drug baron.' He snorted. 'That pillock couldn't deal a hand of poker, never mind a key of crack. Any road, he's so desperate to get out of the shit he's drowning in that he coughs the lot. Next morning, they're round my house mob-handed. The wife was mortified.'

'They charging you?' I asked, swinging a swift kick in towards Dennis's knee.

He sidestepped and twisted round, catching me over the right hip. 'Got to, haven't they? Otherwise they come away from their big stakeout empty-handed. Theft, and obtaining by deception.'

I didn't say anything. I didn't need to. Dennis might have been clean as far as the law is concerned for half a dozen years now, but with his record, he was looking at doing time. I feinted left and pivoted on the ball of my foot to bring my right leg up in a fast arc that caught Dennis in the ribs.

'Nice one, Kate,' he wheezed as he bounced back off the ropes.

'Bit of luck, your punters might decide it would be bad for their reputations if they weigh in as witnesses when it comes to court.' It wasn't much consolation but it was all I could think of.

'Never mind their reputation, it wouldn't be too good for their health,' he said darkly. 'Anyway, I've got one or two things on the boil. Just a bit of insurance in case I do go down. Make sure Debbie and the kids don't go without if I'm away.'

I didn't ask what kind of insurance. I knew better. We worked out in silence for a while. I was upset at the thought of only seeing Dennis with a visiting order for the next couple of years, but there was nothing I could do to help him out, and he knew that as well as I did. Even though we have more attitudes in common than seems likely on the surface, there are areas of each other's lives we take care to avoid. Mostly they're to do with knowledge that either of us would feel uncomfortable about keeping to ourselves. I don't tell him when I'm about to drop people in it who he knows, and he doesn't tell me things I'd feel impelled to pass on to the cops.

After fifteen minutes of dodging each other round the ring, we were both sweating. I lost concentration for a moment, which was all it took.

Next thing I knew, I was on my back staring at the strip lights.

'Sloppy,' Dennis remarked.

I scrambled up to find him leaning on the ropes. I could have knocked the wind out of him with one kick. Or maybe not. I've come into contact with that rock-hard diaphragm before. 'Got a lot on my mind,' I said.

'Anything I can help with?' he asked. Typical Dennis. Didn't matter how much crap of his own he had to sort out, he was still determined to stay in the buddy role.

'Maybe,' I said, slipping between the ropes and heading for the neat stack of scruffy towels on a shelf.

Dennis followed me, and we sat companionably on a bench while we talked. I gave him a brief outline of the Kerrchem case. 'You know anybody who's doing schneid cleaning fluid?' I ended up.

He shook his head. 'I don't know anybody that stupid,' he said scornfully. 'There's not nearly enough margin in it, is there? And it's bulky. Costs you a lot to shift it around, and you can't exactly set up a street-corner pitch with it, can you? There was a team from Liverpool tried schneid washing powder a couple of years back. They'd done a raid on a chemical firm, nicked one of their vans to do the getaway. There were a couple of drums of chemicals in the back, and they decided not to waste it so they printed up some boxes and flogged it on the markets. Nasty stuff. Took the skin off your fingers if you tried hand-washing. Mind you, there weren't any of them "difficult" stains left. That's because there wasn't a lot of clothes left.'

'So you don't reckon it's any of the usual faces?'

Dennis shook his head. 'Like I said, you'd have to be stupid to go for that when there's plenty of hooky gear around with bigger profits and a lot less risk. I reckon you're looking closer to home on this one. This is a grudge match.'

'An ex-employee? A competitor?' Even though it's a long way removed from his world, it's always worth bouncing ideas off Dennis.

Dennis shrugged. 'You're the corporate expert. Is this the kind of stunt big business pulls these days? I'd heard things were getting a bit tough out there, but bumping people off is a bit heavy for a takeover bid.'

'So an ex-employee, you reckon?'

'That's where I'd put my money. Stands to reason, they're the ones with a real grudge, and there's no comeback. And what about them thingumabobs . . . what do they call it? When they give you the bullet and make you sign a bit of paper saying you can't go off and sell their secrets to the opposition?'

'Golden handcuffs,' I said ruefully. I was slipping. That should have been one of the first half-dozen questions I asked Trevor Kerr.

'Yeah well, nobody likes being stuck in a pair of handcuffs, don't matter whether they're gold or steel,' Dennis said with feeling. 'It was me, I'd feel pretty cheesed. Specially if I was one of them boffins whose expertise goes out of date faster than a Marks and Spencer ready meal.'

I stretched an arm round his muscular shoulders and hugged him. 'You're a pal, Dennis.'

'I haven't done anything,' he said. 'That it? You consulted the oracle?'

'That's it. Unless you know an international gang of art thieves.'

'Art thieves?' he asked, sounding interested.

'They've been working all over the country, turning over stately homes. They go for one item and crash in through the nearest door or window. No finesse, just sledgehammers. Straight in and out. Obviously very professional. Sound like anybody you know?'

Dennis pulled a face. 'I'm well out of touch with that scene,' he said, getting to his feet. 'I'm off for a shower. Will you still be here when I'm done?'

I glanced at my watch. 'No, got to run.' Whatever else happened today, I couldn't leave Richard standing around at the multi-screen.

'See you around, kid,' Dennis said, walking off.

'Yeah. And Dennis . . .'

He looked over his shoulder, the changing room door half open.

'If there's anything I can do . . .'

Dennis's smile was as crooked as his business. 'You'll know,' he said.

Back at the car, I hit the phone. Sheila the Dragon Queen tried to tell me Trevor Kerr was in a meeting, but she was no match for my civil servant impersonation. I had good teachers; I once devoted most of my spare time for six months to screwing housing benefit out of a succession of bloody-minded officials.

'Trevor Kerr,' the phone barked at me.

'Kate Brannigan here. I've spoken to the police, who were very interested in what I had to tell them about the fake KerrSter,' I said. 'They said they would investigate that angle.'

'You pulled me out of a production meeting to tell me that?' he demanded.

'Not only that,' I said mildly. It was an effort. If he carried on like this, I reckoned there was going to be a five per cent surliness surcharge on Trevor Kerr's bill.

'What, then?'

'You mentioned you'd had a round of redundancies,' I said.

'So?'

'I wondered if anyone who'd gone out the door had been subject to a golden handcuffs deal.'

There was a moment's silence. 'There must have been a few,' he admitted grudgingly. 'It's standard practice for anybody working in research or in key production jobs.'

'I'll need a list.'

'You'll have one,' he said.

'Have it faxed to my office,' I replied. 'The number's on the card.' I cut the connection. That's the great thing with mobile phones. There are so many black holes around that nobody dares accuse you of hanging up on them any more.

I took out my notebook and rang the number Alexis had given me earlier. The voice that answered the phone didn't sound like Lord Ballantrae. Not unless he'd had an unfortunate accident. 'I'm looking for Lord Ballantrae,' I said.

'This is his wife,' she said. 'Who's calling?'

'My name is Kate Brannigan. I'm a private investigator in Manchester. I understand Lord Ballantrae is the coordinator of a group of stately home owners who have been burgled recently. One of my clients has had a Monet stolen, and I wondered if Lord Ballantrae could spare me some time to discuss it.'

'I'm sure he'd be happy to do so. Bear with me a moment, I'll check the diary.' I hung on for an expensive minute. Then she was back. 'How does tomorrow at ten sound?'

'No problem,' I said.

'Now, if you're coming from Manchester, the easiest way is to come straight up the M6, then take the A7 at Carlisle as far as Hawick, then the A698 through Kelso. About six miles past Kelso, you'll see a couple of stone gateposts on the left with pineapples on top of them. You can't miss them. That's us. Castle Dumdivie. Did you get all that?'

'Yes, thank you,' I said weakly. I'd got it, all right. A good three to four hours' driving.

'We'll look forward to seeing you then,' Lady Ballantrae said. She sounded remarkably cheerful. It was nice to know one of us was.

9

Richard didn't even stir when the alarm cut through my dreams at ten to six like a hot wire through cheese. I staggered to the shower, feeling like my eyes had closed only ten minutes before. Until I started this job, I didn't even know there were two six o'clocks in the same day. Richard still doesn't. I suppose that's why he suggested a club after the latest Steven Spielberg, enough popcorn to feed Bosnia and burgers and beer at Starvin' Marvin's authentic American diner. We'd been having fun together, and I didn't want it to end on a sour note, so I'd agreed with the proviso that I could be a party pooper at one. It goes without saying that we were still dancing at two.

Even a ten-minute power shower couldn't convince my body and my brain that I'd had more than three hours' sleep. Sometimes I wish I hadn't jacked in the law degree after two years, so I could have become a nine-to-five crown prosecutor. I put a pot of strong coffee on to brew while I dressed.

Just what do you wear for a Scottish baron that won't look like a limp dishrag after four hours behind the wheel? I ended up with navy leggings, a cream cotton Aran jumper and a military-style navy wool blouson that I inherited from Alexis. I'd told her in the shop that it made her look too heavy in the hips, but would she listen?

By the third cup of coffee, I felt like I could be trusted to drive without causing a major pile-up. Not that there was a lot of traffic around to test my conviction. For once, it was sheer pleasure to motor down the East Lancs. Road. No boy racers wanting to get into a traffic-lights Grand Prix with my coupé, no little old men with porkpie hats and pipes dithering between lanes, no macho reps waving their mobile phones like battle honours. Just blissful open road spread out before me and Deacon Blue's greatest hits. Since I was going to Scotland, I thought I'd better opt for the native sound. When I left the motorway at Carlisle, it was just after eight. I promised myself breakfast at the first greasy spoon I passed, forgetting what roads in the Scottish borders are like. There was nothing for the best part of an hour, and then it was Hawick. I ended up with a bacon and egg roll from a bakery washed down with a carton of milky industrial effluent that they claimed was coffee.

At a quarter to ten, I spotted the gateposts. When Lady Ballantrae had said pineapples, I was expecting some discreet little stone ornaments.

What I got were two squat pillars topped with carved monstrosities the size of telephone kiosks. She'd been right when she said I couldn't miss them. I turned into a narrow corridor between two beech hedges taller than my house. The road curved round in a gentle arc. Abruptly the trees stopped and I found myself in a grassy clearing dominated by Lord Ballantrae's house. I use the term 'house' loosely. At one end of the sprawling building was a massive square stone tower with a sharply pitched roof. Extending out from it, built in the same forbidding grey stone, was the main house. The basic shape was rectangular, but it was dotted with so many turrets, buttresses and assorted excrescences that it was hard to grasp at first. The whole thing was surmounted by an incongruous white belvedere with a green roof. One of Ballantrae's ancestors either had a hell of a sense of humour or a few bricks short of a wall.

I pulled up on the gravel between a Range Rover and a top-of-the-range BMW. What they call in Manchester a 'Break My Windows'. Like Henry, Lord Ballantrae clearly kept the trippers' coaches well away from the house. By the time I'd got out of the car, I had a spectator. At the top of a short flight of steps like a giant's mounting block a tall man stood staring at me, a hand shielding his eyes from the sun. I walked towards him, taking in the tweed jacket with leather shooting patches, cavalry twills, mustard waistcoat and tattersall check shirt. He was even wearing a tweed cap that matched the jacket. As soon as I was in hailing distance, he called, 'Miss Brannigan, is it?'

'The same. Lord Ballantrae?'

The man dropped his hand and looked amused. 'No, ma'am, I'm his lordship's estate manager. Barry Adamson. Come away in, he's expecting you.'

I followed Adamson's burly back into a comfortable dining kitchen. Judging by the microwave and food processor on the pine worktops, this wasn't part of the castle's historical tour. Beyond the kitchen, we entered a narrow passage that turned into a splendid baronial hall. I don't know much about weapons, but judging by the amount of military hardware in the room, I'd stumbled upon Bonnie Prince Charlie's secret armoury. 'Through here,' Adamson said, opening a heavy oak door. I followed him through the arched doorway into an office that looked nearly as high tech as Bill's.

A dark-haired man in his early forties was frowning into a PC screen. Without looking up, he said, 'With you in two shakes.' He hit a couple of keys and the frown cleared. Then he pushed his chair back and jumped to his feet. 'You must be Kate Brannigan,' he said, coming round the desk and thrusting his hand towards me. 'James Ballantrae.' The handshake was cool and dry, but surprisingly limp. 'Pull up a seat,' he said, waving at a couple of typist's chairs that sat in front of a desk top that ran the length of one wall. 'Barry, Ellen's in the tack room. Can you give her a shout and ask her to bring us some coffee?' he added as he dragged his own chair round the desk. 'How was your journey?' he asked. 'Bitch of a drive, isn't it? I sometimes wish I could ship this place stone by stone to somewhere approximating civilization, but they'd never let me get away with it. It's Grade Two listed, which means we couldn't even have satellite TV installed without some bod from the Department of the Environment making a meal out of it.'

Whatever I'd been expecting, it wasn't this. Lord Ballantrae was wearing faded jeans and a Scottish rugby shirt that matched sparkling navy blue eyes. His wavy hair fell over his collar at the back, its coal black a startling contrast to his milky skin. There was an air of suppressed energy about him. He looked more like a computer-game writer than a major land owner. He sat down, stretching long legs in front of him, and lit a cigarette. 'So, Henry Naismith tells me you're looking for his Monet?' he said.

I tried to hide my surprise. 'You know Henry?' I asked. Let's face it, they both spoke the same language. Their voices were virtually indistinguishable. How in God's name do Sloanes know who's calling when they pick up the phone?

He grinned. 'We met once on a friend's boat. When my wife told me about your call yesterday, I put two and two together. I'd already spoken to a reporter on the Manchester evening paper about these art robberies and when she mentioned a

Monet going missing in Cheshire, I could only think of the Naismith collection. So I gave Henry a ring.'

'The reporter you spoke to is a friend of mine,' I said. 'She passed your number on to me.'

'Old girls' network. I like it,' he exclaimed with delight. 'She did the right thing. God, listen to me. My wife tells me that arrogance runs in the family. All I mean is that I'm probably the only person who has an overview of the situation. The downside of having locally accountable police forces is that crime gets compartmentalized. Sussex don't talk to Strathclyde, Derbyshire don't talk to Devon. It was us who brought to the police's attention the fact that there had been something of a spate of these robberies, all with the same pattern of forced entry, complete disregard for the alarm system and single targets.'

'How did you find out about the connections?' I asked.

'A group of us who open our places to the public get together informally . . .' I heard the door open behind me and turned to see a thirty-something redhead with matching freckles stick her head through the gap.

'Coffee all round?' she said.

'My wife, Ellen,' Ballantrae said. 'Ellen, this is Kate Brannigan, the private eye from Manchester.'

The redhead grinned. 'Pleased to meet you. Be right back,' she said, disappearing from sight, leaving the door ajar.

'Where was I? Oh yes, we get together a couple of times a year for a few sherbets, swap ideas and tips, that sort of thing. Last time we met was a couple of weeks after I'd had a Raeburn portrait lifted, so of course it was uppermost in my mind. Three others immediately chipped in with identical tales – a Gainsborough, a Canaletto and a Ruisdael. In every case, it was one of the two or three best pieces they had,' he added ruefully.

'And that's when you realized there was something organized going on?' I asked.

'Correct.'

'I'm amazed you managed to keep these thefts out of the papers,' I said.

'It's not the sort of thing you boast about,' he said drily. 'We've all become dependent on the income that comes through the doors from the heritage junkies. The police were happy to go along with that, since they never like high-profile cases where they don't catch anyone.'

'What did you do then?'

'Well, I offered to act as coordinator, and I spoke to all the police forces concerned. I also wrote to as many other stately home owners as I could track down and asked if they'd had similar experiences.'

'How many?' I asked.

'Including Henry Naismith's Monet, thirteen in the last nine months.'

I took a deep breath. At this rate, the stately homes of Britain would soon have nothing left but the seven hundred and thirty-six beds Good Queen Bess slept in. 'That's a lot of art,' I said. 'Has anything been recovered?'

'Coffee,' Ellen Ballantrae announced, walking in with a tray. She was wearing baggy khaki cords and a shapeless bottle green chenille sweater. When she moved, it was obvious she was hiding a slim figure underneath, but on first sight I'd have taken her for the cleaner.

I fell on the mug like a deprived waif. 'You've probably saved my life,' I told her. 'My system's still recovering from what they call coffee in Hawick.'

Both Ballantraes grinned. 'Don't tell me,' Ellen said. 'Warm milk, globules floating on top and all the flavour of rainwater.'

'It wasn't that good,' I said with feeling.

'Don't let me interrupt you,' she said, giving her husband's hair an affectionate tousle as she perched on the table. 'He was about to tell you about the Canaletto they got back.'

Ballantrae reached out absently and laid his hand on her thigh. 'Absolutely right. Nothing to do with the diligence of the police, however. There was a multiple pile-up on a German autobahn about a fortnight after Gerald Brockleston-Camber lost his Canaletto. One of the dead was an antique dealer from Leyden in Holland, Kees van der Rohe. His car was shunted at both ends, the boot flew open, throwing a suitcase clear of the wreckage. The case burst open, revealing the Canaletto behind a false lid. Luckily the painting was undamaged.'

'Not so lucky for Mr van der Rohe,' I remarked. 'What leads did they come up with?'

'Not a one,' Ballantrae said. 'They couldn't find anything about the Canaletto in his records. He conducted his business from home, and the neighbours said there were sometimes cars there with foreign plates, but no one had bothered to take a note of registrations.' He shrugged. 'Why should they? There was no indication as to his destination, apart from the fact that he had a couple of hundred pounds' worth of lire in the front pocket of the suitcase. Unfortunately, van der Rohe's body was badly burned, along with his diary and his wallet. Frustrating, but at least Gerald got his painting back.'

Frustrating was right. This was turning into one of those cases where I was sucking up information like a demented Hoover, but none of it was taking me anywhere. The only thing I could think of doing now was getting in touch with a Dutch private eye and asking him or her to check out Kees van der Rohe, to see if he could come up with something the police had missed. 'Any indication of a foreign connection in the other cases?' I asked.

'Not really,' Ballantrae said. 'We suspect that individual pieces are being stolen to order. If anything, I'd hazard a guess that if they're for a private collector, we're looking at someone English. A lot of the items that have been stolen have quite a narrow appeal – the Hilliard miniatures, for example. And my Raeburn too, I suppose. They

110

wouldn't exactly set the international art world ablaze.'

'Maybe that's part of the plan,' I mused.

'How do you mean?' Ellen Ballantrae leaned forward, frowning.

'If they went for really big stuff like the thieves who stole the Munch painting in Norway, there would be a huge hue and cry, Interpol alerted, round up the usual suspects, that sort of thing. But by going for less valuable pieces, maybe they're relying on there being less of a fuss, especially if they're moving their loot across international borders,' I explained.

Ballantrae nodded appreciatively. 'Good thinking, that woman. You could have something there. The only thefts that fall outside that are the Bernini bust and Henry's Monet, but even those two aren't the absolutely prime examples of their creators' works.'

'Can you think of any collectors whose particular interests are covered by the thefts?' I asked.

'Do you know, I hadn't thought about that. I don't know personally, but I have a couple of chums in the gallery business. I could ask them to ask around and see what they come up with. That's a really constructive idea,' Ballantrae enthused.

I basked in the glow of his praise. It made a refreshing change from Trevor Kerr's charmlessness. 'What's the geographical spread like?' I asked.

'We were the most northerly victims. But there doesn't seem to be any real pattern. They go from

Northumberland to Cornwall north to south, and from Lincolnshire to Anglesey east to west. I can let you have a print-out,' he added, jumping to his feet and walking behind his computer. He hit a few keys, and the printer behind me cranked itself into life.

I twirled the chair round and took the sheet of paper out of the machine. Reading down it, I saw the glimmer of an idea. 'Have you got a map of the UK I can look at?' I asked.

Ballantrae nodded. 'I've got a data disk with various maps on it. Want a look?'

I came round behind his desk and waited for him to load the disk. He called up a map of the UK with major cities and the road network. 'Can you import this map and manipulate it in a graphics file?' I asked.

'Sure,' he said. And promptly did it. He gave me a quick tutorial on how to use his software, and I started fiddling with it. First, I marked the approximate locations of the burglaries, with a little help from Ballantrae in identifying locations. I looked at the array.

'I wish we had one of those programs that crime pattern analysts use,' I muttered. I'd recently spent a day at a seminar run by the Association of British Investigators where an academic had shown us how sophisticated computer programs were help- ing police to predict where repeat offenders might strike next. It had been impressive, though not a lot of use to the likes of me.

'I never imagined I'd have any use for one of those,' Ballantrae said drily.

Ellen laughed. 'No doubt the software king will have one by next week,' she said.

Using the mouse, I drew a line connecting the outermost burglaries. There were eight in that group, scattered round the fringes of England and Wales. Then I repeated the exercise with the remainder. The outer line was a rough oval, with a kink over Cornwall. It looked like a cartoon speech balloon, containing the immortal words of the Scilly Isles. The inner line was more jagged. I disconnected Henry Naismith's robbery and another outside Burnley. Now, the inner line was more like a trapezium, narrower at the top, spreading at the bottom. Finally, I linked Henry and the Burnley job with a pair of semi-circles. 'See anything?' I asked.

'Greater Manchester,' Ballantrae breathed. 'How fascinating. Well, Ms Brannigan, you're clearly the right woman for the job.'

I was glad somebody thought so. 'Have there been any clues at all in any of the cases?' I asked.

Ballantrae walked over to a shelf that held his computer software boxes and manuals. 'I don't know if you'd call it a clue, exactly. But one of the properties that was burgled had just installed closed-circuit TV and they have a video of the robbery. But it's not actually a lot of help, since the thieves were very sensibly wearing ski masks.' He took a video down from the shelf. 'Would you like to see it?'

'Why not?' I'd schlepped all the way up here. I wasn't going home before I'd extracted every last drop of info out of Lord Ballantrae.

'We'll have to go through to the den,' he said.

As I followed him back across the hall, Ellen said affectionately, 'Some days I think he's auditioning for *Crimewatch*.'

We retraced my steps back towards the kitchen, turning into a room only twice the size of my living room. The view was spectacular, if you like that sort of thing, looking out across a swathe of grass, a river and not very distant hills. Me, I'm happy with my garden fence. As Ballantrae crossed to the video, I gave the room the once-over. It wasn't a bit like a stately home. The mismatched collection of sofas and armchairs was modern, looking comfortable if a bit dog-haired and dog-eared. Shelves along one wall held a selection of board games, jigsaws, console games and video tapes. A coffee table was strewn with comics and magazines. In one corner there was a huge Nicam stereo TV and video with a Nintendo console lying in front of it. The only picture on the walls was a framed photograph of James and Ellen with a young boy and girl, sitting round a picnic table in skiing clothes. They all looked as if the world was their oyster. Come to think of it, it probably was.

'Sorry about the mess,' Ellen said in the offhand tone that told me she didn't give a shit about tidiness. 'The children make it and I can't be bothered unmaking it. Have a seat.'

She walked over to the windows and pulled one of the curtains across, cutting down the brightness so we could see the video more clearly. I sat down opposite the TV, where daytime TV's best actors played out their roles as a happily married couple telling the rest of us how to beat cellulite. Ballantrae slumped down beside me and hit the play button. 'This is Morton Grange in Humberside,' he said. 'Home of Lord Andrew Cumberbatch. His was the Ruisdael.'

The screen showed an empty room lined with paintings. Suddenly, from the bottom left-hand corner, the burglars appeared. The staccato movements of the time-lapse photography made them look like puppets in an amateur performance. Both men were wearing ski masks with holes for eyes and mouth only, and the kind of overalls you can pick up for next to nothing in any army surplus store. One of them ran across to the painting, pulled out a power screwdriver and unscrewed the clips that held the frame to the wall. The other, holding a sledgehammer, hung back. Then he turned towards the camera and took a couple of steps forward.

Recognition hit me like a punch to the stomach.

10

One of the mysteries of the universe is how I got out of Castle Dumdivie without confessing that I knew exactly who had had it away on his toes with Lord Andrew Cumberbatch's nice little Ruisdael. I was only grateful that James Ballantrae was sitting next to me and couldn't see my face.

After the first seconds of shock, I tried to tell myself I was imagining things. But the longer I watched, the more convinced I was that I was right. I knew those shoulders, those light, bouncing steps. God knows I'd watched that footwork often enough, trying to gauge where the next kick was coming from. I forced myself to sit motionless to the bitter end. Then I said, 'I see what you mean. Even their own mothers wouldn't recognize them from that.'

'Their lovers might,' Ellen said shrewdly. 'Don't they say a person's walk is the one thing they can never disguise?'

She was bang on the button, of course. 'The

video makes it look too jerky for that, I'd have thought,' I said.

'I don't know.' Ballantrae lit another cigarette and inhaled deeply. 'Body language and gesture are pretty individual. Look at the number of crimimals who get caught by the videos they show on *Crimewatch*.'

'Told you,' Ellen said fondly. 'He's dying to go on and talk about his art robberies. The only thing that's holding him back is that all his cronies are terrified about what the publicity might do to their admissions.'

'Yes, but now the cat's out of the bag with that newspaper story in Manchester, there's no point in holding back,' Ballantrae said. 'Maybe I should give them a ring . . .'

'Any chance you could let me have a copy of the tape?' I asked. 'I'd like to show it to Henry Naismith's staff while everything's still fresh in their memories. Perhaps, as Ellen suggests, there might be something in the way these men move that triggers something off. The police reckon they will have gone round the house a couple of times as regular punters, sussing it out, so we might just get lucky if one of Henry's staff has a photographic memory.'

Ballantrae got up and took the video out of the machine. 'Take this one,' he said. 'I can easily get Andrew to run me off another copy.'

I took the tape and stood up. 'I really appreciate your help on this,' I said. 'If anything else should

117

come to mind that might be useful, please give me a ring.' I fished a business card out of my bag.

'What will you do now?' Ballantrae asked.

'Like I said, show the vid to Henry's staff. I'm also hopeful that the story in the *Chronicle* might stir the pot a bit. The chances are that it's not just the robbers themselves who know who they are. Maybe you should think about getting together with your insurance companies and offering a reward. It would make a good follow-up story for the paper and it might just be what we need to lever the lid off things.' I was starting to gabble, I noticed. Time for a sharp exit. I ostentatiously looked at my watch. 'I'd better be heading back to the wicked city,' I said.

'You're sure you've got to go?' Ballantrae asked with the pathetic eagerness of a small boy who sees his legitimate diversion from homework disappearing over a distant horizon. 'I could show you round the house. You could see for yourself where they broke in.'

Amused, Ellen said, 'I'm sure Ms Brannigan's seen one or two windows in her time.' Turning to me, she added, 'You're very welcome to stay for lunch, but if you have to get back, don't feel the need to apologize for turning down the guided tour of Dumdivie's loot.'

'Thanks for the offer, but I need to hit the road,' I said. 'This isn't the only case we've got on right now, and my partner's out of the country.' I really was wittering now. I took a step towards the door. 'I'll keep you posted.'

I drove back to Manchester on automatic pilot, my thoughts whirling. Shelley phoned at one point, but I'm damned if I know what we talked about. When I hit the city, I didn't go to the office. I didn't want any witnesses to the conversation I was planning. I drove straight home, glad for once to find Richard was out.

My stomach was churning, so I brewed some coffee and made myself a sandwich of ciabatta, tuna, olives and plum tomatoes. It was only when I tried to eat it and found I had no appetite that I realized it was anxiety rather than hunger that was responsible for the awesome rumblings. Sighing, I wrapped the sandwich in clingfilm and tossed it in the fridge. I picked up the phone. Some money-grabbing computer took ten pence off me for the privilege of telling me Dennis's mobile was switched off.

Next, I rang the gym. Don, the manager, told me Dennis had been in earlier, but had gone off a couple of hours ago suited up. 'If he comes back, tell him I've been visiting the gentry and he needs to see me, double urgent. I'll be at home,' I said grimly.

That left his home. His wife Debbie answered on the third ring. She's got a heart of gold, but she could have provided the model for the dumb blonde stereotype. I'd always reckoned that if a brain tumour were to find its way inside her skull it would bounce around for days looking for a place to settle. However, I wasn't planning

119

on challenging her intellect. I just asked if Dennis was there, and she said she hadn't seen him since breakfast. 'Do you know where he is?' I asked.

She snorted incredulously. 'I gave up asking him stuff like that fifteen years ago,' she said. Maybe she wasn't as thick as I'd always thought. 'To be honest, I'd rather not know what he's up to most of the time. Long as he gives me money for the kids and the house and he stays out of jail, I ask no questions. That way, when the Old Bill comes knocking, there's nothing I can tell them. He knows I'm a crap liar,' she giggled.

'When are you expecting him back?'

'When I see him, love. Have you tried his mobile?'

'Switched off.'

'He won't have it turned off for long,' Debbie reassured me. 'If he comes home before you catch him, do you want me to get him to give you a bell?'

'No. I want him to come round the house. Tell him it's urgent, would you?'

'You're not in any trouble, are you, Kate?' Debbie asked anxiously. 'Only, if you need somebody in a hurry, I could get one of the lads to come round.'

Like I said, heart of gold. 'Don't worry, Debbie, I'm fine. I've got something I need to show Dennis, that's all. Just ask him to come round soon as.'

We chatted for a bit about the kids, then I rang off. I knew I should go into the office and pick up Trevor Kerr's list of former employees, but I knew

I wouldn't be able to concentrate on it. I switched on the computer and loaded up Epic Pinball. I thrashed the ball round the bumpers and ramps a few times, but I couldn't get into it. My scores would have shamed an arthritic octogenarian. I decided I needed something more violent, so I started playing Doom, the ultimate shoot-'em-up, at maximum danger level. After I got killed for the tenth time, I gave up and switched the machine off. I know it's as bad as it can get when I can't lose myself in a computer game.

I ended up cleaning the house. The trouble with modern bungalows is that it doesn't take nearly long enough to bottom them when you want a really good angst-letting. By the time the doorbell rang, I'd moved on to purging my wardrobe of all those garments I hadn't worn for two years but had cost too much for me to dump in my normal frame of mind. A disastrous pair of leggings that looked like stretch chintz curtains were saved by the bell.

Dennis stood on the doorstep, grinning cheerily. I wanted to smack him, but good sense prevailed over desire. It seemed to have been doing that a lot lately. 'Hiya. Debbie says you've got something for me,' he greeted me, leaning forward to kiss my cheek.

I backed off, letting him teeter. 'Something to show you,' I corrected him, marching through into my living room. Without waiting for him to sit down, I smacked the tape into the video, turned on the TV and pressed play. I kept my back to him while the robbery replayed itself before our eyes. As the two burglars disappeared from sight, I switched off the TV and turned to face him.

Dennis's expression revealed nothing. I might as well have shown him a blank screen for all the reaction I was getting. 'Nice one, Dennis,' I said bitterly. 'Thanks for marking my card.'

He thrust his hands into the trouser pockets of his immaculate, pearl grey, double-breasted suit. 'What did you expect me to do? Put my hands up when you told me what you was looking into?' he said quietly.

'Never mind what I expected,' I said. 'What you did do has dropped me right in it.'

Dennis frowned. 'What is this?' he demanded angrily. 'You know the kind of thing I do for a living. I'm not some snow-white straight man. I'm a thief, Kate, a fucking criminal. I steal things, I have people over, I pull scams. How else do you think I put food in my kids' mouths and clothes on their backs? It's not like I've been keeping it a big fucking secret, is it?'

'No, but . . .'

'What's wrong? You're quick enough to come to me for help because I can go places and get people to talk that you can't. You think I could do that if I wasn't as bent as the bastards you chase? What is it, Kate? You can't handle the fact that one of your mates is a crook now you're faced with the evidence?'

I found myself subsiding on to a sofa. He was

right, of course. I've always known in the abstract that Dennis was a villain, but I'd never had to confront it directly. 'I thought you weren't doing this kind of thing any more,' I said weakly. 'You always said you wouldn't do stuff that would get you a long stretch again.'

Dennis threw himself on to the sofa opposite me. A grim smile flashed across his face. 'That was the plan. Then everything came on top, like I told you. Kate, I could get five for that. My kids shouldn't have to suffer because I'm a villain, should they? I don't want my kids not being able to go to university because their old man's inside and there's no money. I don't want my family living in some bed-and-breakfast dosshouse because the mortgage hasn't been paid and the house has been repo'ed. Now, the only way I know to make sure that doesn't happen is to salt away some insurance money. And the only way I know to get money is robbing.'

'So you've been doing these art robberies,' I said.

'That's right. Listen, if I'd known that you'd done the security on Birchfield Place, I wouldn't have gone near the gaff. You're my mate, I don't want to embarrass you.'

I shook my head. 'If I recognized you, Dennis, chances are someone else might, especially if they put the tape on the box.'

He sighed. 'So do what you have to do, Kate.' He met my eyes, not in a challenge, but in a kind of agreement.

'You don't think I'm going to shop you, do you?' I blurted out indignantly.

'It's your job,' he said simply.

I shook my head. 'No, it's not. My job is to get my clients' property back. It's the police that arrest villains, not me.'

'You've turned people over to the dibble before,' Dennis pointed out. 'You got principles, you should stick to them. It's OK, Kate, I won't hold it against you. It's an occupational hazard. You work with asbestos, sometimes you get lung cancer. You go robbing for a living, sometimes you get a nicking. There's nothing personal in it.'

'Will you get it into your thick head that I am not going to grass you up?' I said belligerently. 'The only thing I'm interested in is getting Henry Naismith's Monet back. Anyway, you're only a small fish. If I want anybody, I want the whale.'

Dennis's lips tightened to a thin line. 'OK, I hear you,' he said grimly. I didn't expect him to fall to his knees in gratitude. Nobody likes being placed under the kind of obligation I'd just laid on him.

'So cough,' I said.

He cleared his throat. 'It's not that simple,' he said, taking his time over pulling out his cigarettes and lighting up. 'I haven't got it any more.'

'That was quick,' I said, disappointed. From what Dennis had told me about his previous exploits in the field of executive burglary, it often takes some time to shift the proceeds, fences being notoriously

124

twitchy about taking responsibility for stolen goods that are still so hot they risk meltdown.

Dennis leaned back in his seat, unbuttoning his jacket. 'A ready market. That's one of the reasons I got into this in the first place. See, what happened was when I realized this court case wasn't going to go away, I put the word out that I was looking for a nice little earner. A couple of weeks later, I get a call from this bloke I know in Leeds. I fenced a couple of choice antique items with him in the old days when I was pursuing my former career. Anyway, he says he's heard about my bit of bother, and he's got a contact for me. He gives me this mobile phone number, and tells me to ring this bloke.

'So I ring the number and mention my contact's name and this bloke says to me he's in the market for serious art. He says he has a client for top-flight gear, flat fee of ten grand a pop for pieces agreed in advance. I go, "How do I know I can trust you?" And he goes, "You don't part with the gear till you see the colour of my money." I go, "How does it work?" And he goes, "You decide on something you think you can get away with, and you ring me and ask me if I want it. I ring you back the next day with a yes or a no."'

'So you embark on your new career as an art robber,' I said. 'Simple, really.'

'You wouldn't be so sarcastic if you knew what a nause it is shifting stuff like that on the open market,' Dennis said with feeling.

'How did you know what to go for? And where to

go for it?' I demanded. I'd never had Dennis pegged as a paid up member of the National Trust.

'My mate Frankie came out a while back,' he said. I didn't think he meant that Frankie had revealed he was a raging queen. 'He's been doing an eight stretch for armed robbery, and he did an Open University degree while he was inside. He did a couple of courses in history of art. He reckoned it would come in useful on the outside,' he added drily.

'I don't think that's quite what the government had in mind when they set up the OU,' I said.

Dennis grinned. 'Get an education, get on in life. Anyway, we spent a couple of months schlepping round these country houses, sussing out what was where, what was worth nicking and what the security was like. Pathetic, most of it.'

I had a sudden thought. 'Dennis, these robberies have been going on for nine months now. You only got nicked a few weeks ago. You didn't start doing this for insurance money, you started doing this out of sheer badness,' I accused him.

He shrugged, looking slightly shamefaced. 'So I lied. I'm sorry, Kate, I can't change the habit of a lifetime. This was just too good to miss. And watertight. We don't touch places with security guards so nobody gets hurt or upset. We're in and out so fast there's no way we're going to get caught.'

'I caught you,' I pointed out.

'Yeah, but you're a special case,' Dennis said.

'Besides, the CCTV wasn't there when we cased the place. They must have only just put it in.'

'So who is this guy who's giving you peanuts for these masterpieces?'

Dennis smiled wryly. 'It's not peanuts, Kate. It's good money and no hassle.'

'It's a tiny fraction of what they're worth,' I said.

'Define worth. What an insurance company pays out? What you could get at auction? Worth is what somebody's prepared to pay. I reckon ten grand for a night's work is not bad going.'

'A grand for every year if they catch you. You'd get a better rate of pay working in a sweatshop making schneid T-shirts. So who's the buyer? Some private collector or what?'

'I don't know,' Dennis said. 'I don't even know who the fence is.'

I snorted incredulously. 'Come on, Dennis, you've done more than a dozen deals with this guy, you must know who he is.'

'I've never met him before this run of jobs,' Dennis said. 'All I've got is the number for his mobile.'

'You're kidding,' I said. 'You've done over a hundred grand's worth of work for some punter whose name you don't even know?'

''S right,' he said easily. 'My business isn't like yours, Kate, I don't take out credit references on the people I do business with. Look, what happens is, every few weeks I ring the guy up with one of

Frankie's suggestions. He gives me the nod, we go out and do the job, and I give him a bell. We meet on the motorway services, we show him the goods, he counts the dosh in front of us, and we all go home happy boys.'

'What about the fakes?'

There was a deathly silence. He ground out his cigarette viciously in the ashtray. 'How did you find out about them?' Dennis asked warily. 'There's been nothing in the papers or anything about that.'

'What happens when it turns out you've nicked a copy?' I asked, ignoring him.

Dennis shifted in his seat, leaning forward with his elbows on his knees. 'You setting me up, or what?' he asked. 'You saying that Monet wasn't kosher?'

'It was kosher,' I said. 'But they haven't all been, have they?'

Dennis lit his cigarette like an actor in a Pinter play filling one of the gaps with a complicated bit of business. 'Three of them were bent as a nine-bob note,' he said. 'First I knew about it was about a week after we'd done the handover when the geezer bells me and tells me. I said I never knew anything about it, and he goes, "I'm sure you were acting in good faith, but the problem is that so was my client. He reckons you owe him ten grand. And he has very efficient debt collectors. But he's a fair man. He'll cancel the debt if you provide another painting for free." So we to and fro a bit, and eventually he agrees that he'll pay us a grand for expenses for the next kosher one we bring him, and we're all square. So we go and do another one, and bugger me if it isn't bent as well.' He shook his head in wonderment.

'Talk about a scam,' he said. 'These bastards with their country houses really know how to pull a con job on the punters. Anyway, we end up having to do a third job, this time for fuck all, just to get ourselves square. I mean, he's obviously dealing with the kind of money that can buy a lot of very vicious muscle. You don't mess with that.'

'But everything's hunky-dory now, is it?'

He nodded, eating smoke. 'Sweet.'

'Great,' I said. 'Then you won't mind putting the two of us together, will you, Dennis?'

11

Once upon a time I had a fling with a Telecom engineer. It didn't end happily ever after, but he taught me more than I'll ever need to know about crossed lines. Along the way, before I accepted that great sex wasn't a long-term compensation for the conversational skills of Bonzo the chimpanzee, I met some very useful people. I met some bloody boring ones too, and unfortunately the crossover between the two groups was disturbingly large. Even more unfortunately, I was going to have to talk to one of them.

After I'd finally convinced Dennis that I wasn't going to back off and that the price of his liberty was putting me together with his fence, it hadn't taken me long to squeeze out of him the phone number of the contact. He'd left, grumbling that I was getting in over my head and I needn't come running to him when the roof fell in. Naturally, we both knew that in the event of such an architectural disaster, the combined emergency services of six counties wouldn't keep him away.

I watched his car drive away, not entirely certain I was doing the right thing. But I knew I couldn't turn Dennis over to the cops. It wasn't just about friendship, though that had been the key factor in my decision, no doubt about it. But I hadn't been lying when I said I wanted the people behind the whole shooting match. Without them, the robberies wouldn't end. They'd just find another Dennis to do the dirty work and carry the can. Besides, I wanted Henry's Monet back, and Dennis didn't have it any more.

After Dennis had gone, I rediscovered my appetite and wolfed the sandwich from the fridge before settling down to the thankless task of calling Gizmo. Gizmo works for Telecom as a systems engineer, which suits him down to the ground since he's the ultimate computer nerd. The first time I met him, he was even wearing an anorak. In a nightclub. I later discovered it was rare as hen's teeth to catch Gizmo out on the town. Normally the only thing that will prize him away from his computer screen is the promise of a secret password that will allow him to penetrate to the heart of some company's as yet virgin network. He's only ever happy when his modem's skittering round the world's bulletin boards. Gizmo would much rather be wandering round the Internet than the streets of Manchester. I thought Bill and I were pretty nifty movers round the intangible world of computer communications till I met Gizmo. Then I realized our joint hacking skills were the equivalent of comparing a ten-year-old's 'What I did on my holidays' essay with Jan Morris on just about anywhere.

I looked Gizmo up in my Filofax. There were several points of contact listed there. I tried his phone, but it was engaged. What a surprise. I booted up my computer, loaded up my comms software and logged on to the electronic mail network that Mortensen and Brannigan subscribe to. I typed a message asking Gizmo to call me urgently and sent it to his mailbox.

The phone rang five minutes later. I'd specifically asked him to call me person to person. The last thing I wanted was to relay my request to him over the Net. You never know who's looking in, no matter how secure you think you are. That's one of the first things Gizmo taught me. 'Kate?' he said suspiciously. Gizmo doesn't like talking; he prefers people to know only the constructed personality he releases over the computer network.

'Hi, Gizmo. How's life?' Silly question, really. Gizmo and life are barely on speaking terms.

'Just got myself a state-of-the-art rig,' he said. 'She's so fast, it's beautiful. So, what's going down with you?'

'Busy, busy. You know how it is. Gizmo, I need some help. Usual terms.' Fifty quid in used notes in a brown envelope through his letter box. He comes so cheap because he loves poking around other people's computers in the same way that some men like blondes with long legs.

'Speak, it's your dime,' he said. I took that for agreement.

'I've got a mobile number here that I need a name and address for.'

'Is that all?' He sounded disappointed. I gave him the number. 'Fine,' he said. 'I should be back to you later today.'

'You're a star, Giz. If I'm not here, leave a message on the machine. The answering machine. OK?'

'OK.'

The next call was to Lord Ballantrae. 'I think I've got a lead,' I told him. 'To the fence, not the principal behind the robberies. But I need some help.'

'That's quick work,' he said. 'Fire away. If I can do, I will do.'

'I need something to sell him. Not a painting, something fairly small but very valuable. Not small as in brooch, but maybe a small statuette, a gold goblet, that kind of thing. Now, I know that some of your associates have taken to displaying copies rather than the real thing. One of those dummies would be ideal, provided that it would pass muster on reasonably close scrutiny. You think you can come up with something like that?' I asked.

'Hmm,' he mused. 'Leave it with me. I'll get back to you.'

Two down, one to go. I dialled a number from memory and said, 'Mr Abercrombie, please. It's Kate Brannigan.' The electronic chirrup of the

Cuckoo Waltz assaulted my eardrums as I waited for whatever length of time Clive Abercrombie deemed necessary to put me firmly in my place. Clive is a partner in one of the city's prestige jewellers. He would say *the* prestige jewellers. That's the kind of pretentious wally he is. We pulled Clive's nuts out of the fire on a major counterfeiting scam a couple of years back, and I know that deep down he's eternally grateful, though he'd die before he'd reveal it to a mere tradesperson like me. His gratitude had turned into a mixed blessing, however. It was thanks to Clive's recommendation that we'd got the case that had put Richard behind bars and me at risk of parting company with my life. By my reckoning, that meant he still owed me.

We were on the third chorus when he deigned to come on the line. 'Kate,' he said cautiously. Obviously I wasn't important enough to merit solicitous inquiries about my health. Not a stupid man, Clive. He's clearly sussed out that Richard and I are not in the market for a diamond solitaire.

'Good afternoon, Clive,' I said sweetly. 'I find myself in need of a good jeweller, and I can't think of anyone who fits the bill better than you.'

'You flatter me,' he said, flattered.

'I'm like you, Clive. When I need a job doing, I come to the experts.'

'A job?' he echoed.

'A little bit of tinkering,' I said soothingly. 'Tomorrow, probably. Will one of your master craftspeople have a little time to spare for me then?'

'That depends on what we're talking about,' he said warily. 'I hope you're not suggesting something illegal, Kate.'

'Would I?' I said, trying to sound outraged.

'Quite possibly,' he said drily. 'What exactly did you have in mind?'

'I don't have all the details yet, but it would involve . . . a slight addition to an existing piece.'

He sighed. 'Come round tomorrow morning after eleven. I'll discuss it with you then.'

'Thank you, Clive,' I said to dead air.

I checked my watch. Half past four. Just time to nip round to the office and collect Trevor Kerr's list of former staff. I swapped the smart clothes for a pair of leggings and a sweatshirt and took my bike. It would be quicker than the car this time of day, and besides, I wanted the exercise. I found Shelley in the throes of preparing the quarterly VAT return. 'Kate,' she said grimly. 'Just the person I wanted to see.' She waved a small bundle of crumpled receipts at me. 'I know it's really unreasonable of me, but do you suppose you could enlighten me as to what precisely these bills are for? Only, by my calculations, we're due a VAT inspection some time within the next six months, and I don't think they're going to be thrilled by your idea of keeping records. "Miscellaneous petty cash" isn't good enough, you know.'

I groaned. 'Can't you just make it up?' I wheedled,

picking up the top receipt. 'This is from the electrical wholesalers; just call it batteries or light bulbs or cassette tapes. Use your imagination. We don't often let you do that,' I added with a smile.

Shelley curled her lip. 'I don't have an imagination. I've never found it necessary. You're not leaving here till you've told me what's what. And if *you* make it up, I can blame you when the VAT inspector doesn't believe me.'

It didn't take me as long as I feared. Imagination is not something I've ever lacked. What I couldn't remember, I invented. There wasn't a VAT person in the land who'd dare question what I needed thirty-five metres of speaker wire for. Having mollified the real boss at Mortensen and Brannigan, I grabbed my fax and headed out the door before she could think of something else that would keep me from my work.

In the short interval that I'd been out, both Gizmo and Ballantrae had been back to me. The name and address attached to the phone didn't fill me with confidence. Cradaco International, 679A Otley Road, Leeds. On an impulse, I grabbed the phone and rang Josh's office. The man himself was in a meeting, but Julia, his personal assistant, was free. I pitched her into hitting the database right away and finding out whatever details Cradaco International had filed at Companies House. I hung on while she looked. Now that everything's on-line, information it used to take days to dig out of dusty files is available at the touch of a finger-tip.

She didn't keep me waiting long. 'Kate? As you thought, it's an off-the-shelf company. Share capital of one pound. Managing director James Connery. Company Secretary Sean Bond. Uh-oh. Does something smell a bit fishy to you, Kate?'

I groaned. 'Any other directors?'

'Have a guess?'

'Miss Moneypenny? M?' I said, resignedly.

'Nearly. Miss Penny Cash.'

I sighed. 'You'd better give me the addresses, just in case.' I copied down three addresses in Leeds. At least they were all in the same city. One trip would check out the directors and the company. 'You're a pal, Julia,' I said.

'Don't mention it. You could do me a small favour in return,' she said.

'Try me.'

'Could you ask Richard if there's any chance he could get me a bootleg tape of the Streisand Wembley concert?' she asked.

I'd never have put cut-glass, upper-middle-class Julia down as a Streisand fan, but there's no accounting for taste. 'It's a bit off his beat, but I'll see what I can do,' I promised.

Time to get back to Ballantrae. He answered on the first ring. 'I think I've got the very thing for you,' he said. 'How does an Anglo-Saxon belt buckle sound?'

'Useful if you've got an Anglo-Saxon belt,' I said.

He chuckled. 'It's a ceremonial buckle, worn by chieftains and buried with them. It's about five inches by two inches. The original is made of solid gold, chased with Celtic designs and studded with semi-precious stones. There are only two known to be in existence. One's in the British Museum, the other's in a private collection in High Hammerton Hall near Whitby.'

'Sounds perfect,' I said. 'Have you spoken to the owner?'

'I have. He's been displaying a replica for the last five months, but I've managed to persuade him to lend it to you. We were at school together,' he added in explanation.

'What's it made of?' I asked.

'The replica's made of lead and plastic, with a thin coating of gold leaf. He says it would fool someone who wasn't an expert, even close up. He says if you sit the two of them side by side, it's almost impossible to tell them apart.'

'Sounds perfect,' I said. 'When can I get it?'

'He's sending it to you by overnight courier. It will be at your office by ten tomorrow morning.'

'Lord Ballantrae, you are a star,' I said, meaning it. So much for the inbred stupidity of the aristocracy. This guy was more on the ball than ninety-five per cent of the people I have to deal with.

'No problem. I want to get these people as badly as you do. Probably more so. Then we can all get back to the business of doing what we do best.'

Speaking of which, I finally got down to doing

something about Trevor Kerr's case. I felt guilty for ignoring the material he'd sent me, but the art-theft case was far more absorbing. I felt it was something I could get to the bottom of single-handed, unlike the Kerrchem case. I found myself inclined to agree with Jackson. This was a case for the cops, if only because they had the staffing resources to cover all the bases that it would take me weeks to get round. Then the little voice in my head kicked in with the real reason. 'You can't stand Trevor Kerr so you don't want to put yourself out for him. And you're desperate to impress that Michael Haroun.'

'Bollocks,' I muttered out loud, seizing the sheets of fax paper with fresh energy. Someone – the indomitable Sheila, I suspected – had conveniently included the job titles as well as the names and addresses of those made redundant. I reckoned I could exclude anyone who worked on the factory floor or in the warehouse. They would have neither the chemical know-how nor the access to sales and distribution information that would allow them to pull a sabotage scheme as complex as this. That left thirty-seven people in clerical, managerial and scientific posts who had all been given what looked like a tin handshake to quit their jobs at Kerrchem.

By nine, I felt like the phone was welded to my ear. I was using a labour-market research pitch, which seemed to be working reasonably well. I claimed to be working for the EC Regional Fund, doing research to see what sort of skills were not

139

being catered for by current job vacancies. I told my victims that I was calling people who had been made redundant over the previous year to discover whether they had found alternative employment. A depressingly low number of Kerrchem's junked staff fell into that category, and they were mostly low-grade clerical staff. Not one of the ten middle managers had found new jobs, and to a man they were bitter as hell about it. Of the chemists, two out of the three lab technicians were working in less skilled but better paid jobs. The four research lab staff who had been laid off were bound by their contracts and the terms of their redundancies not to work for direct competitors. One had taken a job as an analyst on a North Sea oil rig, two of the other three were kicking their heels and hating it, and one was no longer at the address the company had for him. It looked like I had no shortage of suspects.

I stood up and stretched. Richard still hadn't come home, so there was nothing to divert me from work. I couldn't move on with the Kerrchem stuff tonight, but I wasn't quite stalled on the other investigation. The sensible part of me knew I should go to bed and catch up on last night's missed sleep, but I'd had enough of being sensible for one week. I went through to the kitchen, cut open the other half of the ciabatta and loaded it with mozzarella, taramasalata and some sun dried tomatoes. I wrapped it in clingfilm, and took a small bottle of mineral water out of the fridge.

Fifteen minutes later, I was cruising down the M62, singing along cheerfully to a new compilation of Dusty Springfield's greatest hits that I'd found lying around in Richard's half of the conservatory. Never mind the mascara, check out that voice.

I was in Leeds before ten, nervously navigating my way through the subterranean tunnels of the inner ring road, emerging somewhere near the white monolith of the university. The roads were quiet out through Headingley, but every now and again, a beam of light split the night from on high as the police helicopter quartered the skies, trying to protect the homes of the more prosperous residents from the attentions of the burglars. Burglary has reached epidemic proportions in Leeds these days; I know someone whose house was turned over seven times in six months. Every time they came home with a new stereo, so did the burglars. Now, their house is more secure than Armley jail and their insurance premiums are nearly as much as the mortgage.

I slowed as I approached the Weetwood round-about, scanning houses for their numbers. 679A looked like it might be one of an arcade of shops, so I parked up and stretched my legs. I can't say I was surprised to find there was no 679A. There was a 679, though, a small newsagent's squeezed between a bakery and a hairdresser. I walked round the back of the shops, checking to see if the flats above had entrances at the rear. A couple did, but 679 wasn't one of them. I walked back to the car, with plenty to think about. Whoever Dennis's fence was, he was determined to cover his tracks. Using an accommodation address for his phone bills was about as careful as you could get without actually being sectioned for paranoia.

I decided to check out the directors' addresses while I was in the city, but I held out little hope of finding any of them at home. James Connery's alleged residence was nearest, back in Headingley proper. It was number thirty-nine in a street of ten houses. On to Chapel Allerton, where Sean Bond apparently lived in a hostel for the visually handicapped. Penny Cash was even worse off. According to Companies House, she was living on a piece of waste ground in Burmantofts. I doubled back through the city centre, passing the new Health Ministry building up on Quarry Hill, spotlit to look like a set from Fritz Lang's *Metropolis*. Apparently, the place contains a full-size swimming pool, Jacuzzi and multi-gym. Nice to know our hard-earned taxes are being spent on the health of the nation, isn't it?

It was nearly midnight when I got home. Richard's car was parked outside, though I didn't need that clue to know he was home as soon as I touched the front door. It was vibrating with the pulse of the bass coming through the bricks from next door. As I shoved my key in the lock, I could feel exhaustion flow through me, settling in a painful knot at the base of my skull.

I walked through the house to the conservatory.

Richard's patio doors were open, revealing half a dozen bodies in varying states of consciousness draped over the furniture. Techno dance music drilled through my head like a tribe of termites who have just discovered a log cabin. The man himself was nowhere to be seen. I picked a path to the kitchen, where I found him taking a tray of spring rolls out of the oven. 'Hi,' he said. His eyes were as stoned as the woman taken in adultery.

'Any chance of the volume coming down? I need some sleep,' I said.

'That's cool,' he said, a lazy smile spreading across his face. 'Want some company?'

'You've already got some.'

'They can be out of here in ten minutes,' he said. 'Then I'm all yours.'

He was as good as his word. Eleven minutes later, he crawled into my blissfully silent bed. Unfortunately, I'm not into necrophilia.

12

The buckle got to the office before I did, which gave Shelley something to puzzle over. I arrived to find her using it as a paperweight. 'OK,' she said. 'I give in.'

I don't often find myself one up on Shelley, so I decided to drag it out a bit. 'If you can guess, I'll buy lunch,' I said.

'What makes you think you're going to have time for lunch?' she asked sweetly. 'Besides, I told you yesterday, I don't do imagination. You want me to learn how, you're going to have to pay me a lot more.'

I should know better. The woman is the mother of two teenagers. What chance do I have? 'It's a replica of an Anglo-Saxon ceremonial belt buckle,' I said. 'Also known as a honey pot.' Mustering what was left of my dignity, I scooped up the buckle and marched through to my office.

This time Dennis's mobile was switched on. 'I want you to set up a meet for me with your man,'

I said. 'Tell him you vouch for me, and that I've got something really special for him.'

'I'm not sure if he'll go for it,' Dennis tried. 'Like I told you, we have to wait for a yes or a no before we lift stuff. He's very picky, and he likes to be in control.'

'Tell him there's only two in the world. I've got one and the British Museum's got the other one. Tell him it's from the collection at High Hammerton Hall. And it's gold. He should be able to work it out himself from that. Believe me, Dennis, he'll want this.'

'All right,' he said grudgingly. 'But I'm coming with you on the meet.'

'No, you're not,' I told him firmly. 'You're in enough trouble as it is. This is not going to be heavy, Dennis. I can handle one man in a car park. You should know, you train me.'

'I still think you're crazy, chasing this,' he said. 'Your client's going to be better off with the insurance company's readies in his bank account than he is with a poxy picture on the wall.'

'Call it professional pride.'

'Call it pig-headedness,' he said. 'I'll get back to you.'

I went through to Bill's office and opened the cupboard where we keep our stock of technological wizardry. I found what I was looking for in a cardboard box at the back of the top shelf. It's not something we use very often, reeking as it does of *The Man from U.N.C.L.E.*, but given that Dennis's fence seemed to be an aficionado of James Bond, it seemed entirely appropriate to use a directional bug. If that conjures up images of chunky metal boxes stuck to the bottom of cars, forget it. Thanks to modern miniaturization technology, the bugs we've got are about the size of an indigestion tablet. The transmission batteries last about a week, and allow the bug to send a signal to a base unit. The range is about fifteen kilometres, provided large mountains don't get in the way, and the screen gives a read-out of direction and distance. Perfect for tracking the buckle back to source, so long as the fence was going to get rid of it sharpish.

Next stop, Clive Abercrombie, with a brief detour via the terraced streets of Whalley Range to stuff Gizmo's used tenners through his letter box. When I got to the shop, Clive was hovering behind a counter, ostentatiously leaving the waiting-on to the lesser mortals he employs to be polite to the rich. When I walked in, he shot forward and had me through the door to the back of the shop so fast my feet didn't even leave tracks in the shag pile. Obviously, he doesn't want proles like me hanging around making the place look like Ratners. 'In a hurry, Clive?' I asked innocently.

'I thought *you* would be. You usually are,' he replied acidly. 'Now, what was it you wanted?'

I took the buckle out of my handbag. In spite of himself, Clive drew his breath in sharply. 'Where did you get that?' he demanded, extending one finger to point dramatically at the twinkling gold lump.

'Don't worry, my life of crime runs to solving it, not committing it,' I soothed. 'It's not the real thing. It's a copy.'

If anything, he looked even more disturbed. 'Why are you walking around with it in your *handbag?*' he demanded, giving Lady Bracknell a run for her money.

Knowing Clive's weakness for anything reeking of snobbery, I said, 'I'm doing a job for the Nottingham Group.'

'Should I know the name?' he asked snottily.

'Probably not, Clive. It's a consortium of the landed gentry, headed by Lord Ballantrae of Dumdivie. Art thefts. Very hush-hush. I'm very close to Mr Big, and this is a ploy to smoke him out.' I pulled the bug out of my pocket. 'What I need is for one of your craftsmen to incorporate this in the piece. Preferably on the outside. I'd thought under one of the stones.' I handed the bug and the buckle to Clive, who already had his loupe out.

He took a few minutes to scrutinize the buckle which was heavy enough to make a useful weapon, especially if it was attached to a belt. 'Nice piece of work,' he commented. 'If you hadn't told me it was a fake, I'd have had my work cut out to spot it.' Praise indeed, coming from Clive. He unscrewed the loupe from his eye socket and said, 'It'll take a few hours. And it will cost.'

'Now there's a surprise,' I said. 'Just send us an

invoice. Give me a bell when it's ready.' I turned to go back through the shop, but Clive gripped my elbow and steered me further into the nether regions.

'Easier if you pop out the back door,' he said. Half a minute later, I was in the street. I reckoned I deserved a cappuccino made by someone other than me, so I decided to take the scenic route back to the office. For a brief moment, I toyed with the idea of ringing Michael Haroun and suggesting he play truant for half an hour, but I told myself severely that it wouldn't help my pursuit of the art thieves to involve the insurers at this stage. They'd only start muttering about doing things by the book and informing the police. I smacked my hormones firmly on the wrist and drove the length of Deansgate to the Atlas Café, where they claim to make the best coffee outside Italy. I wasn't going to argue. I dumped the car on a yellow line down by the canal basin and walked back up to the chic glass-and-wood interior. I sat by the window, sipping the kind of cappuccino that acts like intravenous caffeine and pulled the Kerrchem papers out of my bag. Time for a file review.

I didn't know exactly what I was looking for. All I knew was that I wanted to find something, anything that would legitimately allow me to postpone or short-circuit the tedious process of doing background checks into all of the redundant staff that I hadn't been able to eliminate on the phone.

On the second read-through, I found exactly what I was looking for.

Joey Morton's supply of KerrSter came from the local branch of a national chain of trade wholesalers, Filbert Brown. His wife couldn't remember which of them had actually made the trip to the cash-and-carry when the fatal drum of KerrSter had been bought, but there was no doubt that that was the original source of the tainted cleanser.

It wasn't much to go on, but it was a place to start. One of the dozens of pieces of normally useless information cluttering up my dustbin brain was the fact that Filbert Brown were a Manchester-based company. I knew this because I passed their head office and flagship cash-and-carry every time I drove from my house to North Manchester. Suddenly energized, I abandoned the hedonism of the Atlas and trotted down the steps to the car.

It didn't take long to skirt the city centre. It took longer to get through to the customers' car park at Filbert Brown. They occupied an old factory building just off Ancoats Street. The area was in the middle of that chaotic upheaval known as urban renewal. East Manchester is supposedly coming up in the world; home of the new Commonwealth Games stadium, spiffy new housing developments and sports facilities. Oh, and roads, of course. Lots of them. Virgin territory for the traffic cones and temporary traffic lights that have become an epidemic on the roads of the Northwest. My political friends reckon it's the government's revenge because most of us up here didn't vote for them.

Considering it was the middle of the morning when all of us small business people are supposed to have our noses firmly to the grindstone, Filbert Brown was surprisingly busy. I walked in without challenge and found myself in a glorified warehouse. It reminded me of those cheap and cheerless back-to-basics supermarkets that we've imported from Europe in recent years. Anyone who did their shopping in Netto or Aldi would have been right at home in Filbert Brown. Me, I always find it incredibly cheap to shop there – they never stock anything I'd want to buy. The same went for Filbert Brown. I know Richard thinks I have an unhealthy obsession with cleanliness, but even I couldn't get turned on by cases of dishwasher powder, drums of worktop bactericide and cartons of paper towels. I was clearly in a minority, judging by the number of people who were happily filling up their trolleys.

I wandered up and down the aisles for a few minutes, getting a feel for the place. One of the things that struck me was how prominent KerrSter was among the cleansers. It occupied the whole width of a shelf at eye level, the key position in shifting merchandise. Compared with the other Kerrchem products, which seemed to be doing just about OK compared with their competitors, KerrSter was king of the castle.

What I needed now was a pretext. Thoughtfully, I wandered back to the car. I always keep a fold-over clipboard in the boot for those occasions when I need to pretend to be a market researcher. You'd be amazed at what people will tell you if you've got a clipboard. I gave my clothes the once-over. I was wearing tan jodhpur-style leggings, a cream linen collarless shirt and a chocolate brown jacket with a mandarin collar. The jacket was too smart for the pitch, so I folded it up and left it in the boot. In the shirt and leggings, I could just about pass. Freeze, maybe, but pass.

I walked briskly into Filbert Brown and strode up to the customer service counter. I say counter, but it was more of a hole in the wall. Customers here clearly weren't encouraged to complain. The woman behind the counter looked as if she'd been hired because of her resemblance to a bulldog. 'Yes?' she demanded, teeth snapping.

'I'm sorry to trouble you,' I said brightly. 'I'm doing an MBA at Manchester Business School and I'm doing some research into sales and marketing. I wonder if I could perhaps have a word with your stock controller?'

'You got an appointment?'

'I'm afraid not.'

She looked triumphant. 'You'd need an appointment.'

I looked disappointed. 'It's a bit of an emergency. I had arranged to see someone at one of the big DIY stores, but she's come down with a bug and she had to cancel and I really need to get the initial research done this week. It won't take more than half an hour. Can't you just ring through and see if it would be possible for me to see someone?'

'We're a bit busy just now,' she said. 'We' was inaccurate; 'they' would have been nearer the mark, judging by the queues at the tills.

'Please?' I tried for the about-to-burst-into-tears look.

She cast her eyes heavenwards. 'It's a waste of time, you know.'

'If they're busy, I could make an appointment for later,' I said firmly.

With a deep sigh, she picked up the phone, consulted a list taped to the wall of her booth and dialled a number. 'Sandra? It's Maureen at customer services. There's a student here says she wants to talk to you . . . Some project or other . . .' She looked me up and down disaparagingly. Then her eyebrows shot up. 'You will?' she said incredulously. 'All right, I'll tell her.' She dropped the phone as if it had bitten her and said, 'Miss Bates will be with you in a moment.'

I leaned against the wall and waited. A couple of minutes passed, then a woman approached through the checkouts. Her outfit was in the same colours as the rest of the staff, but where they wore red and cream overalls, she wore a red skirt and a blouse in the red and cream material. She smiled as she approached, which explained why she'd never get the job in customer services. 'I'm Sandra Bates,' she greeted me. 'How can I help you?'

I gave her the same spiel. 'What I need is a few minutes of your time so you can run through your shelf-allocation principles,' I finished.

She nodded. 'No problem. Come along to my office; I'll take you through it.'

I fell into step beside her. 'I really appreciate this,' I said. 'I know how busy you must be.'

'You're not kidding,' she said. 'But this business needs more women who can give the boys a run for their money. When I was doing my business studies degree at the poly, it was almost impossible to get any of them to spare any of their precious time,' she added grimly. Thank God for the sisterhood.

She ushered me into an office that was marginally bigger than the room off my office that doubles as a darkroom and the ladies' loo. Most of the floor space was taken up by a desk dominated by a PC. The desk surface and the floor around it were stacked with files and papers. Sandra Bates picked her way through the piles and sat in her chair. 'Give me a second,' she said, staring at the monitor.

I used the time to check her out. She looked to be in her late twenties, about my height, her jaw-length light brown hair expertly highlighted with blonde streaks. She was attractive in a china doll sort of way, pink and white complexion, unexceptional blue eyes and a slightly uptilted nose. Her determined mouth was the only contrasting feature, indicating an inner strength that might just give the boys a run for their money in the promotion stakes.

'Right,' she said, looking up and grinning at me. 'What do you want to know?'

'How you decide what goes where on the shelves?' I said. I don't know why I wanted to know that, but it seemed a good place to start if I wanted to get round to KerrSter.

'The general order of the products in the aisles is ordained from above, based on market research and psychological analysis, would you believe,' she said. 'It's the same way that supermarkets decide you get the fruit and veg first and the booze last. I mean, those of us who actually do the shopping know that your grapes get crushed by the six packs of lager, but I suppose they work on the principle that by the time you've cruised the aisles, you feel like you need a drink.'

My turn to grin. 'So what decisions do you actually make on the shop floor?'

'What we decide is what goes where within each section. The received wisdom is that items placed at eye level sell better than those you have to reach up for or bend down to. Now, all the checkouts are computerized, and I can access all the product figures from this terminal here. That way, I can see what stock is moving fast, and make sure we reorder at the right time so that we neither run out nor end up with huge stockpiles. When a particular line starts to outstrip rival products, it automatically goes into the best shelf position so that those sales are maintained or increased. With me so far?'

I nodded. It was all terribly logical. 'Are there any exceptions?'

Sandra nodded approvingly. 'Oh, yes. Lots. For example, when a company brings out a new product, they will often arrange to pay us a premium in return for our displaying it in the most advantageous shelf position. Or if a company's product has been ousted from its top selling position by a rival, they'll offer us a loss-leader price on the product for a limited period in exchange for them getting their old shelf site back so they can try to re-establish their old supremacy.'

'Is that what Kerrchem have done with KerrSter?' I asked.

Sandra blinked. 'I'm sorry?' she asked, sounding startled.

'I was having a browse round before I asked to see you, and I couldn't help noticing how prominent the KerrSter was. And with that guy dying after he opened it, I'd have thought sales would have gone through the floor,' I said innocently.

'Yes, well, it's always been a popular seller, KerrSter,' Sandra gabbled. 'I suppose our customers haven't seen the stories.'

'I'd have thought Kerrchem would have recalled it,' I went on. For some reason, talk of KerrSter was making Sandra Bates twitchy. Rule number one of interrogation: when you've got them on the run, keep chasing.

'They recalled one batch,' she said, regaining her composure.

'Still, I wouldn't buy it,' I said. 'I'm surprised one of their competitors hasn't tried to exploit the situation. In fact, I'm surprised a small company like them outsells the opposition so comprehensively.'

'Yes, well, there's no accounting for customer preferences. Now, if there's nothing more you'd like to know about the shelf-stacking, I have got a lot on my plate,' Sandra said, getting to her feet and waving vaguely at the paperwork on her desk.

I was back on the street inside a minute. Being hustled twice in one morning was bad for the ego. Clive Abercrombie I could understand. But the mere mention of KerrSter had shifted Sandra Bates from cooperative sisterhood to the verge of hostility. Something was going on that I didn't understand. And if there's one thing I hate, it's things I don't understand.

13

I'm no cyberpunk, but I'm knowledgeable enough about hacking to know that I couldn't have penetrated Filbert Brown's computer network on my own. I was sure they had to have a central computer that dealt with all their individual branches. Via that it should be possible to crawl back inside Sandra Bates's data. Way back in the mists of time – say, around 1991 – I could probably have reached first base. Bill has a program that dials consecutive phone numbers till his modem connects with another computer. I could have set that to run through all the numbers on the same exchange as Filbert Brown's head office. It would probably have taken all night to run, but it would have got me there in the end.

However, the powers that be have decided that darkside hackers like us need to be cracked down on, so now they've got their own sophisticated equipment that picks up on sequential dialling like that and traces it. Then the dibble comes and knocks on your door in a very user-unfriendly way. Besides, getting the computer's number was only the start. I'd need a login to get through the front door, and a password to get any further. Ideally, I needed the password of the sysman – the system manager. Most people who are authorized users of a network system have logins which allow them only limited access to the part of the system they need to work with. The sysman is what computerspeak calls a superuser, which means he or she can wander unimpeded throughout the system, checking out each and every little nook and cranny. With Bill's help, I might just have managed to achieve sysman status on the Filbert Brown network. But Bill was on the other side of the world.

That only left Gizmo. I tried his number, and got lucky. 'Wozzat?' a voice grunted.

'Gizmo?'

'Yeah?'

'Kate. Did I wake you?'

He cleared his throat noisily. 'Yeah. Been up all night. What d'you want?'

I told him. He whistled. 'Can't do that one for the usual,' he said.

'But can you do it?'

'Sure, I can *do* it,' he said confidently. 'Getting in shouldn't be a problem. But if you want sysman status, that'll cost you.'

'How much?' I sighed.

'One and a half.'

Trevor Kerr could stand another hundred and fifty quid, I decided. 'Done deal,' I told Gizmo. 'How soon?'

He sniffed. Probably on account of the whizz he'd have snorted to keep him awake all night. 'Few hours,' he said.

'Sooner the better.'

Back in the office, routine awaited. A stack of background information had arrived in the post that morning. I'd been waiting for it so that I could complete a report for a client on the three candidates they'd short-listed for the head of their international marketing division. One of them looked like he'd have a promising career writing fiction. The candidate's degree from Oxford turned out to have been a two-year vocational course at the former poly. His credit rating was worse than the average Third World country's. And one of his previous employers seemed to think that his financial skills were focused more in the direction of his bank account than theirs. All of which would make the selection panel's job a bit easier.

It was just after four when Clive Abercrombie rang to tell me the buckle was ready and waiting. I worked for another hour, then collected it on the way home. Clive's jeweller had done a good job. I was looking for the bug, and I couldn't see it. No way would the fence spot it in the middle of a motorway service station. Back in the car, I checked the receiver was picking it up. Loud and clear.

When I got in, there was a message from Gizmo on my machine. 'Hi. I've got your order ready. I think you should collect it in person. I'll expect you.' I sighed and got back in the car. Just because you're paranoid doesn't mean they're not out to get you. In Gizmo's case, I thought it was a small miracle the hacker crackers hadn't already kicked his door in. In his shoes, I wouldn't trust the phone lines either.

I hit the cash machine on the way, taking myself up to my daily limit. I parked round the corner from his house, just in case he really was under surveillance, and wishing I'd remembered to do the same on my earlier drop. I rang the bell and waited. Nearly a minute passed before the door cracked open on the chain. 'It's me, Giz,' I said patiently. 'Alone.'

He handed me a piece of paper. I handed him the cash. 'See you around,' he said and closed the door.

Back in the car, I unfolded the paper. There was a telephone number, FB7792JS (the login), and CONAN (the sysman's password). I'd bet it was Conan the Barbarian the sysman had in mind, not the creator of the world's first PI. Yet another wimpy computer nerd with delusions of grandeur. I drove home via Rusholme, where I picked up a selection of samosas, onion bhajis, chicken pakora and aloo saag bhajis. I had the feeling it was going to be a long night, and I didn't know if I could rely on Richard to come home with a Chinese.

I brought the coffee machine through to my study and sat down at the computer with the Indian snacks and the coffee to hand. I booted up and loaded my comms program. Dialling the number on the paper brought me a short pause, then the monitor said, 'Welcome to FB. Login?' I typed the digits Gizmo had given me. 'Password?' the monitor asked. 'Conan' I typed. 'As in Doyle,' I said firmly.

The screen cleared and offered me a set of options. The first thing I had to do was to familiarize myself with the system. I needed to know how the different areas were arranged, how the directory trees were laid out, and how to move around to remote terminals. Somehow, I didn't think I'd be having an early night.

By nine, I'd got the basic layout clear in my mind. My mind and a sheaf of scribbled maps and diagrams that strewed my desk top. Now all I had to do was find Sandra Bates's terminal and start sifting her data. Doesn't sound much, does it? Imagine trying to find a single street in Manchester with only the motorway map as a guide. I took a screen break in the shower, brewed another pot of coffee and settled down to do battle with Filbert Brown's computer.

When the phone rang, I jumped a clear inch off my chair. I grabbed it and barked, 'Hello?'

'It's me,' Dennis's voice announced. 'Sorted.' Dennis is another one who doesn't like confiding in the phone system.

'Great. When?'

'Tomorrow. Half past three, eastbound at Harts-head Services.'

'How will I know him?'

'He drives a metallic green Mercedes. He's about forty, five ten, bald on top. Anyway, I told him to look for a tarty-looking little blonde.' Dennis couldn't keep the triumph out of his voice.

'You did what?'

'I didn't think you'd want to go looking like yourself,' he said defensively. 'Kate, these are not people you want coming after you with a clear picture. Wear a blonde wig, stick on the stilettos and the short skirt. And don't drive that poncy coupé. It sticks out like a prick in a brothel.'

'Thank you very much, Dennis,' I said.

Impervious to my sarcasm, he said, 'My pleasure. Be careful out there now, you hear? Let me know how you go on.'

'OK.'

'Be lucky.'

If only it was as simple as that. With a groan, I turned back to the computer. Just after eleven, I made it into Sandra Bates's data. Interestingly, it looked like Sandra had overall supervisory respon-sibility for about half of the Filbert Brown ware-houses in the Northwest, as well as her day-to-day charge of the Ancoats cash-and-carry. She hadn't mentioned that in our brief encounter. I decided to concentrate on Manchester for the time being. The first thing I went for was the purchase orders for Kerrchem. When I reached those files, I printed the lot out. Analysis could wait until a time when I wasn't wandering round someone else's system like an illegal alien. After a bit of searching, I found the till data, sorted product by product. I scrolled through till I found KerrSter and printed that lot out too. Finally, I made myself at home in the invoices section of Sandra's files. That was the first indication I had that there was something going on. As a matter of course, I'd been checking for hidden files as I went along. When I added up the sizes of the individual files in the invoices subdirectory, it came to less than the amount of space the terminal told me the subdirectory occupied. The difference was about the size of one biggish file.

What Sandra Bates had done was clever. She could have made the file a password file, but anyone from head office trying to get into it would have become immediately suspicious. With a hidden file, there was no way of knowing it was there unless you were looking for precisely that, and nothing to trigger off suspicions in a routine trawl. I copied the hidden file on to my own hard disk, not wanting to interfere with it in Sandra's environment, and also copied the visible Kerrchem invoice file. I couldn't think of anything else I needed right then, so I made my way out of the system. If what I already had suggested fresh avenues of inquiry, I could always go back in. I didn't think I'd left any footprints obvious enough for the sysman to notice and do anything panicky like change his password.

The last thing I did was to open up the hidden file and print out the contents of it and the other invoice file. Then, clutching my pile of papers, I staggered off to bed. Richard hadn't appeared, which meant he was probably out on the razz with a bunch of musicians. When he finally came home, he'd collapse into his own bed rather than waken me. Just one of the advantages of our semi-detached lifestyle.

I woke up just before eight, the light still on, the papers strewn all over the duvet and the floor. I hadn't got past page one before sleep had overwhelmed me. I picked up the papers and shuffled them together. I showered, sliced a banana into a bowl of muesli and took breakfast and coffee out into the conservatory. As I ate, I started to read the paperwork. The purchase order for KerrSter showed a sudden hike about two months previously, virtually tripling overnight. Interestingly, they weren't big orders. According to this print-out, Sandra hadn't increased the amount of KerrSter on each order. It was the number of orders that had shot up. That seemed a pretty inefficient way of doing business to me.

I checked back with the till receipts to see when the sudden surge in sales of KerrSter had started. I knew then that I was on to something. If what Sandra Bates had told me was the truth, the increased orders should have been sales-led. But what I was seeing was something very different. The till receipts for KerrSter didn't start to pick up until a few days after the orders increased dramatically. It looked as if the product had been given its starry position before the sales justified it. I was sure Trevor Kerr hadn't been paying them a premium to improve the profile of his product; I couldn't imagine him parting with his company's cash in a deal like that. Trevor struck me as a man who liked his profits, and wouldn't cede them to anyone.

By now, I was gripped by the paper trail. Time for the invoices. First, I went through the accessible KerrSter invoice file. That was when the alarm bells started ringing. The product orders might have tripled, but the invoices hadn't. I double-checked, but there was no mistake. Filbert Brown were still paying Kerrchem for the same amount of cleaning fluid as they had been before the order hike.

That left the contents of the hidden file. It contained the invoices for the remaining two thirds of the KerrSter. There was one crucial difference. The bank account where the electronic fund transfer was sending the money for the extra KerrSter wasn't the same as the bank account on the other, upfront invoices. Whoever Sandra Bates was paying for the KerrSter, it wasn't Kerrchem.

That left me two possibilities. Either somebody at Kerrchem was creaming off a tidy back-door profit for themselves. Or Sandra Bates was dealing with the chemical merchants who were peddling phoney KerrSter with such disastrous results. I knew which theory looked most likely to me.

I checked the clock. Ten to nine. Chances were that management staff at Filbert Brown didn't start work until nine. If I was quick, I could be in and out of their computer before their sysman logged in to find someone else using his ID. To be on the safe side, I should have waited until the evening, but I was behind the door when they were handing out patience.

Two minutes later, I was in the system again. This time, I wasn't looking for Sandra Bates's terminal. I wanted her personnel file. I got into personnel at three minutes to nine. A minute took me to staff personnel files. Once I was there, I downloaded Sandra Bates's file to my own hard disk. I was back out of Filbert Brown by one minute past nine. A couple of minutes later, I was looking at Sandra Bates's CV.

She'd been to school in Ashton-under-Lyne, a once separate town now attached to East Manchester by a string of down-at-heel suburbs. She'd done a degree in business studies at what was then Manchester Poly and is now Manchester Metropolitan University. You'd think when they got their university status that someone would have noticed their new initials translate only too readily to Mickey Mouse University, endorsing the snooty opinions of those who attended 'real' universities. After her degree, Sandra had gone to work for one of the big chains of DIY stores, havens for suburbanites on Sundays and bank holidays. She'd stayed there for a couple of years before joining

Filbert Brown three years previously. She'd had one promotion since then and was pulling down just over twenty grand. The item that really interested me was her address: 37 Alder Way, Burnage. I needed to check out her house at some point today while she was at work. I would probably have to stake her out or do a little bit of illegal bugging to discover who her phoney KerrSter supplier was, and to do that, I needed to get a picture of the set-up in Alder Way.

Before I could do any of that, I had to get dressed and stop by the office. I had plenty of time before the meet with Dennis's fence, so I could at least put off the tart's disguise till later. I grabbed a clean pair of jeans, my Reeboks and denim-look cotton sweater. If I was going to spend the afternoon teetering on stilettos, I could at least spend the morning in comfort.

Shelley was catching up on the filing when I walked in, a clear sign that she was bored. 'Going part-time now, are we?' she asked acidly.

'I've been doing some work on the computer at home,' I said defensively. Shelley has the unerring knack of making me feel fifteen and guilty again.

'A report would be nice now and then,' she said. 'I know I'm only the office manager, but it does help when clients phone if I know where we're up to.'

'Sorry,' I said contritely. 'It's just that most of the things I've been doing for the last couple of days are the kind of things I don't want the clients to know I'm up to. I'll get something down on tape for you by the end of today, promise.' I smiled ingratiatingly. 'Would you like a cappuccino?'

'How much is it going to cost me?' Shelley asked suspiciously. Abe Lincoln wouldn't have said you can fool all the people some of the time if he'd ever met Shelley.

'Can I borrow you and your car this afternoon?' I asked. 'I've got a meet with the fence who's been handling these stolen art works, and I'm going to need to tail him afterwards. He's going to have clocked the coupé, and it's too obvious a car to follow him in. I want you to come out there with me and after the meet, we can swap cars. I go off in your motor, you come back in the coupé.'

'You saying my Rover's common?' Shelley asked.

'Only in a numerical sense. Please?'

'How do I know you'll bring it back in one piece?'

She had a point. In the past eighteen months I'd written off one car and done serious damage to the Little Rascal, the van we've got fitted out with full surveillance gear. Neither incident had been my fault, but it still made me the butt of all office jokes about drivers. 'I'll bring it back in one piece,' I said through gritted teeth.

'What about the Little Rascal?' Shelley demanded. 'You could tail him in that. All you have to do is make sure he doesn't see you getting out of it. Just be there early, out of the car, waiting for him.'

I pulled a face. 'The guy drives a Merc. I suspect

I'd lose him on the motorway. Besides, he's no dummy. He's probably going to wait till he sees me drive off before he takes off himself.'

'So if you drive off, how are we going to swap cars?'

'Trust me. I'll show you when we get there.'

'I get the coupé overnight?' she bargained.

'But of course. I might as well take your car now, since I've got to look unobtrusive in Burnage.'

We swapped keys and I headed off in her four-year-old Rover to Burnage. My first stop was the local library, where I checked the electoral roll. Sandra Bates was the only resident listed at 37. Alder Way was a quiet street of 1930s semis, each with a small garden. I marched boldly up the path of 37 and knocked on the door. There was no reply. There was an empty carport at the side of the house, and I walked cautiously through it and opened the wrought iron gate leading into the back garden. Sandra was obviously as efficient at home as she was at work. There was a line of washing pegged out, drying in the watery sunlight. Whatever the electoral roll said, Sandra didn't live alone. Hanging beside her underwear were boxer shorts and socks. Flapping in the breeze like a phantom among the shirts and blouses were two pairs of overalls. Maybe I wouldn't have to look so far for the mystery chemist after all.

14

I rang the doorbell of 35 Alder Way. I was about to give up when the door opened. I realized why it had taken so long. The harassed-looking young woman who stood in the doorway had identical toddlers clinging on to each leg of her jeans. As a handicapping system, it beat anything the Jockey Club has ever come up with. The twins stared up at me and conducted a conversation with each other in what sounded like some East European language, all sibilants and diphthongs. 'Yes?' the woman said. At least she spoke Mancunian.

'Sorry to bother you,' I said. 'I'm looking for a guy called Richard Barclay. The address I've got for him is next door at number thirty-seven. But there doesn't seem to be anybody in.'

She shook her head. 'There's nobody by that name next door,' she said with an air of finality, her hand rising to close the door.

'Are you sure?' I said, looking puzzled and referring to the piece of paper in my hand where I'd

170

just written my lover's name and Sandra Bates's address. I waved it at her. 'I was supposed to meet him here. About a job.'

She took the paper and frowned. 'There must be some mistake. The bloke next door's called Simon. Simon Morley.'

I sighed. 'I don't suppose he's the one taking people on, then? I mean, I've not got the right address and the wrong name?'

One of the twins detached itself from the woman's jeans and lurched towards me. Without looking down, she stuck her leg out and stopped its progress. 'I shouldn't think so, love,' she said. 'Simon got made redundant about six months ago. He's only started working himself a couple of months back, and judging from the overalls he goes in and out in, he's not hiring and firing.'

I did the disappointed look, but it was wasted on the hassled woman. The pitch of the twins' dialogue had risen to a level she couldn't ignore. 'Sorry,' she said, closing the door firmly in my face.

'Don't be sorry,' I said softly as I walked back to the Rover. 'Lady, you just made my day.' Simon Morley's name had rung so many bells my head felt like the cathedral belfry.

By three o'clock, everything was in place. Shelley and I had driven across the Pennines on the M62, to the Bradford exit, the first past Hartshead Services. We'd turned off on the Halifax road, where I remembered there was a lay-by just after the motorway roundabout. I left Shelley there in her Rover while I zoomed back down the motorway, doubling back so I ended up on the correct side of the sprawling service area. I parked away from the main body of cars and teetered up the car park on the white stilettos I keep in the bottom of the wardrobe for days like these.

I went to the ladies' room to check that I still looked like a tarty blonde. I don't often go in for disguises that involve wigs, but a couple of years before, I'd needed a radical appearance change, so I'd spent a substantial chunk of Mortensen and Brannigan's petty cash on a really good wig. It was a reddish blonde, which meant it didn't look too odd against my skin, which is the typically yellow-based freckle-face that goes with auburn hair. Coupled with a much heavier make-up than I'd normally be seen dead in, the image that peered out of the mirror at me was credible, if a bit on the dodgy side. I'd dressed to emphasize that impression, in a black lycra mini-skirt and a cream scoop-necked vest under my well-worn brown leather blouson. My own mother would have thrown me out of the house.

I touched up the scarlet lipstick and gave myself a toothy grin. 'Show time, Brannigan,' I muttered as I walked back across the car park and leaned against the door of my coupé.

He was right on time. At precisely 3.30, a metallic green Mercedes appeared at the entrance to the car park. He cruised round slowly, before purring to a halt next to my car. The driver was indeed fortyish, though calling him bald on top seemed to be a euphemistic description for someone well on the way to the billiard-ball look. I opened the passenger door and sank into the leather seat. 'Pleased to meet you,' I said.

'Dennis tells me you have something I might be interested in,' he said without preamble. His voice was nasal, the kind that gets on my nerves after about five minutes. 'I don't normally deal with people on a freelance basis,' he added, glancing at me for the first time.

'I know. Dennis explained how you like to work. But I thought that if I showed you what I can do, you might put some work my way,' I said, trying to sound hard-bitten.

'Let's see what you've got, then.' He turned in his seat towards me. His eyes were grey and cold, slightly narrowed. When he spoke, his mouth moved asymmetrically, as if he were gripping an imaginary cigarette in one corner.

'What about the colour of your money?' I demanded.

He leaned across. For a wild moment, I thought his hand was heading for my legs, but he carried on to the glove box. It fell open to reveal bundles of notes. I could see they were fifties, banded into packs of a thousand. There were ten of them. He picked one up and riffled it in my face, so I could see it was fifties all the way through.

Then he slammed the glove box shut again. 'Satisfied?'

'You will be,' I said, reaching into my bag. I took out the buckle, wrapped in an ordinary yellow duster. I opened it up and displayed the buckle. 'Anglo-Saxon,' I said. 'From High Hammerton Hall.'

'I know where it's from,' he said brusquely, taking a loupe out of his pocket and picking up the buckle. I hoped he couldn't hear the pounding of the blood in my ears as he examined it. I could feel a prickle of sweat under the foundation on my upper lip. 'Is this the real thing or is it a fake?' he asked.

I pointed to the twenty-grand car sitting next to us. 'Is that a real Leo Gemini turbo super coupé or is it a fake? Behave. It's the business,' I said aggressively.

'There's been nothing in the papers,' he said.

'I can't help that, can I? What do you want me to do, issue a press release?'

A half-smile twitched at the corners of his mouth. 'You done much of this sort of thing?' he asked.

'What d'you want, a fucking CV? Listen, all you need to know is that I can deliver the goods, and I haven't got a record, which makes me a damn sight better bet than Dennis and Frankie. D'you want this or not?' I held my hand out for the buckle.

'Oh, I think my clients will be happy with this,' he said, pocketing the buckle and the loupe. 'Help yourself.' He gestured towards the glove box, at the same time taking a card out of his inside pocket. I grabbed the money and stuffed it in my bag.

'Cheers,' I said.

He handed me the card. It was one of those ones you get made up on those instant print machines at railway stations and motorway services. I'd passed one minutes before. All it had on it was his mobile number. 'Next time, phone me before you do the job and I'll tell you whether we want the piece or not.'

'No sweat,' I said, opening the door. 'I like a man who knows what he wants.' I closed the door with a soft click and got behind the wheel of the coupé. The fence showed no sign of moving, so I started the engine and drove off. As I joined the motorway, I clocked him a few cars behind me. I stayed in the inside lane, and he made no move to catch me up, never mind overtake me. I left the motorway at the next junction, going round the roundabout twice to make certain he wasn't following me, then I turned down the Halifax road. Shelley got out of the Rover as I pulled in behind her. I jumped out of the coupé and raced for the Rover, pulling off my jacket as I ran. Shelley had left the engine running, as I'd asked her to.

'Speak to you later,' I shouted as I put the car in gear, did an illegal U-turn at the first opportunity and tore back to the motorway. The receiver for the bug beeped reassuringly. He was already five kilometres away from me, and climbing. I floored the accelerator as I rejoined the M62. The car seemed sluggish after the coupé, but it didn't take long to push it up to ninety. I pulled off the wig and ran a hand through my hair. I'd left a packet of moist tissues on the passenger seat of the Rover, and I used a handful of them to scrub the make-up off my face.

According to the tracer screen, the fence's direction had changed slightly. As I'd expected, he'd turned off on the M621 for Leeds. I followed, noting that I'd narrowed the distance between us. He was only 2.7 kilometres ahead of me now. I really needed to be a lot closer before he turned off and lost me in a maze of city streets. Luckily, the M621 runs downhill, and he was sticking to a speed that wouldn't get him picked up by the speed cameras. By the time we came to the Wetherby and Harrogate slip road, I was close enough to glimpse his pale green roof leave the motorway. Fortunately, there was a fair bit of traffic, so I was able to keep a couple of cars between us. In the queue at the Armley roundabout, I pulled on my denim shirt over the vest, completing the transformation from the waist up.

I had a momentary panic when he entered the tunnels of the inner city ring road and the signal disappeared from the receiver. But as soon as we emerged into daylight, the beep came back. I kept him in sight as we approached the complex confluence of roads at Sheepscar, one car behind as he swung right into Roundhay Road. I reckoned he had no idea that he was being followed, since he wasn't doing any of the things you do when you think you've got a tail; no jumping red lights, no sudden turns off the main road, no lane switching.

He stayed on Roundhay Road, then, just by the park, he turned left and drove up Prince's Avenue, through the manicured green of playing fields and enough grass to walk all the dogs of Leeds simultaneously. Where the avenue shaded into Street Lane, he turned right into a drive. I cruised past with a sidelong glance that revealed the Merc pulling into a double garage, then found a place to park round the corner. I kicked off the stilettos and pulled on the leggings I'd left in the car. I wriggled out of the lycra mini and got out of the car, stuffing my feet into my Reeboks. Then I strolled back along Prince's Avenue. Clearly, being a fence was a lot more lucrative than being a private eye. Baldy's house was set back from the road, a big detached job in stone blackened with a century and a half of industrial pollution. Not much change out of a quarter of a million for that one, by my reckoning. Probably the most popular man in the street too; they say good fences make good neighbours! I carried on down the road and bought an ice cream from one of the vans by the park gates. I sat on a wall and ate my cornet, keeping an eye on Baldy's house all the while.

Five minutes later, an Audi convertible pulled in to the drive. A blonde woman got out, followed by two girls in the kind of posh school uniform that has straw boaters in the summer term. From where I was sitting, the girls looked to be in their early teens. The woman left the car on the drive and followed the girls into the house. I finished my ice cream and walked back to the car. I drove around for a few minutes, trying to find a suitable place for a stakeout. Eventually, I parked just round the bend on the forecourt of a row of shops. I couldn't see the whole house from there, but I could see the door and the drive, and I hoped that by not parking outside anyone else's house, I'd escape the worst excesses of the neighbourhood watch. If I was going to have to come back tomorrow, I'd ring the local police and tell them I was in the area on a surveillance to do with a non-criminal matter. What's a few white lies between friends?

I took out the phone and rang the local library and asked them to check the address on the electoral roll. They told me the residents listed at that address were Nicholas and Michelle Turner. At last, I had a name that hadn't come from the pages of Ian Fleming.

Just after six, the woman came out again with the girls, each carrying a holdall. They drove off, passing me without a glance. They came back after eight, all with damp hair. I deduced they'd been indulging in some sporting activity. That's why I'm a detective. At half past eight, I phoned the Flying Pizza, a few hundred yards up the road, and ordered myself a takeaway pizza. Ten minutes later, I walked up and collected it, using their loo at the same time. I ate the pizza in the car, taking care not to drop my olives on Shelley's immaculate carpet and upholstery. At nine, my phone rang. 'Kate? It's Michael Haroun,' the voice on the other end announced.

I jerked upright, ran a hand through my hair and smiled. As if he could see me. Pathetic, really. 'Hello, Michael,' I said. 'What can I do for you?'

'I wondered if you were free for a drink this evening? You could give me a progress report.'

'No, and no. I'm working, and you're not my client. Not that that means we can't have a friendly drink together,' I added hastily, in case he thought I was being unfriendly.

'You can't blame me for trying,' he said. 'I do have an interest.'

'In the case or in me?' I asked tartly.

'Both, of course. When are you going to finish work?'

'Not for a while yet, and I'm over in Leeds.' I hoped the regret I felt was being transmitted through the ether.

'In Leeds? What are you doing there?'

'Just checking out an anonymous tip-off.'

'So you're making progress? Great!'

'I never said I was working on Henry's case,' I said. 'We do have more than one client, you know.'

'OK, OK, I get the message. Keep your nose out, Haroun. I'm sorry you can't make it tonight. Maybe we could get together soon?'

'Why don't you give me a ring tomorrow? I might have a clearer idea what my commitments are then.'

'I'll do that. Nice to talk to you, Kate.'

'Ditto.' After that little interlude, my surveillance seemed even more unbearably tedious. When the radio told me it was time for a book at bedtime, I decided to call it a day. It didn't look like Nicholas Turner or my buckle were going anywhere tonight.

When I got home, I picked up the Kerrchem file I'd left there when I'd got changed earlier. I skimmed the list of former employees, and one name jumped straight out at me. I hadn't been mistaken about Simon Morley. He'd been a lab technician at Kerrchem, made redundant with golden handcuffs six months before. He'd been the one I hadn't been able to contact because he'd moved. At least I knew where he was now. And I had a funny feeling that I knew just what he was doing in his overalls.

15

I pulled up on the forecourt of the shops in Street Lane at five to seven in Bill's Saab turbo convertible. One of the first rules of surveillance is to vary the vehicle you're sitting around in. Luckily, when Bill had gone off to Australia, he'd left me with a set of keys for his house and the car. I'd left Shelley's Rover in Bill's garage, with a message on the office answering machine telling her to hang on to the coupé for the time being. I felt sure this was a hardship she'd be able to bear, always supposing she didn't leap to the conclusion that the reason I wasn't back with her Rover was that her beloved heap was in some garage being restored to its former glory.

It had been a toss-up whose house I was going to sit outside this morning. On the one hand, if I didn't keep close tabs on Nicholas Turner, having the buckle bugged would have been a complete waste of time. On the other hand, Simon Morley's little adventures in cleaning had already cost a man his life. I'd lain awake, tossing and turning to the point where Richard, who normally sleeps like a man in persistent vegetative state, had sat up in bed and demanded to know what was going on. He'd eventually persuaded me to talk the dilemma over with him, something I always used to do but had been avoiding since his involvement in the car fraud case caused us both so much grief.

'You've got to go after the fence,' he finally said.

'Why?'

'Because if you lose him this time, you'll never get a second bite of the cherry. Sooner or later, someone's going to spot that your buckle isn't just a fake but a bugged fake, and then you're going to be on someone's most wanted list. And if this Simon Morley really has killed some bloke accidentally, he's going to be a damn sight more careful what he puts in his chemical soup in future. I'd be surprised if he's still at it. Maybe I should give him a bell; if he's such a shit hot chemist, I know some people who'd be delighted to have him on the payroll.'

I smacked his shoulder. 'I've told you before about the people you hang out with.'

He grinned. 'Only joking. You know I'm allergic to anything stronger than draw. Anyway, Brannigan, you should go for the fence.'

'You sure?' I asked, still doubtful.

'I'm sure.'

'And what about the ten grand?'

Richard shrugged. 'Hang on to it for now. We all need walking-around money.'

'It's a lot to be walking around with. Shouldn't I be paying it back to the insurance company, or somebody?'

'They don't know you've got it, they're not going to miss it. Maybe you should just look on it as an early Christmas bonus for Mortensen and Brannigan.'

'I don't know . . .'

'Trust me. I'm not a doctor,' he said, wrapping his arms around me and nuzzling the back of my neck. Instant goose-flesh. You can't fight your gonads. I hadn't even wanted to try. Michael who?

The Turner household came to life around half past seven. The curtains in the master bedroom opened, and I caught a glimpse of Nicholas in his dressing gown. This time I'd come fully equipped for surveillance. I had a video camera in the well of the passenger seat, cunningly hidden in a bag made of one-way fabric which allowed the camera to see out but prevented anyone seeing in. I had a pair of high-powered binoculars in my bag, and my Nikon with a long lens attached sitting on the passenger seat. And five hundred quid of walking-around money in the inside pocket of my jacket. I'd left the other nine and a half grand with Richard, who had strict instructions to pay it into a building society account which I hold in a false name for those odd bits and pieces of money that it's sometimes advisable to lose for a while.

At quarter past eight, Mrs Turner and her two daughters emerged, the girls in the same smart school uniform. The Audi drove off. Two hours later, the Audi came back. Mrs Turner staggered indoors with enough Tesco carrier bags to stock a corner shop. Then nothing for two more hours. At a quarter to one, Mrs T came out, got into the Audi and drove off. She came back at ten past two, when I was halfway through my Flying Pizza special. If something didn't happen soon, I was either going to die of boredom or go home. Apart from anything else, Radio Four loses its marbles between three and four in the afternoon, and I didn't think I could bear to listen to an hour of the opinions of those who are proof positive that care in the community isn't working.

Half an hour later, the front door opened, and Nicholas Turner came out. He was carrying a brief-case and a suit carrier. He opened the garage, dumped the suit carrier in the boot and reversed out into the road. 'Geronimo,' I muttered, starting my engine. Within seconds, the screen told me that he had the buckle with him. I eased out into the traffic and followed him back through the park.

The traffic was pretty much nose to tail as we came down the hill towards the city centre so it wasn't hard to stay in touch with the Mercedes. I kept a couple of cars between us, which meant I got snagged up a couple of times at red lights, but there wasn't enough free road for him to make much headway. I realized pretty soon he was heading for the motorways, which took some of the pressure off. I caught up with him just before he hit the junction where he had to choose between the M621 towards Manchester and the M1 for the south and east. He ignored the first slip road and roared off down the M1. In the Saab, it was easy to keep pace with him, which was another good reason for having swapped the Rover. I kept about half a mile behind to begin with, since I didn't want to lose him at the M62 junction. Sure enough, he turned off, heading east towards Hull.

We hammered down the motorway, the speedo never varying much either side of eighty-five. He'd obviously heard the same rumour I had about that being the speed cameras' trigger point. When we hit Hull, he followed the signs for the ferry port. I followed, with sinking heart. At the port, he parked and went into the booking office. I got into the queue in time to hear him book the car and himself on to that night's ferry. I didn't have any choice. I had to do the same thing.

By the time I emerged, he'd disappeared. I ran to the car, and saw that the buckle was moving away from the ferry port. He was either going to dispose of it now, or it was going on the ferry with him. Either way, I needed to try and follow him. I drove off in the direction the receiver indicated, grabbing my phone as I went and punching in Richard's number. The dashboard clock told me it was five past four. I prayed. He answered on the third ring. 'Yo, Richard Barclay,' he said.

'I need a mega favour,' I said.

'Lovely to hear your voice too, Brannigan,' he said.

'It's an emergency. I'm in Hull.'

'That sounds like an emergency to me.'

'I've got to be on the half past six ferry to Holland. My passport's in the top drawer of my desk. Can you get it, and get here by then?'

'In my car? You've got to be kidding.'

I could have wept. He was right, of course. Even though it's pretty souped up, his Volkswagen just couldn't do the distance in the time. Then I remembered the coupé. 'Shelley's got the Gemini,' I told him. 'I'll get her to meet you outside the office in five minutes with it. Can you do it?'

'I'll be there,' he promised.

I rang the office, one eye on the monitor, one eye on the road. I was probably the most dangerous thing on the streets of Hull. We seemed to be heading east, further down the Humber estuary. Shelley answered brightly.

'Don't ask questions, it's an emergency,' I said.

'You've been arrested,' she replied resignedly.

'I have not been arrested. I'm hot on the trail of a team of international art thieves. Some people would be proud to work with me.'

'OK, it's an emergency. What's it got to do with me?'

'Hang on, I think I'm losing someone . . .' We'd cleared the suburbs of Hull, and the receiver was registering a sharp change in direction. Sure enough, about a kilometre up the road, there was a right turn. Cautiously, I drove into the narrow road then pulled up. The distance between us remained constant. He'd stopped.

And the phone was squawking in my ear. 'Sorry, Shelley. OK, what I need is for you to meet Richard downstairs in five minutes with the Gemini. He'll leave you his car so you won't be without wheels,' I added weakly.

'You expect me to drive *that*?'

'It'll do wonders for your street cred,' I said, ending the call. I was in no mood for banter or argument. I put the car in gear and moved slowly down the lane, keeping an eye open for Turner's car. The tarmac ended a few hundred yards later in the car park of a pub overlooking the wide estuary. There were only two cars apart from Turner's Merc. There was no way I was going in there, even if he was offering the buckle to the highest bidder. With so few customers, I'd be painfully obvious. All I could do was head back to the main road and pray that Turner would still have the buckle with him.

I fretted for an hour, then the screen revealed signs of activity. The buckle was moving back towards me. Moments later, Turner's car emerged from the side road and headed back into Hull. 'There is a God,' I said, pulling out behind him. We got back to the ferry port at half past five. Turner joined the queue of cars waiting to board, but I stayed over by the booking office. The last thing I wanted was for him to clock me and the Saab at this stage in the game.

Richard skidded to a halt beside me at five to six. He gave me a thumbs-up sign as he got out. He picked up my emergency overnight bag from the passenger seat and came over to the Saab. He tossed the bag into the back and settled into my passenger seat. 'Well done,' I said, leaning across to give him a smacking kiss on the cheek.

'You'll have to stand on for any speeders I picked up,' he said. 'It really is a flying machine, that coupé.'

'You brought the passport?'

Richard pulled out two passports from his inside pocket. Mine and his. 'I thought I'd come along for the ride,' he said. 'I've got nothing pressing for the next couple of days, and it's about time we had a jaunt.'

I shook my head. 'No way. This isn't a jaunt. It's work. I've got enough to worry about without having to think about whether you're having a nice time. I really appreciate you doing this, but you're not coming with me.'

Richard scowled. 'I don't suppose you know where this guy's going?'

'I've no idea. But where he goes, I follow.'

'You might need some protective colouring,' he pointed out. 'I've heard you say that sometimes there are situations where a woman on her own stands out where a couple don't. I think I should come along. I could share the driving.'

'No. And no. And no again. You don't expect me to interview spotty adolescent wannabe rock stars, and I don't expect you to play detectives. Go home, Richard. Please?'

He sighed, looking mutinous. 'All right,' he said, sounding exactly like his nine-year-old son Davy when I drag him off the computer and tell him ten is not an unreasonable bedtime. He flung open the door and got out, turning back to say, 'Just don't expect me to feed the cat.'

'I haven't got a cat,' I said, grinning at his olive branch.

'You could have by the time you get back. Take care, Brannigan.'

I waved as I drove off, keeping an eye on him in my rear-view mirror. As I took my place in the slowly moving queue, I saw him get in the car and drive off. Half an hour later, I was standing in the stern of the ship, watching the quay recede inch by inch as we slowly moved away from the dock and out towards the choppy, steel grey waters of the North Sea.

I spent almost all of the trip closeted in my cabin with a spy thriller I'd found stuffed into the door pocket of Bill's car. The only time I went out was for dinner, which comes included in the fare. I left it to the last possible moment, hoping Turner would have eaten and gone by then. I'd made the right decision; there was no sign of him in the restaurant, so I was able to enjoy my meal without having to worry about him clocking me. I was certain he wouldn't recognize me as the tart with the buckle, but if this surveillance lasted any length of time, the chances were that he'd see me somewhere along the line. I didn't want him connecting me back to the ferry crossing.

On the way back to the cabin, I changed some money; fifty pounds each of guilders, Belgian francs, Deutschmarks, French francs, Swiss francs and lire. Nothing like hedging your bets. The sea was calm enough for me to get a decent night's sleep, and when we docked at Rotterdam, I felt refreshed enough to drive all day if I had to. From where I was placed on the car deck, I couldn't actually see Turner, and the steel hull of the ship didn't do a lot of favours for the reception on the tracking monitor.

Once I was clear of the ship, however, the signal came back strong and clear. For once, Bill's mongrel European ancestry worked to my advantage. He makes so many trips to the continent to visit family that he has serious road maps and city street plans for most of northern Europe neatly arranged in a box in his boot. I'd shifted the box to the back seat and unfolded a map of Holland and Belgium on the passenger seat. Comparing the map to the monitor, I reckoned that Turner was heading for Eindhoven. As soon as I got on the motorway, I stepped on the gas, pushing my speed up towards a ton, trying to close the distance between us.

Within half an hour, I had Turner in my sights again. He was cruising along just under ninety, and there was enough traffic on the road for me to stay in reasonably close touch without actually sitting on his bumper. He stayed on the motorway past Eindhoven. The next possible stop was Antwerp. From my point of view, there couldn't be a better destination. Bill's mother grew up in the city and he still has a tribe of relations there. I've been over with him on weekend trips a couple of times, and I fell in love with the city at first sight. Now, I feel like I know it with the intimacy of a lover.

It was my lucky day. He swung off the E34 at the Antwerp turn-off and headed straight for the city centre. He seemed to know where he was going, which made following him a lot easier than if he'd kept pulling over to consult a map or ask a passer-by for his destination. Me, I was just enjoying being back in Antwerp. I don't know how it manages it, but it still manages to be a charming city even though it's the economic heartbeat of Belgium. You don't normally associate culture with huge docks, a bustling financial centre and the major petrochemical industries. Not forgetting Pelikaanstraat, second only to Wall Street in the roll of the richest streets in the world. Come to think of it, what better reason could a fence have for coming to Antwerp than to do a deal in Pelikaanstraat, since its diamonds are the most portable form of hard currency in the world?

It began to look as if that was Turner's destination. We actually drove along the street itself, diamond merchants lining one side, the railway line the other. But he carried on up to the corner by Central Station and turned left into the Keyserlei. He slipped into a parking space just past De Keyser, the city centre's most expensive hotel, took his briefcase and suit carrier out of the car and walked inside. Cursing, I made a quick circuit of the block till I found a parking garage a couple of hundred metres away. I chose one of the several bars and restaurants opposite the hotel and settled down with a coffee and a Belgian waffle. I was just in time to see a liveried flunkey drive off in Turner's car, presumably taking it to the hotel garage.

I was on my third coffee when Turner re-emerged. I left the cup, threw some money on the table and went after him. He crossed over to the square by the station and walked towards the row of tram stops on Carnotstraat. He joined the bunch of people waiting for a tram. I dodged into a nearby tobacconist and bought a book of tram tickets, praying he'd still be there when I came out.

He was, but only just. He was stepping forward to board a tram that was pulling up at the stop. I ran across the street and leapt on to the second of the two carriages just before the doors hissed shut. Turner was sitting near the front, his back to me. He got off near the Melkmarkt, and I had no trouble following him past the cathedral and into the twisting medieval streets of the old town. He was strolling rather than striding, and he didn't look like he had the slightest notion that he might be followed. That was more than I could say for myself. I kept getting a prickling sensation in the back of my neck, as if I were aware at some subconscious level of being watched. I kept glancing over my shoulder, but I saw nothing to alarm me.

Eventually, we ended up in the vrijdag markt. Since it was too late for the twice-weekly second-hand auction, I could only assume Turner was heading for the Plantin-Moretus Museum. I'd tracked him all the way round Antwerp just so we could go round a printing museum? I hung back while he bought a ticket, then I followed him in. While it was no hardship to me to revisit one of my favourite museums, I couldn't see how it was taking me any nearer my art-racket mastermind.

The Plantin-Moretus house and its furnishings are just as they were when Christopher Plantin was Europe's boss printer back in the sixteenth century. But Nicholas Turner didn't seem too interested in soaking up the paintings, tapestries, manuscripts and antique furniture. He was moving swiftly through the rooms. Then I realized he was heading straight for the enclosed garden at the heart of the rectangular house. Rather than follow him out into the open air, I stayed put on the first floor where I could see what was going on.

Turner sat down on a bench, appearing to be simply enjoying the air. After about five minutes, another man joined him. They said nothing, but when the stranger moved on a few minutes later, he left his newspaper beside Turner's briefcase. Another few minutes went by, then Turner picked up the paper, placed it in his briefcase and started for the exit. The man had definitely been watching too many James Bond films.

I hurried back through the rooms I'd already visited and made it into the street in time to see Turner hail a cab. I ran up the square after him, but there wasn't another cab in sight. I ran all the way up to the Grote Market before I could get a cab to stop for me.

Luck was still running my way. As we turned into the Keyserlei, Turner was walking into the hotel. I paid off the cab and chose another bar to watch from. I'd eaten a bucket of mussels and drunk three more coffees before I saw any action. This time, he walked round the corner into the Pelikaanstraat. A couple of hundred yards down the street, he turned into a diamond merchant's. I wasn't too happy about staking the place out; it's an area where people are understandably suspicious of idle loitering. I'd noticed a slightly seedy-looking hotel on the way down the street, so I doubled back and walked into the foyer. It seemed as handy a place as any to spend the night, so I booked a room. I settled down on a sofa near the door and waited.

I was beginning to think Turner had gone off in the other direction when he finally walked past just before six. This time, I followed him into the hotel, where he headed for reception to pick up his key. I picked up a brochure about daily excursions to Bruges, managing to get close enough to hear him book a table for one in the restaurant at seven and an early-morning call at six. It sounded like he wasn't planning on anything more exciting than an early night. It sounded like a good idea to me.

I had one or two things to see to before I could crash out, but by half past seven, I was sorted. I'd used the hotel phone to check in with Shelley, since my mobile isn't configured to work with the continental system. She was singularly unimpressed with where I was, what I was doing and Richard's car. She was even less impressed when I confessed that her own car was less than a couple of miles from her house, locked safely inside Bill's garage, since I had the keys for the garage lurking somewhere at the bottom of my bag.

Thanks to the wonders of car hire, I was better off than she was. I had my very own Mercedes stashed in the parking garage round the corner. The Saab was safely parked behind a high fence at the Hertz office, and I'd dined on a giant slab of steak with a pile of crisp chips and thick mayo. I hadn't eaten so well on a job for years.

By nine, I was watching CNN in my hotel room, a large vodka and grapefruit juice sweating on the bedside table next to me. I was just about to get up and run a bath when I heard the unmistakable sound of a key fumbling into the lock of my bedroom door.

16

I was off the bed in seconds and in through the open door of the bathroom, hitting the light switches on the way. Whoever was outside the door would have to pass me on their way into the room itself, with only the flickering light of the television screen to guide them. The scrabbling stopped, and an arc of light from the hallway spilled across the carpet as the door opened. A shadow crossed the light, then the arc narrowed and disappeared as the door closed. I tensed, ready to come out kicking.

A hand groped along the far wall, followed by a shoulder. I leapt through the doorway, pivoted on one foot and put all my weight behind a straight kick at stomach level, yelling as loudly as I could to multiply the fear and surprise. My foot made contact with flesh and the body staggered back against the door with a heavy crash, the air shooting out of him in a groaning rush as he crumpled on the floor. I stepped back, keeping my weight on the balls of my feet, and reached for the lights.

Richard was doubled up on the carpet, arms folded defensively over his guts. For once, I was lost for words. I relaxed my fighting stance and stood staring at him.

'Fucking hell,' he gasped. 'Was that some traditional Belgian greeting, or what?'

'It's a traditional private eye's greeting for uninvited visitors,' I snarled. 'What the hell are you doing here?'

Richard struggled to his feet, still clutching his stomach. 'Nice to see you too, Brannigan.' He pushed past me and stumbled on to the bed, where he curled into a ball. 'Oh shit, I think you've relocated my stomach somewhere around my left shoulder blade.'

'Serves you right,' I said heartlessly. 'You scared me shitless.'

'That why you were in the bathroom?' he said innocently.

'What was wrong with the phone? Was it too much for you to handle, a foreign phone system? Besides, how did you get here? How did you find me? Did Shelley tell you where I was?'

Richard stopped rubbing his stomach and eased up into a sitting position. 'I thought I'd surprise you. I don't know, call yourself a detective? I've been tailing you ever since you got off the ferry, and you didn't even notice,' he said proudly.

I moved across the room to the only chair and sat down heavily. 'You've been tailing *me*?'

'Piece of piss,' he said.

He had me worried now. If I'd been so busy watching Nicholas Turner that I hadn't spotted a car as obvious as a snazzy UK-registered coupé on my own tail, it was time I gave up detective work and settled for something like social work where I could get away with a complete lack of observational skills. 'I don't believe you,' I said. 'Shelley told you where I was and you got a flight over here.'

He grinned. For once, it made me want to hit him, not kiss him. 'Sorry, Brannigan. I did it all by myself.'

'No way. I couldn't have missed seeing the coupé on the ferry,' I said, positive now. The Saab had been one of the last cars to board. He simply couldn't have got the coupé on board without me spotting it.

'That's what I thought too,' he said complacently. 'That's why I left it at Hull. I travelled as a foot passenger, which meant I got off the ferry before you. I hired a Merc at the ferry terminal and picked you up as you came off. Then I followed you here. I thought I'd lost you when you got on the tram, but I managed to get a taxi and he followed the tram. Just like the movies, really. I waited outside while you were in that museum, and I hung about just inside the station when you came in here first time around.'

I shook my head in bewildered amazement. 'So how did you get a key for the room?'

His grin was beginning to infuriate me. 'I had a

word with the desk clerk. Told him my girlfriend was here on business and I'd come to surprise her. It cost me two thousand francs. Most I've ever paid for a good kicking.'

Forty quid. I was impressed. 'I suppose you're potless now, are you?' I said sternly.

He looked sheepish. 'Not as such. I forgot to go to the building society with the nine and a half grand, so I brought it with me.'

I didn't know whether to be furious or impressed. There was no doubt the money would come in handy, at the rate I was spending, but I didn't want Richard around on the chase. I had enough to worry about keeping tabs on Turner without having to be constantly aware of what Richard was up to. 'Thanks,' I said. 'I was wondering what to do when I ran out of cash. You can leave it with me when you go home tomorrow.'

He looked crestfallen. 'I thought you'd be pleased to see me,' he said.

I got up and sat down beside him on the bed. 'Of course I'm pleased to see you. I just don't need to have to worry about you while I'm trying to do my job.'

'What's to worry about?' he demanded. 'I'm not a kid, Kate. Look, these are heavy people you're after, there's no two ways about it. You could use an extra pair of eyes. Not to mention an extra set of wheels. If he's going on a long haul, you can't use the same car all the way, and you could lose him while you're swapping over at some car-hire place.

If I stay, we can rent a couple of mobile phones and that way one of us can stay with him while the other one does things like fill up with petrol or stop for a piss.'

The most irritating thing was that he was right. I'd been worrying about that very thing myself. 'I don't know,' I said. I wanted to say, this is my territory, my skill area, my speciality and you're just an amateur. But I didn't want to throw that down on the bed for both of us to look at. The thing that worried me most was that after the debacle when he'd last tried to help me out, Richard felt he had something to prove. And there's nothing more dangerous on a job that needs patience than someone with something to prove.

At quarter past six the following morning, I was sitting in the dark in my rented Mercedes on Pelikaanstraat. Richard was on the Keyserlei, a couple of hundred yards up from the hotel. Whichever way Turner went, one of us would pick him up. I checked the equipment on the passenger seat one more time. Richard hadn't been strictly honest with me the previous evening. Once I'd reluctantly agreed to let him tag along, he confessed that he'd already hired a pair of mobile phones, so convinced was he that I'd see what he called sense.

We'd already agreed on a modus operandi. I would use the bugging equipment to keep tabs on Turner. Richard would sit tucked in behind me. If I wanted to stop to change cars, fill up with petrol or go to the loo, I'd phone him and he'd overtake me. Then, when he had Turner in sight, he'd call me and I'd go and do whatever I needed to. Once I was back on track, Richard would fall back behind me again. That was the theory. I'd put money on it working like a wind-up toy with a broken spring.

I sipped the carton of coffee I'd bought from the vending machine in the station and watched the screen. The buckle wasn't moving yet. I ate one of the waffles I'd bought the evening before. I could feel my blood sugar rising with every mouthful. The combination of sugar and caffeine had me feeling almost human by the time the phone rang at five to seven. 'Yes?' I said.

'Z-Victor one to BD,' Richard said. 'Target on move. I've just pulled out in front of him. Heading for the traffic lights. He's staying in the left-hand lane. Roger and out.'

If he carried on like this all day, I might just kill him by dinner time, I decided. I stepped on the accelerator and swung round the corner. I was just in time to see the two cars turn left at the traffic lights. No way was I going to catch them, so I settled for watching the screen. I caught up with them about a mile from the motorway. It looked like we were heading southeast, towards Germany.

Once we hit the motorway, I called Richard and told him to fall back behind me. I kept a steady two kilometres behind Turner, which was far enough at a hundred and forty kph, and five minutes later Richard appeared in front of me, slowing down enough to slide into my slipstream with a cheery wave. By nine, we'd sailed past Maastricht and Aachen, the bug had seen us safely through the maze of autobahns round Köln, and Bonn was fast approaching on the port bow as we rolled on to the west of the Rhine. The boring flat land of Belgium was a distant memory now as the motorway swept us inexorably through rolling hills and woodland. Somehow, the motorways in Europe seem to be much more attractively landscaped than ours do. Maybe it's just the indefinably foreign quality of the scenery, but I suspect it's more to do with the fact that the Germans in particular have had to take Green politics seriously for a few years longer than we have.

Just before eleven, we crossed the Rhine north of Karlsruhe, with no sign of slowing up. I rang Richard and told him to overtake me and get on Turner's back bumper again. The motorway split just south of the city, the A5 carrying on south and the A8 cutting off east. Unlike Köln, there was no quick way to double back if we made the wrong decision. A few minutes later, he called telling me to stay on the A5. We carried on down the river valley, the wooded hills on the left starting to become mountains, the occasional rocky peak flashing in and out of sight for seconds at a time.

A few kilometres before the Swiss border, the blip on the screen started moving towards me. It looked like Turner had stopped. Judging by the state of my fuel gauge, he was probably buying petrol. I rang Richard and told him to pull off at the approaching services while I carried on across the border. I stopped as soon as I could after waving my passport at Swiss customs and poured petrol into my tank till I couldn't squeeze another drop in. I bought a couple of sandwiches, bars of yummy Swiss chocolate and cans of mineral water, then rushed back to the car. The buckle was still behind me, but closing fast. I rang Richard.

'We both filled up with petrol,' he reported. 'I waited till he'd cleared the shop before I went in to pay, then I followed him through the border. Where are you?'

'In the service area you're about to pass,' I told him. 'You can let Turner get away from you now. If you drive into the services, you can fall in behind me again.' I couldn't believe it was all going so well. I kept waiting for the other shoe to drop.

We carried on past Basel and on to Zürich. By now, we were properly into the Alps, mountains towering above us on all sides. If I hadn't been concentrating so hard on staying in touch with Turner and the buckle, I'd have been enjoying the drive. As it was, I felt as stressed as if I'd been sitting in city rush-hour traffic for the five and a half hours it had taken us to get this far.

We skirted the outskirts of the city and drove on down the side of Lake Zürich. About halfway down the lake, the blip on the screen suddenly swung off to the right. 'Oh shit,' I muttered. I stepped on the accelerator, checking in my mirror that Richard was still with me. The motorway exit was only seconds away, and I swung off on a road that led into the mountains. I grabbed the phone, punched the memory redial that linked me to Richard and said, 'Wait here. Turn round to face the motorway so you can pick him up if he heads back.'

'Roger wilco,' Richard said. 'Call me if you need back-up.'

I carried on, checking the blip on the screen against the road map. Cursing the fact that I didn't have a more detailed map of Switzerland, I swung the car through the bends of what was rapidly becoming a mountain road. A couple of miles further on, I realized that staying on the main road had been the wrong decision, as the buckle was moving further away from me at an angle. Swearing so fluently my mother would have disowned me, I nearly caused a small pile-up with a U-turn that took a thousand miles off the tyres and hammered back down the road and on to a narrow, twisting side road. About a kilometre away from the main drag, the screen suddenly went blank.

I panicked. My first thought was that Turner had met someone or picked someone up who had taken one look at the buckle, spotted the bug and disabled it. Then logic kicked in and told me that was impossible in so short a time. As I swung round yet another bend with a sheer rock wall on one side and a vertiginous drop on the other, I twigged. The mountains were so high and so dense that the radio signal was blocked.

I raced the car round the bends as fast as I could, tyres screaming on every one, wrists starting to feel it in spite of the power steering. I was concentrating so hard on not ending up as a sheet of scrap metal on the valley floor that I nearly missed Turner. With the suddenness of daylight at the end of a tunnel, the road emerged on to a wide plateau about halfway up the mountain. In the middle of an Alpine meadow complete with cows that tinkled like bass wind chimes stood an inn, as pretty as a picture postcard, as Swiss as a Chalet School novel. On the edge of the crowded car park, Turner's pale green Mercedes was parked. And the screen flashed back into life.

Heaving a huge sigh of relief, I drove to the far end of the car park and tried to ring Richard and let him know everything was OK. No joy. I supposed the mountain was in the way again. I got out of the car, took a black beret and a pair of granny glasses with clear lenses out of my stakeout-disguises holdall and walked into the inn. Inside, it was the traditional Swiss chalet, wood everywhere, walls decorated with huge posters of Alpine scenery, a blazing fire in a central stone fireplace. The room was crammed with tables, most of them occupied. A quick scan showed me Turner sitting alone at a table for two, studying the menu. A waitress dressed in traditional costume bustled up to me and said something in German. I shrugged and tried out my school French, saying I wanted to eat, one alone, and did they have a telephone?

She smiled and showed me to a table near the fire and pointed out the phone. I got change from the cashier and gave Richard a quick call. For some reason, he was less than thrilled that I was sitting down to some Tyrolean speciality while he was stuck on the verge of the road with nothing in sight but the motorway and a field of the inevitable cows. 'Go and get some sandwiches or something,' I instructed him. 'I'll let you know when we set off.'

I went back to my table. Out of the corner of my eye, I could see Turner tucking into a steaming bowl of soup, a stein of beer beside him, so I figured I'd have time to eat something. I ordered Tiroler gröstl, a mixture of potatoes, onions and ham with a fried egg on top. It looked like the nearest thing to fast food on the menu. I was right. My meal was in front of me in under five minutes. I was halfway through it before Turner's main course arrived. Judging by the pile of chips that was all I could identify, he was eating for two. Frankly, I could see why he'd made the detour. The food was more than worth it, if my plateful was anything to go by. Definitely one to cut out and keep for next time we were passing Zürich.

By the time I'd finished and lingered over a cup of coffee, Turner had also demolished a huge wedge of lemon meringue pie. If I'd scoffed that much in the middle of the day, I'd have been asleep at the wheel ten miles down the road. I hoped he had a more lively metabolism. When he called for the bill, I took mine to the cashier, rang Richard to warn him we were on the move, and headed back to the car. Minutes later, Turner was heading back down the road, with me a couple of bends behind him.

As we hit the motorway, I had another panic. Where I'd expected to see Richard in his Mercedes, there was a black BMW. As I sailed past, I glanced across and saw the familiar grin behind the thumbs-up sign. Moments later, as he swung in behind me, the phone rang. 'Sierra 49 to Sierra Oscar,' he said. 'Surprise, surprise. I nipped back to Zürich and swapped the cars. I thought it was about time for a change.'

'Nice one,' I conceded. Maybe he wasn't the liability I'd feared he'd be after all. And there was me thinking that he was as subtle as Jean Paul Gaultier. This wasn't the time to reassess the capabilities of the man in my life, but I filed the thought away for future scrutiny.

I figured we must be heading for Liechtenstein, haven for tax dodgers, fraudsters and stamp-collecting anoraks. No such luck. We carried on south, deep into the Alps. Richard was in front of me again, keeping tabs on Turner. The bug kept cutting out because of the mountains, and I was determined that we weren't going to lose him after coming this far. Now Richard was in another car, I felt happy about him staying in fairly close touch.

A few miles down the road, my bottle started twitching. There was no getting away from it. We were heading for the San Bernardino tunnel. Ten kilometres in that dark tube, aware of the millions of tons of rock just sitting above my head, waiting to crush me thin as a postage stamp. Just the thought of it forced a groan from my lips. I'm terrified of tunnels. Not a lot of people know that. It doesn't sit well with the fearless, feisty image. I've even been known to drive thirty miles out of my way to avoid going through the tunnels under the Mersey.

With every minute that passed, that gaping hole in the hillside was getting closer and my heart was pounding faster. Desperately, I rattled through the handful of cassettes I'd grabbed when I'd picked up Bill's car. Not a soothing one among them. No Enya, no Mary Coughlan, not even Everything But The Girl. Plenty of Pet Shop Boys, Eurythmics and REM. I settled for Crowded House turned up loud to keep the eerie boom of the tunnel traffic at bay and tried to concentrate on their harmonies.

Two minutes into the tunnel and the sweat was clammy on my back. Three minutes in and my upper lip was damp. Four minutes in and my forehead was slimy as a sewer wall. Six minutes in and my knuckles were white on the steering wheel. The walls looked as if they were closing in. I tried telling myself it was only imagination, and Crowded House promised they could ease my pain. They were lying. Ten minutes and I could feel a scream bubbling in my throat. I was on the point of tears when a doughnut of light appeared around the cars in front of me.

As soon as I burst out again into daylight, my phone started ringing. 'Yeah?' I gasped.

'You OK?' Richard asked. He knows all about me and tunnels.

'I'll live.' I swallowed hard. 'Thanks for asking.'

'You're a hero, Brannigan,' he said.

'Never mind that,' I said gruffly. 'You still with Turner?'

'Tight as Jagger's jeans. He's got his foot down. Looks like we're heading for *la bella Italia*.'

At least I'd be somewhere I could speak the language, I thought with relief. I'd been worried all the way down Germany and Switzerland that Turner was going to end up in a close encounter that I couldn't understand a word of. But my Italian was fluent, a hangover from the summer before university, when I'd worked in the kitchens of Oxford's most select trattoria. It was learn the language or take a vow of silence. I'd prevented it from getting too rusty by holidaying in Italy whenever I could.

I drove cheerfully down the mountain, glad to be out in the open air again, relieved that we were gradually leaving the mountains behind us. We worked our way round Milan just after five, Richard back behind me, and by seven we were skirting Genoa. This was turning into one hell of a drive. My shoulders were locked, my backside numb, my hips stiff in spite of regular squirming. If they ever start making private eyes work with tachographs, I'm going to be as much use to my clients as a cardboard chip pan. I shuddered to think what this overtime was going to look like on Henry's bill. He'd run out of buckshee hours a while back.

At Genoa we turned east again on the A12, another one of those autostradas carved out of the side of a mountain. I kept telling myself the little tunnels were just like driving under big bridges, but it didn't help a lot, especially since the receiver kept cutting out, giving me panic attacks every time.

Three quarters of an hour past Genoa, the screen told me Turner was moving off to one side. First, he went right, then crossed back left. I nearly missed the exit, I was concentrating so hard on the screen, but I managed to get off with Richard on my tail. We were on the outskirts of some town called Sestri Levante, but according to my screen, Turner was heading away from it. Praying I was going the right way, I swung left and found myself driving along a river valley, the road lined with shops and houses. Sestri Levante shaded into Casarza Ligure, then we were out into open country, wooded hills on either side of the valley. We hit a small village called Bargonasco just as the direction changed on the receiver. A couple of kilometres further up, there was a turning on the left. It was a narrow, asphalt road, with a sign saying Villa San Pietro. The blip on the screen stayed steady. A kilometre away, straight up the Villa San Pietro's drive.

Journey's end.

17

'What now, Sam Spade?' Richard asked as we both bent and stretched in vain attempts to restore our bodies to something like their normal configuration.

'You go back to the village and find us somewhere to stay for the night, then you sit outside in the car in case Turner comes back down the valley,' I told him.

'And what are you doing while I'm doing that?' Richard asked.

'I'm going to take a look at the Villa San Pietro,' I told him.

He looked at me as if I'd gone stark staring mad. 'You can't just drive up there like the milkman,' he said.

'Correct. I'm going to walk up, like a tourist. And you're going to take the receiver with you, just in case the buckle's going anywhere Turner isn't.'

'You're not going up there on your own,' Richard said firmly.

'Of course I am,' I stated even more firmly. 'You are waiting down here with a car, a phone and a bug receiver. If we both go and Turner comes driving back down with the buckle while we're ten minutes away from the cars, he could be outside the range of the receiver in any direction before we get mobile. I'm not trekking all the way across Europe only to lose the guy because you want to play macho man.'

Richard shook his head in exasperation. 'I hate it when you find a logical explanation for what you intend to do regardless,' he muttered, throwing himself back into the driver's seat of the BMW. 'See you later.'

I waved him off, then moved the Merc up the road a few hundred yards. I scuffed some dust over my trainers, put on a pair of sunglasses even though dusk was already gathering, hung my camera round my neck and trudged off up the drive.

There was a three-foot ditch on one side of the twisting road, which appeared to have been carved out of the rough scrub and stunted trees of the hillside. Ten minutes' brisk climbing brought me to the edge of a clearing. I hung back in the shelter of a couple of gnarled olive trees and took a good look. The ground had been cleared for about a hundred metres up to a wall. Painted pinkish brown, it was a good six feet high and extended for about thirty metres either side of a wrought iron gate. Above the wall, I could see an extensive roof in the traditional terracotta pantiles.

Through the gates, I could just about make out the villa itself, a two-storey white stucco building with shutters over the upper-storey windows. It looked like serious money to me.

I would have been tempted to go in for a closer look, except that a closed-circuit video camera was mounted by the gate, doing a continuous 180-degree sweep of the road and the clearing. Not just serious money, but serious paranoia too.

Staying inside the cover of the trees and the scrub, I circled the villa. By the time I got back to the drive, I had more scratches than Richard's record collection, and the certainty that Nicholas Turner was playing with the big boys. There were video cameras mounted on each corner of the compound, all programmed to carry out regular sweeps. If I'd had enough time and a computer, I could probably have worked out where and when the blind spots would occur, but anyone who's that serious about their perimeter security probably hasn't left the back door on the latch. This was one burglary that was well out of my league.

I found Richard sitting on the bonnet of his car on the forecourt of a building with all the grace and charm of a Sixties tower block. Green neon script along the front of the three-storey rectangle proclaimed Casa Nico. Below that, red neon told us this was a Ristorante-Bar-Pensione. The only other vehicles on the parking area were a couple of battered pickups and a clutch of elderly motor scooters. So much for Italian style.

'This is it?' I asked, my heart sinking.

'This is it,' Richard confirmed gloomily. 'Wait till you see the room.'

I gathered my overnight bag, the video camera bag and my camera gear and followed Richard indoors. To get to the rooms, we had to go through the bar. In spite of the floor-to-ceiling windows along one wall, it somehow managed to be dark and gloomy. As soon as we walked through the bead curtain that separated the bar from the fore-court, the rumble of male voices stopped dead. In a silence cut only by the slushy Italian Muzak from the jukebox, we crossed the room. I smiled inanely round me at the half-dozen men sprawled around a couple of tables. I got as cheerful a welcome as a Trot at a Tory party conference. Not even the human bear leaning on the Gaggia coffee machine behind the bar acknowledged our existence. The minute we left by a door in the rear, the conversation started up again. So much for the friendly hospitality of the Italian people. Somehow, I didn't see myself managing to engage mine host in a bit of friendly gossip about the Villa San Pietro.

The third-floor room was big, with a spectacular view up the wooded river valley. That was all you could say for it. Painted a shade of yellow that I haven't seen since the last time I had food poison-ing, it contained the sort of vast, heavy wooden furniture that could only have been built *in situ*, unless it was moved into the room before the walls went up. Above the double bed was a crucifix, and the view from the bed was a massive, sentimental print of Jesus displaying the Sacred Heart with all the dedication of an offal butcher.

'Bit of a turn-off, eh?' Richard said.

'I expect Jeffrey Dahmer would love it.' I sat down on the bed, testing the mattress. Another mistake. I thought I was going to be swallowed whole. 'How much is this costing us?' I asked.

'About the same as a night in the Gritti Palace. Mind you, that also includes dinner. Not that it'll be edible,' he added pessimistically.

After we'd had a quick shower, I set the bug receiver to auto-alert, so that it would give a series of audible bleeps if the buckle moved more than half a kilometre from its current relative position. Then we went in search of food. Richard had been right about that too. We were the only two people in the cheerless dining room, which resembled a school dining room with tablecloths. The sole waitress, presumably the wife of Grizzly Adams behind the bar, looked as if she'd last laughed somewhere around 1974 and hadn't enjoyed the experience enough to want to repeat it. We started with a platter of mixed meats, most of which looked and tasted like they'd made their getaway from the local cobbler. The pasta that followed was *al dente* enough to be a threat to dentistry. The sauce was so sparing that the only way we could identify it as pesto was by the colour.

Richard and I ate in virtual silence. 'What was that you said about it being time we had a bit of a jaunt?' I said at one point.

He prodded one of the overcooked lamb chops that looked small enough to have come from a rabbit and scowled. 'Next time, I won't be so bloody helpful,' he muttered. 'This is hell. I haven't had proper food for two days and I'd kill for a joint.'

'Not many Chinese restaurants in Italy,' I remarked. 'It's on account of them inventing one of the world's great cuisines.' Richard took one look at my deadpan face and we both burst out laughing. 'One day,' I gasped, 'we'll look back at this and laugh.'

'Don't bet on it,' he said darkly.

We passed on pudding. We both have too much respect for our digestive tracts. At least the coffee was good. So good we ordered a second cup and took it upstairs with us. The one good thing about the bed was the trough in the middle that forced us into each other's arms. After the day we'd had, it was more than time to remind each other that the world isn't all grief.

My eyelids unstuck themselves ten hours later. The bleeding heart on the wall wasn't a great sight to wake up to, so I rolled over and checked the receiver sitting on the bedside table. No movement. By nine, we were both showered, dressed and back in the dining room. Breakfast was a pleasant surprise. Freshly baked focaccia, three different cheeses and a choice of jam. 'What's the game plan for today?' Richard asked through a mouthful of Gorgonzola and bread.

'We stick with the buckle,' I said. 'If it moves, we follow. If it stays put and Turner moves, we stay put too and follow Plan B.'

'What's Plan B?'

'I don't know yet.'

After breakfast, Richard took his BMW up the valley past the drive. I'd told him to park facing up the valley and to follow anything that came down the drive, unless I called him and told him different. I sat on a bench on the forecourt of Casa Nico, reading Bill's thriller, the receiver in my open bag next to me. I hoped that anyone passing would take me for a tourist making the most of the watery autumn sunshine. I only had thirty pages to go when the receiver bleeped so loudly I nearly fell off my seat.

I picked it up and stared at the read-out. The buckle was moving steadily towards me. I leapt to my feet and jumped into the car, gunning the engine into life. Still the buckle was drawing nearer. There was a sudden change of direction, which I guessed was the turn from the drive on to the main road. I edged forward, ready to pull out after the target vehicle had passed, one eye on the screen. Seconds later, a stretch Mercedes limo cruised past me, followed in short order by Richard in the BMW.

I slotted into place behind him, and our little

cavalcade made its way back down the valley and into Sestri Levante. The outskirts of the town were typical of northern Italy – dusty, slightly shabby, somehow old-fashioned. The centre was much smarter, a trim holiday resort all stucco in assorted pastel shades, green shuttered windows on big hotels and small *pensiones*, expensive shops, grass and palm trees. We skirted the wide crescent of the main beach and headed along the isthmus to the harbour. As the limo turned on to a quay, I dumped the car in an illegal parking space and watched Richard do the same. I ran up to join him, linked arms and together we strolled up the quay, our faces pointing towards the sea and the floating gin palaces lined up at the pontoons. The great thing about wrap-round sunglasses is the way you can look in one direction while your head is pointing in the other.

From the corner of my eye, I saw the stretch limo glide to a halt at the foot of a gangway. The boat at the end of it was bigger than my house, and probably worth as much as Henry's Monet. The driver's door opened and a gorilla in uniform got out. Even from that distance, I could see muscles so developed they made him look round-shouldered. He wore sunglasses and a heavy moustache and looked around him with the economical watchfulness of a good bodyguard. Martin Scorsese would have swooned.

Satisfied that there was no one on the quay more dangerous than a couple of goggling tourists, he opened the back door. By now, we were close enough for me to get a good look at the presumed owner of the Villa San Pietro. He wasn't much more than my own five feet and three inches, but he looked a hell of a lot harder than me. He was handsome in the way that birds of prey are handsome, all hooked nose and hooded eyes. His perfectly groomed black hair had a wing of silver over each temple. He was wearing immaculately pressed cream yachting ducks, a full-cut, canary yellow silk shirt with a navy guernsey thrown over his shoulders. He carried a slim briefcase. He stood for a moment on the quayside, shaking the crease straight on his trouser legs, then headed up the gangplank without waiting for Turner, who scrambled out of the car behind him.

I pulled Richard into a tight embrace as Turner and the bodyguard went on board, just in case Turner was looking. When they'd disappeared below, we carried on strolling past the *Petronella Azura III*. I can't say I was surprised to see that the expensive motor cruiser was registered out of Palermo.

'Fucking hell,' Richard murmured as we passed the boat. 'It's the Mafia. Brannigan, this is no place for us to be,' he said, casting a nervous look back over his shoulder.

'They don't know we're here,' I pointed out. 'Let's keep it that way, huh?' At the end of the quay, we stared out to sea for a few minutes.

'We're going to pull out now, aren't we?' Richard

demanded. 'I mean, it's time to bring in the big battalions, isn't it?'

'Who did you have in mind?' I asked pointedly. 'This isn't Manchester. I don't know the good cops from the bad cops. From what I've heard of Italian corruption, I could walk into the nearest police station and find myself talking to this mob's tame copper. Can you think of a better short cut to a concrete bathing suit?'

Richard looked hurt. 'I was only trying to be helpful,' he said.

'Well, don't. When I want help, I'll ask for it.' I can't help myself. The more scared I get, the more I bite lumps out of the nearest body. Besides, I didn't figure I was obliged to feel guilty. As far as I was concerned, Richard had drawn the short straw from choice.

I got to my feet and started to stroll back down the quay. After a moment, Richard caught up with me. We were just in time to see the chauffeur and a young lad in shorts and a striped T-shirt trot down the gangplank and start unloading suitcases from the boot of the limo. They ferried half a dozen bags on board, not even giving us a second glance. We walked back to my car and stared at the receiver in a moody silence neither of us felt like breaking.

After about half an hour, Turner and the body-guard came off the yacht and got in the car. 'You want to follow them?' I asked Richard. 'I'll stay here and watch the boat.'

'No heroics,' he bargained.

'No heroics,' I agreed.

He just caught the lights at the end of the road where the limo had turned right. It looked like the chauffeur was taking Turner back to the villa. And judging by the screen, the buckle was now aboard the yacht. One of two things was going to happen now. Either the yacht was going to take off, complete with buckle, or some third party was going to come to the yacht and get the buckle. My money was on the former, but I felt duty-bound to sit it out. The phone rang about twenty minutes later. 'They're back at the villa,' Richard reported. 'Do you want me to wait and see if Turner takes off?'

'Please,' I said. 'Thanks, Richard. Sorry I bit your head off earlier.'

'So you should be. You're lucky to have me.' He ended the call before I could find a retort.

Suddenly the receiver screen went blank. I sat bolt upright. I pulled the connector out of the cigarette-lighter socket where I'd been recharging the batteries and slid the power compartment cover off. I broke one of my nails getting the batteries out in a hurry, and stuffed replacements in. But when I switched on again, the screen was still blank. Given that it wasn't the batteries and the yacht hadn't moved out of range, there was only one possible reason why my screen was blank. Someone had discovered the bug and put it out of action. I took a deep breath and thanked my lucky stars that my name wasn't Nicholas Turner.

Ten minutes later, the lad in the shorts was back on the quayside, casting off. Within twenty minutes, the *Petronella Azura III* had disappeared round the point. Pondering my next step, I drove back up the valley and found Richard sitting in the BMW a couple of hundred yards up the road from the turn-off to the drive. I parked my Merc at Casa Nico and walked up to join him. I filled him in on the latest turn of events. It didn't take long.

'So do we go home now?' he asked plaintively.

'I suppose so,' I said reluctantly. 'I'd like to get inside that villa, though.'

'You said yourself it was impregnable,' he pointed out.

'I know, but I never could resist a challenge.'

Richard took a deep breath. 'Brannigan, you know I never try to come between you and your job. But this time, you've got to back off. Go home, tell the police what you've got so far. They can pick up Turner and they can talk to the good cops over here and get them to look at the villa and the boat. There's nothing more you can do here. Besides, you've got another investigation you're supposed to be working on, in case you'd forgotten.'

Part of me knew he was right. But there is another part of me that responds to being told what to do by doing just the opposite. It overrides all my common sense, and it's one of the reasons why I prefer to work alone. Besides, I knew that all we had was an address and the name of a boat. That wouldn't necessarily take the authorities anywhere at all. I wanted more. But I didn't want to get into that right then. 'Let's book in at Casa Nico for another night,' I said. 'We might as well get an early start tomorrow and shoot straight back to Antwerp in a oner,' I said. 'We don't have to eat there,' I added hastily. 'Sestri Levante looked like it might have a few decent restaurants.'

Richard scowled. 'So why don't we go the whole hog and book in at a decent hotel too?'

'I'd like to stay up here, keep an eye on the place, see if there are any more comings and goings,' I told him. 'You can go down to Sestri and potter round the shops if you want.'

The scowl deepened. 'I'm not some bloody bimbo,' he complained. 'If you're waiting here, I'll keep you company.'

It was a long afternoon. I finished the thriller and Richard started it. We played I-Spy. We played Bonaparte. We played 'I went to the doctor's with . . .' right through the alphabet. The only break was when I nipped back to the Casa Nico to book us a room for the night. I was about to give in to Richard's pleas to call it a day when there was movement. An Alfa Romeo sports saloon shot out of the drive heading up the valley. Even at the speed it was travelling, I recognized the bodyguard behind the wheel. 'Move it,' I told Richard. He pulled the BMW round in a tight arc and shot after the Alfa.

We didn't have far to go. A few miles up the road was a bar whose owner could have taught Nico a thing or two. Even from our slow cruise past, it was obvious that Bar Bargonasco made Nico's look like a funeral parlour. The music was loud and cheerful, the car park didn't look like an apprentice scrapyard and there were more than six people in there. 'Pull up round the corner,' I said.

When the car stopped, I opened the door. 'Where are you going?' Richard said, panic in his eyes.

'I'm going to get into that villa one way or another. If I can't do it Dennis O'Brien style, I'm going to do it Kate Brannigan style. I'm going to chat up the bodyguard.' I shut the door and took off the shirt I was wearing over the cotton vest that was tucked into my jeans. As I was stuffing the shirt into my handbag, Richard jumped out of the driver's seat.

'You're out of your mind,' he yelled at me. 'Have you seen the size of that guy?'

'That's the whole point. He's obviously been hired for his size, not his brains. He probably keeps them in his trousers, which gives me a head start.'

'You'll never get his keys off him,' Richard exploded. 'For fuck's sake, Kate. This is madness.'

'I'm not planning on getting his keys off him. I'm planning on getting him to take me home with him,' I said, starting off towards the bar.

Richard caught up with me two steps further on and grabbed my arm. 'No way,' he shouted.

Mistake, really. In one short, sharp move, I freed myself and left Richard white-faced and clutching his wrist. 'Never, never grab me like that,' I said softly. 'You don't own me, Richard, and you don't tell me what to do.'

For a long moment we stood in a silent standoff. 'I love you, you silly bitch,' Richard finally said. 'If you want to go off and get yourself killed, you'll have to knock me out first.'

'I'll do it if I have to. You better believe me. This is my job, Richard. I know what I'm doing.'

'You'd fuck that gorilla because you think it'll help you nail some mafioso?'

I snorted. 'Is that what this is about? Sexual jealousy? What do you think I am, Richard? A tart? I never said I was going to fuck the guy. If he thinks that's on the agenda, that'll be his first mistake.'

'You think you can sort out a fucking monster like that with a bit of Thai boxing? Brannigan, you're off your head!' Richard was scarlet by now, his hands bunched into fists by his side.

I was inches away from completely losing control, but I had enough sense left not to flatten him. That would be one move that our relationship wouldn't survive. 'Trust me, Richard,' I said quietly. 'I know what I'm doing.'

He laughed bitterly. 'Fine,' he spat at me. 'Treat me like an idiot. I'm used to it, after all. That's what you all think I am anyway, isn't it? Richard the wimp, Richard the pillock, Richard the doormat, Richard the wanker, Richard who lets Kate do his thinking for him, Richard the limp dick who can't be trusted to do the simplest of jobs without ending up in the nick,' he ranted.

'Nobody thinks you're a wimp. I don't think you're a wanker, or any of the other things,' I shouted back at him. 'What happened to you with the car could have happened just as easily to me.'

'Oh no, it couldn't,' he screamed back at me. 'Clever clogs Brannigan would have phoned the police as soon as she found the car. Clever clogs Brannigan would have checked the car to see if there was anything in it there shouldn't have been. Clever clogs Brannigan and the girls would never have got themselves banged up. Because the girls are smart, and I'm just a fucking stupid arsehole *man* who gets put up with because he's marginally more fun than a vibrator.' He stopped suddenly, out of steam.

'I love you, Richard,' I said quietly. It's not an expression I'm given to, but extreme circumstances demand extreme responses.

'Bollocks,' he shouted. 'I'm a fucking convenience. You don't know what love is. You never let anyone close enough. It's all a fucking game to you, Brannigan. Like your fucking job. It's all a game. Nothing ever gets you in here,' he added, thumping his chest like an opera buffa tenor.

He looked so ridiculous, I couldn't help a smile twitching at the corners of my mouth. 'This isn't the time for this,' I said, trying to make my amusement look like conciliation. 'I'd no idea you felt this bad about what happened, and it's important that we sort it out. But we're both tired, we're both under a lot of pressure. Let's leave it till we get home, OK? Now, let me do what I've got to do. I'll see you back at Casa Nico later, OK?'

Richard shook his head. 'You really are a piece of work, Brannigan. You think you can just sweep all this aside like that? Forget it. You can go back to Casa fucking Nico if you want. But I won't be there.'

He turned on his heel and stormed back to the car. As he opened the door, he said, 'You coming?'

I shook my head. He slammed the car door behind him, swung the car round and headed back down the valley. I watched him go, my stomach feeling hollow, my eyes suddenly swimming with tears. Impatiently, I blinked them away. I tried to convince myself that Richard would be back at Casa Nico once he'd calmed down.

In the meantime, I had work to do. Besides, now I needed a lift back down the valley.

18

No woman is a heroine to her dentist. Along with my phobia about tunnels goes my paralysing fear of needles and drills. As a result, I knew I wasn't going to have to rely on anything as crude as physical strength to beat the bodyguard. If Richard hadn't pissed me off so much, I'd have explained it to him. But Watsons who scream at their Holmeses don't get the inside track on methodology.

Picking up the bodyguard was a doddle. Any man who spends as much time as he obviously did on keeping his body in peak condition has to have a streak of vanity a mile wide. He fully expected that if an attractive foreign woman walked into a bar where he was drinking, he'd be the one she'd inevitably be drawn to. And in a country where the native women are so sexually constrained by religion, it's equally inevitable that foreign women who walk into bars alone and with bare shoulders must be whores. My target thought it was his lucky night as soon as I settled on the bar stool next to him and smiled as I ordered a Peroni.

On the short walk to the bar, I'd come up with the cover story that I was a professional photographer, in Italy to take pictures for a coffee-table book of Italian church bell towers. Gianni the bodyguard and his drinking companions fell for it hook, line and sinker, with much nudging in the ribs about women who liked big ones. I suppose they thought my Italian wasn't up to mucky innuendo. By the time I'd finished my first beer, they were competing over who was going to buy the next one. By the time I'd finished my second, his heavy, muscular arm was draped over my naked shoulders and his equally heavy cologne had invaded my nostrils. The hardest part of the whole production number was hiding my revulsion. If there's one thing I hate it's hairy men, and this guy was covered like a shag pile carpet. Just the thought of his shoulders was enough to make me feel queasy.

I was on my fourth beer when I casually let slip that I was staying at Casa Nico and that I'd left my car down there while I walked up the valley. Immediately, Gianni volunteered to drive me back down. Then, of course, he suddenly remembered how terrible the cooking was at Casa Nico. Cue for nods of agreement from his buddies, coupled with nudges and winks acknowledging the cleverness of Gianni's moves. Why, he asked innocently, didn't I come back to the villa with him for some genuine

Italian home cooking. His boss was away, and he was a dab hand with the spaghetti sauce. We could eat on the terrace like the rich folks do, and then, later, he could run me back down to the *pensione*.

I looked up adoringly at him and said how delightful it was to meet such hospitable people. We left a couple of minutes later, accompanied by whoops and grunts from his cronies. In the car, he put a proprietary paw on my knee between gear changes. I fought the urge to lean over and grip his balls so tight his eyes would pop from their sockets like shelled peas. He was the driver, after all, and I didn't want to end up on the river bed looking like spaghetti sauce.

As we approached the villa, he pulled a little black electronic box out of his tight jeans and punched a button. The gates swung open, the Alfa shot through and I got my first full frontal view of the Villa San Pietro. It was magnificent. A modern villa in the style of the traditional houses that front every fashionable resort in Italy. Immaculate pink stucco, green louvred shutters. And a satellite dish the size of a kid's paddling pool. *'Molto elegante,'* I said softly.

'Good, huh?' Gianni said proudly, as if it were all his. The drive swung round the side of the house, past a tennis court and swimming pool and over to a separate, single-storey building. As we drew near, Gianni hit the button on the box again and an up-and-over garage door opened before us. Inside the garage was the stretch limo, Turner's Merc and a small green Fiat van. At the sight of Turner's car, I started to get a bad feeling in the pit of my stomach. Gianni had said we'd have the place to ourselves. But Turner had come back to the villa with him in the afternoon, and his car was still here as proof positive that he hadn't left. Maybe he'd nipped into Sestri for the evening in a taxi. Somehow, I didn't think so. For the first time since I'd started this crazy expedition, I allowed a trickle of fear to creep in. Maybe I should have listened to Richard after all.

We got out of the car and Gianni folded me into a bear hug, his tongue thrusting between my teeth. It felt like my tonsils were being raped. 'What happened to dinner?' I asked as soon as I could get my mouth clear. 'I don't know about you, but I can't think about having fun when I'm hungry.'

Gianni chuckled. 'OK, OK. First the food, then the fun.' He leered and gestured with his thumb towards a door at the side of the garage. 'That's my apartment over there. But we'll go over to the house to eat. My boss has better food and drink than me.'

We walked over to the house, his arm heavy across my shoulders. We crossed a marble patio, complete with built-in barbecue and pizza oven, and entered the kitchen through tall french windows. It was like a temple to the culinary arts. There was a free-standing butcher's block in the middle of the floor, complete with a set of Sabatier knives in their slots. Above it hung a batterie de cuisine. On the blond wooden worktops, there was every conceivable kitchen machine from ice-cream maker to a full-sized Gaggia espresso machine. Bunches of dried herbs hung from the walls, while pots of fresh basil, coriander and parsley lined a deep windowsill to the side. 'He likes to cook,' Gianni said. 'He likes me to cook too, when we have guests.'

'Nice one,' I said. 'Where's the drink?'

He nodded towards a door. 'Through there. There's a wet bar in the dining room. It's got everything. There's white wine in the fridge, and red wine in the cupboard here. Why don't you help yourself?' He moved towards me again and clutched me close, his huge hands cupping my buttocks. 'Mmm, gorgeous,' he growled.

I reached round and let my fingers stray up and down his back. That way I stopped myself thrusting my thumbs into his eyeballs. 'Tell you what,' I whispered, 'I'll fix us some cocktails. I might not be much good in the kitchen, but I'm terrific with a cocktail shaker.'

He released me and leered again. 'I can't wait to experience your wrist action.'

I giggled. 'You won't be disappointed, I promise you.'

I left him staring into a big larder fridge. He hadn't lied about the wet bar. It did have everything. The first thing I did was dredge my phial of Valium out of the bottom of my bag. I'm pretty hostile to pharmaceuticals in general, but without the Valium, I'd have blackened stumps where my teeth should be. I tipped the tablets out. There were six. I hoped that would be enough on an empty stomach to knock Gianni out before I had to test whether I really did have the skills to stop a man in his tracks. I spotted a sharp knife by a basket of lemons and oranges, and quickly crushed the tablets with the blade. Then I took a quick inventory of the bar. What I needed was a cocktail that was strong and bittersweet.

I found the measure and the shaker sitting on a shelf behind me. A small fridge contained a variety of fruit juices, and a couple of bags of ice. I settled on a Florida. Into a cocktail shaker I put three measures of gin, six measures of grapefruit juice, three measures of Galliano, and one and a half measures of Campari. I tossed in a couple of ice cubes, closed the shaker and did a quick salsa round the bar with the shaker providing the beat. 'Sounds good,' Gianni shouted from the kitchen.

'Wait till you taste it,' I called back. I chose a couple of tall glasses and scraped the Valium powder into one. I topped it up with about two thirds of the cocktail mixture and stirred it vigorously with a glass rod. I poured the rest into the other glass and topped it up with grapefruit juice and a dash of grenadine syrup to make the colours match. I swallowed hard, picked up both glasses and walked through to the kitchen. Gianni was chopping red onions with a wide-bladed chef's knife. 'A very Italian cocktail,' I announced, handing the drugged glass to him.

He took it from me and swigged a generous mouthful. He savoured it, swilling it round his mouth before swallowing it. 'You're right. Bitter and sweet. Like love, huh?' The leer was back.

'Not too bitter, I hope,' I giggled, moving behind him and hugging him from behind.

'Not with me, baby. With me, it'll be sweeter than sugar,' he said arrogantly.

'I can hardly wait,' I murmured. I wasn't exactly lying. I moved away and perched on a high stool, watching him cook. The onions went into a deep pan with olive oil and garlic. Next, he chopped a fennel bulb into thin slices and added them to the stewing onions. He took a punnet of wild mushrooms from the fridge, washed them under running water, patted them dry lovingly with paper towels and chopped them coarsely. Into the pan they went along with a torn handful of coriander leaves.

'It smells wonderful,' I said.

'Wait till you taste it,' he said. 'There's only one thing tastes better.' Time for another leer. The temperature was rising in more ways than one. The only good thing about that was the speed at which he was drinking his cocktail.

'No contest,' I said, watching him measure out round grains of risotto rice. He tipped the rice into the pan, stirred it into the mixture for a couple of minutes, then took a carton out of the freezer.

'Chicken stock,' he said, tossing the solid lump into the pan amidst much hissing and clouds of steam. He kept stirring till the stock had defrosted and the pan was bubbling gently. Then he put a lid on, set the timer for twelve minutes and drained his glass.

'How about a salad to go with it?' I asked hastily as he started to move towards me. 'And I'll mix you another drink, OK?'

His eyes seemed to lose focus momentarily and he shook his head like a bull bothered by flies. He rubbed his hands over his face and mumbled, 'OK.' I'd reckoned about twenty minutes for the drugs to take effect, but maybe the amount he'd had to drink on an empty stomach was accelerating things.

I'd barely got the cap off the gin bottle when there was a sound like a tree falling in the kitchen. I tiptoed back to the doorway to see Gianni spread-eagled on the marble floor. For one terrible moment, I thought I'd killed him. Then he started to snore like a sawmill on overtime. I ran across to the butcher's block and picked up the knife. It took seconds to saw off the electric cable from a couple of the kitchen appliances. Tying him up took quite a bit longer, but the snoring didn't even change in note while I was doing it. I took the black box out of his pocket and tucked it in my bag.

I found the cellar door on the second try. A wide flight of stairs led down into the depths. One thing about marble floors is that they make shifting heavy loads a lot easier. I got down on my knees behind Gianni and shoved with all my strength.

Foot by foot, we slid across the gleaming tiles to the doorway. One last push sent him skidding over the first step, feet first. He bounced down the stairs like a sack of potatoes, still snoring. I staggered to my feet. For the first time, I was grateful that Gianni's boss was security conscious. The cellar door had bolts top and bottom as well as a lock on the door. I slid the bolts home and leaned against the door to get my breath back.

When the timer went off, I nearly jumped out of my skin. Automatically, I turned off the gas under the pan. Now the adrenaline surge was slipping away, I realized that I was in fact ravenous. I shrugged. The food was there, I might as well eat. I didn't think Gianni was going to be knocking at the door demanding his share in a hurry.

He might have been the world's worst lecher, but he was a fabulous cook. I shovelled the risotto down, savouring every delicious mouthful. Now I needed coffee. It was going to be a long night. I wished I hadn't chopped the lead off the Gaggia. A search of the cupboards eventually turned up a jar of instant and a Thermos jug. I brewed up and, armed with jug, mug and shoulder bag, I set off to explore.

Whatever Gianni's boss was, he wasn't short of a bob. The public rooms on the ground floor were all marble floored, with expensive Oriental rugs scattered around. The furniture was upmarket repro, all polished to a mirror finish. There was nothing in the dining room, drawing room, morning room or the TV lounge to indicate that this was anything other than the home of a successful businessman. Even the videos lined up in the cabinet by the oversized TV were completely innocuous.

Cautiously, I made my way up the stairs. It was always possible that Turner was a prisoner somewhere inside the villa rather than the victim of my worst imaginings. Six doors opened off the long landing. The first two were lavish guest bedrooms, complete with *en suite* bathrooms. If Gianni's boss ever set up in competition with Casa Nico, the *pensione* down the valley would go out of business within hours. The third door opened on what was clearly the master bedroom. The wardrobes were filled with designer suits and shirts, the drawers with silk underwear and the kind of leisure wear that has the labels on the outside. No trace of a woman in residence. No trace of any papers, either.

The fourth door opened on to a library. It was obviously a reader's library rather than one where the books had been bought by the yard. Modern hardbacks lined the shelves. I noticed a sizeable chunk of crime fiction, but most of the books were by authors I'd never heard of. There was also a whole section of legal textbooks, mostly covering commercial and international law. But again, there were no papers anywhere, unless some of the books were dummies. If they were, they'd be hanging on to their secrets. There was no way I had time to go through that lot book by book.

The fifth door was locked. I left it for a moment and tried the sixth. Another guest bedroom. That told me that either Turner was behind the locked door, or something significant was. Unfortunately, I didn't have my set of picklocks with me. I don't carry them routinely, and when I'd set off on my pursuit of Turner, I hadn't expected to be doing any burglaries. I could of course simply smash the lock with one of the dozens of marble statuettes that hung around in niches all over the place. But I didn't want the villa's owner to know the extent to which he'd been turned over unless I could possibly help it.

I looked up at the door lintel. Gianni's boss was not much bigger than me, so the chances were that the key wasn't sitting up there. I went back to the master bedroom and began a proper search. I got lucky in the bathroom. I'd taken the contents of the bathroom cupboard off the shelves one by one, just to make sure there was nothing behind them. There were two aerosol cans of Polo shaving foam, and one was a lot lighter than the other. I looked more closely at the heavier of the two. Gripping it tightly, I twisted the bottom of the can. It unscrewed smoothly, revealing a compartment lined with bubble wrap. Inside was what looked like a handkerchief. I pulled it out and a bunch of keys tumbled to the floor. 'Gotcha!' I murmured.

The longest of the keys opened the locked door. Inside was a starkly functional office, a sharp contrast to the luxurious appointments of the rest of the villa. I switched the light on, closed the shutters and took a good look around. A basic desk stood against one wall with a computer, a modem, and a fax machine on it. To one side there was a photocopier and a laser printer. Automatically, I switched them on. I noticed a shredder under the desk as I sat down and hit the computer's power button. The machine booted up and I called up the directories. Ten minutes later, my jubilation had given way to depression. Every single data file I'd tried to access was password protected. I couldn't get in to read them. All it would let me do was print out a list of all files, which I duly did.

Muttering dark imprecations, I returned to the main directory. Time for some lateral thinking. In the years since I first started working at Mortensen and Brannigan and discovered the wonderful world of electronic mail, the Internet had grown from the home of academics and a handful of computer loonies like me to the world's bulletin board. The communications software that was running on this machine was a standard business package that I'd used dozens of times before. Even if the files were password protected, I reckoned that the communications program would still be able to transmit them intact to somewhere I could retrieve them later and pass them on to someone who could crack the passwording. All I needed was a local number for the Internet. If I was lucky, there would be one already loaded in the comms program. I started it running and called up the telephone directory screen.

It was my lucky night. Right at the top of the list was the number for the local Internet node – the E-mail equivalent of a postal sorting office. The way the Net works is simple. It's analogous to sending a letter rather than making a phone call. The network is connected by phone lines, and works on what they call a parcel switching system. What happens is you dial a local number and send your data to it. The computer there reads the address and shunts your data down the network, section by section, till it arrives at its destination. But unlike a letter, which takes days if you're lucky, this takes less time than it takes to describe the process.

I used the edit mode to discover Gianni's boss's login and password, then I instructed the computer to connect me to the Internet. Less than a minute later, we were in. I typed in the electronic mail address of the office, then I started sending the files one by one. An hour and a mug of coffee later, I'd sent a copy of every data file in the machine back to Manchester.

Breathing a deep sigh of relief, I switched off the machine. Now it was time for the desk drawers. I unlocked each drawer with the remaining keys on the bunch. The first drawer held stationery. The second held junk – rubber bands, spare computer disks, a couple of computer cables, a half-eaten chocolate bar and a box of Post-it notes. The bottom drawer looked more promising, with its collection of suspension files. No such luck. All the files held was the paperwork for the house: utility bills, receipts for furniture, building work, landscaping, pool maintenance. The only interesting thing was that everything was in the name of a company – Gruppo Leopardi. There was no clue as to who was behind Gruppo Leopardi. And I didn't have the time for the kind of thorough search that might reveal that. I'd already been there too long, and I was getting too tired to concentrate. It was time to make tracks.

I went back over to the window, to open the shutters again. I wanted to leave everything exactly as I'd found it. As I turned back, clumsy with exhaustion, I caught the Thermos jug with my elbow. It sailed off the desk and bounced off the panelled wall under the window. It landed on its side on the floor, apparently undamaged. Not so the wall. The wood panelling where the jug had hit had slowly swung away from the wall, revealing a safe. Eat your heart out, Enid Blyton. If preposterous coincidence is good enough for the Secret Seven, it's good enough for me.

19

If the Brannigans were posh enough to have a family motto, it would go something like, 'What do you mean, I *can't*?' Just because I've never learned how to crack a safe didn't mean I was going to close the panel and walk away. I sat on the floor opposite the safe and studied it. There was a six-digit electronic display above a keypad with the letters of the alphabet and the numbers zero to nine. Beside the keypad were buttons that I translated as 'enter code', 'open', 'random reset', 'master'. That didn't take me a whole lot further forward.

I checked my watch. Ten o'clock. Not too late to make a call. I took the mobile out of my bag and rang Dennis. It would have been cheaper to use the fax phone, but I'd already noticed that Gruppo Leopardi had itemized billing on their phone account and I didn't want to leave a trail straight back to Dennis, especially given that he already had connections with these people via

Turner. Dennis answered his phone on the second ring. 'Hi, Dennis,' I said. 'I'm looking at the outside of a safe and I want to be looking at the inside. Any ideas?'

'Kate, you're more of a villain than I am. You know I haven't touched a safe since Billy the Whip dropped one on my foot in 1983.'

'This isn't the time for reminiscing. This call's costing me a week's wages.'

He chuckled. 'Then somebody else must be paying for it. What does this safe look like?'

I described it to him. 'You're wasting your time, Kate. Beast like that, you've got no chance unless you know the combo,' he said sorrowfully.

'You sure?'

'I'm sure. He might be a sloppy git though, this guy you're having over. He might have gone for something really stupid like the last six digits of the phone number. Or the first six. Or his date of birth. Or his girlfriend's name. Or some set of letters and numbers he sees in his office every day.'

I groaned. 'Enough, already. You sure there's no other way?'

'That's why they call them safes,' Dennis said. 'Where are you, anyway?'

'You don't want to know. Believe me, you don't want to know. I'll be in touch. Thanks for your help.'

I went back to the domestic files and tried various combinations of the phone number and any other number I could find, including the vehicle registrations. No joy. I sat in the boss's chair and looked around me. What would he see from here that would be a constant *aide-mémoire*? I got up and tried the model numbers of the fax machine, the modem and the photocopier. Nothing. I didn't know the boss's birthday, but I had a feeling that a man as security conscious as him wouldn't have gone for anything that obvious.

It was last resort time. What would *I* do if I wanted a code that was random enough for no one to guess, but accessible to me whenever I forgot it? Acting on pure instinct, I hit the power button on the computer again and watched the screen, looking for any six digit combinations that came up during the boot process. I ended up with two, MB 4D33 was part of the operating system ident. And the CD-ROM drive's device model number was CR-563-X. The first string did nothing. But when I entered the second set of digits, the display changed from red to green. I couldn't believe it.

Holding my breath, I hit the 'open' button. There was a soft click and the door catch released. 'There is a God, and she likes me,' I said softly. I opened the safe and stared in at the contents. There was a stack of papers about half an inch thick. On top of them sat a loose-leaf folder, slightly bigger than a Filofax. I took everything out of the safe and moved back to the desk. I started with the folder. First there was a list of names, with dates and figures next to it. Following that were half a dozen pages listing numbered locations. Some of them had ticks beside them, and a couple were crossed out. Castle Dumdivie was on the list, with a tick. So were a few other names I recognized. Next came a list of dates and places followed by a number and letter code – 20CC, 34H, 50,000E, that sort of thing. The fourth column was a number. A little bit of crosschecking, and I realized that the numbers corresponded to ticked locations on the list, and, in the cases I knew about, the dates were all two to four weeks after the burglaries. Finally, there were several pages of names, addresses and phone numbers. Halfway down the third page, I spotted Turner. I wasn't sure what all of this meant, but I was beginning to have the glimmerings of an idea.

I opened the clasps of the folder and put the pages through the photocopier. While they were feeding through, I looked at the other papers. Some of them were legal contracts, and I couldn't make head nor tail of them. Others were handwritten notes which seemed to refer to meetings, but although I understood most of the words, I couldn't get a lot of sense out of them. There were a few business letters, mostly of the 'thank you for your letter of the fifteenth, we can confirm the safe arrival of your consignment' type. The final bundle of papers were draft accounts of Gruppo Leopardi. I copied the lot.

Once I'd finished, I replaced everything in the safe, exactly as I'd found it. I had the papers, but I wanted a little bit of insurance, just in case anything happened on the way home to deprive me of my photocopies. The fax machine was the best source of that insurance, but I didn't want to send the stuff to my office number for the same reason I'd used the mobile to phone Dennis. It needed to go somewhere secure, but somewhere large enough for it not to be obvious who specifically it had gone to. Ideally, it also had to go somewhere that even the Mafia would think twice about storming mob-handed.

There was only one place and one person I could think of that fitted the bill. Detective Chief Inspector Della Prentice, top dog on the Regional Crime Squad's fraud task force. This wasn't her bailiwick, but Della's still the only copper I'd trust with anything that might put me at risk. I'd worked with Della a couple of times now since we'd first been introduced by Josh Gilbert. They'd been at Cambridge together, and although their fascination with finance high and low had taken them in radically different directions, they'd stayed close enough for Josh to recognize that Della and I are kindred spirits. Since our first encounter, we'd become close friends. I knew if I faxed this wodge of incomprehensible paperwork to Della, she'd tuck it away safely in her drawer till I turned up to explain its significance.

I took a sheet of paper out of the stationery drawer and scribbled a cover sheet. 'Fax for the urgent and confidential attention of DCI Prentice, Regional Crime Squad. Dear Della, Vital evidence.

Please keep safe until I can fill you in on the deep background. I'll call you as soon as I get back. Thanks. KB.' That should do it, I thought, dialling her departmental fax machine. God knows what the duty CID would make of a hundred-page fax from Italy in the middle of the night.

By the time I'd finished, it was after two. I bundled up my photocopies, stuffed them in an envelope and tucked the lot into my bulging bag. Time to get the hell out of here, as far away as possible. I had a horrible feeling that I knew what had happened to Nicholas Turner, probably because of my bug, and I didn't want to end up the same way. There wasn't a trace of the guy in any of the spare bedrooms, which put paid to any comforting ideas about him having nipped into Sestri in a taxi for dinner.

I switched everything off and locked the desk drawers again. Satisfied that it all looked just as it had when I'd walked into the office, I got out, locking the door behind me. I replaced the keys in the dummy can, hoping that my memory of how the contents of the cabinet had been arranged was accurate. I trotted down the stairs and back to the kitchen. I put my ear to the cellar door. Silence. I had a momentary pang of conscience, wondering what would happen to the big man when he came round and found himelf tied up in the dark for an indefinite period of time. Then I reminded myself that he was probably directly responsible for whatever had happened to Turner, and I stopped feeling guilty. Besides, judging by the pristine condition of the villa, I reckoned there must be a maid who came in every day to polish the floors, the furniture and the kitchen equipment. By the time she arrived, Gianni would probably be bellowing like a bull.

I let myself out of the French windows and stood on the patio, weighing up what to do next. I had the black box that would open the gates for me, but I didn't know where the security system was controlled from, and the cameras would still be rolling. I wasn't keen on finding myself the star of the Mafia equivalent of *Crimewatch*, so I decided to help myself to one of the vehicles, just to keep myself hidden from the all-seeing eyes by the gate. You can only do so much with computer enhancement, and I reckoned the combination of the darkness and the obscurity of being inside a car would make sure I couldn't be identified.

A quick sortie in the garage revealed that the keys for all the vehicles were hanging on the board where Gianni had deposited his set earlier. I settled on the van, on the basis that it was the least memorable of the three. I opened the door, threw my bag on the passenger seat and climbed behind the wheel. I was just about to stick the key in the ignition, when something stopped me.

I don't believe in sixth sense or second sight or seventh sons of seventh sons. But something was making the hair on the back of my neck stand up, and it wasn't love at first sight. I took a deep breath and looked over my shoulder into the back of the van.

At once I wished I hadn't. There's only one thing comes in a six-feet-long, heavy-duty black bag with a zipper up the front. It didn't take many of my detective skills to decide that I'd probably solved the mystery of Nicholas Turner's disappearance.

I was out of the van in seconds. I stood in the garage, leaning against the wall for support, my breath coming fast, clammy sweat in my armpits. The combination of shock and exhaustion was making my limbs tremble. I don't know how long I stood there like that, frozen in horror, incapable of movement, never mind decisive action. It's one thing to think somebody might be dead. It's another thing entirely to find yourself sitting in a van with their mortal remains. Especially when you're the one who's responsible for their present state.

It was only fear that got me moving again. Hanging around the Villa San Pietro was about as clever a move as a mouse going walkabout in a cattery. My first instinct was to dive into the Alfa and put as much distance between me and the villa as fast as I could. I was halfway across the garage when I realized that wasn't an answer I could live with. It was my bug and my fake that had got Nicholas Turner murdered. I couldn't just walk away and let the people who'd had him killed dispose of the body and wash their hands of the whole business. If I left him here, that's exactly what would happen. I couldn't just drive to the nearest police station and tell them what I knew. They might be on the villa's payroll, for a kickoff. And even if they weren't and I did get them to believe me, I couldn't think of a cover story that wouldn't leave me facing charges of false imprisonment, assault, deception, breaking and entering, and probably the murder of Aldo Moro.

I thought about waking Della and bringing her up to speed so we could do it through official channels, but by the time we'd got the wheels of justice rolling, there would be no evidence of murder at the villa, the body would be miles away, and even if it did eventually turn up, there would be nothing to connect it to Gianni and his boss.

Taking a deep breath, I opened the back of the van. Before I did anything else, I needed to be sure it really was Turner in the bag. Gingerly, I reached out for the tab of the zip and pushed it away from me. It wouldn't budge. I could feel my stomach begin to turn over as I gripped the slick, rubberized bag with one hand and forced the zip down. A few inches was all I needed. Nicholas Turner's eyes stared up at me out of a face grey in the stark fluorescent light of the garage. I gagged and whipped round just in time for the contents of my stomach to miss the van and hit the floor. I stood there, hands on my knees, throwing up till my stomach and throat were raw. Shaking and sweating, my fingers slippery on the body bag, I managed to pull up the zip. Turner's face showed no signs of how he had met his end, but

I'd have been willing to bet it hadn't been a brain tumour.

I don't remember how I managed it, but somehow I got back behind the wheel and drove out of the garage. All I could think of was getting out of there and putting some distance between me and the Villa San Pietro. I hurtled down the drive, punching the steering wheel in frustration as the gates took their time opening. I shot down the track so fast I nearly lost it on one of the bends. The shock of that sobered me enough to slow me down to a more reasonable speed. As I hit the main road, I realized I'd have to move the Mercedes away from Casa Nico, since Gianni knew that was where I was staying, and I couldn't guarantee I'd get back to the car before he was released from his prison.

I left the van parked on the verge by the villa turn-off and jogged the couple of kilometres back to the *pensione*. There was no sign of the BMW. So much for expecting Richard to see sense and come back. I drove the Merc back up the valley, past the van, looking for somewhere to stash it. About a kilometre further on, there was a cluster of houses and a mini-market. I left the car just off the main road and half jogged, half staggered back to the van. I didn't pass another car the whole hour.

I turned the van round and headed back towards Sestri Levante. I reckoned I needed to leave the van somewhere no one would notice if it was parked for a few days. I thought about finding some remote forest track in the mountains, but I vetoed that. It would be difficult to find the right place in the dark, it would be impossible for me to remember where it was with pinpoint accuracy, and it wouldn't be easy for me to make my way back to the Merc. I didn't want to leave it parked on a street, because I didn't know how long it was going to take to get anyone to listen to my tale, and after a day or two in Italian sunshine, the van wasn't going to smell too appetizing. What I needed, ideally, was an underground car park where no one would pay attention.

Either I needed a big city, or a swanky resort where people left their cars in the hotel car park for a few days. The solution popped out of my memory just as the autostrada junction hove into sight. The picture postcard village of Portofino, star of a thousand jigsaw puzzles, its harbour lined with picturesque houses painted every colour of the ice-cream spectrum. I'd been there a couple of years before with Richard, and remembered the big car park, half underground, where tourists left their cars to avoid completely choking the centre of the former fishing village.

I drove into Portofino just after 5.00 a.m. It's probably the only time of day when there isn't a queue to get into the village. I drove straight into the car park, taking a ticket at the automatic barrier. I left the van on the lowest level and walked up the stairs to the street. The pale light of dawn was just beginning to brighten the eastern sky as I strolled down to the harbour. There were a few boatmen around in the harbour, but I didn't want to draw too much attention to myself by asking any of them how soon I could get out of the place. I tried to look like an insomniac tourist enjoying the peace and quiet, and wandered down the quayside to where the pleasure boats departed. I was in luck. At nine, there was a boat that went to Sestri Levante and on to the Cinque Terre beyond.

I walked on round the harbour and found a bench that overlooked the bay. Using my bag as a pillow, I put my head down and managed to doze off. Strange dreams featuring Gianni's chef's knife and bodies that climbed out of bags and into passenger seats prevented it from being a restful sleep, but I was so exhausted that even the nightmares couldn't wake me up. The sound of a pleasure steamer's hooter jerked me into wakefulness just after eight, and I staggered back into the village, bought myself a couple of sandwiches and a cappuccino from a café and headed for the pleasure boat.

I don't remember much about the sail. I was too jittery from lack of sleep and the horrors of the night. I kept nodding off, and starting awake, nerves jangling and eyes staring in paranoia. I couldn't stop thinking about Turner's wife and those two daughters. Not only had they lost a husband and father, but they were going to find out about it in a blitz of police and media activity.

In spite of the fact that arriving on dry land brought me nearer to the enemy, I was glad to be off the boat. Somehow, I felt more in control. In Sestri, I found the tourist office and discovered where I could catch a bus up the valley. The next one left in twenty minutes, and I was first on it, complete with brand-new sun hat. I sat at the back, slouched low in my seat. As Casa Nico approached, I put my sunglasses on and pulled the hat forwards. The bus was so much higher off the road than a car would have been that I was able to look right down on Casa Nico. As the bus rounded the bend beyond the *pensione*, I looked back. Parked behind the building, where I wouldn't have been able to spot it in a car, was Gianni's Alfa.

I got off at the next stop and walked cautiously past the alley where I'd left the Merc. It was still there, and no one seemed to be watching it. I doubled back behind the houses and came up the alley from the far end. I crept into the car, not even slamming the door shut until I had the engine running. Then I shot out on to the main road and headed up the valley, away from Casa Nico and the Villa San Pietro, my foot hard on the accelerator, my eyes on the rear-view mirror. As I joined the autostrada, I wondered how long Gianni would stake out the *pensione*. It was worth the loss of my overnight bag not to have him on my tail.

Nigel Mansell couldn't have got to Milan airport faster than I did that day. I dumped the car with the local Hertz agent and headed for the terminal. I'd just missed a flight to Brussels, but there was one to Amsterdam an hour later. If I could only stay awake, I could pick up Bill's Saab in Antwerp, catch the night ferry from Zeebrugge and be home the following morning some time. Frankly, I couldn't wait to feel British soil under my feet.

I had half an hour to kill in the international departure lounge. I thought I'd better give Shelley a ring before she decided tracking me down was a job for Interpol. She answered on the first ring, and I could hear relief in her voice. I knew then it must be bad, since Shelley never lets on that anything's beyond her competence.

'Thank God it's you,' she said. 'Where are you? You've got to get back here. There's been another death.'

20

I nearly dropped the phone. My first thought was, how the hell had Shelley found out about Nicholas Turner? Her voice cut through my panic. 'Kate? Are you still there? I said there's been another death involving KerrSter.' This time round, I heard the whole sentence.

'Oh fuck,' I groaned.

'Where *are* you? Trevor Kerr is reading me the riot act every ten minutes. I've managed to stall him so far, but if you don't speak to him soon, he's threatening to sack us and go to the press saying the reason for the second death is your dereliction of duty,' Shelley continued, her voice betraying an agitation I'd never heard from her before.

'I'm at Milan airport. On the way to Amsterdam, *en route* for Antwerp. I'll have to leave Bill's car in Belgium and get a flight straight back to the UK. When did this happen?'

'This morning. An office cleaner. They found her dead beside a new drum of KerrSter. It looks like another case of cyanide poisoning, according to Alexis. Incidentally, she wants to talk to you too.'

I glanced over at the gate. They hadn't started boarding us yet. 'Is Kerr still in his office?'

'He was five minutes ago,' Shelley said. 'He's had the Merseyside police all over his factory this afternoon.'

'I'll call him and stall him,' I said. 'I'm sorry you've had all this shit to deal with on your own. If it's any consolation, this trip's been a nightmare. I've already had one close encounter with death today. I'm not sure if I'm up to another one.'

'You're all right?' Shelley demanded anxiously.

'I wouldn't pitch it that high. I'm in one piece, which is more than I can say for Turner.'

'Oh my God,' she said, sounding stricken.

'Look, it's OK. Let me talk to Kerr. I'll call you from Amsterdam. There's a flight gets in to Manchester about half-seven tonight. See if you can get me a seat on it. I don't care if it's business class, club class or standing in the toilet, just get me on it.'

'Will do. I'll hang on here till I hear from you,' she promised. 'For God's sake, be careful.'

It was a bit late for me to take heed of that warning. I took a deep breath, bracing myself for battle, and rang Trevor Kerr. Not even my powers of imagination had prepared me for his onslaught. For two straight minutes he ranted at me, with a string of obscenities that would have won him admiration on the football terraces but didn't do a lot for me. I made a mental note to bump that surliness surcharge up to ten per cent. When he paused to regroup for a second outpouring, I cut in decisively. 'I'm sorry you've had a difficult day, but you're not the only one,' I said grimly. 'I have been pursuing my inquiries into your problem as fast as I can. I've made a lot of progress, but I needed a crucial piece of information that I've not been able to get hold of yet. Now, I'm meeting someone in an hour's time who can tell me what I need to know,' I continued, raising my voice to cut through his crap.

'Bullshit!' he hollered like a bear with its leg in a gin. 'You've been doing fuck all. Give me one good reason why I shouldn't fire you this fucking minute.'

'Because if you do, some other private eye with half my talent is going to have to start from square one because you'll have to sue me to get one single scrap of the information I've already uncovered.'

That silenced him for all of ten seconds. 'I'll tell the police you're withholding information,' he blustered.

'Tell them. Inspector Jackson knows me well enough to realize that shoving me in a cell won't make a blind bit of difference to what I have to say for myself.'

'You can't treat me like this,' he howled, the ultimate spoilt bully.

'If you want us to discuss this like reasonable adults, you can meet me this evening in the bar of the Hilton at the airport at eight o'clock,' I said. 'Otherwise, I'm taking my bat and ball home, Mr Kerr.' Out of the corner of my eye, I could see my fellow passengers disappearing through the gate. 'It's up to you,' I said, replacing the phone.

The flight to Amsterdam seemed never ending. I stared gloomily out of the window, feeling more guilty than a Catholic in bed with a married man. My meddling had cost Nicholas Turner his life. Meddling I'd done while I should have been nailing down my suspicions about the product-tampering racket. If I'd done that job properly, the culprits would be answering Inspector Jackson's questions now and maybe the woman who had died would still be alive. I should never have taken Trevor Kerr's case on when I was in the middle of another demanding investigation. But I had to be smart, prove to the world that I was twice as good as any reasonable private investigator needed to be. I'd been trying to show Bill that I was more than capable of being left to run the agency single-handed. All I'd done so far was get two people killed.

Not only that, but I'd fractured my relationship with Richard, perhaps beyond repair this time. All because I was determined to be the big shot, doing things my way. I began to wonder why I was bothering to go back. On my present form, the only people I'd be keeping satisfied were the undertakers. I had the best part of nine grand in my bag, a car waiting at Antwerp. In all my working life, I've never been closer to running away.

When it came to the crunch, I couldn't do it. Call it duty, call it stubbornness, call it pure bloody-mindedness. Whatever it was, it propelled me off that plane and over to the check-in desk for the flight to Manchester. Shelley had come up trumps. I was booked on a seat in business class. I had ten minutes to give her a quick ring and tell her I was meeting Kerr at the airport hotel. Slightly reassured, she told me again to take care. She was warning the wrong person.

They had that evening's *Chronicle* on the plane. CLEANER'S MYSTERY DEATH hit me like a stab in the guts. Even though she'd died in Liverpool, Mary Halloran had made the front page in Manchester because of the KerrSter connection and because it gave the paper the chance to rehash the Joey Morton story. Feeling accused by every word, especially since they came under the by-line of Alexis Lee, I read on. Mrs Halloran, forty-three, a mother of two (oh God, another two kids I'd deprived of a parent . . .), had started her own commercial cleaning firm after she was made redundant by the city council. The business had grown into a real money-spinner, but Mrs Halloran liked to keep her hand in on the office floor, presumably to stay in touch with her roots. She had a regular stint three mornings a week in a local solicitor's office, where she started work at half past five. Normally, she worked with another woman, but her partner had been off sick that week. Mrs Halloran's body had been found outside the cleaning cupboard on the first floor by one of the solicitors who had come in just after seven to catch up on some work. She was slumped on the floor beside an open but full container of KerrSter. The police had revealed that the postmortem indicated Mrs Halloran had died as a result of inhaling hydrogen cyanide gas.

The pathologist must have been quick off the mark, I thought. Not to mention in possession of a nasty, suspicious mind. After Joey Morton's death I'd checked my reference shelves, which had confirmed what I'd already thought – death by cyanide's a real pig to diagnose. It happens almost instantaneously, and there's not much to see on the pathologist's slab. Maybe a trace of frothing round the mouth, possibly a few irregular pink patches on the skin like you get with people who suck too long on their car exhausts. If you get the body open quickly, there might be a faint trace of the smell of bitter almonds in the mouth, chest and abdominal cavity. But if you don't get your samples pdq, you're knackered because the cyanide metamorphoses into sulphocyanides, which you'd expect to find there anyway. The only reason they'd picked up on it right away in Joey's case was that the barman who discovered his body noticed the smell and happened to be a keen reader of detective fiction.

The Merseyside police were being pretty cautious, and there was a stonewalling quote from

Jackson, but reading between the lines, you could see they were talking to each other already. Trevor Kerr was on the record as saying he was confident that there was no problem with the products leaving his factory and he was sure that any investigation would completely vindicate Kerrchem. Never one to miss the chance for a bit of speculation, Alexis had flown the kite of industrial sabotage, but she had no quotes to back her up. No wonder she wanted to talk to me. I wondered if Trevor Kerr had told her I was working for him as part of his attempt to get out from under.

By the time the plane landed, I could have done with a couple of lines of speed. I'd had a stressful couple of days with almost no sleep, and the coffee I'd been mainlining in the air was starting to give me the jitters rather than simply keeping me awake. I was just in the mood for Trevor Kerr.

I reclaimed my bags by ten to eight and pushed them through customs on a trolley, like a sleepwalker. Halfway down the customs hall, I felt a hand on my shoulder and heard a voice say, 'Step this way, madam.' I looked up blearily at the customs officer, inches away from tears. The last thing I needed right now was to explain my bizarre assortment of possessions, ranging from a box of maps to a wad of cash and a radio receiver.

'What's going on?' I asked.

'Just follow me, please,' he said, leaving me no choice. We walked across the hall to a door on the far side. I was aware of several curious stares from my fellow passengers. The customs man showed me into a small office and closed the door behind me. Leaning against the wall, exhaling a mouthful of smoke, stood Detective Chief Inspector Della Prentice, a wry smile on her lips. Her chestnut hair was loose, hanging round her face in a shining fall. Her green eyes were clear, her skin glowing. She'd clearly had more than two hours' sleep in the last thirty-six. I hated her.

'You look like you had a rough flight,' she said.

'The flight was fine,' I told her, slumping into one of the room's plastic bucket chairs. 'It's just the last two days that have been hell.'

'Anything to do with the collected works that was waiting on my desk this morning?' she asked.

I groaned. 'More than somewhat. I realize it won't have made a word of sense to you, but I needed to send it somewhere safe.'

'Come on,' Della said, shrugging away from the wall. 'I'll drive you home and we'll talk.'

'I'm meeting a client at the Hilton,' I said, glancing at my watch. 'Two minutes from now. On a totally unrelated matter,' I added.

Della looked concerned. 'You sure you're up to that?'

I laughed affectionately. 'The copper in you never quite goes off duty, does it? I'm in a fit state for you to give me the third degree, but let me near a client? Oh no, I'm far too knackered for that.'

Della gave me a playful punch on the shoulder. 'I can't imagine that your client's planning to run you a hot bath laden with stimulating essential oils or to cook you a meal while you luxuriate with a stiff Stoly and grapefruit juice. And if he is, maybe I should call Richard and let him know the competition's hotting up.'

My head fell into my hands. 'Not one of your better ideas, Della,' I sighed.

'Oh God, you've not been checking out the insurance man's endowments, have you?' she giggled.

'Thank you, Alexis,' I said, getting wearily to my feet. 'And thank you for your confidence in me, Della. Come on, then. You can give me a lift over to the Hilton so I can talk to the client. Then you can take me home and I'll tell you all about it.'

One of the good things about having the cops meet you at the airport is that they get to park right outside the door without the traffic wardens turning their windscreens into scrapbooks. We drove across to the Hilton in blissful silence, and I left Della in reception with strict instructions to get me out of there in no more than ten minutes.

Trevor Kerr was planted in an armchair in the corner with a brandy glass in front of him. I sat down opposite him. He didn't offer me a drink. 'So what have you got to say for yourself?' he demanded by way of greeting. 'I've had a hell of a day thanks to your incompetence. The police have turned my bloody factory upside down, questioning everybody. God knows what today's production figures will be like.'

'Somebody is making fake KerrSter. They're releasing it on to the market via a little scam they've got going with one of the major wholesale chains. I know how the scam works and I know who's pulling it. The only thing I don't yet know is where they're manufacturing the stuff,' I said in an exhausted monotone. I just didn't have the energy to let Trevor Kerr wind me up.

His red face turned purple. 'Who is it? Who's doing this to me?' he shouted, leaning forward and banging the table with his fist. Several distant drinkers turned towards us, curious. The Hilton's bar isn't a place that's used to raised voices that early in the evening.

'It's a former employee, who clearly wasn't too impressed with the golden handcuffs you slapped on him,' I said.

'I want a name,' he demanded, his voice lower but his expression no less menacing. 'And an address. I'm going to break every bone in his fucking body when I get my hands on him.'

I shook my head, weary of his incontinent anger. 'No way.'

'What the hell do you think I'm paying you for, girl? Give me the name and address!'

'Mr Kerr, shut up and listen to me.' I'd reached the end of my rope and I suspect it showed. Kerr fell back in his seat as if I'd hit him. 'A client hires me to do a job, and I do that job. Sometimes I come up against things that make people want to take the law into their own hands. Part of my job is stopping

265

them. If I give you that name and address, and you go round there and give this bloke a good seeing to, you won't thank me tomorrow when you're in a police cell and he's sitting in his hospital bed free and clear because there isn't a shred of tangible evidence to tie him to the fake KerrSter or these killings. Sure, he'll have a sticky couple of hours down the nick, but unless we find where this stuff is being made and connect him directly to it, all we have is a chain of circumstantial evidence.' Kerr opened his mouth to speak, but I waved a finger at him and carried on. 'And I have to tell you that because of the way I've collected some of that circumstantial evidence, we're not going to be able to produce it for the police. We can tell them where to look, but we can't show them all we've got. We *need* the factory. I'm not keeping the name from you out of bloody-mindedness. I'm doing the job you paid me for, and I intend to finish it before somebody else dies. Do you have a problem with any of that?' I challenged him.

'Your name will be mud in this town,' he blustered.

'For what? Keeping my client out of jail? Mr Kerr, if I ever get the faintest whiff that you have bad-mouthed me to a living soul, our solicitors will slap a writ on you so fast it'll make your eyes water. If you want this case clearing up, and your good name restored, you'll give me till this time tomorrow to come up with the final piece of evidence that we need to hand this mess over to the police.'

Before he could answer, the barman appeared at his shoulder. 'Excuse me? Miss Brannigan?'

'That's me,' I said wearily.

'Phone call for you. You can take it at the bar.'

Thank you, Della. Without a word to Kerr, I got up and went to the phone. 'Time to go,' Della said.

'I'll be right with you.' I replaced the phone and returned to the table. 'I have to go now,' I said. 'Frankly, Mr Kerr, there are plenty more productive things for me to be doing than talking to you. I'll be in touch.'

Della was as good as her word. While I soaked in a bath laced with refreshing essential oils, a cold drink sweating on the side, she knocked together a chicken and spinach curry from the contents of the freezer. Wrapped in my cuddly towelling dressing gown, I curled up in a corner of one of the sofas and tucked in. I hadn't been able to face food on the flight, and as soon as the first forkful hit my mouth, I realized I was absolutely ravenous. As we ate, I gave Della the rundown on the case. 'And so I sent you the stuff from the safe,' I ended up.

Della nodded. 'I've been through it, as far as I could get with an Italian dictionary. What's your conclusion?'

'Drugs,' I said. 'They're swapping art for drugs. Those number and letter combinations – 20CC, 34H, 50,000E. I make that twenty kilos crack cocaine, thirty-four kilos heroin, fifty thousand tabs of Ecstasy. Once you've taken a painting out of its frame, it's a lot more portable than the cash equivalent, and a lot easier to smuggle. It's costing them next to nothing to acquire the stolen art, and it's got a sizeable black-market value, so they can swap it for a much greater value in drugs than they've initially laid out to have it stolen.'

Della nodded. 'I think you're right. Kate, you know I'm going to have to pass all this on to other teams, don't you? It's not my field.'

I sighed. 'I know. And somebody's going to have to liaise with the Italians so they can send someone to pick up Nicholas Turner's body. But I can't handle going through all this with some sceptical stranger tonight.'

'Of course you can't. And before you talk to any other coppers, you need to have Ruth with you. They're going to put a lot of pressure on you to come up with the original source that put you on to Turner in the first place. I've got a shrewd idea who that might be, but I don't see any need to pass my suspicions on.'

I smiled gratefully. She was right about Ruth. I'd broken the law too many times in the previous couple of days to be prepared to talk to the police without a solicitor. And my buddy Ruth Hunter is the best criminal solicitor in Manchester. 'Thanks, Della,' I said. 'Can you start the ball rolling tomorrow? I warn you now that I'm not going to be available for questioning till the day after. I've got something else to chase that I can't ignore.'

Della looked doubtful. 'I don't know if they'll want to wait that long.'

'They'll have to. Watch my lips. I'm not going to be available. I won't be in the office, I won't be here, I won't be answering my mobile.'

Della grinned. 'I hear you. I'll leave a message on the machine.' She gave me the copper's once-over look. 'You need to sleep, Kate. Speak to me tomorrow, OK?'

After Della had gone, I went next door. No sign of the coupé, which wasn't surprising if Richard had chosen to drive back. He might have made tonight's ferry out of Rotterdam, or he might have decided to take the long way home. I was still furious with him, but something inside me didn't want it to end here. I climbed into his bed, drinking in the smell of him from his pillows.

Call me sentimental. On the other hand, if you've just handed the police a stack of information pointing straight to a Mafia-style drug-running operation, sleeping in your own bed might not seem to be the safest option.

21

Some mornings you wake up ready to take on the world, feeling invincible, immortal and potentially omniscient. This wasn't one of them. I'd set Richard's *Star Trek* alarm clock for seven, which meant I'd had a straight eight hours' sleep before Captain James T. Kirk intoned, 'Landing party to *Enterprise*, beam us up, Scotty,' but I was in no mood to boldly go. I felt rested, but the hangover you get from guilt is infinitely worse than the one that comes from drink.

I dragged myself next door, called a cab and dived into the shower. I dressed in the last clean pair of jeans, a dark blue shirt and the new navy blazer, and managed half a cup of instant before the taxi pulled up outside. I picked up Shelley's Rover from Bill's garage, making a mental note to ring Hertz in Antwerp and ask them to hang on to Bill's car till I could get back over to pick it up. I was parked at the end of Alder Way by eight.

For once, I didn't have long to wait. At ten past,

Sandra Bates left the house with a tall, skinny bloke in overalls. She passed me without a glance in her little Vauxhall Corsa. Clearly her feminism didn't extend to boycotting products that indulge in blatantly sexist advertising. The man I took to be Simon Morley followed in a two-year-old Escort. I slipped into the traffic a couple of cars behind him.

When we reached Kingsway, he turned left, heading away from the city centre. I had no trouble staying in touch with him as we drove down the dual carriageway. We went out through Cheadle, past Heald Green, and on into Handforth. He turned left in the centre of the village, out past the station. We drove through a housing estate, then, just as we reached open country, he turned right. A couple of hundred yards down the road, there was a turning on the right, leading to a small industrial estate. I pulled up and watched as he parked outside a unit that wasn't much bigger than a double garage.

As he disappeared inside, I cruised into the estate and parked further down the road, outside a company that made garden sheds. Just after nine, a battered Transit van pulled up behind Morley's car. The two lads in overalls who got out looked as if they should still be in school. You know you're getting old when even the villains start looking young. I gave it another ten minutes, then I grabbed my clipboard and the bag containing the video camera, and headed for the unmarked warehouse.

I knocked on the door and marched straight in.

At one end of the room were a couple of tall vats with taps on the bottom of them. On a platform behind them, one of the lads was emptying the contents of a white plastic five-gallon drum into a vat. The other lad was halfway down the room, pushing a trolley that held gallon drums identical to the ones Kerrchem used for KerrSter. Simon Morley had his back to me, doing something at a bench on the far wall. Compared to the high-tech world of Kerrchem, this was a medieval alchemist's cell.

The lad pushing the trolley looked over at me, and called, 'Can I help you, love?'

At the sound of his voice, Simon Morley whirled round, consternation written all over his face. 'Who are you?' he demanded, crossing the room towards me.

'Is this Qualcraft?' I asked, casually swinging my bag through a gentle arc, hoping the video was getting the full flavour of the premises. 'Only, there's no name on the door, and I've got an order for Qualcraft, and I can't seem to find them.'

By now, Simon Morley was feet away from me. He looked like the classroom swot twenty years on, gangling limbs, acne scars and glasses that were constantly slipping down his sharp nose. 'You've come to the wrong place,' he said nervously. 'This isn't Qualcraft.'

If I hadn't stepped backwards, he'd have trodden on my trainers. 'Sorry,' I said. 'You don't know where Qualcraft is, do you?'

'No,' he said.

I smiled. 'Sorry to have bothered you.' I carried on backing out the door. Morley closed it firmly behind me, and I heard a key turn in the lock.

I pressed my ear to the door and heard him say, 'How many times have I told you to keep the door locked?' He said something more, but he was obviously moving back to his workbench, since I couldn't make out the words.

Back at the car, I checked the video on playback. The picture was slightly hazy, but the vats and the gallon drums were clearly discernible, along with a nice clear shot of Morley's face. I set the video camera up on the dashboard and waited. I rang Shelley and filled her in on what had happened to me in Italy and told her to call me as soon as she heard from Richard. 'Don't worry if you get diverted to the message service,' I added. 'I'm trying to avoid the cops, so I won't actually be answering the phone.' Wonderful thing, technology. If I don't want to take calls on my mobile, I can divert them to an answering machine. Then, when I want to pick the messages up, I simply dial a number and it plays them over to me.

By eleven, I'd had messages from Della, Mellor from the Art Squad, a superintendent from the Drugs Squad, Alexis and Michael Haroun. I didn't feel like talking to any of them, but I made myself ring Michael. I still had a client, after all, something I'd kind of lost sight of as I'd chased across Europe. And Henry needed insurance. If I could convince

Michael Haroun that the art thieves' racket was over for the time being, maybe he'd be a little more flexible about Henry's premium.

Michael was in a meeting, but I made an appointment with his secretary for three o'clock. I figured I'd be through here by then. Next, I took out my micro-cassette recorder and dictated a full report on the KerrSter scam. I'd drop it off with Shelley on my way to meet Michael so I could hand the client a copy this evening. I'd also be dropping off a copy with Inspector Jackson, just so Clever Trevor couldn't go taking the law into his own hands.

There was movement at the warehouse just after noon. I hit the record button on the video and taped Simon Morley and the two lads loading up the van with pallets of schneid KerrSter. Simon went back indoors with one of the lads, and the van took off. I followed at a discreet distance. I needn't have bothered. If I'd just driven straight to Filbert Brown's Manchester HQ, I'd have been able to film them arriving just as easily.

I was gobsmacked at their sheer cheek. Two people had died because of their crazy product tampering, yet they were still milking the racket for all it was worth. The more I thought about it, the more disturbing I found that. Simon Morley might well be crazy enough to carry on putting people's lives at risk in his vendetta against Kerrchem. But Sandra Bates hadn't struck me as a woman who would go along with random murder. I know people do ridiculous things for love, but I couldn't get the scenario into a credible shape at all.

But if Sandra Bates and Simon Morley weren't bumping people off, who was? It went beyond the bounds of credibility to imagine two lots of blackmailing saboteurs. I know coincidences do happen, but this wasn't one I could buy into. I closed my eyes and groaned. All this time and effort and I had a horrible feeling I wasn't any nearer the killer than I had been at the start.

Michael looked delighted to see me, greeting me with an unprofessional kiss on the lips. The tingle factor was still firing on all four cylinders, I noted as I moved away and sat demurely on the opposite side of the table from him. 'You've been keeping a very low profile,' he complained jocularly. 'I've been trying to reach you for days. Your secretary keeps telling me you're unavailable. I was beginning to think you'd gone off me.'

'She wasn't bullshitting,' I said. 'I genuinely have been unavailable. I've been out of the country. The good news is that you're not going to have any more trouble from this particular gang of art thieves.'

He leaned forward, his eyes surprised and interested. 'Really? They've been arrested?'

'Let's just say the market's collapsed,' I replied. 'Take it from me, the racket's over and done with. So you can safely reinsure Henry Naismith's property. They won't be back for a second bite of the cherry.'

Michael ran a hand through his dark hair and shook his head. 'This is incredible. What on earth have you been up to? It all sounds very unorthodox.'

'That's a word,' I said.

'You're going to have to tell me more than that,' Michael said, his face and voice equally determined. 'It's not that I don't believe you. But I have to explain myself to higher powers, and they're not going to be overly impressed if I tell them I've taken a particular course of action on the say-so of a private eye who isn't even our employee.'

I was growing bored with this story already, and I was still going to have to repeat it more times than the sole survivor of an air crash. 'Look, I can't go into great detail. I've still got a lot of talking to do to the police, and there are going to be arrests to come. The bare bones go like this. I got a tip-off from a good source as to who was fencing the goods. I tracked him back to an international criminal consortium who have been using art works as payment in kind for drugs. The fence is out of the game for good, and the police will be closing in on the rest of the syndicate. Without a guaranteed market, the thieves won't be doing any more robberies. I promise you, Michael, it's all over.'

He looked up from the pad where he'd been taking notes. 'You're sure? You don't think the fence is going to start up again once everything quietens down?'

I closed my eyes briefly. 'Not unless you believe in communications from beyond the grave,' I said.

Michael's mouth opened as he stared at me with new eyes. 'He's dead?' His voice was incredulous.

'Very.'

'You didn't . . . ? It wasn't . . . ?' A flicker of fear showed in his eyes.

I snorted with ironic laughter. 'Please,' I said. 'I didn't kill him, Michael, I only set him up. And my payoff was getting to discover the body.'

He looked faintly queasy. I can't say I blamed him. 'Is there any chance of recovering any of the stolen paintings?' he asked.

I shrugged. 'I shouldn't think so. I'm afraid you're going to have to bite the bullet and cough up. But like I said, you won't be having any repeat business from this team.'

'What can I say?' He spread his hands. 'I'm impressed. Look, I can't make any promises at this stage, but I'd be interested in working with you in future. On a more official basis.'

'Fine by me. Anything you need sorting, give us a call and we'll talk.' Normally, I'd have been punching the air in jubilation at landing a client as major as Fortissimus. Today, all I could muster was a moment's satisfaction. Fortissimus had been too expensive an acquisition.

I got to my feet. 'And on a personal note,' Michael added, his eyes crinkling in a smile, 'when can I see you again?'

'Tomorrow night?' I suggested. 'Meet me in the

bar at the Cornerhouse at half past seven?'

'Fine. See you then.'

I sketched a wave and moved towards the door. He bounded to his feet and caught up with me on the threshold. He tried to put his arms round me in a hug, but I backed off. 'Not in business hours,' I said defensively. 'If we're going to work together, we need some ground rules. Rule one, no messing about on the company's time.'

His mouth turned down ruefully. 'Sorry. You're absolutely right. See you tomorrow. Stay lucky.'

I stopped off at the Cigar Store café for a bite to eat and a cappuccino, then went back to the office to pick up the Kerrchem reports from Shelley. 'Nice work,' she remarked as she handed me two neatly bound copies.

'Yeah,' I said, my lack of conviction obvious.

'So what's the problem?'

I told her my reservations about Sandra Bates and her boyfriend. At the end of my tale, Shelley nodded sympathetically. 'I see what you mean,' she said. 'Are you going to front them up and see what they've got to say for themselves?'

'I hadn't planned on it,' I said. 'I was just going to hand over the reports to Trevor Kerr and the cops and let them get on with it. I can't pretend murder isn't police business, can I?'

'No, but if they're not the killers, maybe you should go and talk to them. They might have some useful ideas as to who actually is doing the killing.'

She was right, of course. Before I blew their lives out of the water, I should at least talk to Sandra Bates and Simon Morley. 'What if they leg it?' I protested weakly.

'If you drop off the reports with Kerr and Jackson and go straight round there, they won't have time to leg it, will they? This isn't a lead that Jackson's going to sit on till morning, is it?'

Half an hour later, I was walking up the path of 37 Alder Way. I'd sent Kerr's copy of the report round by motorbike courier, and I'd left Jackson's copy with his sergeant. I estimated I probably had a maximum of half an hour before the police came knocking.

Sandra Bates opened the door. Her first reaction was bemused bewilderment, then, clearly remembering what I'd been asking about, she tried to close the door. I stepped forward, shoving my shoulder between the door and jamb. 'What's going on?' she demanded.

'Too slow, Sandra,' I said. 'An innocent woman would have spoken sooner. We need to talk.'

'You're not a student,' she accused me, eyes narrowing.

'Correct.' I handed her one of my business cards. 'I'm Kate Brannigan. I'm working for Kerrchem, and we need to talk.'

'I've got nothing to say to you,' she said desperately, her voice rising.

From inside the house, Simon Morley's voice

joined in. 'What's going on, Sandra?'

'Go *away*,' she said to me, shoving the door harder.

'Sandra, would you rather talk to me about industrial sabotage or to the police about murder?' I replied, leaning back against the door. 'You've got ten seconds to decide. I know all about the scam. There's no hiding place.'

Simon's tall figure loomed behind Sandra in the hall. 'What's . . . ? Wait a minute, you were at the factory this morning.' He looked down at Sandra. 'What the hell's going on?'

'She's a private detective,' Sandra spat out.

'Simon, we need to talk,' I said, struggling to maintain a responsible façade with my shoulder jammed painfully between two bits of wood. 'I know about the fake KerrSter, I've got videos of your factory and your delivery run this morning, I know exactly how Sandra's working the fiddle at her end. You're already in the frame for product tampering and attempted blackmail. Do you really want two counts of murder adding to the list?'

'Let her in,' Simon said dully. Sandra looked up pleadingly at him, but he simply nodded. 'Do it, love,' he said.

I followed them into a living room that came straight from Laura Ashley without any intervening application of taste. I chose an armchair upholstered in a mimsy floral chintz, and they sat down together on a matching sofa. Sandra's hand crept out and clutched Simon's. 'There's no way you can wriggle out of the scam,' I said brutally. 'But I don't think murder was on the agenda.'

'I haven't killed anybody,' Simon said defiantly, pushing his glasses up his nose.

'It doesn't look that way,' I said.

'Look, I admit I wanted to get my own back on Kerrchem,' he said.

'The golden handcuffs?' I asked.

He nodded. 'That was bad enough, but then I found out they were refusing to give me a proper reference.'

I frowned. Nobody at Kerrchem had indicated that anyone had left under a cloud. 'Why?' I said.

'It was my department head, Keith Murray. He screwed up on a research project I was working on with him and it ended up costing the company about twenty grand in wasted time and materials. It was just before the redundancies were going to be announced and everybody was twitchy about their jobs, and he blamed me for the cockup. Now, because of that, personnel say I can't have a good reference. So I've ended up totally shafted. Never mind waiting six months, I'll be waiting six years before anybody gives me a responsible research job again. Kerrchem owes me.' The words spilled out angrily, tumbling out in the rush of a normally reticent man who's had enough.

'So you decided to take it out in blackmail?'

'Why not?' he asked defiantly.

'Apart from the fact that it's illegal, no reason

at all,' I said tartly. 'What about the two people who died?'

'That's got nothing to do with us,' Sandra butted in. 'You've got to believe us!' She looked as if she was about to burst into tears.

'She's right,' Simon said, patting Sandra's knee with his free hand. 'The papers said they'd died from cyanide poisoning – that's right, isn't it?' I nodded. 'Well, then,' he said. 'All the stuff I've been using is over-the-counter chemicals, mostly ones Sandra's picked up through work. I've got no access to cyanide. I've got none in the warehouse or here. You can search all you like, but you can't tie us in to any cyanide. Look, all we wanted was to get some money out of Trevor Kerr. Why would we kill people if that was what we were trying to do? It'd be daft. You pay off somebody who's wrecking your commercial operation, you do it quiet so the opposition don't get to hear about it. You don't go to the police. You don't pay off murderers. You can't hide murder.'

'What about the note? The one that came after the first death? That implied there would be more if Kerrchem didn't pay up,' I said.

This time, Sandra did start crying. 'I said we shouldn't have sent that one,' she sobbed, pulling her hand away from Simon and punching ineffectually at his chest.

Gently, Simon gripped her wrists, then pulled her into a tight hug. 'You were right, I'm sorry,' he told her. Then he turned back to me. 'I thought if we pretended to be more ruthless than we were, Kerr might cough up. It was stupid, I see that now. But he got me so mad when he just ignored the first note and nobody seemed to notice what we were doing. I had to make him pay attention.'

'So if you're not doing the killings, who is?' I demanded, finally getting round to the reason why I'd put myself through another harrowing encounter.

I was too late. Before Simon could answer, the doorbell rang, followed by a tattoo of knocking. 'Police, open up,' I heard someone shout from the other side of the door. I thought about making a run for it through the back door, but the way my luck had been running lately, I'd probably have been savaged by a police dog.

The pair on the sofa had the wide-eyed look of rabbits transfixed by car headlights. By the time they got it together to let the cops in, their front door was going to be matchwood. With a sigh, I got to my feet and prepared for another jolly chat with Detective Inspector Cliff Jackson.

22

My encounter with Jackson reminded me of the old radical slogan: help the police, beat yourself up. After listening to the usual rant about obstructing the police, withholding evidence and interfering with witnesses, I needed a drink. I was only a couple of miles away from the Cob and Pen, the pub where Joey Morton had breathed his last, which clinched the decision.

If they'd gone into mourning over the death of mine host, it hadn't been a prolonged period of grief. It was pub quiz night, and the place was packed. In the gaps between the packed bodies, I got the impression of a bar that had been done out in the brewery version of traditional country house: dark, William Morris-style wallpaper, hunting prints, and bookshelves containing all those 1930s best sellers that no one has read since 1941, not even in hospital out-patients' queues. No chance of anyone nicking them, that was for sure.

I bought myself a vodka and grapefruit juice

and retreated into the furthest corner from the epicentre of the quiz. I squeezed on the end of a banquette, ignored by the other four people surrounding the nearby table. They were much too involved in arguing about the identity of the first Welsh footballer to play in the Italian league. There was no chance of engaging any of the bar staff in a bit of gossip, not even lubricated with the odd tenner. They were too busy pulling pints and popping the caps off bottles of Bud. I sipped my drink and waited for an interval in the incessant trivia questions. Eventually, they announced a fifteen-minute break.

The foursome round my table sat back in their seats. 'John Charles,' I said. They looked blankly at me. 'The first Welshman to play in Italy. John Charles.' Amazing the junk that invades your brain cells when you live with a football fan.

'Really?' the lad with the pen and the answer sheet said.

'Truly.'

The one who'd been rooting for Charles against the other three grinned and clapped me on the back. 'Told you so,' he said. 'Can I get you a drink?'

I shook my head. 'I've got to get off. But thanks all the same. I'm surprised you didn't all know the answer. I'd have thought anybody who was a regular in Joey Morton's pub would have been shit hot on all the football questions.'

They all looked momentarily embarrassed, as if they'd caught me swearing in front of their mothers. 'Did you know Joey, then?' the pen-pusher said.

'We met a couple of times. My fella's a journalist. Bad business.'

'You're not kidding,' another said with feeling. 'Now, if you'd said it was Mrs M. that took a breadknife to him, I wouldn't have been half as surprised. But dying like that, a casual bystander in somebody else's war, that's seriously bad news.'

'You thought his wife had done it?' I asked, trying to keep my voice light and jokey.

They all snorted with laughter. 'Gail? Get real,' Penpusher said scornfully. 'Like Tez said, if it had been a breadknife job, nobody would have been gobsmacked. Them two fighting behind the bar's the nearest thing you used to get to cabaret in here. But rigging up a drum of cleaning stuff with cyanide? Nah, Gail's too thick.'

'When Gail writes the daily specials up on the board, there's more spelling mistakes than there are hot dinners,' another added. 'She probably thinks cyanide's a perfume by Elizabeth Taylor.'

'Must have been a hell of a shock, then. I guess it hit her hard,' I said.

The one I'd backed up gestured over his shoulder with his thumb towards the bar. 'Looks like it, doesn't it?'

I looked across. 'Which one's Gail? I never met her, just Joey.'

'The bottle blonde with the cleavage,' Penpusher said.

I didn't have to ask for more details. Gail Morton's tumbled blonde mane looked as natural as candy-floss, and the bra under her tight, V-necked T-shirt didn't so much lift and separate as point and aim. As I looked she served a customer, giving a laugh that revealed perfect teeth and healthy tonsils. 'A bit of a merry widow,' I remarked.

'Widow's weeds up until the funeral, then back to normal.'

I began to wonder if my eager inquiries down the line of industrial sabotage had shunted Jackson off the right track. After all, it's one of the great truisms that when wives or husbands die of unnatural causes, the prime suspect is the spouse. I was going to have to eat more than my usual portion of humble pie with Jackson if Gail Morton turned out to be Joey's killer. But that didn't explain why Mary Halloran had died. Time to go and pick some more brains.

I made my excuses and left. I headed east out of Stockport, and soon I was on the edge of the Pennine moors. About a mile before I hit Charlesworth village, I turned right on to a narrow road whose blacktop had been laid so recently it still gleamed in my headlights. The road climbed round the side of a hill and emerged in what had originally been a quarry. In the huge horseshoe carved out of the side of the hill stood ten beautiful stone houses, each individually designed by Chris.

For as long as I'd known them, Chris and Alexis had cherished the dream of building their own home, designed by Chris to their own specifications. They'd joined a self-build scheme a few years back, and, after a few hiccups, the dream had finally become a reality. Chris had swapped her architectural skills for things like plumbing, bricklaying, carpentry and wiring, while Alexis had served as everybody's unskilled labourer. The site was perfect for people who get off on a spectacular view, looking out through a gap in the Pennines to the Cheshire plain. There isn't a pub within three miles, the nearest decent restaurant is ten miles away, and if you run out of milk at half past nine at night, you're drinking black coffee. Me, I'd rather live in a luggage locker at Piccadilly Station.

The house wasn't quite ready to be inhabited yet. A small matter of connection to the main gas, electricity, telephone and sewage systems. So for the time being Alexis and Chris were living in an ugly little caravan parked in their drive. It must have been a bit like going out for dinner to the best restaurant in town with your jaw wired up.

The light was on in their van, so I knocked. Chris opened the door in her dressing gown, blonde hair in a damp, tousled halo round her head. Seeing me, a broad grin split her face. 'Kate!' she exclaimed, then made a point of leaning out and scanning the area beyond me. 'And you made it without a team of native bearers and Sherpa guides.'

'Sarcasm doesn't become you,' I muttered as I followed her into the claustrophobe's nightmare. The caravan was a four-berth job which might conceivably have contained a family for a fort-night's holiday. Right now, it was bursting at the seams with the worldly goods that Chris and Alexis simply couldn't do without. Once they'd packed in their work clothes, their casual clothes, a couple of shelves of books, a portable CD player with the accompanying music library, two wine racks, a drawing board for Chris and the files Alexis deemed too sensitive to trust to her office drawers, there wasn't a lot of room left for bodies.

Alexis was sprawled on the double bed watching the TV news in a pair of plaster- and paint-stained jogging pants and a ripped T-shirt, her unruly hair tied back in a ponytail with an elastic band. She greeted me with a languid wave and said, 'Kettle's just boiled. Help yourself.'

I made a cup of instant and joined the two of them on the bed. It wasn't that we were planning an orgy; there just wasn't anywhere else to sit. 'So what brings you up here in the hours of darkness, girl?' Alexis asked, leaning across me to switch off the TV. 'You finally decided to tell me why you've been doing a Cook's tour of the EC?'

'I bring greetings from civilization,' I told her. 'Cliff Jackson's just arrested two suspects in the Kerrchem product-tampering scam.'

I had all her attention now. Alexis pushed herself into an upright position. 'Really? He charging them with the murders?'

'I don't know. If he does, he'll be making a mistake,' I said.

'So, spill,' Alexis urged.

I gave her the bare bones of the tale, knowing she wouldn't be able to say much in the following day's paper because of the reporting restrictions that swing into place as soon as suspects are charged with an offence. But the details would be filed away in Alexis's prodigious memory, to be dragged out as deep background when the case finally came to court. And she wouldn't forget where the information came from.

'And you believe them when they say they had nothing to do with the two deaths?' Chris chipped in.

'Actually, I do,' I said. 'Breaks my heart to say so, but I don't think the job's finished yet, whatever Cliff Jackson decides to charge them with.'

Alexis lit a cigarette. Chris pointedly cracked the window open an inch and moved out of the draught. 'I know, I know,' Alexis sighed. 'But how can I possibly be a labourer without a fag hanging out of my mouth and a rolled up copy of the *Sun* stuffed in my back pocket? Anyway, KB, I suppose this means that you're here for access to the Alexis Lee reference library?'

'You can see why she's an investigative reporter, can't you?' I said nonchalantly to Chris.

'So what do you want to know?' Alexis asked.

'Tell me about Joey Morton,' I said. First rule of murder investigation, according to all the detective novels I've read: find out about the victim. Embarrassing that it had taken me so long to get there.

'Born and raised in Belfast. Came over here with a fanfare of trumpets that said he was going to be the next George Best. Unfortunately, the only thing Georgie and Joey had in common was their talent for pissing it all up against the wall. United took him on as an apprentice, but they didn't keep him on, and he never made it past the Third Division. Gail believed the publicity when she married him. She was expecting the days of wine and roses, and she never forgave him for not making the big time. So she gave him the days of bitter and thorns. They fought like cat and dog. When we were living in the Heatons, we used to pop into the Cob and Pen occasionally for a drink and the spectator sport of watching Joey and Gail tear lumps out of each other.'

'So why didn't she leave him?' I asked.

Alexis shrugged. 'Some people get addicted to rowing,' Chris said. 'You watch them at it and imagine how stressed it would make you to live like that, but then you realize they actually thrive on it. If they ever found themselves in agreement, the relationship would die on the spot.'

'Also, where would she go? It's not a bad life, being the *grande dame* of a busy pub like the Cob,' Alexis added. 'Besides, Joey was a staunch Catholic. He'd never have stood on for a divorce.'

'Now she's got it all,' I said. 'She's got her freedom, and presumably the brewery aren't going to chuck her out of the pub as long as it keeps making money.'

'And the insurance,' Alexis said. 'Word is, Joey was worth a lot more dead than he ever was in the transfer market.'

'All of which adds up to a tidy bit of motive for Mrs Morton,' I said. 'But if she's behind Joey's murder, how does Mary Halloran's death fit in?'

'Copycat?' Alexis suggested.

'Maybe, but cyanide isn't exactly a common household chemical. I wouldn't know how to get my hands on it. Would you?'

Alexis shrugged. 'I've never wanted to kill her enough,' she joked, grabbing Chris and hugging her. A sudden pang of envy took me by surprise. All too painfully, I could remember when Richard and I were as easy and warm together. It felt like a long time had passed since then. I wanted that back. I just didn't know any more if I could recover it with Richard or if I was going to have to start all over again on the wary process of love.

I must have shown something on my face, for Chris looked at me with a worried frown. 'You all right, Kate?' she asked.

'Not really,' I said. 'Me and Richard have had a major falling out. We parted company in Italy a couple of days ago, and I've not heard from him since. I'm just not sure if we can fix it this time.'

I could hardly bear the love and concern on their faces. Chris pulled free from Alexis and leaned over to hug me. 'He'll be back,' she said with more confidence than I felt.

'Yeah, but will he be back with a bricklayer to build a wall across the conservatory?' I asked bitterly.

'If Richard needed a brickie, he'd have to ask you where to find one,' Alexis said. 'You don't get rid of him that easy, girl.'

'He's obviously not very happy,' I told them. 'He said he's pissed off with everybody treating him like he's a pillock.'

'Maybe he should stop behaving like one, then,' Alexis said. 'Ever since he got himself arrested, he's been walking around like a dog waiting for the next kick. Wait till he comes back, girl, I'll take him out for a drink and put him right.'

I couldn't help smiling. That was one encounter I'd pay for a video of. 'Anyway, I don't want to talk about my troubles,' I said briskly. 'I've got too much to do trying to put right all the cockups I've made this week to worry about Richard. Did he have any dodgy contacts, this Joey Morton?'

'Not that I've heard. He hung out with one or two moody people, but that was probably for the so-called glamour as much as anything. He was probably into a few bits and pieces on the side, but he wasn't a player.'

So I wasn't looking for some gangster that Joey had double-crossed on a deal over stolen Scotch. 'What's the score with this Mary Halloran?' I asked.

'I haven't been over there myself, but I've still gorra few good contacts in Liverpool,' she said, becoming more Scouse by the syllable. 'This Mary

Halloran, she was a real grafter. The only out-of-the-way thing about her was that her staff actually liked her. They said she was a great boss, good payer, dead fair. According to them, she lived for her kids and her old man, Desmond. Our Desmond is apparently devastated. My mate Mo went round to try for a talk for the *Post*, but the guy was too distraught. She said he just burst into tears, then one of the relatives did the Rottweiler and saw her off.'

'This Desmond. Has he got a job?'

'He's got his own business too. Not as successful as Mary's by all accounts, but he does OK. He's a photographer. Does portraits mainly. Dead artistic, according to Mo. Specializes in unusual printing techniques and special effects stuff. Not your weddings and babies type. Charges about five hundred a shot, apparently. God knows where he gets clients. The only pictures I've ever seen of people in Liverpool with that kind of money are in police mugshots and wanted posters.'

'And no connection between the Hallorans and the Mortons?'

'Nothing that's come up so far. The only thing they've got in common, except for the way they died, is that they've left their surviving partners a lot better off than they were before. Mo says the girls that worked for Mary Halloran reckoned she was well insured. Had to be. If anything happened to her, the business was bound to suffer a bit, because Mary was one of those who had to take charge of everything herself.'

'Maybe they did a *Strangers on a Train*,' Chris volunteered. 'You know, I'll do your murder, you do mine.' We both looked at her, gobsmacked. 'It was only a suggestion,' she said defensively.

'The only point in doing something like that is when the murder method's one where having an alibi puts you in the clear. Like a shooting or a stabbing,' Alexis finally said. 'A delayed-action thing like this, there wouldn't be any point.'

'Nice idea, though,' I mused. Suddenly, a huge yawn crept up on me and shook me by the scruff of my neck. 'Oh God,' I groaned. 'I'm going to have to go, girls. If my overdraft was as big as my sleep deficit, the bailiffs would be kicking my door down.'

I leaned over and hugged the pair of them. 'You never know,' Chris said. 'He might be there when you get home.'

It's just as well Chris is such a good architect. She'd never make a living as a fortune teller.

23

The answering machine was flashing like a sex offender. I played back the long chain of messages against my better judgement. I'd had enough coppers on the line to staff my very own Tactical Aid Group minibus. But the one message I really wanted wasn't there. I hated myself for letting Richard's childish behaviour get to me, but that didn't make it any easier to escape. I ignored the rest of the messages and crashed out in my own bed. Deep down, I knew the Mafia weren't after me. Sleeping in Richard's bed the night before had been nothing but a self-indulgence I wasn't about to allow myself again.

I woke up just after eight, my head muzzy with the novel experience of a proper night's sleep. The phone was ringing already, but I had no problem ignoring it. I took a long, leisurely bath, deciding on my plans for the day. I'd told Della I'd be prepared to talk to the Art Squad and the Drugs Squad, but I had other ideas now. A few hours' delay wasn't going to make a whole lot of difference to their investigation, and I was determined to press on with my inquiries into the KerrSter murders as fast as I could. The last thing I wanted was another head to head with Cliff Jackson, and the best way to avoid that was to move as fast as I could while he was still working out what to do with Sandra Bates and Simon Morley.

After breakfast, I filled the washing machine with the first load of dirty clothes. Glancing out of the kitchen window, I noticed an unfamiliar car parked in one of the residents' bays. I didn't have to be Manchester's answer to Nancy Drew to work out that an unmarked saloon with a radio aerial and two men in it was a police car. The only thing left to wonder was which squad it belonged to. I wasn't about to pop over and ask a policeman.

I pulled the blonde wig out of its bag and arranged it on my head, adding the granny glasses with the clear lenses and a pair of stilettos to give me a bit of extra height. Then I nipped through the conservatory into Richard's house and out his front door. The two bobbies gave me a cursory glance, but they were waiting for a petite redhead from next door. That told me Della wasn't responsible, even indirectly, for their presence; she'd have told them about the conservatory. Which left Jackson.

Of course, the car was in the clear, since I was still driving Shelley's Rover. She'd tried the previous afternoon to persuade me to swap it for Richard's Beetle, but I played the card of professional necessity and managed to hang on to hers for the time being. I headed out of town towards Stockport and got to the Cob and Pen while the cleaners were still doing their thing. The bar stank of stale tobacco and sour beer, somehow more noticeable when the place was empty. 'I'm looking for Mrs Morton,' I told one of them.

'You from the papers?' she asked.

I shook my head. 'I'm representing Kerrchem, the company who manufacture the cleanser Mr Morton was using when he died.' Nothing like a bit of economy with the truth. Let them think I was here to talk about the compensation if they wanted.

The woman pursed her lips. 'You'd better go on up, then. It's going to cost your lot plenty, killing Joey like that.' She gestured towards a door marked 'Private'.

I smiled my thanks and opened the door on to a flight of stairs. The door at the top had a Yale, but when I tapped gently and turned the handle, it opened. 'Hello?' I called.

From a doorway on my left, I could hear a voice say, 'Hang on,' then the clatter of a phone being put down on a table. Gail Morton stuck her head through the doorway and said sharply, 'Who are you? What are you doing up here?'

'The cleaners sent me up,' I said. 'My name's Kate Brannigan. I'm a private investigator working for Kerrchem.'

She frowned and cast a worried glance back through the doorway. 'You'd better come through, then.' She moved back smartly into the room ahead of me and swiftly picked up the phone, swivelling so she could keep an eye on me. 'I'll call you back,' she said firmly. 'There's some private detective here from the chemical company. I'll ring you after she's gone . . . No, of course not,' she added sharply. Then, 'OK then, after one.' She replaced the phone and turned to face me, leaning against the table as if she were protecting the phone from hostile attack.

All my instincts told me that phone call was more than some routine condolence. Something was going on. Maybe it was nothing to do with anything, but my instincts have served me too well in the past to ignore them. I wanted to know just who she'd been talking to who needed to know a private eye was on the premises. 'Sorry to interrupt,' I said. 'Hope it wasn't an important call.'

'You'd better sit down,' she said, ignoring the invitation I'd dangled in front of her.

The room was as much of a cliché as Gail Morton herself. Dralon three-piece suite, green onyx and gilt coffee table and side tables, complete with matching ashtrays, cigarette box and table lighter. Naff lithographs in pastel shades of women who looked like they'd escaped from the pages of those true-romance graphic novels. The room was dominated by a wide-screen TV, complete with satellite decoder. I chose the chair furthest away from Gail.

She moved away from the telephone table and sat down opposite me. She leaned forward to take a cigarette from the box on the table, her deep-cut blouse opening to reveal the tanned swell of her breasts. Philip Marlowe would have been entranced. Me, I felt faintly repelled. 'So what have you come here for?' she asked. 'Have they sent you to make me an offer?'

'I'm afraid not,' I said. 'Kerrchem hired me to try to find out who tampered with their product.'

She gave a short bark of laughter. 'Trying to crawl out from under, are they? Well, they're not going to succeed. My lawyer says by the time we're finished with your bosses, they'll be lucky to have a pot to piss in.'

'I leave that sort of thing to the lawyers,' I said mildly. 'They're the only ones who can guarantee walking away rich after tragedies like this.' I thought I'd better remind her of her role as grieving widow.

'You're not kidding,' she said, dragging deep on her cigarette. In the unkind daylight coming through the window, I could see the incipient lines round her mouth as she kissed the filter tip. It wouldn't be long before her face matched her personality. 'So what do you want to know?'

'I've got one or two questions you might be able to help me with. First off, can you remember who actually bought the KerrSter?'

'It could have been me or Joey,' she said. 'We used to do the cash-and-carry run turn and turn about. KerrSter was one of the things that was always on the list, and we usually had a spare drum in the cupboard.'

'Who made the last trip?'

'That was Joey,' she said positively. Given when the affected batch had gone out, that meant Joey had purchased the fatal drum.

'Where are your cleaning materials kept?' I asked.

'In a cupboard in the pub kitchen.'

'Is it locked?'

She looked at me scornfully. 'Of course it's not. There's always spills and stuff in a pub. The staff need to be able to clean them up as and when they happen, not leave them for the cleaners.'

'So anybody who works in the pub would have access?'

'That's right,' she said confidently. 'That's what I told the police.'

'What about private visitors, friends or business associates? Would they be able to get to the cupboard?'

'Why would they want to? Do your friends come round your office and start nosing about in the cleaner's cupboard?' she asked aggressively.

'But in theory they could?'

'It'd be a bit obvious. When people come to visit, they don't usually swan around the pub kitchen on their own. You must know some really funny people. Besides, how would they know Joey was going to open that particular container?'

Before I could ask my next question, a voice from the stairwell shouted, 'Gail? There's a delivery down here you need to sign for.'

Gail sighed and crushed out her cigarette. 'I'll be back in a minute.'

As soon as she left the room, I was on my feet. I wouldn't be getting a second chance to check out what had set my antennae twitching. I took my tape recorder out of my bag and pressed the record button, then I picked up the phone and put the machine's in-built mike next to the earpiece. Then I hit last number redial. The phone clicked swiftly through the numbers, then connected. A phone rang out. I let it ring a dozen times, then broke the connection and gently replaced the phone.

I heard steps on the stairs and threw myself back into my chair. When Gail entered the room, I was sitting demurely flicking through the pages of the *TV Times*. 'Sorted?' I asked politely.

'I hate paperwork,' she said. 'But then, so did Joey, so we've got a little woman that comes in every week to keep the books straight.'

'Did your husband have any enemies?' I asked. Eat your heart out, Miss Marple.

'There were plenty of people Joey would happily have seen dead, most of them football managers. But people tended to like him. That was his big trouble. He was desperate to be liked. He'd never stand up for himself and make the bosses treat him properly. He just rolled over,' she said, years of bitterness spilling into her voice. 'I told him, you've got to show them who's in charge, but would he listen? Would he hell as like. Same with the brewery. I'd been on at him for ages to talk to them about our contract, but he just fobbed me off. Well, they'll know a difference now it's me they've

302

got to deal with,' she added vigorously. Knowing the corporate claws of brewery chains, I thought Gail Morton was in for a nasty surprise.

'So, no enemies, no one who wanted him dead?'

'You're barking up the wrong tree,' she told me. 'You should be looking for somebody at that factory who has it in for their bosses. Joey just got unlucky.'

'You benefit from his death,' I commented.

Her eyes narrowed. 'It's time you were on your way,' she said. 'I'm not sitting here listening to that crap in my own living room. Go on, get out of it.'

I can take a hint.

When I walked into the office, Shelley had a look on her face I'd never seen before. After a couple of minutes of awkward conversation, I worked out what it was. The shifty eyes, the nervous mouth. She was feeling guilty about something. 'OK,' I said heavily, perching on the corner of her desk. 'Give. What's eating you? Is it having to lie to the police about where I am?'

'I don't know what you mean,' she said sniffily. 'Anyway, I'm black. Isn't lying to the cops supposed to be congenital?'

'Something's bothering you, Shell.'

'Nothing is bothering me. By the way, if you want your coupé back, it's on a meter round the corner. I wouldn't mind having my Rover back.' She couldn't meet my eyes.

'Has he been here?' Try as I might, I couldn't keep my voice cool.

303

'No. He came round the house about eight o'clock this morning. I asked him to talk to you, but you're too good a teacher. That man of yours has really learned how to ignore. I was going to phone you, but he was gone by then, so it wouldn't have been a whole lot of use.'

'Did he say where he was going?' There was a pain in my stomach which was nothing to do with what I'd had for breakfast.

'I asked him, but he said he wasn't sure what he was doing. He told me to tell you not to waste your time looking for him.'

I looked away, blinking back tears. 'Fine,' I said unsteadily. 'Though why he should think I can spare the time to chase him . . .'

Shelley reached out and gripped my hand. 'He's hurting in his pride, Kate. It's going to take him a bit of time, that's all.'

I cleared my throat. 'Sure. I should give a shit.' I walked through to my office. 'If anybody wants me, I'm not here, OK?'

I closed the door and sat down with the tape recorder. I'd recorded the number dialling on high speed, and now I played it back on the lower speed setting so I could more easily count the clicks. Given the way my luck had been running lately, the call I'd interrupted had probably been made *to* Gail, and all I was going to end up with was the number of her dentist.

I wrote the numbers down on a sheet of paper. Unless Gail made a round trip of eighty miles every time she wanted her teeth fixed, it looked like I'd struck gold. The number I'd recorded from her telephone was a Liverpool number. On an impulse, I marched through to Bill's office, where the phone books live, and picked out a three-year-old Liverpool directory. I looked up Halloran. There it was. Desmond J. Halloran, an address in Childwall. The number didn't match.

'It ain't over till it's over,' I said grimly, picking up the phone and calling Talking Pages. I asked for portrait photographers in Liverpool. The second number she gave me matched the number on the sheet of paper. DJH Portraits. I didn't think Ladbrokes would be offering me odds on those initials not standing for Desmond J. Halloran.

I shut myself back in my office and rang Paul Kingsley, a commercial photographer who occasionally does jobs for us when Bill and I are over-stretched or we need pictures taking in conditions that neither of us feels competent to handle. Paul's always delighted to hear from us. I suspect he read too many Batman comics when he was a lad. I got him on his mobile. 'I need your help,' I told him.

'Great,' he said enthusiastically. 'What's the job?'

'I want to check out a photographer in Liverpool. I need to know how his business is doing. Is he making money? Is he on the skids? That kind of thing. Do you know anybody who could colour in the picture?'

'That's all you want?' He sounded disappointed. It was worrying. This is man whose assignments for us have included spending a Saturday night in an industrial rubbish bin, and standing for three days in the rain in the middle of a shrubbery. In his shoes, I'd have been delirious with joy at the news that his latest task for Mortensen and Brannigan involved nothing more hazardous to the health than picking up a phone.

'That's all I want,' I confirmed. 'Only I want it yesterday. DJH Portraits, that's the firm.'

'Consider it done,' he said.

My next call was to Alexis. 'All right?' she greeted me. 'Has dickhead turned up?' I told her about Shelley's encounter with Richard. 'That doesn't sound like goodbye to me,' she said. 'You want my advice, give your insurance man a bell. Show Richard you're not sitting around waiting for him to decide it's time to come home.'

'Strangely enough, I'm seeing him for dinner,' I told her.

'Nice one. Don't do anything I wouldn't do.'

'That doesn't give me a lot of scope on a date with a fella, does it?'

'Exactly. Now, what was it you wanted?'

'You still got your contact in Telecom accounts?' I asked her.

'You bet. Like the song says, once you have found her, never let her go. What are you after?'

'I want the itemized bills for the last six months on three numbers,' I said. 'One Manchester, two Liverpool. How much is that going to rush me?'

'It's usually fifty quid a throw. I'll ask her if she'll give you the three for a hundred and twenty.

306

You want to give me the numbers, I'll pass them on?'

I read the three numbers over to her. 'Soon as poss,' I said.

'If I catch her now, she'll fax them to you when she gets home tonight. That do you?'

'It'll have to.'

'Is this something I should know about, KB? I mean, I'm the woman you were pumping last night about mysterious deaths in Manchester and Liverpool.'

I chuckled. 'If I said it was a completely unrelated matter, would you believe me?'

'Girl, if the Pope himself told me it was a completely unrelated matter, I wouldn't believe him. You've got no chance. You want to share this with me?'

'Do your own investigations,' I told her.

'I'll catch up with you later. Have fun with the insurance man. I'll expect a full report tomorrow.'

'Only paying clients get full reports,' I laughed. I replaced the receiver and swung my feet up on to the desk. A vague shape was forming in my mind, but there were still too many questions that needed answering. Not least of them was the one Gail Morton herself had raised. If someone had been targeting Joey Morton specifically, how could they be sure he would be the person to open the fatal container?

I was still worrying at that point when Paul called back. 'DJH Portraits,' he said. 'Desmond Halloran. One-man band. He used to work with another guy, doing the usual weddings, babies and pets. But he fancied himself as a bit of an artist, so he set up on his own, doing specialist portrait work. I'm told his stuff is really good, but the problem is that using the kind of processes he does is very labour intensive, as well as costing a fair bit on the chemicals. He was keeping his head above water to begin with, but the way the recession's been biting, nobody's got the cash to spare for fancy photographs that come in at five hundred quid a throw. My contact says he reckons he must be running at a loss these days. That what you wanted to hear?'

'Smack on the button,' I said.

'This wouldn't have something to do with the fact that his wife has just popped her clogs, would it?' he asked eagerly, ever the boy detective.

'Now, Paul, you know I never divulge confidential client information.'

'I know. Only, my mate, he says Desmond only kept afloat because his wife's business was a raging success and she subsidized him. He was wondering how Desmond's going to go on now.'

Another piece of the jigsaw fell into place. 'Thank you, Paul,' I said. 'Send me an invoice.' It was a long shot, but if Desmond Halloran was having an affair with Gail Morton and they wanted to ditch their partners and run off together, they'd need something to live on. Quite a big something, if my impressions of Gail were accurate. But if Desmond divorced Mary, she'd doubtless hang on to the kids and to her business, leaving Desmond potless. And

I suspected that Desmond potless was a lot less attractive to Gail than Desmond loaded.

Before I could do anything more, the door to my office opened and Della walked in. She looked at me, eyes reproachful, and gently shook her head. 'Running out on Cliff Jackson I could understand,' she said. 'But running out on a promise you made to me? Kate, you checked your brains in with your bags at Milan and forgot to pick them up at the other end.'

She didn't need to say any more. I could beat myself up. She was right. When I start letting my friends down, I know my life's starting to spin out of control. I got to my feet. 'I'm sorry,' I said inadequately. 'You're right. You deserve better.'

'Shall we go?'

I nodded. On the way out, Shelley said, 'Sorry, Kate. I can lie to most people, but not to the rest of the team.'

'No need to apologize,' I said. 'I'm the one in the wrong. You better phone Ruth and tell her to meet me at . . . where, Della?'

'Bootle Street,' Della said.

'Oh, and Shelley? I think I might be a while. Better ring Michael Haroun at Fortissimus and tell him I need a rain check tonight.'

I followed Della out to the waiting police car. I knew I was damn lucky not to be under arrest. I just didn't feel like I could risk walking under ladders.

24

It seemed to take longer to recount Richard and Kate's excellent adventure than it had taken to experience it. Asking the questions were Inspector Mellor from the Art Squad, who remembered me from our earlier encounter at Henry's, and Geoff Turnbull from the Drugs Squad, who thankfully owed me one on account of information received in a previous investigation that had provided him with a substantial feather in his cap. Della sat in on the interview, probably to make sure my brief didn't change my mind and persuade me to opt for the Trappist approach.

Even so, by the time I'd answered everyone's questions, it was past midnight. I'd come clean about all of my nefarious activities, on the advice of Ruth Hunter, my nonpareil criminal solicitor and, incidentally, one of the tightknit group of my female friends which Richard refers to as the Coven-ment – witches who run the world. 'After all,' she pointed out drily, 'all your law-breaking took place outside their jurisdiction, and I rather think the Italian police are going to have enough to worry about without bothering you with such trivial charges as assault, kidnap, false imprisonment, burglary, data theft, concealing a body, and failing to report a murder.'

Ruth, Della and I ended up eating steak in one of the city's half-dozen casinos. The great advantage with them is that they stay open late and the food's cheap. It's supposed to act as an incentive to make people gamble. I don't know how effective it is; most of the gamblers that night were Chinese, and none of them looked like a juicy steak was on their agenda. Not as long as the roulette wheels were still spinning. 'Cliff Jackson's still going to want to talk to you,' Della pointed out after we ordered.

'I know. His goons were sitting on my doorstep this morning.'

Ruth groaned. 'What now, Kate? Haven't you broken enough laws for one week?'

'That's not why Cliff Jackson's after me,' I said stiffly. 'It's just that I've been doing his job for him, and now I've tracked down his saboteurs, he probably wants to know who the real murderer is.'

Della and Ruth both choked on their drinks. 'Oh ye of little faith,' I complained. 'Anyway, I want to stay out of his way until I've got the whole thing done and dusted. If I leave the job half done, he'll only mess it up and arrest the wrong person. He's got form for it.'

'Isn't it about time you went back to white-collar

crime and left the police to deal with these dangerous criminal types?' Ruth demanded. 'It's not that
I think you're incapable of looking after yourself.
It's just that you keep involving Richard, and he's
really far too accident-prone to be exposed to these
kinds of people.'

'I don't want to discuss Richard,' I said. 'Anyway,
Della, what have Mellor and Turnbull been doing
for the last forty-eight hours with the info I handed
them on a plate?'

'Luckily, Geoff's already had dealings with his
opposite numbers in Europe about organized drug
trafficking, so he was able to cut through a lot of
the bureaucratic red tape. It turns out his Italian
oppos have been taking a long hard look at Gruppo
Leopardi and its offshoots, so the info you brought
out of there has slotted in very nicely. You were
right, by the way. They've been organizing art
robberies all over Europe, not just in the UK,
and using the art works as payment for drug
shipments,' Della said. 'With the data you stole,
it looks like they'll be able to set up a sting that
will pull in some of the big boys, for a change.'

'What about Nicholas Turner?' I asked.

Della fussed with a cigarette and her Zippo. 'They
found his body in the van, where you left it. A
couple of the lads went over to Leeds this morning
and spoke to his wife. She's denying all knowledge
of anything shady, of course. She's going for the
Oscar as the grieving wife of a legitimate art and
antiques dealer. Grieving she may well be, but

nobody believes for a minute she's as innocent as she wants us to think. Apart from anything else, there's evidence that she's accompanied him on several of his trips to the Villa San Pietro.'

'He still didn't deserve to die,' I said.

Ruth shrugged. 'You take the money, you take the risks that go with it. How many lives have been destroyed by the drugs Turner was involved in supplying? Half the people I defend owe not a little of their trouble to the drug scene. I wouldn't lose any sleep over Turner, Kate.'

I didn't.

Jackson's goons were on my doorstep again the following morning. I figured that by now he'd probably be staking out the office as well. I rang Shelley. 'Have you got company of the piggy variety too?'

'Of course, sir. Did you want to talk to one of our operatives?'

That told me all I needed to know. 'Is it Jackson himself or one of his gophers?'

'I'm afraid our principal isn't in the office at present.'

I'll say this for Shelley, nothing fazes her. 'There should have been an overnight fax for me,' I said. 'Can you stick it in an envelope and have it couriered round to Josh's office? I'll pick it up there.'

'That's no problem, sir. I'll have Ms Brannigan call you when she comes back to the office. Good-bye now.'

Whoever said blondes have more fun obviously didn't garner the experience wearing a wig. I went through the disguise-for-beginners rigmarole again and made my exit through Richard's bungalow, pausing long enough to do a quick inventory of his wardrobe. If he'd been back, he hadn't taken any significant amount of clothing with him. His laptop was gone, though, which meant he was planning to be away long enough to get some work done.

I arrived at Josh's office ten minutes after the fax, and settled down at an empty desk to plough through the phone numbers. It was a long, tedious process of crosschecking, made worse by the fact that Alexis's contact had come up with a more detailed breakdown of calls than the customer receives. The fax she'd sent listed every call from all three numbers, even the quickies that don't cost enough to make it on to the customer's account. But at the end of it, I'd established that there were calls virtually every day between Desmond Halloran's office number and the private number of the Cob and Pen. There were also a couple of long calls from the Hallorans' home number to the pub.

There was one other curious thing. A Warrington number cropped up on both bills. I checked the dates. Every Monday, a call a few minutes long was logged on one bill or another. It appeared most often on Desmond's office bill, but it was there half a dozen times on the Cob and Pen's account too. Of course, I had to ring it, didn't I?

'Warrington Motorway Motel, Janice speaking, how may I help you?' the singsong voice announced.

'I'm meeting someone at the motel today. Can you give me directions?'

'Certainly, madam. Where are you coming from?'

'Manchester.'

'Right. If you come down the M62 and take junction nine, you go left as you come off the motorway and right at the first roundabout. We're the first turning on the left, just after the bridge.'

'Thank you,' I said. 'You've been most helpful.' If I had my way, Janice was going to be a lot more helpful before the day was out.

There was nothing to mark out the Warrington Motorway Motel from the dozens of others that sprang up around the motorway network in the late Eighties. A two-storey, sprawling red-brick building with a low-pitched roof, a car park and a burger joint next door, it could have been anywhere between the Channel Tunnel and that point on the edge of the Scottish highlands where the motorways run out. Rooms for around thirty quid a throw, TV but no phone, no restaurant, bar or lounge. Cheap and cheerless.

Late morning wasn't a busy time behind the reception desk. Janice – or someone who'd stolen her name badge – looked pleased at the sight of another human being. The reception area was so small that with two of us present, it felt intimate. On the way over, I'd toyed with various approaches. I'd decided I was too strung out to try for subtlety. Besides, I still had a wad of cash in my bag that had no official home.

I dropped one of my cards on the desk half-way through Janice's welcome speech. Her pert features registered surprise, followed by an air of suppressed excitement. 'I've never met a private detective before,' she confided, giving me the wide-eyed once-over. I hoped I wasn't too much of a disappointment.

I followed the card with a photograph of Gail I'd persuaded Alexis to lend me. 'This woman's a regular here,' I stated baldly. 'She comes here once a week with the same bloke.'

Janice's eyes widened. 'I'm not supposed to release information about guests,' she said wistfully.

I leaned on the desk and smiled. 'Forgive me being so personal, Janice, but how much do they pay you?'

Startled, she blurted out the answer without thinking. 'A hundred and seventy pounds a week.'

I opened my bag and took out the five hundred I'd counted out on the way. I placed it on the desk and pushed it towards her. 'Nearly three weeks' money. Tax free. No comebacks: I don't even want a receipt.'

Her eyes widened. She stared at the cash, then at me, consternation clear in her face. 'What for?'

'All I want to know is how often they come and how long they stay. I want to know when they're due here next. Then I want to book the room next door. Oh, and five minutes in their room before they arrive. There's no reason why anyone should know you've helped me.' I nudged the money nearer to her.

'It's for a divorce, isn't it?' she said.

I winked. 'I'm not supposed to release information either. Let's just say this pair shouldn't be doing what they've been doing.'

Suddenly, her hand snaked out and the dosh disappeared faster than a paper-wrapped prawn off Richard's plate. She tapped Gail's photograph with a scarlet fingernail. 'She's been coming here with this bloke for about a year now. They always book as Mr and Mrs Chester. It's usually a Wednesday. They arrive separately, usually about half past two. I don't know when they leave, because I go off at half past four.'

I nodded, as if this was exactly what I'd expected to hear. 'And when are they booked in next?'

'I think you've dropped lucky,' she said, consulting her screen. 'Yeah, that's right. They've got a room booked today.' She looked up at me, smirking. 'I bet you knew that, didn't you?'

Again, I winked. 'Maybe you could let me into the room they'll be in, then book me in next door?'

Eagerly, she nodded. Funny how excited people get when they feel like they're part of the chase. 'I'll give you their key,' she said. 'But bring it back quick as you can.'

I picked up the key and headed for the lift. Room 103 was a couple of doors down the corridor from the lift. The whole floor was eerily silent. I let myself in, and gave the room a quick scan. I could have drawn it from memory, it was so similar to every motel room I'd ever camped out in. Because I hadn't been able to get into the office to pick up proper surveillance equipment, I'd had to rely on what I could pick up from the local electronics store. A small tape recorder with a voice-activated radio mike hadn't made much of a dent in my payoff from Turner. I took out my Swiss Army knife and unscrewed the insipid seascape from above the bed. I stuck the mike to the back of the picture with a piece of Elastoplast, then screwed it back on to the wall. There was a gap of about a quarter of an inch between the picture and the hessian wallpaper, but I didn't think Gail and Desmond were there for the décor.

I quickly checked the mike was working, then I was out of there. I returned the key to Janice and went over to the burger joint for supplies. I settled down in my room with a giant cheeseburger, fries, a large coffee and a bag of doughnuts. I stuck the earpiece of the tape recorder in my ear and waited. I couldn't believe myself. I felt like I was playing the starring role in the worst kind of clichéd private-eye drama; staking out the seedy motel for the couple indulging in illicit sex. All I needed was a snap-brimmed trilby and a bottle of bourbon to feel like a complete idiot.

While I was waiting, I rang Michael Haroun. 'Sorry about last night,' I said. 'I was helping the police with their inquiries.'

'They *arrested* you?'

'Behave. They only wanted a friendly chat. They were just a little insistent about having it right that minute.'

'My God, you like to sail close to the wind, don't you?'

'My yachting friends tell me that's where you have to be if you want to travel fast,' I said. What was it about this man that brought out the portentous asshole in me?

'So is this a social or professional call?' he asked.

'Purely social. I wanted to offer you dinner tomorrow as a penance for cancelling yesterday.'

'You cook, as well as everything else?'

'I do, but that's not what I had in mind. How does the Market sound?'

'Fabulous. My favourite restaurant in town. What time?'

'I'll see you there about half past seven,' I promised. To hell with Barclay.

The feeling of wellbeing that I got from talking to Michael didn't last long. There's nothing more boring than sitting around in a featureless motel room waiting for something to happen. Patience and I aren't normally on speaking terms, so I always get really edgy on jobs like this. It's not so bad doing a stakeout in the car; at least I can listen to the radio and watch the world go by.

But here, there was nothing to do but stare at the walls.

The monotony broke around twenty past two. My earpiece told me that the door to the next room had closed. At once, I was on the alert, my free ear pressed to the wall. I heard the toilet flush, then, a few minutes later, the door closed again. There was a mumble of what sounded like greetings and endearments, irritatingly incomprehensible. At a guess, they were still in the passage by the bathroom, rather than in the room proper.

More mumblings, then gradually, I could make out what they were saying.

'. . . taking a risk,' a man's voice said.

'You said what I told you to, didn't you?' Gail's voice. Unmistakably.

'Yeah, I told my mother I needed some time on my own, that I was going for a drive and would she look after the kids.'

'And did she act like she thought you were behaving oddly?'

'No,' the man admitted.

'Well, then,' Gail said. There was the instantly recognizable sound of kissing, the groans of desire. 'I needed to see you,' Gail went on when she next surfaced. 'I wanted you so bad, Dessy.'

'Me too,' he said. More of the kind of noises you get in Tom Cruise movies. I half expected to hear 'Take my breath away' swelling in the background.

'We did it, you know,' Gail said exultantly in the

next break. 'We're going to get away with this. Nobody suspects a thing.'

'What about that private eye? You sure she doesn't know anything?'

'Positive. She was just on a fishing expedition, that was obvious. If she'd had anything solid to go on, she'd have let me know. Cocky bitch.'

I wasn't the only one who was cocky. Only I had better reason to be. I checked that the tape was still running.

'Have you seen the news?' Gail asked.

'What news?' Desmond said, sounding nervous.

'About the chemical company,' she said. 'It was all over the *Evening Chronicle* and the local TV news.'

'We haven't had the TV on much. We're supposed to be in mourning,' Desmond said cynically. 'What's been going on? Are they admitting liability?'

'Better than that,' Gail said. 'Apparently, somebody's been trying to blackmail Kerrchem. Product tampering, they said it was. The police have arrested a man and a woman. Hang on, I've got the paper in my bag.' There was the sound of rustling, then silence.

Then Desmond let out a low whistle. 'Fantastic!' he exclaimed. 'The icing on the cake. Nobody's going to look twice at us now, are they?'

Famous last words, I thought to myself.

'Exactly. It's turned out even better than we planned. The police might think I had a motive for wanting rid of Joey, but they're not going to bother digging around in my life when they've got a perfect pair of scapegoats.'

And even though his access to photographic chemicals meant Desmond Halloran could probably get his hands on cyanide without too much trouble, I reckoned the police weren't even going to think about suspecting him while they had Simon and Sandra behind bars. Besides, according to Alexis, the Hallorans were supposed to have an idyllic marriage. No one had an inkling that Desmond Halloran's Wednesday afternoons were spent in a motel room near Warrington.

The smooching noises had begun again. Then Gail said, 'In a year or so, when we've got to know each other because of the court cases we'll be filing against Kerrchem, no one will be surprised when we decide to get married. After all, we'll have had so much in common.'

Desmond giggled, an irritating, high-pitched whinny. Never mind his murderous instincts, that giggle alone should have put any reasonable woman off him for life. 'Talk about coincidence,' he cackled. 'I bet those two blackmailers are sweating.'

After that, things got a lot less interesting for me, though Gail and Desmond obviously thought different. There was a lot of kissing and groaning and embarrassing lines like, 'Give it to me, big boy'. Then they were grunting like a pair of Wimbledon champions. I pulled out the earpiece in disgust. It's not that I'm a prude, but it felt like this pair were shagging in an open grave. I sat patiently on the bed, watching the winking red light on the tape machine that told me it was recording. After an hour, I reckoned I'd got more than enough to nail the scumbags.

It was time to go and play at good citizens.

25

I dumped another oner on Janice's desk. 'You've got an office through the back?' I asked.

She nodded, never taking her eyes off the money. 'I'd like to use the phone there for a couple of minutes. I know you're not supposed to allow customers access to your phone, never mind your office, but if anyone kicks off, tell them I said it was an emergency.' I winked again. Strange how I develop that tic whenever I'm sharing my wealth with the less fortunate.

Janice lifted the access flap at the side of the reception desk and I went through to the tiny office, closing the door behind me. I rang the familiar number of Greater Manchester police and asked for the Stockport incident room. The detective who answered didn't seem very keen to put me through to Inspector Jackson. He told me firmly that anything I had to say to the boss could equally be said to him. Clearly a man desperate for Brownie points. 'I know he wants to talk to me,' I insisted.

'He wants to talk to me so badly that he's had two of his lads sitting outside my house for the last two days.'

'Hold on,' he said grudgingly. 'I'll see if he's free.'

Jackson came on the line immediately. 'At last,' he said grimly. 'Why have you been avoiding me, Miss Brannigan? I thought you were very hot on civic duty the last time we spoke.'

'I'm sorry, Inspector, I've been a bit busy. And I knew you wouldn't be very keen to take me seriously since the last criminals I handed over to you weren't exactly what you were looking for.'

He sighed. 'Cut the smartarse remarks and get to the beef,' he said. 'When are you coming in to talk to me?'

'I rather thought you might want to come to me,' I said sweetly. 'I have something I'd like you to hear. I'll happily play it over the phone, though I don't know how well you'll be able to hear it.'

'If you've been interfering with my case again . . .' he said heavily, letting some unspoken threat hang in the air. I wasn't scared; I've been threatened by experts.

'Just listen, please.' I pressed play and held the speaker of the cassette player up to the mouthpiece of the phone. I'd rewound to the crucial exchange where Gail had conveniently outlined the murder plan. I let the tape run for a few minutes, then clicked it off. 'The voices you just heard are Gail Morton and Desmond Halloran. I've only just made this recording. The pair of them are still in Room 103 at the Warrington Motorway Motel. If you hurry, you might just catch them at it.'

As I replaced the receiver, I heard a splutter of rage from Jackson. Like the man said, I'm into performing my civic duty. I didn't want him to waste time cursing me out when he should be jumping in a motor and shooting over here, sirens blaring and lights flashing.

I thanked Janice politely for the use of her phone and handed back my room key. I went out to the car park and sat in my car. I don't know what I was planning to do if they'd left before the police got there, but I didn't have to make any decisions. A bare twenty minutes after I'd called, a pair of unmarked police cars screamed into the car park. I was impressed. They must have really hammered it.

Jackson jumped out and ran across to my car. He looked as if he wanted to hit me. 'They still in there?' he demanded.

'Present and correct.'

'Wait here,' he commanded.

'My pleasure,' I said.

Jackson went back to his officers and the six of them went into a huddle. After a moment, the only woman there peeled off from the main group and walked across to my car. She opened the passenger door and plonked herself in the seat next to me. 'It's nice to be trusted,' I commented drily.

She grinned. 'After the way you've been giving

him the runaround, just be grateful you're not cuffed to the back bumper of his motor,' she said. 'I'm Linda Shaw, by the way. DC Shaw.'

'Kate Brannigan,' I said.

'Oh, I know exactly who you are, Ms Brannigan. My guv'nor says you've got something for us?'

I watched Jackson lead his troops into the motel. I had a momentary pang of sympathy for Janice. I hoped the six hundred would be enough to make her feel reasonably cheerful about having been had over. Once they'd gone inside, I took the tape out of the recorder and handed it to Linda Shaw. 'I take it this will come under the heading of anonymous tip-off when the case comes to court?'

'I'd imagine so. I don't think giving your agency good publicity is high on my guv'nor's Christmas list. Now, where else would you expect us to go looking for evidence that might strengthen our case?'

I liked Linda Shaw. She spoke my language. None of the bluster or intimidation of her boss had rubbed off on her. Like me, she'd developed her own style, complete with techniques that got quicker results than the heavy-handed approach without alienating everyone along the way. I made a mental note to mention her name to Della. Any woman trying to make it through the male-dominated hierarchy of the police needs all the help she can get. I stared straight ahead and said, 'For it to get as far as murder, this affair must have been going on for a while. I'd have thought the hotel records would indicate how long. So they must have had some means of communication. If I had access to that sort of information, I'd take a long hard look at the phone bills at the Cob and Pen and at DJH Portraits.'

Linda smiled and took out her notebook. As she scribbled a reminder to herself, she said, 'You do realize you're going to have to come back with us and give a full statement this time? Not just about this, but about the Kerrchem sabotage?'

I sighed, resigned to my fate. 'I spent yesterday evening in the nick helping the Art Squad and the Drugs Squad with *their* inquiries. Much more of this, and I'm going to be asking for overtime.'

Linda chuckled. 'You've got more chance of getting it out of your clients than out of our budget. Listen, would you prefer it if I took your statement?'

Another careerist. But this time, it suited me to go along. 'Do you really think Jackson's going to give up the opportunity to make my life seriously uncomfortable?'

Linda nodded towards the door of the motel. A man I took to be Desmond Halloran was stumbling towards the car park, wearing nothing but a pair of jeans and a policeman on each arm. 'I think Inspector Jackson's going to have his hands full with those two. Just thank your lucky stars that from here on in, you're a bit player.'

Next came Gail Morton, more respectable in leggings, scoop-necked T-shirt and the kind of fashion leather jacket that makes you angry on behalf of the cow. Jackson held her firmly by one arm, with the other two officers bringing up the rear. The lovers were each thrust into a separate car, and Jackson came over to us.

'I'll see you back in Stockport,' he said darkly to me, his eyes menacing behind the tinted lenses.

'I thought the police were supposed to be grateful for cooperation from members of the public,' I said airily.

'We are,' he snarled. 'What we don't like is smartarses who think they know how to do our jobs.'

He walked away before I could come up with a snappy rejoinder. Probably just as well. I didn't want to miss tomorrow night's date with Michael Haroun. I started the car and pulled in behind the two police motors. 'If they smash the speed limit on the way back, I want immunity from speeders,' I told Linda.

'You don't have to keep up with them,' she pointed out. 'I do know where we're going, even if you don't.'

'Listen,' I said. 'Your boss is so paranoid about me that if I disappear from his rear-view mirror he's going to put out an all-points bulletin to stop and shoot me on sight for abducting a police officer.'

'You're probably right. He's just brassed off because he was looking at the angle of possible collusion between the two bereaved spouses. Unfortunately, we're handicapped by having to operate inside the law, so we hadn't managed to make as much progress as you,' Linda said ironically.

'Touché. I'll remember that when I'm making my statement.'

'I would, if I were you. Certain of my colleagues would love to have something to charge you with.'

I reached over and pulled my mobile out of my bag. 'I'd better cover my back, then.' Ruth was going to be thrilled. Much as she loved me, holding my hand twice in two days was stretching our friendship more than somewhat.

For the second night running, I was in a police station past midnight. Most of the time had been spent hanging around while Linda Shaw acted as liaison with Jackson, returning every now and again to ask me fresh questions, most of which I didn't have the answers to. No, I didn't know how they met. No, I didn't know exactly what chemicals Halloran had used. No, I didn't know where he bought his chemicals. Eventually, in exasperation, Ruth said, 'Detective constable, do you believe in God?'

Linda frowned. 'What's that got to do with it?'

'Do you believe that my client is God?'

Linda tipped her head back, stared at the ceiling and sighed. 'No, Ms Hunter, I do not believe that your client is God.' Waiting for the punch line.

'Then why do you expect her to be omniscient?

We've been here for seven hours and my client has cooperated fully with you. Now we've reached the point where either you arrest her, or we're going home to bed. Which is it going to be, Ms Shaw?'

'Give me a minute,' she said. She was back in just over five. 'You can go now. But we may have some more questions for Ms Brannigan.'

'And she may or may not answer them,' Ruth said sweetly as we headed out the door.

When I got home, there was still no sign of Richard. I was too wound up to sleep, so I switched on the computer and played myself at snooker until my eyes were so tired I couldn't tell the reds from the black. I staggered off to bed then, only to dream of Gail Morton running naked across green fields pursued by a gigantic white cue ball.

The next morning, I had to deal with the depressing job I'd been avoiding ever since I'd got back from Italy. I drove out to Birchfield Place, noticing that the leaves were starting to fall. I hate the autumn. Not because it heralds winter or symbolizes the death of the year or anything like that. I just hate the way fallen leaves turn to slime on country roads and bring on four-wheel drift as soon as you corner at anything more than walking pace.

It was one of the days the house was open to the public, and I found Henry hiding from the masses in his little office in the private apartments. He didn't look particularly pleased to see me, which I put down to the pile of paperwork threatening to topple over and cover his desk. But the upper classes never let mere irritation interfere with their manners. 'Hello, Kate,' he said, pushing back his chair to stand up as I walked in. 'Good to see you.'

'And you, Henry.' I sat down opposite him.

'Mr Haroun from the insurance company tells me you've been having a rather exotic time lately,' he said. I thought I detected a slight note of reproach in his voice.

'Exotic. Now, there's a word,' I said. 'I'm sorry you heard it from him rather than directly from me, but I've been a bit hectic the last few days, and I thought the main priority was to make sure you could get reinsured at a decent premium as fast as possible.'

'Oh, absolutely, you did quite the right thing. And you must let me have your bill for your trip to Europe. It sounds utterly dreadful, but the one positive thing to come out of it is that Mr Haroun has agreed to pay some of your bill as a quid pro quo for your putting a stop to these burglaries.' All of a sudden, he'd gone motormouth on me.

I looked at him. 'Don't you want to know about your Monet?' I asked.

He flushed. 'Mr Haroun said you hadn't managed to recover it. I . . . I didn't want to remind you of your lack of success in that respect when you'd been so successful otherwise.'

The smell of bullshit filled my nostrils. 'What I didn't tell Mr Haroun is that the painting showed up in the paperwork,' I said. 'What it looked like to me was that the painting had been received by the drug runners, but hadn't yet been swapped for a consignment of drugs.' I sat back and let Henry work that one out for himself. Right from the start, I'd been convinced he was holding out on me, and an idea of why was starting to form at the back of my mind.

'You mean it might still turn up?' he asked. Too nervously for my liking.

'It's possible,' I said. 'But there could be another explanation.'

By now, he wasn't even trying to meet my eyes. 'I'm sorry, I'm not following you.' He looked up, caught my glance and looked away, his boyish smile self-deprecating. 'I'm obviously not as well up in the ways of criminals as you, Kate.'

'You want me to spell it out, Henry? You've been nervous about this investigation right from the start. I worked with you on the security for this place, and I think I got to know you well enough to realize you're not the sort of bloke who gets wound up about something like a burglary where no one's been hurt. So there had to be another reason. I only grasped it some time during the fourth hour of close questioning by the Art Squad. Henry, if what you had nicked off your wall is a Monet, I am Marie of Romania.'

26

There was a long silence after I dropped my bomb-shell. Henry stared blankly at the papers in front of him, as if they'd inspire him to an answer. Eventually, I said quietly, 'The rules of client confidentiality still apply. You'd be better off telling me what's going on. Then, if what they stole from you does turn up, we're ready with a story to cover your back.'

He glanced up at me quickly, then looked away again. He was pink to the tips of his ears. 'When my parents died, there wasn't a lot of money. I did my sums and realized that with a cash injection, I could make this place work. I was talking over my problem with an old friend who had had a similar dilemma himself. He told me what he'd done, and it seemed like a good idea, so I did the same thing.' More silence.

'Which was . . . ?' I prompted him.

'After I'd had the Monet authenticated for insurance purposes, I took it to this chap my friend knew. He's an awfully good copier of paintings. No talent of his own, just this ability to reproduce other people's work. Anyway, once I had the copy, I sold the original privately to a Japanese collector, on the strict understanding it would never be publicly exhibited.' Henry looked up again, his eyes pleading for understanding. 'I didn't want to admit what I'd done, because the Monet is one of the main visitor attractions at the house. People come here to see the Monet because they're interested in his work, people who otherwise wouldn't cross the threshold. And no one ever noticed, you know. All those so-called experts never spotted the swap.' He perked up as he pointed out his one-upmanship.

'And then when the thieves took the copy, you couldn't own up because that would mean admitting to the insurers that you'd been lying all along,' I said, feeling depressed at the thought of the risks I'd taken over a fake.

'I've been feeling terrible about taking their money under false pretences,' he admitted. 'But what else can I do? If I tell the truth now, they'll never reinsure me, and I'll never get cover anywhere else. I've painted myself into a corner.'

'You're not kidding,' I said bitterly. 'Not to mention putting my life at risk.'

Henry sighed. 'I know. I'm sorry about that. I simply didn't know how to tell you the truth. You've no idea what a weight off my mind it is to have told someone at last.'

'Yeah, well, the Catholics wouldn't have stuck

with confession all these years if it didn't have some therapeutic effect. The thing is, Henry, now I know for sure what I already suspected, I can't sit back and watch you defraud Fortissimus to the tune of seven figures. I've done some hooky things for clients over the years, but this is a few noughts too far,' I said, the iron in my voice matching the anger inside me.

He met my stare at last, panic sparking in his blue eyes. 'You said this came under client confidentiality,' he accused. 'You can't betray that confidence now!'

My first inclination was to say, 'Watch me,' and walk. But I'd got to like Henry. And I believed him when he said he was sorry about the shit I'd been through. Besides, it doesn't do in my business to get a name for selling your clients down the river. 'Henry, this isn't about betrayal. You're making me party to a million-pound fraud,' I said instead.

'But even if it does come out, there will be no suggestion that you knew about it. After all, if you'd known the painting was only a copy, you wouldn't have made such strenuous efforts to recover it,' he argued persuasively.

'But I'd know that I knew,' I said. 'That's the bottom line for me.'

Henry ran a hand through his gleaming hair. 'So what did you come back here for this morning, Kate? To get the truth and then throw me to the wolves?'

His words stung. 'No, Henry,' I told him sternly.

'I hoped you'd tell me the truth, that's true. But I don't want to shaft you. What I think we can do is stitch up a deal.'

He frowned. 'You want a cut, is that it?' Luckily for Henry, he sounded incredulous. If he'd seriously offered me a bribe, all bets would have been off.

'No, Henry,' I said, exasperated. 'What I mean is that I think I can do a deal with the insurance company.'

'You're going to *tell* them I was trying to defraud them?'

'I'm going to tell them what an honest man you are, Henry. Trust me.'

An hour later, I was waiting to see Michael Haroun. I'd taken the time to get suited up in my best business outfit, a drop-dead gorgeous, lightweight woollen tailored jacket and trousers in moss green and grey. This was going to be such a difficult stunt to pull off that I was going to need all the help I could get. Call me manipulative, but this was one occasion where I was willing to exploit testosterone to the full.

I only had to hang on for ten minutes, even though the claims receptionist had warned me he was in a meeting that could take another half-hour. That's the power of hormones for you. Michael grinned delightedly at me, plonking himself down next to me on the sofa. 'What a great surprise,' he said. 'I hope you've not come to call off our dinner date tonight?'

'No way. This is strictly a business meeting,' I told him. I didn't let that stop me brushing my knee against his.

'Right. Well, what can I do for you, Ms Brannigan?' he said teasingly.

'This is all a bit embarrassing, really,' I said.

He raised one eyebrow. Sexy, or what? 'Better get it over with, then.'

I pulled a wry face and tried to look innocent. 'I've just come from our mutual client, Henry Naismith. He's finally got round to clearing out some boxes of papers that were lurking in a dark corner of the cellar at Birchfield Place. And he found something rather disturbing.' I paused for effect.

'Not the Monet, I hope,' Michael joked.

'Not the Monet. What he did find was a bill of sale, and a note accompanying it in his father's writing.' I took a deep breath. 'Michael, the Monet was a fake. Henry's father had it copied a couple of years before he died. He secretly sold the original to a private collector on the understanding it would never be displayed publicly, and the fake's been hanging on the wall ever since.'

I'd never believed the cliché about people's jaws dropping till then. But there was no other way to describe what had happened to Michael's face. 'A fake?' he finally echoed.

'That's about the size of it.'

'It can't be,' he protested. 'We had an expert go over all those paintings when we first insured

Birchfield for Naismith. He authenticated all of them.'

I shrugged. 'Experts can be wrong. Maybe he was misled by the paperwork. I'm told the Monet had an immaculate provenance.'

'I don't believe this,' he exploded. 'We used the leading expert. Shit!' He turned away for a moment. Then, slowly, he swung round to face me. 'Unless we're really talking about your client, not his father.'

He was smart. I like that in a man, except when I'm up against him. I opened my eyes wide, aiming for the injured innocent look. 'What is this, Michael? I come here telling you your company's just saved itself a million quid payout and you're giving me a bad time? For Christ's sake, look at the bottom line here!'

His eyes narrowed. 'You're telling me he's dropping the claim?'

'As far as the painting is concerned, of course he is. He now knows the painting was a fake, he sent me to tell you the painting was a fake. If he was as dishonest as you're trying to make out, he could just have kept his mouth shut and pocketed the readies. Come to that, would he be paying to send me schlepping halfway across Europe in a head-to-head with the Mafia over something he knew was a copy? All Henry wants to do is set the record straight and sort out the reinsurance on what's left of his art collection.'

By now, Michael was scowling. 'And how do

we know the rest of the collection aren't fakes too?'

'They're not. Henry is willing to let you do any tests you want to on the other paintings. Experts, X-rays, whatever. He'll stand by the results. Michael, you owe us a bit of leeway here,' I continued, building up a head of righteous anger. 'If it hadn't been for the investigation Henry instigated, this bunch of robbers would still be emptying your clients' stately homes more regularly than the phases of the moon. Thanks to Henry, that problem has gone away. And now his honesty is saving you a sizeable hole in your balance sheet. Can't you just be grateful for that?'

I watched his eyes as he calculated his way through what I'd just told him. After a few moments, the clouds cleared and he smiled. 'I have to hand it to you, Kate,' he said. 'You are one smart operator. We have a deal. We don't pursue your client for fraud, and we reinsure, subject to more than the usual checks. In exchange for which, your client withdraws his claim in respect of his stolen Monet. Get him to put that in writing, will you?'

I held out my hand. 'Deal.'

Michael shook my hand, holding on to it rather longer than was necessary. 'I do realize I've been listening to *Jackanory*, but this is an outcome I can live with,' he said, needing to end the negotiation in the driving seat.

I let him. I'd got what I wanted. I stood up. 'See you tonight.'

'Half past seven, the Market Restaurant. I'll be there.'

By the time I'd walked back to the office, my brain felt like a bombsite. For once, Shelley took pity on me, leaving me alone to work my way through the pile of paperwork that had accumulated while I'd been roaming the mean streets. After my recent adventures, I was longing to get back to the relative peace of a tasty bit of computer fraud or even some routine process serving.

Alexis rang just before lunch, demanding to know what part I'd played in the dramatic arrest of Gail Morton and Desmond Halloran. Her own researches had come up with how the couple had met. Apparently, Halloran had been doing a portrait of one of Gail's friends and she'd gone along for the session to keep her mate company. It had seemingly been lust at first sight. There was a warning, if I'd needed one, about the consequences of letting physical attraction cloud one's judgement.

In exchange for that nugget, I gave Alexis the lowdown as deep background, and promised her the full story on the drugs-for-art scam just as soon as the various police forces had coordinated their efforts and done their sweep-up of the villains.

When I came off the phone, Shelley wandered into my office with a memo. 'New client,' she said. 'He's got a chain of record shops in the Northwest and his stock seems to be shrinking rather more than it should be. I've set up a meeting for you in the main lounge of the Charterhouse at half past three. OK?'

'Fine,' I sighed. 'Make that the last business of the day, would you? I need some quality time with my bathroom.'

'No problem,' Shelley said. Nothing ever is to her. Sometimes, I hate her.

I walked through the impressive doors of the Charterhouse Hotel at twenty-five past three. The huge red bullshit Gothic building, complete with looming tower, is one of Manchester's landmarks. It used to be the headquarters of Refuge Insurance and occupies a vast block on the corner of Oxford Road and Whitworth Street, bordered on a third side by the brown and sluggish River Medlock. Inside, the decorative glories of Victorian tiling and wood panelling have been left miraculously intact, a monument to a time when labour and materials were cheap enough to make every public building a cathedral to commerce.

I checked at the reception desk, but no one had been asking for me, so I settled down in a chair where I could comfortably see both entrances and where anyone coming in would be bound to see me.

At 3.32, Richard walked in. I breathed in sharply, while my stomach contracted in a cramp. At first, he didn't see me, since he was heading single-mindedly for the reception desk. I had a moment or two to study him. He looked satisfyingly hollow-cheeked, the shadows under his eyes visible even at ten yards. I reminded myself sternly that he probably hadn't been pining, merely enjoying too many late nights on the razz with the rockers. He was wearing Levis and a baggy Joe Bloggs T-shirt under the leather jacket I'd bought him in Florence. As I watched him talk to the receptionist, I felt a pain in my chest.

I saw the receptionist shake her head. He looked around then, and saw me for the first time. I tried to keep my face frozen as our eyes locked. He took an uncertain step in my direction, then stopped.

I stood up and moved a couple of steps away from my chair. It was a Mexican standoff. Shackled by pride and stubbornness, we remained firm, neither willing to be the one to back down. Before the dead-lock could set in stone, a familiar voice from behind my shoulder boomed out, 'This isn't *High Noon*, you know. You're supposed to use your gobs.'

I swung round to see Alexis emerge from behind a pillar. 'You bastard,' I said.

'I didn't set this up just to watch the pair of you imitating Easter Island statues,' she complained, walking over to stand midway between us. 'Now, one step at a time, approach.'

By this time, both Richard and I were clearly fighting not to smile. In sync, we moved towards each other. God knows what the receptionists were making of the scene. When only Alexis stood between us, she stepped back and said, 'I'm out of here. Get it sorted, will you? The pair of you are doing everybody's heads in.'

I suppose she left then. I wasn't paying attention. I was too busy staring at Richard and remembering all the reasons I felt bound me to this man. Thinking too how right he'd been to resent people's perception of him as a wimp, when actually he's the strongest man I know. He's strong enough to step back and let me get on with my own life, strong enough never to make demands he knows I can't meet, strong enough to understand that our relationship gives both of us what we need without all the crap neither of us wants.

Somebody had to speak first, and I reckoned it might as well be me. 'I missed you,' I said.

'Me too. I'm sorry,' he added, his voice cracking.

'Me too.' I reached out a hand across the space between us. He linked his fingers with mine. 'We need to talk,' I said.

Then he smiled, that cute smile that cut me off at the knees the first time I encountered him in a sweaty nightclub, minutes before he reversed straight into my car. 'Later,' he said. 'Let's book a room.'

Richard was pouring the last of the vodka from the mini-bar into a glass for me when I noticed the time. I hoped Michael Haroun wouldn't still be waiting in the restaurant two hours after we'd arranged to meet. Deep down, I knew I didn't really care if he was. Sure, picking up some business from Fortissimus would have been nice. But being grown-up means recognizing that some prices are way too high to pay.